New York Times bestselling author

LISA UNGER

"A compelling storyteller . . .
She makes it impossible to stop reading."
—*The Charlotte Observer*

Praise for *CRAZY LOVE YOU*

"Unger's skillful portrayal of complex and traumatized characters makes her latest psychological thriller one that will keep readers engaged from start to finish. . . . [An] imaginative tale, which may be the author's best work yet."
—*Library Journal* (starred review)

"Riveting . . . This is a complex, intricate story, yet the pages fly by as Ian, the most unreliable narrator since Nick Dunne in *Gone Girl*, leads us on a wild ride in this superb psychological thriller. Unger is at the top of her game here."
—*Booklist* (starred review)

"She scores another bull's-eye with this one. Classic Unger and a surefire hit."
—*Kirkus Reviews*

"Suspenseful . . . Will keep readers hooked."
—*Publishers Weekly*

"Kept me reading like a madwoman, desperate to find out what happens next. This is a haunting, compulsive tale that will have you under its spell long after you've closed the book."

—Tess Gerritsen

"When I tell you I could not put this book down, I mean I COULD NOT PUT THIS BOOK DOWN!!! It is dark and twisted and captivating and full of endless surprises. I promise you're in for a wild ride."

—John Searles

"Mesmerizing and unnerving from its first pages to its stunner of an ending, Lisa Unger's *Crazy Love You* is a tale you won't soon forget."

—Megan Abbott

"Unger has outdone herself. I've been a fan of hers for years but this is hands down my favorite book she's written. It has all the twists and turns we've come to expect from her, along with a delightfully unreliable narrator, and a psychological depth that is as poignant as it is shocking."

—Gregg Hurwitz

IN THE BLOOD

"[A] brisk, crafty, and fascinating psychological thriller ... Offers plenty of good, scary fun—scenes that will make readers jump . . . [and] a reveal that will surely elicit a satisfied gasp. . . . *In the Blood* is a complex mosaic as well, one that's tricky, arresting, and meaningful."

—*The Washington Post*

"A great, scary psychological thriller ... Prepare to be scared. Creepy characters, gripping plot, chilling description—this novel is a perfect weekend read."

—*Minneapolis Star Tribune*

LISA UNGER

CRAZY LOVE YOU

A NOVEL

POCKET BOOKS

NEW YORK LONDON TORONTO SYDNEY NEW DELHI

Pocket Books
An Imprint of Simon & Schuster, Inc.
1230 Avenue of the Americas
New York, NY 10020

This book is a work of fiction. Any references to historical events, real people, or real places are used fictitiously. Other names, characters, places, and events are products of the author's imagination, and any resemblance to actual events or places or persons, living or dead, is entirely coincidental.

This Pocket Books paperback edition January 2024

POCKET and colophon are registered trademarks of Simon & Schuster, Inc.

Simon & Schuster: Celebrating 100 Years of Publishing in 2024

For information about special discounts for bulk purchases, please contact Simon & Schuster Special Sales at 1-866-506-1949 or business@simonandschuster.com.

The Simon & Schuster Speakers Bureau can bring authors to your live event. For more information or to book an event, contact the Simon & Schuster Speakers Bureau at 1-866-248-3049 or visit our website at www.simonspeakers.com.

Manufactured in the United States of America

10 9 8 7 6 5 4 3 2 1

ISBN 978-1-6680-3446-0
ISBN 978-1-4516-9122-1 (ebook)

To Sally

*Superstar editor, champion, and friend. Every novel
we have worked on together is better for your involvement.
Thank you for your expertise, insight, and passion.*

As I pulled up the long drive, deep potholes and crunching gravel beneath my wheels, towering pines above me, I was neither moved by the natural beauty nor stilled inside by the quietude. I did not marvel at the fingers of light spearing through the canopy, dappling the ground. I did not admire the frolicking larks or the scampering squirrels for their carefree existence. No. In fact, it all made me sick. There was a scream of protest lodged at the base of my throat, and it had been sitting there for the better part of a year. When it finally escaped—and I wasn't sure when that might be—I knew it would be a roar to shake the world to its core.

It was supposed to have been an auspicious year for me. According to all the astrological predictions—if you believe in that kind of thing—I was to have found security at home, success at work—rewards for all my labors. Megan, the sweet and willowy girl of my dreams—the kind of girl who asked the universe for what we needed, and who dwelled "in a place of gratitude," and who regularly walked around burning sage and whispering her good thoughts—was no match for the tide of shit that was headed our way.

I should have told her not to bother. Part of me knew that I was only keeping it all at bay—the darkness, the bad luck, the ugly turn of circumstance, the destroyer waiting in the shadows. But I *wanted* to believe in her, in us. And for a time I did. Maybe it was all worth it, everything that followed, for the moment in which I was able to live in the sun with her. But now that moment makes the dark seem so much deeper, so much less penetrable by any kind of light.

I snaked along the winding, narrow path in my banged-up old Scout, steeling myself for the sight of the house, which waited just around the next bend. It shouldn't have even been there. I'd finally scheduled it for demolition; should have done so long ago.

Megan and I talked about building our dream home in its place. Or rather *she* talked about it, and I made noncommittal noises. I might have known the house wouldn't allow itself to be destroyed. In fact, maybe that was where I'd gone too far into my new life. It was one thing to move on. It was quite another to try to level the past, to pave it over and build it back as you would like it. That wasn't allowed. Not for me.

And then there it was, as rickety as it was defiant. As fragile as it was indestructible—shutters askew, siding faded and slipping, yard overgrown, porch sagging. As I turned a hard corner with the mean winter sun setting behind me, it rose into view, looked bigger than it had a right to be. The sky behind it was orange and black, the trees dark slashes against the gloaming.

Oh, Meg had plans for this place—our country home, just a few short hours from the city. It was to be our retreat, a place where I would write far from the distractions and temptations of our urban life. No, we wouldn't have wireless up here. It would have been our place to unplug. But those were *her* plans, not mine. As far as I was concerned, self-immolation was a more desirable option.

As I came to a stop, the whole place seemed to vibrate with malicious glee. The scream dropped into my belly and became a hard ache in my gut as I climbed out of the truck. How is it possible that I am back here? I asked myself. A place I fled, vowing never to return. Now it's the only place I have left. Megan would have something to say, like: *It's the universe forcing you to confront the thing you dreaded most. It's taken everything from you because that's how important this is. What lesson is it asking you to learn?* In fact, that's precisely what she had said.

Man, I ached to hear that bright and positive voice, to hear that vibration of love and confidence. But now, when I called her, I only got the clipped and professional tone she'd used for her voice mail. *I'm not available at the moment. Please leave a message.* She wasn't answering my calls. I left long rambling messages; I wasn't even sure she listened to them. Her last words to me:

We don't have anything left to discuss, Ian. Don't call me until something changes.

I don't know what that means, I pleaded.

But there was an expression she wore when she looked at me now—sad, disappointed, and angry. And that look was the only answer she gave me before she left me on our bench in Central Park by the *Alice in Wonderland* statue. It was the last place I'd seen her. I watched her walk away, huddled into herself against the cold. She moved quickly past a little girl who was chasing a boy around the circle. The boy was crying but the girl was laughing, oblivious or indifferent to the fact that the game was frightening him.

I think I called Megan's name, because the children stopped and looked at me, both of them staring with mouths formed in perfect Os of surprise. Their nanny hurried over and shuttled them away from me, casting a disapproving look in my direction. But maybe I didn't say her name. Maybe I said something else. Whatever it was I said, or yelled, Megan hadn't stopped. She moved faster as if she was afraid, as if she couldn't wait to be away from me. Why was she afraid of me? How could she be? I had watched until she was absorbed into the throbbing crowd of New Yorkers shuttling through the park on their various ways to various important things.

Now the thud of the hatch closing reverberated like a gunshot in the silence. I had one large black duffel bag, my leather art portfolio, my supply box. I slung the bag over my shoulder and left the portfolio and art supplies for later. The air was frigid, my bare hands raw and painful from just a few moments of exposure.

Then I turned to face the house. For the first time I noticed that lights were burning inside—one upstairs in my old bedroom and one downstairs in the small living room. Outside, darkness had fallen completely and suddenly like a shroud. There was movement inside and I wasn't in the least surprised. I wasn't angry or afraid, though I should have been both.

This was it. Rock bottom. The way I saw it, I could lie down, a pile of shattered bones, until I slowly bled out, fading into a blissful, delicious nothingness. Or I could pull myself up, one broken limb at a time, and fight my way back to Megan, to the life we were trying to build. The decision wasn't as easy as you might think. When the darkness calls, it's a siren song—magical, hypnotic, and nearly impossible to resist. You *want* to go. It's so easy to do the wrong thing, the bad thing. All you have to do is give in.

On the front step, I could smell her, that mingling of perfume and cigarette smoke and something else. A helix of fury and desire twisted in my belly as I pushed through the door. And she stood there, as wild and beautiful as she had always been—her hair a riot of white and gold and copper, her linen skin, her eyes the moonstone blue of terrible secrets. *Priss.* She took the stance of victory, legs apart, arms akimbo, a slight smile turning up the corners of her mouth. I almost laughed. I let the door slam behind me.

"Hello, Priss." My voice didn't sound right. It sounded weak, had the tenor of defeat. She heard it. Of course she did. And her smile deepened.

"Welcome home, asshole."

PART ONE

There Was a Little Girl

CHAPTER ONE

It was the garbage truck that woke me. Rumbling, beeping down Lispenard Street. It crashed over the metal plate in the road, creating a mind-shatteringly loud concussive boom. And with my sudden, unwanted wakefulness came the waves of nausea, the blinding pain behind the eyes. I emerged jaggedly into the land of the living, rolled out of bed, and stumbled through my loft to the bathroom. Gripping the sink, I peered at myself in the mirror—three days since my last shave, my hair a wild dark tangle, blue shiners of fatigue, my skin pale as the porcelain bowl I'd soon be hugging. Not looking good.

"Oh God," I said.

But the words barely escaped before the world tilted and I dove for the toilet, where the wretched contents of my belly exited with force, leaving only an acidic burn in my gullet.

I slid down to the ground. On the blessedly cool tile floor, I tried to piece together the events of last night. But there was nothing, just a gaping hole in my memory. I should have been alarmed that I had absolutely no recall of the previous evening. You probably would have been, right? But, sadly, that was the normal state of things. I know what you're thinking: *What a loser*.

Loser. Weirdo. Queer. Douchebag. Freak. Shitbag. Fugly. Tool. And my personal favorite: Fatboy. Yes, I have been called all of these things in my life. I have been shunned, beaten, bullied. I have been ignored, tortured, teased, and taunted. My middle school and high school life were the typical misery of the misfit, though mine had an especially sharp edge because I was feared as well as hated. And so my punishments were brutal. I barely survived my adolescence. In fact, I barely survived my early childhood. I might not have survived either if it hadn't been for Priss.

Of course, it wasn't just Priss who helped me through. My mother did love me, though it seems odd to say that now. I think that's truly what saved me, what kept me from turning into a raving lunatic—though some people think I'm just that. My mom was the kind of mother who spent *time*; she wasn't just going through the motions of caregiving. All those hours with her reading to me, drawing with me, doing puzzles, looking up the answers to my endless questions in big books in the library—they have stayed with me. They have formed me. She loved stories, and she made up endless tales on the fly—the monster who was afraid of cake, the fairy who couldn't find her magic, the butterflies that carried children off to dreamland. And she was a painter, a deep and compelling artist.

She gave those things to me, and that's what I kept after she and my sister were gone. I took solace in those gifts in my bleakest moments. Everyone else forgot those things about her in the wake of her final deeds. But I never did. She only exists for me as she was in those times before my sister was born—when we were all happy and nothing ugly had leaked into our lives. And when I hadn't yet met Priss, who would change everything for me. For good or bad, it's impossible to say.

Of course, I wasn't thinking about any of that as I lifted myself off the floor and stumbled back to bed. The sun was high in the sky, too high for anyone my age to still be buried under the covers. Unpleasantly bright and sunny, the room was spinning and pitching like a carnival ride. I couldn't have gotten up if I wanted to.

Anyway I wasn't Fatboy anymore. I shed all that extra weight before I came to New York City on an art scholarship. I started running, and later boxing at a crappy gym on Avenue D. I got a cool haircut and grew a goatee. When I look in the mirror today (okay, not *today* exactly), the angry, unhappy kid I used to be—he's nowhere to be found. And the town where I grew up, that sad boy, that shitty life—I shed it like I did my old clothes that no longer fit, that hung off me like an old skin. I stuffed it all into a big plastic bag and shoved it down the trash chute. Good-bye. It was that easy. It really was. At least it was for me.

Now, in some circles, I'm the *shiznay*. My graphic novel series, *Fatboy and Priss*, is what they call a cult hit—not a mainstream success, necessarily, but something that every geek and weirdo, every comic book and graphic novel freak in the country knows about. I live in a loft in Tribeca, which is also my studio. (Read: I'm rich, *suckas*! Okay, well, I rent. I'll own when the movie deal comes through and my agent says that should be any time now.) I publish a book a year, which I write and illustrate. I'm working on a novel. There's an option for film. At Comic Con, I'm mobbed. Oh, the geek boys, they love me. They stand in long, snaking lines with their carefully maintained copies of my graphic novels, waiting for my signature.

Of course, it's not me that they care about, or even Fatboy. It's Priss. She is every boy's wet dream—with her wild hair and huge breasts, her impossibly narrow waist and her long, shapely legs. How my hands love drawing her, how I love putting the blue in her eyes, sketching the valentine curve of her ass. Priss loves Fatboy in spite of his many flaws. And she kicks ass, while Fatboy is a wuss, sensitive and artistic but weak. Priss is a powerhouse—she fears nothing and her wrath is a force to be reckoned with. No one messes with Fatboy, or they answer to *her*. It's Fatboy and Priss against the world.

Is she real? Is there a real Priss? they want to know.

Of course, I tell them.

Where is she, dude?

It's a secret, I say. And they don't know if I'm messing with them or not, but they laugh, give me a knowing wink. Even though they know nothing. Priss is a mystery. Even I can't quite figure her out.

On that day, the day I met Megan, I hadn't seen Priss in a while. Priss and I had been slowly drifting apart—spending less time together, getting into less trouble. You know how it is with your childhood friends. You reach an awkward point in your relationship where you've gone in different directions or are starting to. You start to judge each other maybe, agree less, and bicker more. Priss still wanted to raise hell, get drunk or high, get wild. But I had responsibilities, deadlines, meetings.

Still, I looked at her face every day on my drawing table. It was an intimate relationship, my hands always on her, my mind always on her—but that was just on paper, the version of her that lived and breathed within the panels of my books. For Fatboy, she was lover, avenger, and friend. Once upon a time she was all those things for me as well. Somehow, somewhere along the line, for me the real Priss and the one on the page had kind of morphed into one.

The truth was that the more I had of her in ink, the less I wanted or needed her in life. I was okay with that, because my relationship with Priss has always been complicated—*really* complicated—and not always pretty. Like everything in life, she was easier to deal with on the page.

"You don't own me," she said during one of our last conversation-slash-arguments. "Just because you put me in these neat little boxes, have me saying and doing what you want, you think you do. But that's not me."

"I know that," I told her.

"Do you?"

I think what I liked about Megan, the first of many things I liked, was that she was nothing at all like Priss. And I mean nothing—not physically, not energetically. Megan was the good girl, the nice one, the one you took home to your parents. Well, not my parents. My father is dead, and my mother, Miriam, is, shall we say, indisposed. But *one's* parents. She was the woman who would take care of your children, take care of you. There aren't many of them, these types of girls. When you see one, you better be smart enough to recognize her. Lucky for me, I was.

By four o'clock, my blinding, take-me-to-the-emergency-room hangover was starting to abate. In the sundry bargains I'd made with God that day, I'd sworn off booze, pot, blowing deadlines, and being mean to people who didn't deserve it. I'd done penance on the marble floor of my extraordinary bathroom, clinging to its cool, white surfaces, moaning. I'd made Technicolor offerings to my low-flow toilet. And a wobbly redemption was mine. The pain, the nausea, the misery had faded, and my body was looking for nourishment of the greasiest kind.

The late-afternoon light was still impossibly bright, the traffic noise deafening, as I went uptown for the only thing that could save me: a burger, fries, and malt from the Shake Shack in Madison Square Park. I waited on the eternal line, bleary and tilting, and finally made my way to the park bench near the playground to eat.

I liked watching them, those children of privilege, those New York City angels who see their high-powered parents for approximately three hours a day. They are coiffed and impeccably dressed, already wearing the blank expression of entitlement and neglect. They are tended to by nannies of various shapes and colors who always seem mindful that the children are, at once, their charges and their employers. An odd line to walk, I always thought. How terrible for all of them. Children don't want power; they can't handle it. And while I watched this frightful dynamic play out on little stages throughout the park—a tantrum on the jungle gym, a struggle over swings, a child weeping on the slide while her nanny chatted with another nanny, back turned, oblivious—I saw Megan.

She was not the kind of girl I'd usually notice. Typical of the Fatboy turned fairly-decent-looking-moderately-successful guy, my tastes ran to the cheap and flashy. I liked a blonde, one who wasn't afraid to show a little skin, wear leather and denim, sport heels high and spiky, painted nails, glossy lips. You know, strippers. Other than Priss, I'd never really had a woman in my life, not a *relationship* per se. And Priss didn't really count, for all sorts of reasons.

Megan's glossy brown hair was struggling free of its stubby ponytail as she wiped the nose of a towheaded boy. She had a scrubbed-clean look to her, not a drop of makeup. Her black ballet flats were scuffed and worn. Her jeans had dirt on the knees. And yet a kind of innocent, peaceful beauty lit up her features.

"Are you okay?" she said to the little boy, who was crying in a soft, not-too-bratty way. And her voice was so gentle, so full of caring that it lifted me out of myself. I don't think anyone other than my mother had ever talked to me so sweetly. I longed to be that little boy in her care. *No,* I wanted to tell her. *I'm not okay. Can you help me?*

"Want to go home and get cozy?" she asked the little boy. "Are you tired?"

"Yeah," he said, looking up at her with big eyes. Milking it. And I knew just how he felt. It's so nice—and so very rare—when someone understands how you feel.

"Your mom will be home soon," she said. "We need to get dinner ready anyway."

I watched her gather up his little backpack and put him in his stroller. Her face, somehow pale and bright, somehow sweet and smart, somehow kind and strong, was the prettiest face I'd ever seen. But of course there was something else there, too. It wasn't all light. Wasn't there also a bit of shadow? A dark dancer moving beneath the surface? Yes, there was just a shade of something sad.

I started thinking about how to draw her, how I'd capture all the things I saw in just those few moments that our lives intersected. Faces are so hard because they are more than lines and shadows. They are about light, but a light that comes from inside and shines out.

So badly did I want to see her face again that—I am embarrassed to say—I followed her up Park Avenue South to a Murray Hill brownstone. I watched from the corner as she took the little boy out of his stroller, folded it up, and carried them both inside. The light was dim by then; it had turned to evening, the wintery afternoon gold fading to milky gray.

The artist wants to capture everything beautiful and make it his own. There is such a hunger for that. I went home and tried to draw her that night. But I couldn't get her; she eluded me. And so I had to chase.

They went to the park every day. And every day I was there, unbeknownst to them, finding a perch outside the playground that was close enough to watch her and just far enough away not to arouse any suspicion. Because that's what people love: a weird-looking single guy with no kids lingering around a park where children are playing.

But on the third day, she saw me. I *saw* her see me. She looked at the boy—his name was Toby. Then she said something to another young woman, a gorgeous super-model of a nanny with café au lait skin and dark kinky hair beneath a red kerchief. That other one had a stare like a cattle prod and she turned it on me. Men had writhed in agony beneath that stare; I was certain of it. They'd liked it a little, too, I bet.

Then I was getting up and walking away, trying not to look like a caught stalker running for my life. I heard the clang of the playground gate, and her voice slicing over the traffic noise, the kids yelling, laughing, a siren fading down Broadway:

"Hey," she called. "Hey! Excuse me!"

I thought about running; I really did. But imagine what a freak, a coward I would have been if I did that. I could never go back. I'd never see her again. And I was still trying to get her face right. All that light, and that subtle shadow, too—was it worry, anxiety, maybe even a tendency toward depression? I still didn't have her on the page. So I stopped and turned around.

She was scared and mad, her eyebrows arched, her mouth pulled tight. All the other nannies were watching us from the playground fence, moving close together, staring like an angry line of lionesses against the hyena eyeing their adopted cubs.

"Hey," she said. "Are you following us?"

"Uh," I said. I looked up at the sky, then down at the silver-green-purple pigeon strutting near my foot. He cooed, mocking me. "No. No. Of course not."

She did a funny thing with her body. She wasn't quite squared off with me; she tilted herself away, ready to run if she needed to, back to the safety of the playground. "This is the third day I've seen you here."

I held up the Shake Shack bag, offered a little shrug. I didn't have to *try* to look sheepish and embarrassed. I was.

"I eat here on my break," I said. "I'm sorry."

"Oh," she said. She deflated a little, drew in a deep breath. "Oh. Okay."

Woop, Woop, said the police car on Madison, trying to push its way through traffic. *Woop*.

Was she going to apologize? I wondered. If I were writing her, what would I have her do? I'd like to get that little wiggle in her eyebrows, that tightness of uncertainty around her eyes, the just-barely-there embarrassed smile. It's all those little muscles under the skin; they dance in response to limbic impulses we can't control. It's their subtle shifting and moving that make expression.

"It's just something you have to look out for, you know?" she said. She looked back at the playground and gave a little wave. The tension dissipated, the line blurring, the nannies began talking among themselves. "When you watch kids at the playground. Especially here in the city."

I nodded. "Yeah," I said. "I get it. No worries."

"Okay."

Nope. She wasn't going to say she was sorry. Because she didn't believe me. She knew I wasn't there on my break. But she also knew I wasn't stalking the kids. She started moving back toward the playground. I saw Toby looking at her through the fence.

"Meggie," he called. "What's wrong?"

"I'm okay, Toby," she said. "Go play. I'm watching you."

She started moving away, going back to him. I didn't want her to.

"I saw you a couple of days ago," I admitted. It just kind of came out.

She turned back, and I came a step closer. She didn't back up. I looked up at the sky again, the bare branches, the little brown birds watching us. "I think you're the prettiest girl I've ever seen. I've been looking for a chance to talk to you."

I've never been much good at anything but total honesty. Sometimes it works for you. Then I saw it: a brief, reluctant smile. And I knew I wasn't sunk—yet. I tried to remember that I wasn't the loser kid on the school playground. I wasn't Fatboy anymore. I was okay to look at; I had money. She could like me. Why not?

"Really," she said flatly. She looked down at her outfit, another winner—faded jeans, a stained white button-down, a puffy parka with a fur-lined hood, scuffed Ugg boots. She gave me a half-amused, half-flattered look.

"Really," I said.

I could see her scanning through a list of replies. Finally: "That's the nicest thing anyone has ever said to me."

I was sure that wasn't true. She looked like the kind of girl to whom people said nice things all the time.

"There's more where that came from," I said. I went for a kind of faux-smarmy thing. And this time she smiled for real.

"Meeegaaaan," called Toby, whiny, annoyed.

She backed away again toward the playground, blushing in a really sweet way.

"Want to get a coffee?" I asked.

"Uh," she said. "I don't know. This is weird."

I waited, still thinking to myself: I'm okay. Chicks dig me. I get laid with some frequency. I don't always pay for it. I'm not a stalker.

"When?" she asked, still moving backward.

"Tonight," I said. "What time do you get off?"

I couldn't let her go without making her agree to see me again. I knew what would happen if she had too much time to think about it. Because I could already tell what kind of girl she was.

She came from money; she had nice, concerned parents probably living somewhere close by. How did I know this? There's a way a woman carries herself, a shine, an inner cleanliness, when she comes from love and privilege.

It takes a certain amount of confidence to walk around Manhattan looking like a bit of a mess. She was pretty, probably smoking hot underneath those baggy clothes. She could have shown it off like every other beautiful girl in the city. But she didn't need to; she didn't care who was looking. And you don't feel that way, not ever, unless your parents told you and showed you how special you are. That's how I knew.

If she had too much time to think about me, about our encounter, if she told her best friend, her employer, or God forbid her mom, they'd talk her out of seeing me again. Maybe tomorrow she'd decide it was better to go to another park for a while.

"Seven," she said. "I get off at seven."

"Meet me here at seven, then. Seven fifteen."

"Maybe," she said. She moved an errant strand of hair away from her eyes. "I don't know."

"I'll wait."

"I don't know," she said again. And that time it sounded more like a no.

She was gone then, disappeared behind the playground gate. And I turned around, leaving quickly. I knew as I walked downtown that if she didn't come back at seven that night, I might not see her again.

"Why did you come back?" I would ask her much later.

"Because I felt sorry for you," she said. She gave me a kind of sympathetic smile, a light touch to the face. "You looked like a person who needed something."

"I was *needy*? *That's* why you came back—not because I was hot or charming or magnetic? Not because you wanted me?"

"No. Sorry." Then that laugh, a little-girl giggle that always made me laugh, too.

"I *did* need something," I said. I ran my hand along the swell of her naked hip. "I needed you. I needed this life."

"Aw," she said. "And I came back because you were sweet. I could see that you were really, really sweet."

But *I* didn't make it back to the park that night at seven. Guess why.

Priss.

CHAPTER TWO

I'm not saying I didn't love my baby sister. I loved her as much as any ten-year-old *could* love a crying, clinging, alien little monkey who was always on *my mom*, who wouldn't let anyone sleep, and who drew all the attention formerly showered on *me*.

Let's face it; she was annoying. She stayed home while I had to go to school. Family members, neighbors, friends all dropped by with gifts for *the Baby*—and P.S., *none* for me. The Baby slept in bed next to my mother, where I hadn't been welcome in years. Still there was something cute about little Ella—her little fingers that clung to mine, her gooey, toothless smile, that little leg-kicking thing that babies do. I liked looking at her—when she wasn't bawling.

She's your responsibility, too, my mom told me. *She'll love you so much, adore you if you're nice to her.*

What does "adore" mean?

It means she'll love you forever.

I liked the sound of that. But my mom and the Baby seemed like a closed circle, with eyes only for each other. My mom was always looking at her with this blissed-out smile, and the Baby was always looking for her, even when my dad or I was holding her. Even when my mom was hugging me, or reading to me, the Baby was right there. I knew it was wrong to be angry and jealous, so I kept it inside. But my dad saw it, thought it was funny, a reason to tease me.

"Now you know how *I* felt when *you* came along," he said. "Sucks, doesn't it?"

It did suck. It really did. As a grown-up, I know that those feelings are normal. Every little kid with a new sibling has them. Plus, there was a big gap in our ages; I was way too used to being the center of my mom's universe. Ella was a "happy surprise," my mother said. They'd tried for years to have another child and finally gave up.

And then we got our little miracle, later than expected but still wonderful! Right, Ian?

Yeah, right, Mom.

I had dark thoughts about my little sister, ill wishes that shame me even now. And I had them until I realized that Ella needed me.

I came home from school one midwinter day and the house was dark. My mom wasn't in the kitchen; there was nothing cooking on the stove. This was weird, because my mom was always in the kitchen, and all the lights were always on, and there was always music playing on the stereo. But all I could hear when I walked in was my sister crying. I followed the sound and found my way to her nursery. She was red-faced and writhing; her wet diaper had seeped through to the sheets beneath her.

When she saw me she gave a couple of hard sniffles, some ragged breaths, then stopped crying. I lowered the side of the crib the way my mom had showed me, and I lifted her out. She was maybe two months old.

"It's okay," I told her. She was stinky, and I turned my face away from her. I laid her down on the changing table and unbuttoned her little onesie, took off her wet diaper.

"Ew, Ella," I said. "Gross."

She was watching me with her intense dark-eyed baby stare.

"I'll clean you up," I told her. "Don't worry."

I remember thinking that it wasn't as gross as I'd expected. I'd watched my mom change her a hundred times, so I kind of knew what to do. I held her legs and wiped her bottom, got a clean diaper from the drawer, and put it on her. I was just a kid; I'm sure I made a mess of it. But I was super proud of myself. Ella was kicking her legs and cooing by the time I was done. I picked her up and carried her to my parents' bedroom. My mom was just a lump underneath the covers.

"Mom," I said.

"Get her away from me," she said. The words were thick and flat, and I remember a kind of sickness in my belly at the sound of it. I had never heard her say anything like that before.

"She was wet," I said.

"Take her downstairs," she said. "I'm so tired. I haven't slept in days."

I stood waiting. Who was this woman in the bed? Not my mom, not the baker of cookies, singer of songs, LEGO builder, crayon artist, cartoon watcher. She was some wraith, dark and shrunken.

"Go, Ian," she said. "Please."

So I took Ella and we went downstairs. I was way too young to be taking care of a two-month-old baby. But I knew enough to support the head, watch out for the soft spot. There was a bottle of formula in the fridge. I couldn't reach the microwave and I wasn't allowed to use the stove. So I ran it under warm water the way I'd seen my mom do, leaving poor Ella on the floor, where the cat sniffed at her and she made soft noises.

Then I picked her up and fed her. She drank that bottle as if she hadn't eaten all day, and maybe she hadn't. I called my neighbor after that, and said my mom wasn't feeling well. And then Mrs. Carter came over and I watched television, forgetting really everything that had passed that afternoon.

Kids don't think about anything but themselves most of the time—so I wasn't that concerned about why my mom was in bed and not taking care of Ella. But I do remember that I started to love my sister that day. And I knew that Mom was right; if I was nice to Ella, she'd adore me. She'd love me forever. Turns out we wouldn't have that long.

Honestly, I tried not to think about my sister much. Or my mother. I have been guilty of doing what it takes to bury most of my memories and feelings related to both of them. I'm not especially creative when it comes to that— from junk food to booze to drugs, there are few poisons with which I haven't experimented. I've found a million ways to keep the demons in a comfortable, quiet stupor, lazing around on my inner couches.

But I wasn't a *total* mess at the point of my life when I met Megan. I still drank too much—but what thirty-year-old single Manhattanite didn't? Maybe not every-one drinks until they black out, or wakes up with big black gaps in his memory of the evening before, nameless women in his bed, or finds himself in a stranger's apart-ment in the Bronx. But whatever. I wasn't doing drugs the way I used to with Priss—there weren't as many bar fights, disorderly conduct citations, etc. I wasn't as often finding myself in the company of questionable people, doing things I'd later regret. At least that's what I told myself at the time.

Looking back, though, I can see that I was either working, or drunk, or high or hung over most of the time and that kept most of my inner ugliness at bay. I wasn't doing much thinking about anything too deep. I was in a comfortable, if toxic, stasis. I might have stayed there for-ever. But Megan was about to shake things up big-time.

• • •

After talking to Megan in the park, I hustled back to my loft to take a shower and make myself pretty for my date. I was excited—giddy even. I felt a lightness that I hadn't felt in a long, long time. I was Tony in *West Side Story*: something was coming, something big. This was the moment on which my whole life would pivot and I could feel the electricity building. So it was something of a gut punch to find Priss sitting on the steps that led up to my apartment building.

"Hey, stranger," she said.

"Hey," I said. I tried to shoot her a smile, but it felt fake and I wondered if she could tell that I wasn't that happy to see her. "What's up?"

"It's been a while," she said. She turned a strand of that wild red hair around her finger. There was no way to capture all those shades of color—white and copper and gold. I had never gotten it quite right, mainly because it always seemed to be changing.

"It has," I said. I came to stand beneath her and she looked down at me, resting her hand on the metal railings. A woman walked by and glanced at us strangely.

"What are you looking at?" Priss called. She was like that, always causing trouble, reacting to the slightest thing. When I was with her, I tended to be the same way. I followed the woman with my eyes, embarrassed. But she just shuttled on down the street like a good New Yorker, never looked back.

I walked up the stairs and stood by the door. I pulled my phone from my pocket and looked at the time. It was almost five o'clock.

"Did you get your work done today?" she asked.

"Some," I lied. I'd been drawing pictures of Megan all day. I had a deadline looming but it wasn't close enough to motivate me. I'm an eleventh-hour kind of guy; pressure is my friend.

She nodded, unconvinced. She knew me better than anyone did, better than I knew myself. And that wasn't always a good thing.

We stood there in a bit of a standoff. The sky was growing dark, and the black-gray gloaming seemed heavy with the portent of snow. The wind danced a plastic bodega bag down the street; it lofted and whispered and I found myself watching it. It was graceful, a twist of light and shadows, a spiral of ghostly movement. There is beauty in almost every ordinary thing. If Priss hadn't been there, I'd have pulled my camera from my pocket and chased it down the street, taking video. Then I'd have gone home and studied how it moved, how the light shifted and changed to communicate movement to my eye. I might have tried to sketch it into a few panels, tell a story about it. Who had been carrying it? What had it held? Why had it been discarded? Stories are everywhere if you're looking for them.

"Earth to Ian," she said. Her tone had a sharp edge that made me jump a little. "Are we going in?"

"Yeah," I said. "Sure."

I let us in and we walked down the long concrete-and-marble lobby, past the alcove of mailboxes, toward the hammered-metal elevator door. I stared at my lumpy and distorted reflection. All my giddiness had faded. The fatigue I always felt around Priss started to pull at my shoulders and the lids of my eyes. She ran a long slender hand through her hair, shaking it a little like a mane.

She was talking, but I wasn't listening. Instead, I was just watching the way her lips moved around her words, how the candy-pink flesh puckered. I was noticing how her tongue darted out to moisten her lips, how she thrust her right hip out and dug her hands into her pockets. I'd spent many years observing Priss and putting her on the page, but I still wasn't sure I had her. She defied capture like any wild thing.

Up in the loft, she disappeared into my bedroom and came back out with the treasure box. It was a small black suitcase on rollers where I kept my weed and all my sundry illegal paraphernalia. We started calling it the treasure box back in the days when I was high all the time—not just weed, but pills and occasionally blow. I stopped short of things like heroin and crack. But not Priss. She'd do anything.

"I don't want to get high," I said. I made myself busy in the kitchen, taking dishes from the sink and putting them in the dishwasher when normally they would have just sat there until the maid came. "I have plans."

I took a coconut water from the stupidly big Sub-Zero and focused on opening it and pouring the cloudy liquid into a glass.

I heard the hiss and snap of the lighter, the sharp intake of her breath. Then the scent of the weed hit me—sweet and sleepy, warm and earthy. I could imagine the green twisting line of smoke hooking me under the nose like a ghost finger and pulling me toward the couch.

"Oh, really," said Priss. She locked me in that icy blue stare. "You have plans?"

That's the last thing I remember clearly. I vaguely recall sinking into the couch. Just one hit, I thought. It'll relax me. I won't be such a spaz when I meet up with Megan. It was that killer weed from Hawaii that my publicist had given me. *Don't smoke it if you have anything you want to do that day. It'll bake you completely*, she'd warned. I remember Priss, her breath on my neck, her hands down my pants.

Priss, come on. Don't do this to me.

And then, somehow, it was eleven o'clock. The apartment was completely dark except for the television, which was tuned to TCM and Grace Kelly was kissing Jimmy Stewart. And I awoke to the kind of wistfulness I always feel when watching old films, something about a lost beauty, a simplicity to story and character that was never coming back. And then it hit me that I'd stood Megan up, that Priss was gone. The joint had been smoked down to a roach, and it lay cold on the table, surrounded by ash.

CHAPTER THREE

"I screwed up. I am *really* sorry."

Really. If I had a nickel for every time I'd said those words. But Megan didn't care what I had to say. She was pretending I was invisible. She didn't look at me as she walked by, big backpack slung over her shoulder, earbuds in, gaze to the sidewalk. It was my third day waiting outside the brownstone for her to get off work. I know: stalker. Finally, she turned around at the corner, stopping me in my tracks with a cold, angry stare.

"If I see you out here again, I am going to call the police," she said. She looked around, but everyone on the street just kept walking, staring at screens, listening to music. New York can be such a lonely, deserted place, even in a crowd.

She glanced back at me, exasperated. "I mean, who *does* things like this?"

"I just wanted to explain," I said. I kept my distance. I wasn't trying to scare her. I couldn't believe how badly I had screwed up; I hated what she must have thought of me. I wanted to fix it. Somehow, I *had* to fix it.

"Okay, fine," she said. "Explain."

I really wanted to lie, tell her I got hit by a car or rescued a kid from a burning building. But I stammered over the truth. Told her that I had a friend, a life-long friend, and whenever she was around bad things happened. I told her that we got high and I passed out. When I was done, Megan just looked at me, mouth open in awe, eyes wide.

"Did you just tell me that you stood me up because you got high with another girl?" she asked. "*This* is what you've stalked me for three days to tell me?"

She was incredulous, disappointed, but I could tell that she was also a little amused. Something glittered in those dark eyes. She wasn't a prude. She knew about life and what a mess it could be.

"Well, it's more complicated than that."

"How is it more complicated?"

"I can explain that, too," I told her. "But it's a longer story."

She shook her head, looked at the sky above her. When she looked back at me, she didn't seem as angry.

"I don't even know your name," she said.

"It's Ian. Ian Paine."

She blinked, as though she might have recognized my name. She looked just geeky enough to know about my books. Especially tonight when she was wearing thick-framed, tortoiseshell glasses. I loved that look, the pretty girl hiding behind a dorky façade. I found myself wondering about her underpants. Were they plain cotton bikinis? No, I was betting that they were a little sexy . . . a bright color, maybe some lace.

"Well, *Ian Paine*," she said. "You're an asshole."

She started to walk away but I moved after her. I put a very gentle hand on her arm. She spun back toward me, looking a little afraid. I released her, feeling ashamed that I had touched her. It was a breach of her very clear boundaries. I took a step back.

"You're right," I said when she didn't race off. "But not totally. I am not a *total* asshole, in spite of all evidence to the contrary. I am not that guy. I am not the guy who meets you in a park, begs you for a date, and then stands you up."

"But you *are*," she said. She couldn't keep the sadness out of her voice. "You *are precisely* that guy. But the joke's on me. *I* actually showed up. *I* even waited awhile. So what does that make me—desperate? Sad? Just really, really dumb?"

I lifted my palms in a gesture of surrender, supplication, then I put them to my chest in prayer hands. Which I hate. I hate people who do that.

"If you give me one more chance," I said, "I swear I will never let you down again."

It started to snow right at that second, and the lights on the cars around us seemed to glow brighter, and there was a crescendo of street noise. It was such a New York moment, so gritty and lovely, so discordant and musical all at once. We stood there looking at each other, and we both knew. Our lives were supposed to intertwine right then; we were supposed to wrap around each other, if not forever, then for a time. It was critical, unavoidable. Or maybe it was just me. There was something about her, something good and clean and smart. And I needed all of that in my bad, dirty, stupid life.

"There's a place on Madison," she said. "Let's go right now. We'll have a coffee. And if after that I still think you're an asshole, I'll tell you so. And then you'll leave me alone, like, forever."

I lifted my palms again. "It's a deal."

I started talking as we walked toward the coffee shop.

I grew up in a town called The Hollows. It's about a hundred miles from New York City, but it might as well be another planet. It is its own floating orb, a complete system. Plenty of people in The Hollows have never left town, and they're happy about it. Both my parents were raised there. They each left to go to college, but for different reasons found their way back. Because, you see, The Hollows has a sucking vortex. You might try to leave. It might even let you go for a time, but eventually it forces you to return.

My mother went home because she couldn't get a job right away after college. She had to move in with her parents. She tried to write a novel and get a job as a journalist at a newspaper—any paper, anywhere in the country.

Eventually, she found work at *The Hollows Gazette*. It was supposed to be a placeholder job, something to do until she got the job she wanted at a place like the *New York Times*, the *Chicago Tribune*, or the *San Francisco Chronicle*. This was back when people still wanted to work at a newspaper, of course. She was good, too. She had a journalism degree from Columbia University. She could have worked anywhere, done anything. I'm not sure why it never happened for her.

I made the mistake of coming back here, my mom said to me once, not too long ago. *Maybe this place doesn't let you leave twice.*

While she was job-hunting, my mom met my father, Nick Paine, at Jake's Pub, the local bar—I know, how romantic. They fell in love, got married a year later. *Was he the right man? Was he what I had hoped for? Maybe what I liked about him was that he was there. He wasn't another dream that might or might not come true.*

And to hear my mother tell it, a kind of inertia settled over them: they inherited the house after my paternal grandfather passed. My father was growing a contracting business: No Paine Construction. (Get it? Clever, right?) Then, the next thing she knew, my mom was pregnant with me. *And that's pretty much it. Once you're a mom, once you're in love with your kid, you don't have as much ambition for other things. At least I didn't.* But she wasn't bitter about it. I have always known my mother loved me. I was enough for her; I never thought otherwise. You'll think this is weird later, when you know more. But it's true.

And so I grew up in the house where my father grew up. It wasn't the very same house. My parents gutted the old place and remodeled it in 1980. But it was the same foundation, the same frame, the same twenty-acre tract of land. Some people think that's cool. I'm not one of them.

There was another structure on the property, too, an old cabin that sat out by the creek. I found it when I was out exploring. I was happy that afternoon, giddy with my newfound personal freedom. I hadn't been allowed out on my own before. But when my sister came along, some of the restrictions formerly placed on me suddenly lifted. My father was in charge of me more and more, and he wasn't one to sit down and read or play games or paint out in the garage. *Go out and play.* That was his parenting philosophy. *Find something to do with yourself.*

At first I hung around the yard and rode my bike up and down the long drive. I remember not understanding what he'd meant by "finding something to do with myself." My mother had always had some idea, an activity or craft. Or I'd spend hours poring over my comic books. But Dad wanted me to go outside; he didn't think reading for hours alone in your room was a good thing. *You need some exercise, kid. Get out of your head.* He wasn't bookish—he was about building things and sports and exploring. He didn't get my proclivity for art and story. He didn't get *me*.

So, at first I just drew on the walkway with big chalk—

monsters and superheroes, men with guns, buildings on fire, and other images from the comic books that were my obsession. I played fetch with our dog, Butch, a tiny little Yorkie who had also suddenly found himself off Mom's lap.

And then one day, those woods just started talking to me. My mom was sitting on the porch nursing Ella, the dog at her feet. She got up and went inside, and the leaves in the trees started whispering. I was weeding the garden for her, a task I actually enjoyed for some reason. That was the first time I heard what I would later come to think of as the Whispers.

At first I thought it was the sound of voices out in the woods, light and airy, a crowd of kids playing. Then it just sounded like the wind rustling in the leaves. Then it was the echo of laughter, bright and magnetic. The sound pulled me to my feet and I walked to the edge of the woods. The trees—oak, sycamore, birch—were tall, their lush tops creating a thick canopy that cast the woods into semidarkness. I stood there listening, felt a smile creep over my face. I looked back at the house, and it seemed empty. Lonely. My mom hadn't returned to the porch. Only Butch stood there looking at me, his tail wagging uncertainly. He gave an uneasy bark, did a little shuffle with his feet.

And I just moved into the trees, the golden sun streaming through breaks in the canopy, and I walked and walked—jumping over puddles, turning rocks with a big stick, watching birds on the branches and squirrels scurrying up trunks. I had never been in the woods without my mother, and I felt grown-up and brave. The Whispers had grown quiet and I had forgotten all about the sounds that had lured me.

I'm not sure how far I walked before I came upon a little gray house. I never knew it was there; no one had ever mentioned it, and I had never seen it when I'd been out with my mother. There was a rusted propane tank, clearly in disuse. And a water barrel was tipped over and covered with moss. The roof sagged and the windows were broken. It might have been white once; I could see streaks of old paint that had been weathered away to gray. It was a sterling discovery: a house in the woods, a fort, a secret hideaway! I still remember the excited jolt I felt, the disbelief that something so cool was just steps from my own home. Why had my dad never told me about it?

I walked the perimeter—finding an old cloth doll buried in leaves, one button eye missing, black with age and dirt. There was a rusted tricycle so decrepit that it looked like it might crumble with a touch. I heard the Whispers again, giddy with excitement. And then it sounded like a voice, someone singing. As I came around the side of the small structure, I realized that it *was* a real voice. Standing there in the doorway was a girl about my age. She was rail thin and pale, but with a wild head of red hair and the bluest eyes I'd ever seen. She wore a white dress printed with roses and a pair of soft leather sandals. I was too young to wonder what in the world a little girl was doing out in the woods alone. She was simply another kid, out exploring, just like me.

"Hi," she said.

"Hi," I answered.

I was already a bit of a pudgeball, already the butt of jokes at school. I didn't have any friends, couldn't climb the rope in gym class, was picked last for every team. The cliché kid loser. I wasn't quite Fatboy yet, but I was headed that way fast. So I braced myself against whatever insult the girl might hurl at me. Even to this day, I always steel myself on meeting someone. People are so thoughtless and cruel; you never know what offhand comment they might toss out.

"Want to play?" she asked, the way only a kid will ask another kid. That's something you lose as an adult, that ability to just hang out with whoever might happen to be around. But little people get it; love the one you're with.

"Sure," I said. "What do you want to play?"

"Hide-and-seek," she said.

And so we played—running, darting between trees, covering ourselves with leaves, crouching behind logs. She was a very good hider, quiet and not prone to giggling before being found, as I was. I always laughed, giving myself away. I remember noticing how her hair changed color in the different shades of light, and thinking she was the prettiest girl I'd ever seen. But these thoughts were fleeting. I was a kid, only about playing and having some company. She could have been anyone—boy, girl, skinny, fat, pretty, ugly. It wouldn't have mattered. When it came to friends, I had already learned not to look too closely, to just be grateful that anyone wanted to be with me. We ran around until the sky started to grow dark and I began to think my mother would worry.

"I have to go," I told the girl.

"Come back tomorrow," she said.

"I'll try."

That was Priss. We were ten years old.

My mom was standing on the porch, calling my name, when I came back. I'd heard her from a distance, her voice thin and light on the air, and had started to run toward her. By the time I reached the porch I was breathless.

"Ian, where have you been?" she said. "Since when do you run off into the woods by yourself?"

"Dad said I could," I answered, climbing the steps to the porch and letting her take me in her arms. I was already almost as tall as she was, and tended to pull away from her hugs. That day I wanted her to hold me—and she did, but her embrace was bony and weak. When I looked up at her, she seemed tired and gray. She hadn't showered and her hair was dirty, hanging in greasy strands around her face. Her eyes were glassy and her stare distant.

I started to tell her about Priss, but Ella cried out and my mother drifted away toward the sound. My dad pulled up in his big truck with take-out food—all we ever ate now—and called to me to help get things inside. I looked back at the dark doorway through which my mother had disappeared. That was the first day that I knew something was really wrong with my mother. Even now, I don't know what it was precisely. My father kept saying that she was just tired because of the baby, but that didn't seem right. It was as if she was shrinking, disappearing.

Coffee with Megan turned into dinner, turned into her coming back to my place. She wouldn't *sleep* with me, but she did stay over. We lay in my bed all night talking. I never talked so much in my life. I had never been so sober with a woman, so wide open. I told her everything—about my sister, my mother, and Priss. There was something about her . . . those kind eyes, the soft understanding noises she made, the way she held my hand, the way our fingers entwined. With dawn breaking outside my window, we wrapped around each other, still in our clothes. I tried and failed not to get hard, and she let me kiss her. It was the sweetest torture, so wonderfully painful to want her so badly, to have her so close.

"Let's not rush and make a mess of this," she whispered.

"Okay," I said, nearly delirious with desire. The feelings I had for her even then were so big, so pure, I'd have done anything she asked. She was the first woman I had ever spent the night with not drunk, not high. Pathetic, I know. With Megan, I was all myself, and she still wanted to be near me. I pulled her closer, burying my face in the hollow between her shoulder and her neck. *Oh, please*, I begged the universe, *don't let me fuck this up*. We drifted off like that. And I dreamed about Priss. She wasn't happy.

CHAPTER FOUR

We were playing out in the woods, and the dark crept up on me. It had a way of doing that when I was playing with Priss. One minute, we were romping about in the sun; the next, night was upon us. The sky was the blue pink of late dusk. The trees were dancing in a strong wind, the colors shifting from cheerful hues of green and white to menacing shadows of gray and black. My mother had taught me how to look at things with an artist's eye.

You see that tree? she'd asked one day. *What color do you see?*

The leaves are green, I'd said. *The trunk is brown.*

Look closer, she said. *There are so many colors. The yellow of the sunlight shining, the black of the shadows and dark spaces, the white of the veins, the beige of the dead leaves. Nothing is ever just one color, or even two.*

She was right, of course. The world was a riot of color, and always changing with the light. Nothing was still or solid or predictable. I had never seen anything the same way after that.

"I have to go," I told Priss.

She reached out for me and grabbed my arm. Her grip was cool and strong. She hadn't touched me before and I was surprised by the feel of her. She was electric.

"Don't," she said. It was just a whisper among the Whispers. "It's not safe."

She was wearing that same dress again. It was threadbare and ripped at the hem. I had asked her a couple of times where she lived and she just pointed away from my house. *Over there*, she'd say. But I knew there were no houses for miles. The only building that was close was an old church that was long condemned and about to be torn down.

It didn't much matter to me then. Kids don't care about things like that. They only know the moment and whether it's good or bad. And when I was with Priss, it was all good. I could run and play, laugh, be free. I could forget about the various little miseries of my life.

I was being bullied at school and it was getting worse every day. My mother rarely got out of bed now. My grandmother had moved in to take care of Ella and me because my dad couldn't stay home from work any longer. I rarely saw him. He was gone before I woke, home just before I went to bed. And now the house smelled of cigarettes and burned coffee. My grandma Madge wasn't horrible; she just wasn't my mom. She wasn't a good cook, or much of a housekeeper. She was always reading or watching television; I was a bit of an interruption, not an unhappy one, but an interruption just the same.

When I was in the woods with Priss, none of it mattered. The simple pleasure of her companionship was a salve. She always wanted to play what I wanted to play— spies or pirates or bank robbers. She was game for looking for frogs, or climbing trees. She didn't care if she got wet or dirty. She never cried when she fell or skinned her knee. I might, though, and then she sat beside me, rubbing my back until I felt better, or goofing around until I laughed. She was a good friend, the best I'd ever had.

"Just stay awhile," Priss said.

But the sky was dark. And I knew I had to go even though I didn't want to. I had no idea in what condition I'd find my mother lately—sleeping, catatonic, manic, seminormal. Meanwhile, no one had an adequate explanation for what was wrong with her.

"It's the baby blues," my grandmother said. "It will pass. She had it after you were born for a time."

"She did?" This had seemed like hopeful information. My grandmother shrugged. "Not this bad, though."

My mother drifted around like a ghost, when she left her room at all. And Ella wailed all the time. She wanted Mom, too. And I felt sad for my baby sister, almost as sad as I felt for myself.

Of course, now I know that my mother was in the throes of postpartum depression, heading fast toward postpartum psychosis. Why no one knew this at the time, I'm unsure. It wasn't unheard-of in the eighties, even if it wasn't the media buzzword that it is today. Maybe that's what happens when you live in a backwater burg. Substandard medical care is no joke. Why didn't anyone help her? Why didn't anyone help us? There isn't anyone left to answer for it now.

"What do you mean it's not safe?" I asked Priss that night.

"Just stay here with me."

She was moonlight, almost translucent in the dark. And her eyes glowed with intent. "You belong here with me."

I liked the way it sounded. And a part of me believed it was true. But the thought of Mom and Ella, even my dad, pulled me away from her. That was my home and family; I knew I belonged there with them more than anyplace else, imperfect as we all were.

"I have to go," I said again.

"Not yet," she pleaded.

"You should go home, too," I said. "Won't your mom be waiting for you?"

"No," she said. "She won't."

There was something about her then—something angry, almost possessive—and the Whispers grew louder, more insistent. They didn't want me to go either. A strange, dark dawning cast a shadow over me and I started to run.

I ran with the shadows turning into ghouls and the world growing blacker all around me. I fell once and skinned my knee on the ground, tearing my jeans. Even now, I don't know why I ran or why I was so afraid. Some shine, some psychic connection to my mother or my sister maybe. I believe in that shit, you know. That we are connected to each other in twisting and indelible ways even if we are too stupid to know it most of the time. Maybe Ella was calling me, and a part of me, deep inside, heard her.

When I got to the clearing where our house sat, my grandmother's old minivan was gone. Later she'd tell me that she went out to run some errands. Both my mother and Ella were asleep last she checked, and she needed some things for supper. She'd called for me but I hadn't answered. She hadn't planned to be gone more than half an hour, but the store was crowded and traffic unusually heavy in town. She was gone closer to an hour. It shouldn't have mattered. It wasn't her fault, though I know she blamed herself until the day she died.

I saw my mom on the porch, rocking in that chair she loved. She wore the long white nightgown that I swear she'd been wearing for a month. I was washed over with relief when I saw her. She was fine; everyone was fine. Then the silence hit me like a hammer. It was so quiet.

"Where's Ella?" I said as I approached my mother. She looked like shit, seriously. Her face was drawn and her cheekbones jutted out beneath the blue-black valleys under her dark eyes. Her mouth, usually so full of smiles and words of love, was just a tight black line. I remember feeling a little angry with the woman before me. *What did you do with my mom?*

Her collarbone strained against her skin, and her dirty nightgown hung off of her as if she were just a wire hanger.

"She's sleeping," she said.

Through the window, I could see the television with the VCR sitting on top of it. It was just after five, according to the glowing green numbers of the digital clock. Ella should have been wailing for her bottle.

"Did you feed her?"

She stood up then, and put her hands on my shoulders. "Don't worry about Ella," she said. "Ian, I haven't been taking very good care of you. I'm sorry."

Her voice was flat and her eyes glistening.

"It's okay, Mom," I said.

"No," she said. "It isn't. I need to take better care of you. You're my baby, too. My first baby."

She put an arm around me and led me inside. I almost went with her. I leaned against her and she tightened her grip around me. "A mommy needs to take care of her babies, no matter what," she said. "Come inside. It's time for your bath."

But then I heard that voice again, calling from the woods. And I looked out and saw a glowing orange light among the trees. My mother didn't seem to hear. It was Priss; it was the Whispers.

It was something else altogether.

Ian. And the voice was inside my head somehow, and outside, too, all around me. But my mother kept moving us inside. She opened the door. *She's going to kill you.*

And even though it was so far from any reality I had ever known with my mother, I knew in my bones that the words were true.

Still, I didn't break away from her right away. I loved

being close to her; I wanted to be near her. I had missed her so, so much. I almost went inside with her. I wanted to go with her, wherever she planned to take me. And, if I had, what would have happened? Would she have led me to the bath she'd drawn for me? Would I have climbed inside, sunk into the warm water? Would I have let her bathe me, even though I had long since started taking my own showers, shutting the door when I used the toilet? Maybe. I might have let her, the way I let her lie beside me when she read my stories, the way I climbed into her bed at night when my father was away. Even at ten going on eleven, I was still more baby inside than big kid and I was nowhere near not needing and wanting my mom all the time. I might have let her do anything to me, just to be close to her. Isn't that how it works for everyone? We'll let our parents do anything to us.

But it was that light, that voice, that led me away from her. It grew louder, more ubiquitous, more urgent. And finally, just before I crossed the threshold into the house, I ducked from underneath my mother's arm, and ran to the woods toward that light, and answered the call of that voice that sounded like the tinkling of bells.

I heard my mother calling after me, her voice frantic, panicked.

"Ian," she shrieked. "Come back here."

But I didn't. I ran and ran and ran back to that small house in the woods. She wasn't there. Priss was nowhere to be seen. I found a corner and huddled there crying and cold.

After a while I wasn't sure what had happened. What had I seen? Why had I run? When it was fully night and the moon rose and the sky was a field of stars, I must have drifted off. Or maybe I was in a kind of shock. But that's where they found me, my father and the police. I heard them moving through the woods, calling my name in big, booming, urgent voices. Ian! Ian Paine!

I tried to hide, to make myself very small. I remember not wanting them to find me, because once they did, my life was going to be different. I didn't want to hear the horrible things they were going to tell me.

That was the night my sister died. They called it crib death; that's what they do in a town like The Hollows. They hush, they keep secrets, they don't tell. They bury it all deep in the ground where it rests, but maybe not forever. We all knew the truth. My mother killed my sister that night, and she would have killed me. The bath was drawn and waiting. But Priss saved me; she called me to her, called me into the woods. It was the first time she saved my life, but it wouldn't be the last.

"So, when do I get to meet Priss?" Megan wanted to know.

Wow. Never, I wanted to say.

Meg was the only person who knew everything about the history of my relationship with Priss. And she was understandably curious. As things were getting serious with us, it was a topic that came up more and more. But Priss had disappeared. After the events that caused me to stand Megan up, Priss had kept her distance, as she was prone to do when she'd misbehaved. And that was fine with me. It wasn't like I was going to call her and ask her if she wanted to meet my new girlfriend.

"We're not really speaking at the moment," I told her.

Meg and I were meandering through the Union Square farmers market. It was a lazy Saturday morning. We'd gorged ourselves at the Coffee Shop and now we were grocery shopping. Megan shared my obsession with food, which is important to a crazed foodie like myself. Food is life. If you don't like to eat, you don't like being alive. That simple.

"Yeah," she said. "But you've been friends a long time. Friends don't break up forever, do they?"

"Don't they?" I said. We walked past a stand with farm-fresh eggs. "I think friends break up all the time."

"So that's it?" she said. "She's just not a part of your life anymore?"

"She'll always be a part of my life," I said with an easy shrug. "She's the main character in my books."

In the next stall, Meg picked out some kale and an earthy-looking gentleman with dirt under his fingernails and thick-muscled forearms stuffed the vegetable into her reusable sack. How green this girl was. She was as crunchy, recyclely, fair-tradey, organic as you could get and still be fun to hang out with. How I despise the self-importance of all those greenies. Really? You think you're going to save the planet with your hybrid car and recycled toilet paper? It's too far gone, my friends. Way too far.

I could tell by the silence that followed us from the organic produce to the artisan soap stand that she was still thinking about the whole Priss thing. I had already figured out a few things about Megan in the month we'd been together. One was that she didn't talk until she had *really* thought about what she wanted to say. Any long silence was pregnant with her analysis of the situation, her meticulous choosing of the right words to express herself precisely. She was a thoughtful person. Really, she couldn't have been more different from Priss, who was subject to the most terrible rages. Priss exploded, top blowing, her anger like lava spilling over, burning and melting and destroying everything in its path. Once it cooled and hardened, she might be sorry. But it was always too late. The damage she did often couldn't be undone.

"Well," said Megan, inspecting a handmade bar of lavender soap. "I'll just put it out there that I'd like to meet her. But, you know, it's totally up to you."

"Okay," I said. I lifted a bar of lemon sage to my nose and felt my sinuses tingle. "Yeah. I'll think about it."

Wrong answer. She got quiet and was still quiet after a stroll downtown, through Washington Square Park. It's not like she was *mad*; she wasn't freezing me out. She just seemed introspective, not chatty.

But she perked up a bit as we wandered through some galleries and shops in SoHo. Eventually, we looped back uptown and got a table at Miss Lily's, a Jamaican place on Houston with some unbelievably hot supermodel waitresses and spicy beef patties that make you weep with delight. (I know. Didn't we just eat? So what.)

Even though the conversation moved on as we took our seats and we were talking about everything else, I could tell by the way Megan looked at me in the silences that she was still wondering about me, about the variety of reasons I might not want her to meet Priss. I pretended not to notice her slightly distant energy. Note to self: When a woman says, "It's totally up to you," she doesn't mean it. Not at all.

"How's Toby doing?" I asked, just to get her talking. We took a table by the window. There was a guy in the corner playing a steel drum, singing a reggae song I didn't recognize. I wondered how long it would be before he started with the Bob Marley tunes—the only reggae music even remotely familiar to rich white Manhattanites.

I was gratified to see Meg brighten up considerably. She loved that kid—even though I didn't see what was so great about him or why she seemed to like her job so much. She could be doing a lot more with her time. And I wondered if her attachment to him was a way of avoiding what she really wanted to do, which was to write.

She was working on a novel that she hadn't let me read. She said it was about a couple that loses a child, and how the loss impacts their lives and the life of the child that's left. Megan's older brother had died in childhood—a drowning accident. She said her book wasn't about that precisely, but that it was the seed, the inspiration.

We had that weird thing in common, the loss of a sibling in childhood—both of them drowned, her brother by accident, Ella on purpose. So—very different events. But still, grief scars us. We carry its mark. I had thought about it a little bit, wondered if that was the sadness I'd seen in her that first day—if I had connected to it in some deeply subconscious way. When I lost Ella I was older than Megan had been when she lost her brother. I still thought of Ella every time I heard a baby cry—which thankfully wasn't that often. How much did Megan think about her brother?

"Oh, he's good," she said. "Toby's such a smart kid. You know, he read to me last night? It might have just been that he memorized stuff I have read to him, but it was cool."

She'd been Toby's nanny for two years. She never intended to work for the family for so long, she'd told me. It was supposed to have been a placeholder job while she looked for something in publishing. But her job hunt hadn't gone well, even though her father was a pretty well-known nonfiction writer. And she got attached to Toby and his parents, so she was still there. She said the job gave her time to write, but I didn't think she was doing much of that.

"He's a good kid," I said. "I mean that he seems like it. Not bratty. It seems like you really love him."

She had a strange expression on her face, like she might cry, but she didn't.

"It's funny," she said. "I never told anyone this before."

"What?" I reached over for her hand and laced my fingers through hers. She had the softest skin. Just touching it made me want her. Ladies, men are like this. We are always thinking about sex and how to get it, even when you think we're sharing a deep, emotional moment with you. We *are*—but we're still thinking about sex.

"Sometimes when I'm with Toby, I wonder if he's like Josh would have been at that age. You know, my brother who died."

It was one of the first things she'd told me about herself. How he'd died before she ever knew him; she had been just a baby. There were only a few pictures of him around, and she said her parents rarely discussed him. She'd had a hunger to know more about him but was always afraid to ask. I had the sense that somehow the loss of him had defined her in certain ways, though she hadn't talked about it after her initial mentioning of it until now. We were connected like that. I'd be thinking about something and it would come up suddenly in conversation—like now.

"Do you think that's why you're so attached to him?" I asked.

It seemed like a natural conclusion to draw, one I thought she'd already come to herself. But I could tell the question surprised her. She pulled her hand back and I regretted asking it. I had struck a nerve without meaning to.

"I'm sorry," I said. "I didn't mean anything by that."

She looked down at her cuticles, then ran a hand through her thick, dark hair. She wasn't wearing a lick of makeup, and even in the bright light washing in from outside, the skin on her face was peaches-and-cream flawless. There was a wet sparkle to her eyes. How could I get that on the page—that look of raw, surprised emotion?

"My parents think that working for Toby's family is holding me back," she said. She took a sip of the strong black coffee she'd ordered. "They think I should be spending more time on the book, or looking for another kind of job."

The waitress came and set some water glasses on the table. The air was heavy with the smell of roasting meat and jerk spices—cinnamon, thyme, allspice, garlic.

"I have all these things I say to them, like Toby's family needs me, and it pays the bills without taking up every second of my time, or it's not a career but a job that I leave at the end of the day. That's all true without being the whole truth. You're right. I've grown really attached to Toby." She paused. "But I never thought that it might have something to do with Josh."

I wanted to say something, to make her feel better.

"There's nothing wrong with taking care of Toby, if you're happy doing it," I said. I could have left it there. But I added, "As long as you're not letting it keep you from doing what you really want to do."

She nodded but didn't say anything. I could tell she was thinking about it. I touched her leg under the table.

"I wish I'd had a hot nanny when I was a kid," I said.

She laughed then, and the heavy moment grew lighter. We ordered lunch—jerk pork belly hash and Jamaican rancheros, plantains, and beef patties. And just like that we were back to where we were before our conversation about Priss. It was early days, but looking back, I see that we both hauled a lot of baggage into our new relationship.

After lunch, we parted ways. My deadline was drawing closer—and I'd been so wrapped up in Megan that I hadn't been working much. We made out on the corner of Seventeenth and Broadway for a couple of minutes, like our bodies couldn't stand to be apart. As I moved away from her, I thought I saw a familiar flash of red in the crowd at the market and I felt a little twinge of fear—the bad boy getting caught.

"What's wrong?" asked Megan.

"Nothing," I said. I had literally broken a sweat.

She put a hand on my cheek, her brow wrinkled with concern. "You look—scared."

"No," I said. I put on a smile. "Sorry. Just thinking about work."

"That deadline getting close?" she said. She gave me an apologetic smile. "I'd better stop distracting you."

"Please don't," I said. And I kissed her again.

"I'll see you later," she said, pulling away. "Maybe I'll use the thought of your working hard to spur me to work on *my* novel."

"Good idea," I said. "When do I get to read?"

She laughed a little, and didn't answer. "I'll probably just take a nap."

I let her drift away into the crowd. "See you later?" I called after her.

"Call me when you're done."

And then she was gone. I wanted to go after her. But instead, I forced myself to walk home, thinking about Fatboy.

Fatboy is a loser. He's a towering, slovenly, acne-riddled, stuttering fool. He is an object of ridicule and bullying. His mother is locked away in a mental hospital. His father is an emotionally absent, razor-tongued asshole. But Fatboy does have a few things going for him. He's smart, with nearly a genius-level IQ. And he's an artist of exceptional talent. With a charcoal pencil in his hand, he is a master, a virtuoso, a superhero. And he has one friend, a girl named Priss.

Priss is everything Fatboy isn't. She's gorgeous; she's powerful; she's wild. She doesn't take crap from anyone. There's only one problem with her. She's batshit crazy. She's vindictive, vengeful, and full of rage on Fatboy's behalf. She likes to get even with the people who wrong him. And no one can see her but Fatboy.

So that's why when Priss does things that are out of control, even criminal, Fatboy often takes the rap. No one believes that Priss exists. They think Fatboy is crazy, just like his nut-job mother.

And that's basically the premise for my graphic novels. They're about poor Fatboy, just trying to get along, bullied and abused by everyone around him. And about how Priss gets even on his behalf. But then Fatboy has to get himself out of the trouble that Priss gets him into. The series has evolved over the years. Fatboy starts out as a middle schooler. Then it's high school, then the Cooper Union art school. Then he goes to work for Marvel Comics. Then he strikes out on his own as an indie. Yeah, he's a comic book creator and artist—meaning he conceives the story and creates the art—pencil, ink, and color, and he can (wants to) write all the dialogue and text, except he has a partner who does that part.

And all the while Priss is fighting Fatboy's battles. She hurts people who hurt him. And over the years her violence has escalated. In the last book, she kills someone. So now Fatboy is trying to put some distance between himself and Priss. Because at heart, he's a nice guy. He didn't want his writing partner to die just because the guy was trying to screw Fatboy out of his rightful percentage of the money.

Fatboy never wanted to hurt him; they were friends. His partner thought there should be a sixty-forty split in his favor. *After all*, his partner reasoned, *I am doing all the writing. The writing is the story.* But no, the art is the story. Without it, there's nothing. Not in comics. The battle was heated, and nasty words were exchanged. His partner, who Fatboy always thought was his best friend, called him ugly names and insulted his art.

And a week later, Fatboy's partner was dead. Hit by a car. It was an accident, a tragic accident; a hit and run. Only Fatboy knows that Priss had something to do with it—though she denies it—and so he's trying to spend less time with her.

He's stronger now, older. He has lost weight; he's looking good. His skin has cleared up, and his cool goatee and fashionable stubble cover the acne scars. He's not a beaten-up little boy anymore who misses his mother. He is coming of age. He is wiser, more secure. He is respected. Basically, he doesn't need Priss to fight his battles anymore. He's met someone, a nice girl whom he thinks he might love.

He still loves Priss. Of course he does. But things have been taking a turn—her rages are darker and more violent. She's not always nice to him anymore. She seems angry a lot of the time. Yes, Fatboy still loves Priss. But he's a little afraid of her now. Maybe he always has been.

Priss was in my apartment when I got home. (Which really annoyed me. The super has a thing for her, and all she has to do is ring his bell and he lets her in. And she does . . . ring his bell, that is.) She was lying on my couch, holding a recent drawing of Megan in her hand. I came in and let the door shut behind me, went to the refrigerator for a coconut water. I really love that stuff.

"Who's this?" she asked, not looking at me.

"A friend," I said easily. "A girl I met."

"Pretty," she said. She let the paper drift down to the floor. I could see that it was a sketch of Megan sleeping, one I'd done quickly before she woke up this very morning. "In a common way."

"She's all right," I said. Better to downplay it. Priss was the jealous type, jealous of anyone or anything that interested me too much. She used to just get mad at the people who hurt me. But somewhere along the line that changed. She was mad at more things, more often, and I couldn't predict what would set her off.

"Are you going to put her in the book?" she said. She was looking at me now. "A new character in your story?"

I blew out a breath. "Nah," I said. "Nothing like that."

She didn't say anything, but that silence swelled, took up some air in the room.

"I need to take a leak," I said.

I went into the bathroom and closed the door, a vein in my neck throbbing with anxiety, a flush creeping up my cheeks. I took a few deep breaths. I got these minor panic attacks sometimes when Priss was around. I stayed in there a few minutes, trying to pull myself together. She was in the kitchen when I came out.

"So what's her name?"

She was drinking from my carton of coconut water, drained it. Then she set it down on the marble countertop. Outside someone leaned hard and angry on a car horn. The sound seemed to go on for ages, before wailing up the street.

"Meg," I said. The word caught in my throat and ended with a little cough.

"Cute."

She snaked her arm around my neck and pressed her body tight into mine. My arms moved around her as if they had minds of their own.

"Priss, I really have to work," I said. "This is a bad idea."

"Is it?"

A familiar electricity connected us, drawing us into each other, blurring the lines of our bodies. And then her mouth was on mine, and I could feel everything else slipping away—Megan, my plans for work that day, all my good intentions. Priss was a drug. One hit and I was in her thrall. Her breath was hot; her flesh was soft. There was no way for me not to have her. When she was good, she was very, very good and all that.

I lifted her easily and she wrapped her legs around me, let me carry her to my bed. She had always made me feel like a man, even when I was just a kid. She was raw power, until she was in my bed, where she was suddenly so sweet, so yielding when she wanted to be.

"I miss you," she whispered. "Don't leave me."

Her words were vines, twisting and pulling at me. She was a little girl, alone in the woods. She needed me.

I lowered her down and slowly pressed my weight on top of her. The sound of my name on her breath shot me through. We were tugging at each other's clothes. Then her soft, hot lips were on mine, her arms around my neck. The power, the pull of flesh on flesh. Was any man ever strong enough to resist it? Then I was inside her, the heat of it almost too much to bear. Her helpless moaning rolled through me.

I always lost myself to her, the goodness that I knew dwelled deep inside her. She was bad, very bad sometimes. Still, I loved her and had for most of my life. Even as I drowned in pleasure, I was distantly aware of how terrible I'd feel later. But in that moment, it didn't matter, not even a little.

I woke up and it was dark. There was something unpleasant in the air and it took me a second to realize what it was: smoke. I leaped from the empty bed and stumbled to the kitchen. There was a stack of drawing paper, or what was left of it, on top of the Wolf range. All the burners were raging with blue-orange flame, and the industrial hood vent was humming like a tornado, lifting the smoke and ashes up into its powerful vacuum. I ran over, quickly turning off the burners and reaching under the sink for the fire extinguisher—which I couldn't figure out how to work. But the pages were all gone by the time I got there anyway, consumed to ash. I didn't spend any time wondering what Priss had set on fire. All my drawings of Megan.

CHAPTER FIVE

The days after my sister died were characterized by silence. There was a small, grim service in the Episcopal church in town, a tiny coffin draped in white roses standing beside a spray of lilies. My grandmother wept, a choking, inconsolable sound that was part moan, part cough. My father was stoic, a firm grip on my thigh his only concession to grief. His big hand shook. I hated his touch. But I felt bad enough for all of us not to brush him away. My mother was a zombie, drugged and locked away in the hospital. *Your mother needs to rest. It's the worst kind of grief, to lose a child*, my grandmother told me. No. Worse to lose a mother, surely. No one had said the words to me; no one told me what she had done. But I knew.

These things happen, son, my father said. *It's horrible, but sometimes babies stop breathing. We all have to try to go on.*

Do kids sometimes stop breathing? I asked. *Kids like me.*

He looked at me strangely, something sad and frightened twisting up his face. He put his hand on my shoulder. *No, Ian*, he said. *That's not going to happen.*

I believed him. Because even though he was often harsh, often distant, I knew he was strong and right about most things. He'd never told me a thing that later turned out not to be true. I didn't like my father that much. But I trusted him to take care of me in the important ways—food, clothing, shelter, the naked truth about the world.

Your mother will get better and come back to us.

And even though he was wrong about that, I know he believed it at the time.

After the service, I couldn't wait to go home, and to rush out to the woods with Priss. There was a long procession of cars behind us, following us to the reception the ladies of the neighborhood had put together at our house. When we got out of the car, friends, neighbors, coworkers, and people I'd never met formed a circle around my father, offering their condolences. I slipped away, stopping near the edge of the woods to see if anyone noticed me. But no one did.

Priss was waiting by the pond, holding a revoltingly large bullfrog.

"Look," she said. She held up its gelatinous, black-brown body. "It's HUGE."

She handed it to me. I sat beside her and started to cry. At first it was just a whimper.

"Are you okay?" she said.

Then I was choking on sobs, wailing. The frog hopped away, and I laid my head in Priss's lap, where I wept in a way I had never wept before. She never touched me, just sat there waiting.

"How did you know?" I asked her finally, when the sobs subsided, even if the tears hadn't dried up yet.

"I just know these things," she said. And she didn't sound like a ten-year-old girl. "They told me."

I knew she meant the Whispers, even though I didn't have a name for them yet. I kept weeping, and must have eventually fallen asleep. It was the sound of my father's voice that woke me.

"Son," he said. "Wake up. I was worried."

I looked around for Priss, but she was gone. I let my

father take me home, even though it was the last place I wanted to be.

After she set fire to those drawings of Megan, Priss didn't come around. She was mad at me, mad enough to stay away. And I was relieved, even though I didn't imagine that the separation was permanent.

Megan brought up meeting her again, one afternoon after we'd returned to my place from Whole Foods. Megan had been spending more time in the loft and was dismayed by the total lack of anything edible in the kitchen—nothing fresh in the fridge, no pasta, rice, or beans in the cabinets. So we'd decided to stock the kitchen, and we were both a little giddy about it.

I wasn't one of those guys who was afraid of commitment. I *wanted* to play house with Meg. I loved that she had a toothbrush in my bathroom, that her T-shirts and undies came back with my stuff in the laundry delivery. It seemed very serious, very intimate to be in a grocery store together, wandering the aisles, discovering new stuff about each other—how I'm allergic to apple skins, how she hates olives but loves olive oil.

She was stacking cans of San Marzano tomatoes in the cupboard when she said, "So I've been thinking about Priss. You said I could meet her sometime. Are you ready for that?"

The question made me freeze. It was obvious that Sunday-afternoon grocery shopping was a big tell about the course of our relationship. We were getting more serious and it was time for our lives to merge a bit more. It was right for her to want that. But I didn't want Priss anywhere near my relationship with Megan.

"Yeah," I said. "I've been meaning to talk to you about it. Priss and I have had a really big falling-out, actually. I haven't seen her or even talked to her in quite a while."

Clunk. Clunk. Clunk. Now she was shelving some black beans.

"A falling-out about what?" she asked.

She closed the cabinet door and folded up one of the reusable sacks we'd bought to haul home the groceries. God forbid we should use the free brown paper bags. I put the sparkling mineral water in the fridge, hiding behind the big metal door.

"Uh," I said stupidly. I let the door close and she was leaning against the countertop, looking at me in that way she did, sweetly inquiring, curious, concerned. "You know, there's never been anyone serious in my life, except for her. And she feels we're outgrowing our friendship. It's not working anymore. We don't bring out the best in each other. The last time I saw her, we fought. She stormed out and we haven't spoken since."

It sounded lame, but Megan was nodding. Anyway it was better than: *I fucked her and then she set all the pictures I'd drawn of you on fire.* I was trying to be honest with Megan, but telling her this would be going too far. She didn't even know about those pictures; I'd shown her one and that was it. She didn't need to know that there was a stack of fifty. Or had been. And she definitely didn't need to know I'd slept with Priss. You probably think I'm a jerk, and you might be right.

"That must be hard for you," she said. There was no edge to it, nothing sharp or sarcastic. "She means a lot to you. You've loved her a long time."

There was a twist in my middle, and my cheeks suddenly burned hot—I did miss Priss. But it was a toxic relationship. She connected me to a dark part of myself; I wasn't sure I could finally grow up with her in my life. I said as much to Megan.

"I'm sorry," she said. She moved into me and I held on tight to her. "Maybe after there's some distance, you can renew your relationship. She might need some space to change and grow, too."

This made sense—for normal people. But Megan didn't know Priss. Megan had a whole stable of friends—from childhood, from college. All her old boyfriends were still hanging around in the guise of friendship. She was a magnet, drawing people to her and keeping them forever.

"I don't know," I said. I took in the scent of her hair. "She's volatile, unstable. A lot would have to change."

And not just with Priss. With me, too. I'd have to stop wanting her so bad. I'd have to stop getting high and hopping into bed with her every time she showed up.

"Well," Megan said. She moved away and patted me on the chest, looked up with that sweet smile. She was an angel. Really, she was. "I still want to know her. So, if you repair your relationship with her, maybe we can work on that."

"Okay," I said. "Definitely." It was never going to happen.

She took some "ancient wheat" (whatever the hell that means) pasta out of the sack and put it in the cabinet next to the fridge.

"So," she said. She closed the cabinet and looked at me shyly. "Speaking of meeting people."

Megan asked me to come out to her parents' Long Island beach house for the weekend. It was a big step, but I surprised myself by accepting. Her mother was a research librarian; her father was an author of some note—nonfiction, big historical books about wars, and periods in history that no one remembered except your grandfather. But he had racked up the big reviews, had been twice nominated for the National Book Award.

And he'd won the Pulitzer for a series of articles he'd written decades ago for the *New York Times* on Nazi war criminals who had remained at large. So, yeah, I'd already Googled him.

He didn't have a website, too old school for that. But there were some pictures of him online. And honestly? He looked like a prick. In the author photo on his publisher's website he gazed at the lens down his long nose over a pair of reading glasses, holding a pen in one hand, his arm resting on a desk. He was unapologetically bald and wrinkled. There were tall shelves of books behind him, the obvious backdrop. What would he think of a guy who wrote graphic novels for a living? Not too much, I guessed. I felt the niggle of inferiority that comes from being a genre writer. People always think you're not as good as "real writers." Of course, most people don't know shit about art or writing or anything else.

"My dad's a sweetheart," Megan said. She had squealed with excitement when I said yes, and she'd been chattering ever since about the house, about her parents, about how excited they were to meet me. "You're going to like him."

But then girls like Megan always think their daddies are sweet. And they may actually *be* sweet to their daughters. It was everyone else in the world who found them to be intolerable gasbags. In fact, she still called him "Daddy," as in: "Daddy wants us to be there by three on Friday so we can walk on the beach before dinner. It's kind of a thing."

"Sure," I said. "Sounds good."

I cringed, imagining what Priss might say if she'd heard Megan say those words, and how easily, how eagerly I acquiesced. I already loved Megan truly, madly; maybe I had from that first day in the park. I thought of little else. I would have done anything for her even in those early days. (Except put her in a room with Priss.)

"Meg," I said. My heart was thumping with nerves. "I love you. I mean it. I crazy love you."

We hadn't said it before, though I'd come close a couple of times. I'd always chickened out. She put her hands to her mouth and her eyes filled.

"I love you, too," she said. She laughed a little. "I crazy love you, too."

We made out in the kitchen for a while, and then I picked her up and carried her to the bedroom. And we made love the way we did—sweetly, tenderly, respectfully. There was no pain, nothing rough, no grunting or deep, involuntary moaning. There was no moment where it seemed like a struggle for dominance. There was no nail digging; I didn't try to hold her down while she fought against me. It was normal-people sex. It was the way real, not-deeply-fucked-up people expressed physical love. I could get used to it.

Anyway, her parents turned out to be a bit of a surprise. *Daddy* picked us up at the train station the following weekend in a brand-new champagne-colored Range Rover that I knew cost about $100K. I knew because I wanted it and couldn't afford it. (I did all right, but there's money and then there's *money*.) I had an old Scout that I kept up in The Hollows, parked in the garage of a house I couldn't stand to visit. I went up and got it on the very rare instances that I was inspired to leave the city.

Daddy leaped out of the vehicle as we approached, looking fit and youthful, and gave his daughter a big bear hug, planting a kiss on the top of her head. Then he turned to me.

"Aw, man, Ian Paine," her dad said. He pumped my hand, and wore a bright, goofy smile. "I'm a big fan of *Fatboy and Priss*. I've always wanted to do a comic book."

I'm pretty sure my jaw dropped open. Even though "comic book" wasn't quite right (these days we called them graphic novels), I was still flattered.

"Wow, thanks," I said. "I'm honored to meet you, sir."

Maybe he was just blowing smoke up my ass, trying to be cordial. But it was nice. And I felt like a jerk for not reading even one of his books before we made the trip out to his home. That would have been the respectful thing, the grown-up thing to do.

But you're not a grown-up, Priss had said once. *You're a man-baby. Your self-involvement is so total, you don't even know that you're supposed to think of something other than your own appetites and neuroses.*

I didn't know if she was right about me or not. Sometimes she was, sometimes she wasn't. But I suppose I was as self-involved as any jerk-off my age. If Megan's dad—*Call me Binky, everyone does!*—was offended by my not mentioning his work or even pretending that I had any familiarity with it, it didn't show.

That afternoon passed in a happy blur—starting with a blustery blue-gray walk along the white shelly beach. Megan held hands with her dad and I trailed behind a little, but okay. I already knew she was a daddy's girl. Her mom whipped up a lovely meal of homemade gnocchi and butternut squash and salad, which I helped to serve, putting down plates on a table set with flowers and fresh-baked bread in a basket while Megan poured water into crystal glasses.

Her father broke out the perfect wine—a 1997 sauvignon blanc from New Zealand. (Anyway, Binky said it was the perfect wine. What did I know? It tasted good enough to me.) There was a fire in the fireplace; her mother's amateur oil paintings on the wall. And we talked—like, really talked—about life and the world, and current events. There was zero bickering, no arguing. There were no lashes of anger, subtle trading of insults. They liked one another—husband and wife, parent and child. Megan's father asked about my work, my process, the union of art and story. I found myself waiting for someone to get impatient, to say something crappy. But no, nothing. There was one light nudge from Megan's mom about when Meg might think about moving on from her nanny job and "get more serious" about her writing. Megan still hadn't let me read her novel, but I knew it had to be good. She had a writer's soul—she was a compassionate observer, a careful, gentle person, a beautiful spirit who saw a reflection of that beauty in everything around her—even me.

"It's a good job for me right now," she said to her mom, without a touch of defensiveness. "I can write when Toby naps and at night. You don't want me to move home, do you?"

Her mom smiled. She was a stunner like her daughter—dark hair, fair skin, a kind of radiance that was more than the sum of her features. She wasn't someone you'd hit on, exactly. But Julia was someone you would admire, like a painting or a sculpture.

"I'd love it if you moved home," Julia said. And anyone could see that she meant it, in a kind of girlish, let's-have-a-slumber-party way.

"But that's not the way you raised me, is it?" Megan lifted a glass to her mom, gave her a mischievous grin.

A mock sigh. "I suppose not. See, Ian, when you raise a strong, independent child to honor her own ideas—that's what you get."

"Besides," said Megan. "Toby makes me a better person—more loving, more patient, more forgiving. And I think those things make me a better writer."

"Just wait till you have one of your own," said her mother. She laid a hand on her daughter's and the moment was almost too sweet to be real.

My inner skeptic railed and raged inside. *No one's family is like this!* he said. *It's an act!* My own family, even at the best of times, had been the exact opposite of this one. I suppressed the urge to do something horrible, like knock over a glass, just to see how they all reacted. Would anger flash across Julia's face, or annoyance across Binky's? Would Megan rush to clean it up, worried that the peace had been disturbed? Would a thousand little fissures be revealed? Truth dwelled in the first moment of surprise. It had a way of pulling back the curtains. But I behaved. I didn't *want* to break the spell.

"Mom," said Megan, blushing. She cast her eyes down, pushed some gnocchi around her plate.

"No rush, dear," said Julia. "I'm just saying."

Julia was a real woman, with a full, lush body and thick tresses. There was just enough gray—slivers of white throughout—to know the color, still rich in tone and highlights, was natural. She ran a hand down the back of Megan's hair, a gentle, loving gesture. No clinging subtext, no nitpicking or teasing.

Megan and I cleared the table and did the dishes together. It was easy—easy to be with her, easy to be with them. As I was rinsing the dishes, the red of the sauce mingling with the orange of the squash and the pearl white of the soap bubbles in a beautiful gory swirl, Megan came up behind me and wrapped her arms around my middle, resting her head against my back.

"Thank you," she said.

"For what?"

"For being here," she said. "It means something to me."

"To me, too," I said. I turned around and took her into my arms; she rested against me. Megan did a lot of hugging, a lot of wrapping me up in her arms, cuddling in bed, snuggling when we watched television. I'd never experienced this with anyone before, not even with my mother, as far as I could remember, who was always affectionate enough before Ella came. It was very easy to get used to. I'd taken to hugging my pillow when we slept apart.

"This is really nice," I said.

Julia, who was coming in with wineglasses, stopped in the doorway and smiled at me, then quickly turned around and left to give us privacy.

Before we left that weekend, I found a quiet moment and asked Binky if I could marry Megan. I hadn't really planned to do it this the first weekend, but I was a little swept away by Binky and Julia's domestic bliss. The whole asking-for-permission thing seemed like a silly and antiquated tradition, but I knew that's how Megan would want it. Binky was surprised, but polite enough not to be an asshole about it.

"You haven't known each other that long, have you?" he asked. We sat on the porch in two heavy Adirondack chairs looking out at the Atlantic. The ocean beat against the shore, a churning mass of gray and green and white. The sky was an ominous gunmetal gray and a flock of gulls were screaming, diving into the surf and coming up with thin silver fish writhing in their mouths.

"Did you know Julia very long before you knew you

loved her?" I asked. "Like *knew* you would love her forever?"

"About five minutes, actually," he said. His gaze stayed
on the sea for a moment, then rested on me. "And her dad
told me to fuck off when I asked for her hand. He didn't
want her marrying a writer. He wanted her to have some
stability."

I had to laugh. I couldn't imagine anyone more stable
than Binky—he was the dad you always wanted, loving
and present, kind and wise. We should all be so stable.

"But it's not just about those first five minutes," he
went on.

"Is this where you tell me that marriage is about hard
work and commitment?" I was trying to keep the moment
light, and I felt like we already had a pretty good rapport.
But his face was serious, though not unkind.

"No," he said. "This is where I tell you that *life* can be
hard, really hard. And you know a thing or two about that,
I guess. Megan told me some about your history."

I kept quiet. Normally, I didn't like it when rich old
men tried to tell me something about life. Because those
dinosaurs never seemed to know as much as they thought
they did. But Binky was different. He moved in the
country-club set, but he was born and raised in Detroit.
His dad worked on the line at Chrysler for thirty-five
years. His parents struggled to make ends meet, and he
got beat up on the playground, and he paid his own way
through school. So I took a sip of the beer he'd given me
and shut the fuck up for once in my life.

"But I don't mean the big stuff—tragedy and money
problems," he said. "I mean the day-to-day, the workaday
world, marriage and paying bills and parenthood. It can
wear you down, if you let it. And that love, that passion
that brought you together? The shine rubs off a little.
Never forget those first five minutes, when you thought

how much you loved each other was the only thing that mattered. Because in truth it *is* the only thing that matters. That love is what gets you through all the other stuff."

"That's good advice," I said. But it didn't mean anything to me, not then. I look back on who I was in that moment—a punk, stupid and arrogant. I am ashamed of that guy in ratty jeans and scuffed-up Vans, a Death or Glory T-shirt. Even my tattoos, which I really loved, only seemed to prove what a child I was. I had the Batman symbol inked on my left pectoral, and Dark Phoenix down my right arm. Dark Phoenix, her form, her raw power—she ate a star and caused a supernova that destroyed an entire planet—was a big part of my inspiration for capturing Priss on the page. That tattoo was a full panel including the famous quote *You and I are quits now, X-Men. Our paths will cross no more. My destiny lies in the stars.* Even though I was wearing a jacket and neither tattoo was visible at the moment, we both knew they were there. I think Binky knew that I could never make Megan truly happy. She wanted a man like her father. And I was half the man that Binky was, if that.

I could tell he wanted to say something more, but he didn't. He just raised his glass to me.

"Welcome to the family, son," he said.

"Thank you, sir," I said. As we clinked pilsners, the flames on the Dark Phoenix tat licked out from my cuff.

You don't belong here, Priss would surely say. *And you know it.*

CHAPTER SIX

Ever take a dodge ball to the face? It hurts. It also makes you mad. The body doesn't like it when the head is threatened, and it releases a blast of adrenaline to make you stronger, faster, to defend yourself. That might have been part of the reason I lost it in gym class that very first time I *really* lost my temper.

Ah, gym class. Remember it? Institutionally sanctioned torture for society's misfits. God help you in America if you are not thin and fit, attractive, athletic, and coordinated, driven to win at any cost. God help you if you are broken or sad, or even just cerebral, or artistic, or just want to be left alone. You will be told in a million different ways—directly, subliminally—just how deficient you are. But nowhere will the message be delivered with more naked brutality than in a middle school gymnasium.

Mikey Beech was the king of my nightmares, big and muscular, even at twelve. Charming, handsome, athletic—baseball in the summer, wrestling in the fall. And, for whatever reason—maybe because I was his foil, his physical and energetic opposite—he had it in for me. Once upon a time, in kindergarten, we'd been friends—when we'd had the same *Star Wars* lunch boxes and I used to go over to play with his new puppy. Now he wrote BABY KILLER on my locker, aimed at my gut when he pitched softballs to me, fake-coughed when I was up at the board in algebra, pushing out his various taunts—*Fatboy, Lardass, Shithead*—under his breath.

Mostly I just bore it, ate it, swallowed it whole. I was a pussy like that, not equipped to push back. But it was the dodge ball that was the final straw, delivered hard and fast, a direct hit to my face. I was stunned, blood gushing over my shirt onto the floor.

"Oh, shit," he said, laughing. "Shit, Fatboy. I'm sorry. It was an accident, Coach."

I sat on the bleachers for a while, ice on my face, seething, thinking dark, horrible things about Mikey Beech. Then, even though my nose was still bleeding, Coach Jackass seemed to think a few laps around the court would do me good. *Walk it off, Paine!* As soon as he had an opportunity, Beech tripped me. I went down on my face.

Again.

The pain was so white hot, so electric, that I saw stars. As Beech emitted his very particular brand of derisive, mocking laughter, and all the other kids joined in, something happened to me. A kind of red veil came down, a white noise crowded out all other sounds.

Witnesses—the other kids who stood around gawking, and the teachers, too—said I turned into a berserker. I issued a string of expletives so vicious and foul that I nearly got expelled for those alone. I leveled unspeakable threats. They said I rose up to my full height, which was quite impressive even then, and launched myself at Beech, but was stopped by the coach and the other boys before I could land on him. With the blood pouring from my face and my hands raised in big claws over my head, one of the girls claimed that I looked like a "horror-movie monster." They say Mikey Beech cowered and ran.

But the really scary thing was, I didn't remember it that way. All I remembered—all I remember to this day—was crying like a girl, being carried out. I remember wailing, hurting. The coach had me under the arms, his assistant was holding my ankles. They'd picked me up off the ground where I had lain roaring in anger and carried me down the hallway to the nurse's office. I lay on a cot, curled in a ball, while she called my father from an adjacent room.

"Poor thing," I heard the nurse say to my father. "He must be under so much stress. How's his mom doing?"

"Oh," she said after a pause. "I'm so sorry."

My mom had problems, big ones. She'd had them all her life. Brutal bouts with depression, a psychotic break in college. She had been on and off medication most of her life since late adolescence. The early years of her marriage to my father, when she was working, were the most stable and productive she would have. She'd suffered postpartum after I was born, but apparently she'd snapped out of it pretty quickly. Still, she was a prime candidate for postpartum psychosis after a second child. But The Hollows was a backward place, a small town in the sticks. So maybe the doctor didn't know to be watchful. Maybe my father was in denial. Maybe that's why no one helped her. Poor Ella.

But as a kid, I didn't think about any of that. All I knew was that my mother killed my sister, and she would have killed me, too, if I hadn't run from her. And worse than that, everyone in The Hollows knew it, too. Even though everyone pretended to think that Ella had died from SIDS. It was one of the Whispers. The secret truths of that town, only spoken of in hushed voices, that carried on the wind and lived deep in The Hollows Wood. The Hollows knew how to keep a secret, forever.

My father came to the school a while later after my gym class meltdown and picked me up.

"Feeling all right?" he said when I got in the truck. I shut the door and fastened the seat belt around my big belly.

"I'm fine."

"What happened?"

I gave him the recap as I remembered it. He nodded, seemed to search for words then opt for silence. We drove home that way, with him looking straight ahead and me looking out the window at the passing landscape, hating every tree and leaf and wide green field and pretty house.

I was a kid who needed help. I needed someone to talk to, to work out all the pain, the dark thoughts, the twisting anger and fear with which I lived daily. I needed my father to step in at school about the bullying. I needed him to come home at night and have dinner with me, throw a ball around the yard. But he wasn't that kind of man. He was a blue-collar guy, a hardcase. You shouldered the burdens of your life and you didn't complain. You worked hard and you walked off whatever blows were dealt you. That's what he expected of me, and I knew it.

"Your grandmother's home," he said in front of the house. I got out and he drove away, back to work.

My grandmother had moved in permanently to take care of me while my father worked. She was a funny old woman who played cards on Thursday night, said novenas at the church on Mondays, and thought the Crock-Pot was the best invention of the modern age. I would come home to find her reading a romance novel beneath the dim light of a reading lamp—unless she was out playing poker with her girlfriends at the rec center.

She looked up when I walked in, peering at me over her reading glasses. I knew that both my eyes were black, but she didn't say anything. Her gaze just lingered longer than normal.

"How was your day?" she asked carefully.

"Fine," I lied. I waited for her to say something about the incident or at least to ask why I was home early. But she just pulled herself to her feet.

"Learn anything new?"

"Nope."

"Good." She issued a smoky laugh, gave me a pat on the shoulder. "Want a snack?"

You might be picking up on the fact that my family was not big on talking. No, we liked to bury our pain deep. We took the bumblebee approach to life's problems: ignore them and hope they will go away.

"Sure," I said.

The kitchen was always stocked: shiny, crinkly bags of Doritos; orange dusty Cheetos; greasy, salty Ruffles potato chips. Crisp white boxes of Twinkies, Pop-Tarts, Moon Pies, Devil Dogs, and cellophane-wrapped bulk packages of Snickers and Mars bars lined the pantry shelves. The freezer was full of Pizza Rolls, Hungry Man meals, ice cream sandwiches, Fudgsicles, chocolate-covered bananas. There were hot dogs, chicken nuggets, Tater Tots, onion rings, crinkle fries. My grandmother thought Fruit Roll-Ups were healthy. *Have some fruit*, she'd say, unwrapping one. I ate them by the dozen.

Did she notice that I was growing obese? That my face was a minefield of acne? I think, in her way, she was trying to comfort me. She could do nothing else. She couldn't bring my sister back to life, or bring my mother home, or make my father pay attention to me. But she could give me treats after school.

And it *was* a comfort, all that fat and sugar and chemical flavor. I looked forward to those junk-food feasts. I missed my mother desperately, was still crying myself to sleep at night. I would dream of my bawling baby sister, and wake up wishing I could hear her crying. I was a pariah at school, taunted, beaten. Fatboy, Psycho, Blubber

Butt, Pizza Face. They were afraid of me; I could see that. I had been touched by something unthinkable and it frightened them. It frightened me. But gorging on junk food was pleasure. It was my first drug.

My grandmother was beside me. She put a hand on my shoulder, gazed at me through thick glasses. She had a light down of fuzz on her upper lip.

"If you let them hurt you now, they'll hurt you all your life," she said.

I didn't know what to say, so I said nothing. She pushed herself to standing and walked slowly out of sight and then returned. She handed me a bag of frozen peas for my black eyes and another plate of Chips Ahoy! for, presumably, my bruised psyche.

What was she suggesting I do? I didn't ask. How was I supposed to keep people who hated me from hurting me?

"You have no reason to be ashamed," she said. "What happened wasn't your fault."

"I know," I said.

That's what grown-ups always say to kids and no kid yet has ever believed it.

After I had stuffed myself, my grandmother went back to her reading. Our big talk concluded, I left the house and she didn't stop me. Priss was always there, waiting by that falling-down gray shack. That day, she stood by a tall oak and I remember thinking how she seemed such a part of the place, like she could just sink into the tree and become a shadow in its trunk or a small dark hollow. She was wispy and ephemeral, always just about to slip away somehow.

"What happened to your eyes?"

I told her about the dodge ball, the hard trip to the ground.

"Who?" she asked.

"A kid named Mikey Beech."

She nodded, as though she knew him. But she didn't go to school with me.

"You can't let him get away with it," she said.

I knew that even though she was just a girl, there was something about her that was older, wiser, more worldly. She played games like a kid, but talked like a grown-up sometimes.

"If you let him get away with it, things will only get worse." She kicked at the ground, dusting up some sticks and leaves.

"What can I do?"

"Hurt him worse than he hurt you."

Some people have the capacity, even the desire, to hit back at their attackers. Others just curl up in a ball and wait for the blows to stop falling. That was me, even then. I didn't want to hurt people, even when they hurt me. What does that make me?

"I can't," I said.

What a pussy! I heard Mikey say as they carried me away weeping, even though he'd been cowering from me just moments earlier. What can I tell you? School, at least where I grew up, was an unforgiving playing field.

Priss looked at me, a darkness shifting behind her eyes. But she wasn't angry or disappointed.

"Then *I* will."

I didn't know what she meant or what she thought she could do. She was a little girl in a dress, skinny and dirty, with scraped knees and a wild head of hair that looked as if it had never seen a brush. I thought she was just talking. Kids have no real power—so they brag and lie, make up stories.

"Just forget it," I said. But there was something in her face, a kind of hard determination that I found a little frightening.

"If you let them hurt you, they just keep hurting you."
It was a weird echo of my grandmother's words.

She rubbed at her arms; it was cold and she was shivering. I took off my sweater and handed it to her. But she just shook her head.

"What do you want me to do?" I asked again.

I didn't want to hear what she had to say, and yet I *did* want to. I wanted someone to tell me what to do about my life. But in the end Priss didn't say anything. She tilted her ear up to the wind. Those voices, their rise and fall, their giggles and howls, gossipy titters and knowing laughter . . . I heard them all the time now but was only distantly aware of the sounds, like a kind of white noise in my life.

"Listen," she said.

And I did.

That night I dreamed about fire—great licking orange flames reaching into the starry sky. I heard screaming and smelled the burning wood, felt the ache of smoke in the back of my throat. I was happy in that dream, watching those flames. Fire was all energy, all power, using the very air around it to grow stronger, burn brighter. I felt the heat of it on my face.

When I woke, I heard sirens far off in the distance. I walked to my window and there was Priss standing in my front yard, smiling. She looked tiny and white. I thought if I ran down to see her, she'd be gone by the time I got there, evaporating into the mist that hung in the air. Or was it smoke? I felt a mingling of fear and glee.

Someone burned down Mikey Beech's house that night. Over the next couple of days, the rumor started at school that it had been me. And eventually, the police came knocking.

CHAPTER SEVEN

There are a couple of recurring characters in my comic. One is the detective who has always suspected that Fatboy is responsible for all the crime and mayhem that seems to surround him, and not Priss. The detective is a little bit obsessed with Fatboy, because the kid has been getting away with things for too long. There's never any real proof, always an alibi or some conflicting evidence that gets Fatboy off the hook. The detective—tall and big through the shoulders with a jaw like a mountain and fists the size of Volkswagens—lurks, like a haunting specter. He's always in the shadows watching, waiting for Fatboy to fuck up and reveal himself as the psycho the detective believes him to be.

Then there's the shrink who acts as Fatboy's voice of reason. He is small and thin and I always draw him in his chair, with lots of sharp angles, with a big notebook on his lap. He has a shiny pate, and wire-rimmed glasses. He makes affirming noises, and says things like: "Ian, have you ever considered that Priss is your way of expressing the anger you won't allow yourself to express against your mother?" He doesn't believe in Priss either, thinks she's a product of Fatboy's shattered psyche. Fatboy, according to the doctor, never recovered from the trauma of having his mother try to kill him.

There's Fatboy's mother, whom he visits in the mental hospital once every book. She is characterized by her wide, dark eyes. I draw her thin and pale, hair ragged and wild as lightning bolts. She has peered over the other side of sanity, and seen things there that have destroyed her. She is a walking ghost, eaten alive by guilt and fear. She always has something cryptic to say, which later winds up making sense.

Then there's the psychic who talks to the dead. She is gray and birdlike, wasted by a life spent conversing with spirits. I find her to be the most unsettling character in the series. Because she *does* believe Ian. And she knows exactly who Priss is.

All of these characters are *based* at least in small part on real people from my life, though each of them is his or her own thing. The characters in my books are not real people, but real people serve as the seed from which they grew.

The books are dark, really dark. Graphically violent and ugly, and getting worse. Lately my editor has been asking me to tone it down. He is worried that Fatboy is not as sympathetic as he used to be. He used to be the victim, and Priss his avenger. But something about that energy has started to change—because Fatboy isn't a kid anymore.

He is a grown man now, and quite a successful one at that. He isn't picked on and abused. He really doesn't need Priss to fight his battles anymore. And she's a little upset about it; the balance of power has started to shift.

Lately, she's been picking fights and making trouble for Fatboy—like the whole thing with his writing partner. And Fatboy is starting to wonder whether Priss really has his best interests at heart anymore. Maybe he was just her excuse to do bad things. He no longer wants her to do those things on his behalf. But she still wants to do them. And he is not doing anything to stop her.

"So where are we going with this?" my editor, Zack,

asked over lunch at the Noho Star, a post-trendy eatery on Lafayette. Big and roomy, always crowded with arty types, square-paned windows looking out on the gritty avenue, the place served everything plus awesome Chinese.

"What do you mean?" I asked. There was a weird energy to this lunch he'd called, like he had something to say. I didn't really have time for it, because I was past my deadline for the next book (which he should know since he was e-mailing me every Monday asking how it was all going), and I was completely stalled.

I hadn't talked to Priss since she burned those pictures of Megan. And a big part of me was hoping that she was gone for good. But, to be honest, since she *had* gone, I was having a hard time working. She was slipping away from me on the page. I couldn't hear her voice. I had developed an eye twitch from stress.

"So the last couple of books," he said. "You know, the numbers are down."

"Right," I said. "The economy and the whole e-book thing."

He nodded slowly, pushing up his dark-framed glasses, which I strongly suspected he didn't need to wear. He was a kid, wiry and practically bouncing with energy, a thick field of dark stubble on his chiseled face, a mop of curls he clearly made no effort to tame. He looked like a Labradoodle.

"I just wonder if it has to do also, some, *maybe*, with the change in tenor of the comic itself."

"Change in tenor?"

"You know, Fatboy has always been kind of hapless. Kind of a nice guy in bad circumstances. And Priss has been a hero, like a defender of the weak and whatnot. And I think your readership really connects with that. I think they all wish they had a Priss around."

Yeah, let's face it, my average reader is probably a lot

like Fatboy. The world hasn't exactly been kind—many of my fans have neither genetics nor circumstances on their side. They wish for a Technicolor world where geeks are cool, and superpowers are the reward for some type of terrible accident or victimization, and women are flawless and easy to understand, with huge tits and heart-shaped mouths. Comic book girls only want a hero, a man with a true heart. The world of classic comics is very simple; there's a clear code, a concrete set of rules. Good is good and evil is evil. Heroes triumph eventually and bad guys never win. There are no gray areas. It's a nice place to live. And let's face it; I have never wanted to live anywhere else.

"But in the last couple of books, Priss has turned into a villain, hasn't she?"

"Well . . ." I said. Was that true?

"I mean, she isn't helping Fatboy anymore. She's *hurting* him."

I didn't know what to say.

"I mean, she *killed* his writing partner," said my editor. He was getting more excited. It was one of the things I'd always liked about him; he was really into the whole *Fatboy and Priss* story world.

"I liked that character and I think a lot of people did," Zack went on. "He handled all the business so that Fatboy could just stay buried in the story, where he belonged. So it was a big surprise; I mean you must have read all the chatter and online reviews about it."

He paused here and looked at me with raised eyebrows. There *had* been a lot of angry chatter. And the reviews were pretty brutal. But that's the one thing with having taken a lot of abuse in your life; you tend to be pretty numb when it comes to other people and the shitty things they have to say about your work. I gave him a quick nod of acknowledgment, took a sip of water.

"And now there's Molly, who's a really nice girl for

Fatboy. She loves him. But how is it going to all work, you know? Do you really think Priss is going to let Fatboy find a nice girl and settle down? Do you think she's just going to ride off into the sunset on her Harley?"

I felt something clench in my gut. No, she wouldn't. Of course she wouldn't.

"So what are you saying?" I asked.

He took a deep breath, and looked at me hard. "I think it's time for Fatboy to get Priss under control. There has to be some kind of big conflict between them, and Fatboy has to win."

I looked at Zack; he was practically vibrating. What *was* he saying?

"Fatboy is a grown man now. He's a successful writer; he wants to get married. He's not a victim of the world anymore. But he's morphing into Priss's victim. He has to man up and tell Priss that he doesn't need her anymore."

"Break up with her?"

"Right," said Zack. He moved his head in a slow, careful nod, made a steeple of his fingers. "But she won't allow that, will she?"

"What are you saying?" I was dimly aware that it was like the third time I'd asked him this question.

"You know what I'm saying, Ian. Don't you?"

I pushed my plate away. Suddenly the garlic shrimp didn't look very appetizing.

"You're saying that Priss has to die."

Zack took off his glasses and rubbed at the red indentation they'd left on his nose. I'd never seen a man with nicer nails, square and pink, buffed, cuticles white and neat. He was right, of course. It's why I was stuck in the book. I couldn't go forward because there *was* no way forward. Fatboy knew that Priss had turned on him, that the dark energy he'd always relied upon was starting to work against him. He had to break away from Priss and it wasn't going to be pretty.

"And then what happens to the series?"

"Maybe you move on?" Zack said with a shrug. "Come up with a new idea. Your next big thing; I know you have a million ideas in that head of yours. These things can't always go on forever. Fatboy grew up; he's a man. Maybe you should just let him have a life. Write the best last book you can, I mean really bust it out, no holds barred. Write the most exciting, darkest, wildest *Fatboy and Priss* you ever have. Then let's brainstorm some new ideas."

I don't really remember leaving the restaurant. I think I made some affirming noises and then zoned out, getting kind of internal about the whole thing. I walked out of there in a daze and started back to the loft. I remember the day was warm and humid, the sky threatening rain.

Fatboy break up with Priss? It was unthinkable. Yet I knew Zack was right. It was time. At first, the thought filled me with a sick dread. But then came a rush of giddy excitement. A fresh start, a shedding of all the old baggage, the person I used to be, the hold Priss had over me. I could walk into my life with Megan free and clear of all of the negativity from my past. I could come up with a new idea, a hundred of them. It was that easy, just pen to paper. If only I could get Priss out of my head once and for all.

I couldn't wait to get back to the loft. I was more inspired than I'd been in months.

But back at my place, I made the mistake of going online, checking e-mail, cruising through the social networks. It was all the usual stuff, notes from readers around the world—angry at Fatboy, in love with Priss, asking for more sex in the books. There were a couple of people who had posted pictures of themselves wearing Fatboy masks.

I have crazy fans. And since my publisher, Blue

Galaxy, started a merchandising initiative, the fans seem to have gotten crazier. For a promotion at the last Comic Con, my publisher produced one thousand Fatboy masks. It was a hideous rubber face, complete with jowls and riddled with red-and-white plastic acne. It had a head of wild black hair and gaping holes for eyes, and a wide, maniac smile. They sold out the entire run and went back into production after the convention and began to sell them online, sent out a bunch to fulfill orders from various independent comic book shops around the country.

When the masks first came out, fans would send me pictures of themselves wearing them at parties, at the office, at home, alone in front of their computers. Then Blue Galaxy started a promotion where if you posted a picture of yourself somewhere with the mask, you were automatically entered into a contest to win free comics. So then the number of pictures I received increased tenfold. I have to tell you, it freaked me out. It was a scary-looking mask; it was utterly beyond me why anyone would wear it. After all, *I* couldn't wait to shed the Fatboy I used to be.

Then a couple months after the release of the mask, some thug in the Bronx wore one during the commission of an armed robbery in which a store clerk was killed. There was a rash of other incidents—someone in a mask robbed a taxicab driver, someone menaced a couple of girls as they were leaving a club, and exposed himself. Another man wore one while running naked through Washington Square Park. The bad publicity this generated increased orders exponentially. The last I heard, there were over fifty thousand masks out there, mainly in California and the tristate area where my books were most popular.

I had one of the masks resting on a Styrofoam head, sitting on the shelf by my computer. I put it on once and looked in the mirror. I never put it on again. But I reached up now and took it off the shelf, held it in my hand. It was the cheapest possible piece of rubber, made in China, probably toxic.

"Fatboy," I said. "Who are you without Priss?"

He didn't answer.

CHAPTER EIGHT

Fatboy is coming home from his partner's funeral. The sky is black and it's raining hard. Lightning is splitting the sky above him. But Fatboy doesn't run. He walks, slow and hulking, up Lispenard Street, the buildings thick and gray, seeming to bend in on him. He is crushed, grieving for his friend. And he's angry, angry because he knows Priss had something to do with his partner's death. As he approaches his building, a flash of lightning outlines her unmistakable form—the flip of her hair, the curve of her hips, the narrowness of her waist. He draws closer and they stand in the rain, looking at each other.

"Priss, what did you do?"

"Only what you wanted me to do."

"No. It's not what I wanted. I never wanted you to hurt anyone."

"Bullshit. There's a rage inside you, Ian. A big one—it's a beast. You keep it locked away because it scares you. But the beast talks to me. He tells me what you want. And I do the things you can't do yourself."

"You're wrong. You're the beast. You do what you want."

He walks past her and pushes open the door. The thunder and lightning, the heavy downpour—it's right above them. Priss stands soaked in the street, legs apart, hands on her hips.

"We're done, Priss. I'm sorry, but we are."

She laughs.

"I mean it. I don't want you in my life anymore. You helped me once, many times. You were strong when I was weak. You

saved me one night long ago, and I'm grateful. But I'm not weak. And I don't want you to hurt anyone else."

"It's because of her, isn't it? Molly." Priss says her name like a taunt. Her face grows twisted and ugly in her anger. But Fatboy doesn't back down.

"No," he says. "It's because of me. I'm a man, not a little boy anymore. I need to stand on my own now."

"The world's an ugly place," she says. "Bad things happen. They happen all the time."

"I know," he says. "Thank you for protecting me. But it's okay. You don't need to do it anymore."

"Do you think it's going to be that easy?"

Her rage is growing, her face becoming redder, uglier. She's getting bigger, her hair blowing around her like a mane of fire.

"You think you just walk away from me?" Her voice is a roar that mingles with the thunder.

"No," he says. "I'll miss you every day."

"That's sweet," she says. "But that's not what I meant."

"Good-bye, Priss," says Fatboy.

He walks inside and leaves her raging as the storm grows more violent—thunder, lightning, howling wind. He leans his back against the door, as if to hold it closed. And he weeps, sinks to the ground. He knows it's not the end. But it's the beginning of the end. And things are going to get ugly.

CHAPTER NINE

I took Megan up to The Hollows to meet my mother, Miriam. I wouldn't have asked it of her, but she wanted to go. My grandmother and father have both passed on. My maternal grandparents both died when I was a baby, my paternal grandfather before I was even born. Bad genes on both sides.

My mother is the only family I have. She has been diagnosed with paranoid schizophrenia and she lives her life in a medicated fog as a resident of a psychiatric hospital where she also works in the library and assists in the art therapy department, drawing a small stipend.

My mother is destitute, and the costs of her care are mostly covered by Medicaid. I pay for anything that isn't covered. She is a model patient, has some off-grounds privileges, but mainly she has no desire to leave the premises. The world is too ugly, too frightening for her. Too full of demons and sinister characters, bad memories. But really, I think, it's the crushing guilt that keeps her in the little world she has constructed for herself. She is a woman who killed her own child, and there is no changing that. There is no moving on, not for her.

"You don't find it weird? That I still see my mother?" I asked Megan as we settled into our seats on the train. We sat in the quiet car on the Acela, but some jerk a few rows back was talking loudly into his cell phone. "*Well, we haven't had the returns we expected and it might be time to dump, yaknowwhatImean, Chuck?"*

Megan wore a little frown as she pulled her laptop out of her bag. Then she looked at me, giving me the full light of her eyes. "I think it's the measure of who you are. Your devotion to her moves me."

She talked like that; she really did.

"I mean," she said, "people don't get it, how much courage it takes to not only forgive, but to love. You love her. I can see that."

"She's sick," I said. "She needs me."

Megan smiled, and her smile was so warm and loving that I bowed my head. I wished I could crawl inside that smile and live there for all of my days.

"I know she does," she said. "And you need her because she's your mother, no matter what she's done."

"It wasn't *her*, Megan. She had postpartum psychosis," I said to the ground. My voice sounded urgent and pleading to my own ears. "She was someone else then. My real mother, before she got sick . . . I *wish* you could have known her."

"I do know her," she said. She put a warm and gentle hand on my leg. "I know her through you."

I still couldn't meet her eyes. She was too sweet, too earnest. I didn't deserve her. Instead, I looked out the window at the platform. A woman was rushing for the train. A homeless guy slept on the bench, covered with sheets of newspaper. A little girl stared at me with a curious tilt of her head while her mother chatted on her cell phone.

"Thank you for doing this," I said, finally turning back to her. I don't know how much time had passed since she'd spoken. But she was okay with me being awkward and reticent. I never had to talk with Megan. She seemed to understand me without words.

"I want to help you take care of her," she said.

"I'm not doing a very good job," I admitted. "I don't go see her as often as I should."

"I think you're doing what you can. Let me help you do a better job," she said.

And I agreed because it was a relief to have Megan in my life. And there had been no one to share this with, not since my father died. Even when he realized that my mother would never get better, that he couldn't fix the thing that had broken inside of her, he didn't turn away from her. But he wasn't a man who could handle the idea that some things stay broken and you have to carry the pieces around and forget that you ever thought they might be mended. After he was gone, I carried them alone, even though I wasn't any better at it than he had been.

And so we took the train up north, and got a cab from the station, and I took Megan to the place where I grew up: The Hollows. As we pulled through town, and out onto the rural road that led to my childhood home, I waited for her to be horrified, for her to ask me to take her back to the train station.

I was prepared to never see her again after she knew what I came from. How could someone who came from such a good, clean life want someone who came from so much ugliness and misery?

But all she said was, "It's so beautiful up here. So peaceful."

She was looking at the sky and the trees, and the quaint little town center that had been gentrified and grown wealthy in recent years. People had moved from the city, bringing with them a taste for fine restaurants and money to shop at trendy boutiques. And it was actually kind of a nice place to live now. That is, if you liked living in the middle of fucking nowhere, where the woods were haunted and people went missing, died mysteriously, or killed their own babies with, what seemed to me, unusual frequency.

But anyway, as far as "pretty" goes—okay. I guess there was a kind of prettiness to The Hollows. That's what Megan seemed to see when we pulled up that long drive to my old house. It was mine now; my father put it in my name before he died.

"We could do something with this someday," she said. The cab was pulling away and I felt that constriction of my airways that I always felt when I returned home. "If we get tired of the city."

"Meg," I said. I put my hands on her shoulders and looked her dead in the eye. "Hear this. We are never living here. This place is a hell mouth."

She leaned in to give me a chaste little kiss, a patient smile. "Come on. It's not that bad."

Could she hear them, I wondered, the Whispers? *I* could hear them all around me. But no, she was glamoured by the towering pines and the swaying sycamores, by the larks and the squirrels and the big fluttering monarch butterflies. She would hear them, though, if we stayed for any length of time. She was sensitive and open. Eventually, she would sense the darkness here. But I wasn't going to allow that to happen.

"If you don't like the house, we could tear it down," she said. Yes, she was the child of privilege. If you don't like something, break it apart, build something all new. Poor people accept their lives, work with what they have, understand implicitly that some things cannot be changed. But the rich think they can bend the world, the very universe, to their will. I wonder who's right.

"We could build any kind of house we wanted here." She looked dreamy. Had she not heard me? Did she think I was joking? "It could be a retreat, a place to write."

"Yeah, maybe," I said. I didn't want a full-blown confrontation. "Someday."

Like never.

It was strange watching her walk through those rooms, over the worn shag carpet, past the white refrigerator, up the shallow stairs. She moved into the room I'd inhabited as a kid. No doubt she expected it to be preserved as was her bedroom at Binky and Julia's. Her old room had not been converted into a guest room, or a work space, or a place for the treadmill. It was a living shrine to an adored only child. It looked like a teenage Megan could happily return at any moment and bounce onto her pink cloud bed and lounge among her debate-team trophies, and framed artwork, and dolls and stuffed animals and pictures of her friends. You could almost hear her chatting on the phone, getting ready for prom, crying when she broke up with her first boyfriend.

My dad had kept the twin bed in my old room, the plaid comforter. But all my old stuff—books and toys and games, sketches, models—was boxed up in the basement. He had put a desk in my room, used it as a place to pay bills and whatever else. He wasn't a sentimental guy. He didn't like the comics I wrote. I am not sure he ever bought one. There weren't any of them on the bare shelves, no pictures of me, of our family even before everything.

"Was this your room?" Megan asked. She sat on the bed.

"Yeah," I said. I was embarrassed by my old bedroom suddenly. Felt the urge to make excuses for my dad. But in the end, like usual, I didn't say anything.

"Hmm," she said. She kept her cheerful demeanor, but I could see she was disappointed by the room's sparseness. She wanted to know who I was as a kid. "It's a good size."

Out in the garage, we got in the rumbling old Scout, took it into town, and filled it up with gas. I recognized the attendant immediately as my high school's former star jock, homecoming king, all-around-most-likely-to-succeed fuckhead who had made my life a living hell: Mikey Beech.

He didn't recognize me, or if he did, he hid it well. He looked like shit, I was happy to note. He'd packed on a good fifty pounds and was carrying it all in his face and his gut. And—P.S.—he was pumping gas for a living at thirty-something. Most likely to succeed at being a loser, looked like. He still had arms like sledgehammers, though.

Meg went into the little shop to get herself a bottle of water and to scan the paltry aisles for some kind of dairy-free, gluten-free, organic snack. And I stayed in the driver's seat, letting the homecoming king pump my gas and squeegee my windows.

"Check your oil?"

"Why not?" I said.

I saw the recognition flash across his face just as Megan climbed back into the car with a bottle of water and a package of nuts. She held up her purchases and I felt the heat of Mikey's gaze.

"Local," she informed me with a note of triumph.

"Awesome," I said. She hefted the door closed and it shut with a heavy thud.

"This old Scout held up okay," Mikey said. He leaned his big hands on the door.

"Sure did," I said.

I didn't look at him, swallowing back the tightness in my throat that always preceded a conflict of any kind. *What a pussy!* I could hear them all laughing. The sting of it endured more than any physical injury I'd ever suffered. *Sticks and stones can break your bones but words can break your heart.* My mother had said that to me once. I know, very helpful. It stayed with me.

But Mikey Beech didn't say anything more, just gave me the bill and I paid cash and gave him a flashy tip. His eyes bored into my neck.

"Keep the change," I said without looking at him.

"Have a good one." He gave the hood a friendly pat.

But he said something as I pulled away. It was low and under his breath, like a growl. I didn't hear it, didn't want to hear it. In the rearview mirror I saw the nasty, taunting bully I knew him to be. His face was twisted in an ugly grimace.

"People are so nice here," said Megan.

"Yeah," I said. "Real nice. For a bunch of rednecks."

She snorted, gave me a little nudge. "Don't be such a New Yorker."

I found it funny and a little sad that my mother had clearly tried to pull herself together for Megan. She had put on a dress I sent her three years ago. It hung off her thin frame, looking like a muumuu even though I think it was a size six or something. She had also tried to apply a little bit of blush and lipstick. She looked like a doll in a horror movie, broken and frightening, even though she was smiling when we entered the dayroom.

I'd offered to take her out to lunch, more because I didn't want to shock Megan with the full misery of my mother's situation. But my mother refused to leave the hospital and Megan said it was fine. She didn't want there to be any secrets between us, things about our lives that we hid from each other. We both knew we were going to be together forever. I hadn't actually popped the question yet, but I had my plan in place.

We ate sandwiches in the hospital cafeteria. And, in spite of my mother's frighteningly bad application of makeup, she and Meg seemed to hit it off. They were gentle with each other, kind and soft-spoken. But they were both that way anyway, so I guess it shouldn't have come as any surprise.

"Ian tells me you're a writer," my mom said. She was just nibbling at the chicken salad sandwich that sat in front of her. Megan and I were both almost done with our meals, but Mom had barely eaten. She hardly consumed enough to keep herself alive. I wondered if this was one of the ways she punished herself, or maybe it was just that the food was total shit here.

"Well," said Megan, "I'm working on a novel, that's true. But right now I'm a nanny to a four-year-old boy named Toby."

"Oh, that's such a nice age," said my mother. She touched but didn't pick up her sandwich and I noticed how dry and red the skin on her hands was, how her nails were bitten to the quick. "I remember when Ian was four. Everything is so magical—Christmas, Easter. They still believe in all the wonderful things."

"That's so true," Megan said. "Toby asked me the other day about fairies. And I thought if I told him that they were real, that they played in the park and lived in the trees, he'd believe me. I envy that, that willingness to believe in magic."

"We lose it," my mother said. She looked out the window with something wistful on her face. "We have to let that go."

"I know," said Meg. "Luckily there's plenty of real magic—like love, music, poetry. There are stars that are light-years away, stars that died a millennium ago and yet they're still sparkling in our night sky. There's springtime and the birth of children. Those things are magical, too."

My mother smiled at that; it was bright and sudden and took me by surprise. I hadn't made my mom smile like that in years. Her smiles at me were always heavy with sorrow and regret.

"You're right," she said. And I could see that Megan had given her something, a positive thought to cling to in dark hours. It might have been more than anyone had given her in a long time, even me. My mother and I were so wrapped up in each other, in our terrible past, that we hardly gave each other anything except bad memories, and a sad, tattered kind of love.

They chatted on about ordinary things, like Megan's college days, and my mom's dreams of becoming a journalist. I kind of zoned out a bit, checked my e-mail on my iPhone, looked at my Facebook page. I heard my mom say, "Don't put that novel off too long. You'll never have more time than you have right now."

"My mom always tells me that," Megan said.

It was so strange, seeing these two women I loved, so different, from such totally different phases of my life. One all dark, one light. And yet they fit together, yin and yang. I guess I was happy. I also wanted to leave, take Megan away from here, from my mother. I didn't want anything from my past to leak into my future. I kept seeing a rusted barrel with toxic waste eating through the metal, breaking it down from the inside, starting to drip out in a noxious lime-green ooze.

In the truck on the way back to the house, Megan cried.

"She seems so fragile," she said. I pulled over because it wasn't just a few little tears and sniffles. She was sobbing. "But she must be so strong inside. I can't imagine living with it—the pain, the guilt."

"It wasn't her," I said. I know; I said that already. But I thought it should be repeated—because people don't seem to get it when I say it. My mother seemed like another person altogether during that time. Herself, but not at all herself—as if someone else was living in her body and looking out through her eyes. "It was the person she is when she's not well. I think she disassociates, or something. That's the only way I can explain it. And she has never put herself back together, not really. She couldn't live on her own, I don't think."

Megan dug some tissues out of her purse, wiped at her nose and eyes.

"If we fixed up the house, we could spend some time here," she said. She looked at me over her tissue. "You could see her more often. Maybe it would help you both."

There it was, the pull of The Hollows, luring me back. On the sweet lilt of Megan's voice, it almost seemed appealing. I could see the house we'd build, imagine taking my mother out to lunch more than once every few months. That's how it got you; it wove itself into your now, seduced the people who didn't know better. My mother had warned me about this. *Don't let it bring you back here.*

"Yeah, maybe," I said.

"That's what you say when you mean no," she said.

I smiled a little inside. Megan already knew me better than anyone had—even Priss. Priss only knew a former version of me. She didn't know the me that I was with Megan. Megan balled up her tissue, started picking it apart. She was pretty even when she cried, a pink flush on her cheeks and the tip of her nose, under her deep brown eyes.

"It hurts to be back here. I hate it," I said. "This place is evil."

"I know you feel that way," she said. My hand rested on the gearshift, and she laid her palm on top of it. "I know you do. But you give it too much power. Bad things happen everywhere, not just here. We live in New York City; horrible things happen every day."

"It's different."

"It's *not*."

I put my head in my hands and rubbed away at the headache that had settled there. The Hollows activated all my allergies, too. My sinuses were swollen, my eyes itchy and red. I could tell she was about to say something. She drew in a deep breath. But then she stayed quiet.

"You know what?" she said after a few moments. Her voice was gentle. "Just forget it for now. One step at a time, okay?"

"Okay."

"Let's get back to the peace and safety of Tribeca," she said. I heard the smile in her voice, even though I was still staring at my palms.

"Yes," I said. "Let's."

We went back to the house first, though. It was clean inside, if outdated, containing all the same furniture my father had when he died five years earlier, stuff we'd had in the house since I was a kid—a hideous plaid couch, beige shag carpet, a gigantic television in a wooden cabinet.

I had a monthly cleaning service come in, someone also to maintain the property. I guess I was keeping it for my mother, if she ever wanted a place to live outside the hospital. I hadn't believed until recently that she'd want to stay hospitalized in one way or another forever.

She'd had a brief stint at a halfway house a couple of years ago, but it wasn't six months before she had a psychotic break and they found her down by the Black River, just sitting, rocking in her nightgown. But, of course, she'd never go back to the house. How could she? I don't know why I was keeping it. It was on this first visit with Megan that I began to consider tearing the house down. Maybe Meg was right. Time to level the past and rebuild, re-create. She made me believe it was possible.

We turned out the lights, shut off the water, which I had turned on to run the faucets. I decided to take the Scout back to the city, park it in a garage. We could use it to run errands and such, do all those things that people who are about to play house do—go to IKEA and drive out for weekends in the Hamptons. It was a hunk of junk, but there was a cool factor, too. My dad had run our blue 1970 International Scout 800A into the ground, using it to haul materials around. And I had never put the money into having it restored. So it was pretty banged up, but it still rocked. Binky loved Scouts and I was eager to show it to him. Yeah, I was already kissing up to my future father-in-law.

As we walked out to the truck, the sun moved behind the clouds. And before she opened the door, I saw Megan look into the woods and frown. An uncharacteristic sadness had settled over her as we got into the car. It reminded me of that darkness I had seen in her that first day, that open window where the rain can come in. I wondered if she'd heard the Whispers. But I was afraid to ask.

CHAPTER TEN

"So Fatboy and Priss are breaking up?"

Priss was sitting on my couch when I got home that evening. On entering the loft and seeing her there, I'd felt a little shock, a little chill slither through me. What if Megan had been with me?

"You can't do this anymore," I said.

I put down the bag I'd carried in from Whole Foods. Megan was coming over later to cook dinner. She had to spend a few hours with Toby while his mom went to the doctor.

"You're grocery shopping now? Wow, she's really domesticating you. The most wholesome thing I've ever seen you eat is pizza."

"That was a long time ago," I said. "A lot about me has changed. You just don't want to see it."

She issued a throaty laugh, put her feet up on the coffee table. Her legs were long and toned, the heels on her boots hard spikes, the toes coming to sharp points. She put her hands behind her head and made a point of pushing out her chest.

"People don't change. You know that."

"Don't they? I think people change all the time." I actually didn't think this. People might change on the outside—they got old, they got fat. But the core? It stays the same for life.

"Has Mikey Beech changed much?" she asked.

I didn't answer her, just slipped off my jacket and slung it over the bar stool. Mikey Beech was a sore subject between us.

"Did you have a nice visit home?" she asked. "Is The Hollows as lovely and idyllic a place as ever?"

Still nothing. I just started unloading the groceries. I didn't have to talk to her. She didn't have a right to be there. I put the almond milk in the fridge, the peanut butter in the cupboard. Then I felt rather than heard her come up behind me. She was a heat source; whenever she was near, my whole body burned.

"Tofu? You must be joking." She picked up the package and then let it fall with a smack onto the granite counter. I picked it up defensively and put it in with the vegetables.

I closed the heavy metal door, and she was there. She smelled of cigarettes and cinnamon. Even up close, she was flawless—not a blemish on her white skin, her mouth a perfect valentine, those eyes, that buzzing neon blue, dazzling me. She leaned in close.

"Don't let her turn you into one of those millennium nerds, Ian," she whispered. "One of those neutered, so sensitive, stay-at-home-dad types."

She wrapped her arms around me. There was nothing in me that wanted to push her away, even though I knew I had to. I wanted her, always. She used to be a tonic, someone who made me stronger than I had a right to be. But somehow she'd become a poison. Every time I drank from her I became sicker, less right with myself and the life I was trying to build. But I still wanted the taste of her on my tongue.

"Let's talk," I said, unwrapping myself from her embrace.

"Uh-oh," she said. She pulled a little pout and I moved over to the dining table. She followed and sat across from me, but not before grabbing a beer from the fridge. She drank a big swallow and put the bottle on the table between us, where it sat sweating, as if beckoning me to drink.

"Look," I said. "Things with Meg are serious. I am going to ask her to marry me."

She let go an unpleasant cackle. "Why would she marry *you*?"

Her question echoed my own dark thoughts. Why *would* she marry me? I literally brought nothing to the table except a little cash and a crazy mother. Meanwhile, she had a vast network of friends, a loving family—all of whom had welcomed me into their circle with open arms. She had beauty, grace, talent, intelligence. I, on the other hand, was just a grown-up, cleaned-up version of Fatboy. I wrote comic books for a living.

I had been worried enough to ask Megan why she loved me. *Because I can feel your goodness*, she told me. *You're kind and smart and a great fuck. I love you. You. The heart of you. That's all I need.*

"Because she loves me. And I love her," I said. "There isn't another reason."

"Aw," Priss said. Her face had gone a kind of ash gray; her mouth was a thin, tight line. "That's sweet. I'm happy for you."

"You'll always be a part of me," I said. It was a gentler, easier scene than I had written on the page. You never have any of the big drama in real life that you do on the page. I guess that's a good thing. "But you're so angry. I need some space, Priss. I've changed."

"And I haven't."

I looked down at my hands; they were stained with different colors of ink—a splatter of red on my palm, blue under my nails, yellow on the knuckles. She *had* changed. We'd grown up together; she'd gone from girl to teenager to woman right before my eyes. She'd grown stronger, more powerful, older, as I had. She'd also grown darker, harder. There were no soft places to her anymore. Even when we had sex, it was often rough and hungry. I had scratches on my back and ass where she dug her nails into my flesh. It felt good in the moment, the pain. But it ached and burned for days. But I found I couldn't say any of that. Somehow, though, it hung in the air between us.

"I'm not the angry one, Ian," she said. And, in fact, she seemed more sad than angry. Had I expected her to rage? Was I disappointed that she just seemed . . . bored? "You are."

She got up and left without another word. When the door slammed, I felt a sob well up from inside me. I choked it back hard. Boys don't cry, especially not over girls.

"I can't believe you would even come up here," Megan said.

The wind almost took her words away. It was not the night I'd hoped for, blustery and a little wet. But even with the bad weather, the tourists were out in force, crowding to the edge of the observation deck of the Empire State Building, taking pictures and videos with iPhones and iPads. In fact, it was as if we were surrounded by a wall of devices, the view around us duplicated a hundred times on little screens. Was it ever good enough to just *see* anything anymore? Must everything be recorded?

"I need the perspective for research," I told her. "I need to experience the panorama."

"I know, I know. But you are such a *cool* guy." She put air quotes around the word, teasing me. "And this is *so* not cool."

"What?" I said, suddenly worried. "I thought this was your favorite place in the world. You told me that."

"It *is*," she said. She wore a girlish smile, and moved to the edge and looked down. The city spread out before us, a matrix of light and movement, a place in constant motion, growing and changing every second. It *was* cool to see it from so high. It *was* magical in the dimming of late afternoon, all the lights below us punching and twinkling against the city gray. "But I'm not cool. I've never loved anything like I love this city."

"Funny you should say that," I said. I said it a little too loudly—nerves had me feeling clumsy and awkward. I had my fist closed around the light blue box in my pocket. I bought her a *crraazy* ring—a huge diamond. The Tiffany Soleste, a carat and a half. Cost 30K—'cuz that's how I roll, yo.

She looked at me with an inquiring smile. If she knew what I was about to do, she hid it well.

"Because that's how I feel about you," I said. "I've never loved anyone like I love you, Megan."

I backed away from her and sank down onto my knee. I know, I know—it's corny but you gotta do it. It's not right if you don't. The crowd of tourists parted around us and everyone turned to look, all the girls smiling. Megan's eyes were wide, her hand over her mouth.

I took out the box and opened it. "Meg, will you marry me?"

She nodded and started to cry, dropped to her knees, and I took her in my arms. Everyone around us started to cheer and clap. It was the perfect silly, iconic moment I knew she wanted—something sweet and ironic all at once. I was quite pleased with myself, I must say.

"I love you," she whispered. "Yes, yes, yes!"

We stood and I slipped the ring on her finger.

"Oh my God, Ian," she said. "It's gorgeous."

It glinted with that internal fire diamonds have; it really was mesmerizing. And big—like really big. On her hand, it looked like a cartoon engagement ring. I could tell right away that it embarrassed her, the size of it.

"Look at that ring!" someone said. And Meg glanced around with a shy smile. She pulled it in close to her body.

We floated through the rest of the evening—we had dinner at DBGB downtown, had drinks afterward at Beauty & Essex, then drifted home tipsy and laughing, holding on to each other.

"I've never been this happy," I told her. "I mean it, never."

"Neither have I," she said. But I could tell she didn't mean it the way I did. I had *literally* never been happier, because my life up to now had been pretty barren in the joy department. But Meg had been in love; she'd been happy in her life before me. She hadn't experienced the same levels of fear, pain, and trauma that I had. She didn't know how good it felt to just feel normal good after feeling so bad.

Love is an anesthetic, isn't it? It dulls all the pain, pushes back all your worries, quiets your inner demons. You're ten feet tall and bulletproof. With Meg in my life, I felt like I could do anything.

The next day, she made me take the ring back to Tiffany & Co. We went together and she picked out a smaller, pink, heart-shaped solitaire that was a third of the price. I couldn't help but think that Priss would have wanted an even bigger ring. And she'd probably have wanted a car, too. She had big appetites and enough was never enough. You could tell that the pale, WASPy salesgirl thought Megan was nuts. But that's how my girl Meg rolls—and if more people rolled like she did, the world would be a better place.

After we exchanged her ring, we drove out to the

Hamptons, where Binky and Julia opened a bottle of champagne and drank a toast to us on the porch.

"May you be as happy as we have been," Julia said.

She was all choked up, and Binky looked on, smiling with only his mouth. His eyes were worried. But maybe *every* father's eyes are worried when his little girl is about to get married. That's what I told myself anyway.

CHAPTER ELEVEN

Within twenty-four hours of the fire at Mikey Beech's house, the police came to my door. It was my first run-in with Detective Jones Cooper and it wouldn't be my last. My father answered the door and there was some good-natured backslapping. They'd known each other since grade school. My dad had done some of the restoration work on the Coopers' house in town. The Hollows was one of those places, everyone knew everyone forever.

"So what brings you around?" my dad asked finally. I was sitting at the top of the stairs out of sight.

"Funny thing," said Detective Cooper. "You heard about the fire at the Beeches'."

"Oh, yeah," said my dad. "Bad luck. Good thing no one was hurt."

"That's just the thing," said Cooper. "Bad luck didn't have anything to do with it. Someone started that fire. Came in through the basement and poured gasoline around the lower level, set a blaze. It was arson."

"Oh my goodness," said my dad. "That's awful."

His tone had turned wary, though. I heard them move into the living room, my dad offering the detective a seat.

"Who would do such a thing? Why?"

"We're looking into all the possibilities. But there's one I just want to check off my list. Some people say that Mikey and your son have been having some big problems at school. Mikey hurt Ian the other day, gave him a black eye. Is that right?"

"Well, Ian's no tattletale," said my dad. "He said he had a fight and we left it at that."

Actually, it was two black eyes. And they hadn't healed completely yet, so the answer should have been obvious. And I thought it was interesting that Cooper used "Mikey" instead of Mike or Michael. "Mikey" sounded almost affectionate, like he had already taken sides.

"Okay," said Detective Cooper. "Mikey hit Ian in the face with a dodge ball. Then later in the same gym period, Mikey tripped him. The coach said that it did seem to be an accident, though you never can tell with a kid like Mikey. He's a bit of a problem; all the teachers say so. But as they were taking Ian to the nurse's office, your son, according to folks who were there, was enraged, screaming. He said, 'I'm going to burn your house down, mother-fucker.'"

My dad issued a low grunt of a laugh.

"You obviously don't know my boy," said my father. "He wouldn't hurt a fly."

"I know that's always been true," said Cooper. "But there's been a change in your son since his mom . . . went away. According to his teachers, he's sullen, withdrawn, prone to violent verbal outbursts. I know you've been called in about it."

There was a heavy silence.

Then, "We've been through a lot here, Cooper. My mom has moved in to help out. But a boy needs his mother and she's just not ready to come home yet. I'm doing my best."

My dad sounded different, not like the pompous hard-ass I'd always known him to be. He sounded sad.

"I get that," said the detective. "But he threatened Mikey Beech. And there's a neighbor who witnessed someone matching your son's description around the Beeches' neighborhood that night."

"Wait a second," said my dad. His voice had gone up an octave. I leaned myself against the cool wall and remembered the dream I'd had about fire.

"What are we talking about here? Ian's just a boy. You're telling me you think he burned down someone's *house*?"

"I don't think anything," said Jones easily. "Let's not get ahead of ourselves. But I do have to look around, with your permission, Nick. And I need to talk to Ian."

"Sure," he said. "Look around. We have nothing to hide."

My dad was a smart man, but he was naive. He should have refused and called a lawyer, made them get a warrant, just to be on the safe side. But he didn't think like that. The accusation seemed outlandish to him, impossible. His instinct was to throw the door wide open.

"This is about my wife, right?" Now some of his old fight had returned. That angry, don't-fuck-with-me tone was back in his voice. "She's crazy, so he must be, too."

"No, nothing like that," said Detective Cooper. "You know me better. I'm just doing my job."

My father came to stand at the bottom of the stairs and looked up at me as if he'd known I'd been sitting there.

"Come on down, buddy," he said. He wasn't a gentle man. But he was gentle with me that day. And tired—I remember he looked so tired. Of course, I never saw him as a forty-year-old man who'd just lost his daughter, whose wife was hospitalized, whose son was about to be questioned by the police for arson. He was just my dad—a permanent fixture in my life, but someone I loved far less than my mother.

Even when I was older, we never talked about how he handled it all. We never talked about anything really, me and my dad. Even when he was dying, and I came up every week to help out at the house and sit with him in the hospital. We just talked about the weather, the Knicks. I'd read to him from the newspaper; he'd rail about how *the whole goddamn system was broken*. He'd tell me that the septic tank didn't have too many years left in it. He couldn't take care of my mother's bills anymore at that point, though he'd sold the business to his partner for a pretty healthy sum. His illness was eating up most of his savings. We talked about what would be left, and how my mother could get Medicaid after he was gone. And what I would be able to cover. But we never talked about anything real.

"The police have a few questions for you," he'd said that day.

I came down the stairs and loped self-consciously into the room. The detective asked me about what I'd said to Mikey and I told him that I'd never said it. Because I hadn't. All I did when Mikey hit me in the face was cry like a girl; I hadn't raged and threatened. I hadn't burned his house down. But I wished I had. I wished I wasn't such a scared, helpless wuss. Though I didn't say that to Jones Cooper.

He looked around the house, the garage. But there was no physical evidence, no half-empty gas cans or open boxes of matches in my room, or in the garage, or anywhere. Someone started a rumor at school, and it was pure bullshit. Anyway, I knew who had started the fire and why. And while that made me feel guilty, my dad was right: I was no tattletale. I wasn't going to tell on Priss. But I think Jones Cooper picked up on that guilty vibe. He kept at me for like an hour—walked with me from my room, to the garage, out to the shed in the back of the house. My dad kept looking out at the woods, and back at me. But he didn't say anything. Cooper kept asking me to repeat what happened at school. Wanted to know when was the last time, on the night of the fire, that my dad had checked on me. Had I ever snuck out of the house before? The Beech house was just a quick bike ride away; couldn't I easily have made it there on my own? My dad seemed to have an answer for everything. He'd looked in on me at midnight. No, I'd never snuck out. Ian's not that kind of kid; he's afraid of the dark. Did he sound disappointed in me? That I was a scaredy-cat and a wuss. Did he wish I was the kind of kid Jones Cooper seemed to think I was? Cooper was looking at me hard. He had a kind of penetrating gaze; nothing would get away from him. Anything bad or hidden in you started to squirm under that stare.

"Just tell Detective Cooper the truth and it will be okay," my dad said at the beginning of the conversation. And that's what I did. I told him that I didn't know anything about what happened that night. Other than some nightmares, and Priss showing up in my front yard, and an odd, twisting feeling of guilt in my belly—all of which I kept to myself—I had nothing to tell.

After we'd finished his probe of our property, we came to sit at the wobbly kitchen table. It was smeared with something sticky, and my father brushed away a few crumbs. The room was dirty in a way it never had been when my mom was there—grease spots on the backsplash, dishes in the sink, dust bunnies in the corners. My grandmother, I may have mentioned, was not much of a housekeeper.

"Son," Cooper said, "I'm just going to ask you outright: Did you start that fire? I know the Beech boy has been giving you a hard time. Maybe you wanted to teach him a lesson. I can understand that."

"No, sir," I said. "I didn't. I wouldn't. I wouldn't hurt anyone like that."

He looked down at his laced fingers and then back at me. It was the truth and he knew it. "I just wouldn't," I said again. "Even if I wanted to."

He gave me a slow nod. "And what about the witnesses that saw someone who looked like you that night?"

I shook my head. "I don't know. I guess a lot of people might look like me in the dark."

Our conversation seemed to satisfy him. And after some hushed words exchanged with my father in the front room, he left. I stayed at the table, my throat suddenly dry, my heart thumping with adrenaline. I was afraid and I didn't even know why.

My father came in after Cooper left and sat beside me. He drew in and released a breath. I knew he was wishing for a cigarette. But he'd quit for my mom's sake a couple years back, and my dad never broke a promise.

"Tell me, Ian," he said quietly. He looked scared, too—which only made me more scared. "Tell me what you didn't tell him."

So I did.

It was twilight when we walked out into the woods, the gloaming settling like a blanket. I picked my way through the trees with my dad trailing behind me and brought him to the place where I'd first met Priss. The place they'd found me the night my sister died. But there was nothing there—the ramshackle, one-room house, the rusted-out propane tank, the windows with glass long shattered into oblivion. It was all gone. I walked closer and could see that the broken pieces of an old foundation were buried beneath leaves and debris. I just stared at it, my whole body hot with confusion, embarrassment. My father had insisted that there was nothing out there, not anymore. There *had* been an old place, but the city made him tear it down years ago. It was unsafe, threatening to fall, he told me.

He pointed over to a large oak a few feet from the foundation. "We found you there the night your sister passed, crouched into that indentation in the trunk. Not inside any house."

I looked up into the purple sky I could see between the canopy of the treetops. A crow sat on a branch, looking at me with its glassy black eye, its blue feathers glinting in the remaining sunlight. I waited for it to caw at me, but it didn't.

"It used to be out here when I was a kid," he said. And there was something strange in his voice. I turned to look at him. He had his hands buried deep into his pockets, was rocked up a little on his toes.

"It was kind of spooky, all run-down and creaky. I don't know whoever lived in it. Before our time. Some folks thought it was, you know, haunted." He looked embarrassed, glanced at me oddly.

Then, "Of course, that's just kids talking, right? But I was happy enough to have it torn down."

He moved closer, kicked lazily at some leaves. "I cheaped out, though, you know? I should have had them dig up the foundation."

He looked at it regretfully. I could sense that there was something he wasn't saying. But I didn't want to know what it was.

"Dad."

"Let me show you something."

He started walking, and I followed. He knew his way around The Hollows Wood. Our property backed up right against the state-owned land, and he'd been romping about it all his life. He seemed more at home there than I'd seen him anywhere.

He was an awkward guy, not great with words. He did okay with a certain kind of man—which was why his partner did all the sales and customer service at No Paine Construction while my dad supervised the workers, made sure the jobs got done.

My dad was the kind of guy who unwittingly said inappropriate things, laughed too loud, looked red-faced and awkward anywhere off a construction site—at school functions, on the soccer field, at church. And when he drank, which wasn't often, he was downright mean. He got quickly belligerent and unkind. My parents didn't have many friends even when times were good, and I think he had a lot to do with it.

As we walked, the Whispers chattered—nervous, excited, gleefully malicious. I looked at my father, wondering if he could hear them, too. But he didn't seem to hear anything, kept his gaze straight ahead.

The sun faded from the sky as we walked and my dad, always prepared, pulled a flashlight out of his pocket. The shadows danced around, shifting and changing in the wind. It seemed like we walked forever, with the sky growing darker and the moon getting brighter, casting the world in silver blue.

Finally, we came up behind the ruined old church. It was little more than a pile of stones and one wall that cut a jagged shape against the night.

"What are we doing here?"

"We used to play out here," he said.

He moved near what was left of the building, and kicked at a crumpled old beer can that lay there, shining his light on what looked like the remains of a bonfire. The moon was high and bright now, not full but almost, and the stars were making their early-evening debut, weak and distant.

"Have you been out here before?" he asked me.

"No," I said.

But I *had* been out there before with my mother. It seemed like a long time ago—before she'd gotten pregnant with Ella. We'd just been walking in the woods and we'd stumbled on this place. It wasn't on our property;

it was over the line into the state forest. It had been a beautiful day, sunny and warm, and the building site and grounds were covered with tall, high grass and wildflowers. There were hundreds of monarch and azure butterflies that day, dragonflies hovering, and birds singing in the trees. We were dazzled by its prettiness.

"Oh my goodness," my mom said that day. She was herself then, funny and happy. "It's magical. Fairies could live here."

"There are no such things as fairies," I'd said. I was still feeling bitter about the whole Santa and Easter Bunny thing, having recently had those myths busted by some little asshole at school. "Nothing magical is ever real."

She picked a tall purple snapdragon and looked at me with a patient smile.

"If it were real, it wouldn't be magic," she said. "Real is dull and flat, two-dimensional. Magic is anything you want it to be. It sparkles."

"But it's not *real*," I said. "It doesn't *exist*."

Dragons and Hobbits, elves, flying reindeer, Oz, Narnia, the Shire, castles and princesses, warlocks, witches—all the cool stuff was pretend, made up. You couldn't go to any of those places, couldn't be touched by any of those things except in the pages of a book, or in your own imagination. You couldn't *be* anyplace but the dull, ugly, boring real world. I guess that was my coming-of-age—as a kid and as a writer and artist. I didn't like the world the way it was, with all its disappointing truths. I liked it better inside a book, or in a world I'd created myself.

"Poor Ian," she said. She walked over to me and wrapped me up. "You're too young to be so serious."

My mother and I had continued until we came to a cluster of tilted gravestones, almost hidden among the leaves of grass. She bent down to one and moved the grass aside. She let out a little sigh and moved to the next, a tilted Celtic cross.

"It's sad, isn't it?"

I came up close behind her, peered over her shoulder. We moved from grave to grave, looking at names and dates.

They were all children.

"No," I told my father that night. "I've never been here."

He must have heard my voice raise a defensive octave, but he only gave a quick nod. After a moment, he said, "Your mother used to come here. I didn't want her to, but she did."

He walked over toward the graves.

"She thought I was being superstitious, not wanting her to be here when we were trying to have a baby. There were three miscarriages, Ian."

"What's a miscarriage?"

"Uh," he said. He wiped at his eyes, then ran a hand over the crown of his head. He wasn't crying, but he was as close as a man like him could get. "When a woman loses the baby she's carrying. It doesn't get born."

I didn't totally understand what he meant at the time. How did someone *lose* a baby? I knew she'd wanted another child; she was always talking about a brother or sister for me, oblivious to the fact that I didn't want one at all.

I followed my father, even though I didn't want to. Something pulled me along after him, trailing the beam of his flashlight. I always thought of him as big and powerful. But there in the woods, he looked small.

The Whispers grew louder, a kind of rushing through the leaves. I didn't know why he had brought me out there, and I wanted to go home. But not home as it was then. Home as it used to be, with my mom in the kitchen and Ella in her crib, and the lights on, and everything clean and warm and right.

I looked around for Priss, expecting her to step out of the trees. Then I could show her to my father. And he could ask her about the fire. He could ask her the questions that I didn't dare. But she wasn't there. That was the thing about Priss. She was never there when you needed her to be. She never got you out of trouble, only into it. But I wouldn't figure that out until much later.

My father knelt down beside one of the headstones that stood askew like gray, rotting teeth. I hung back. I had cried back on that day with my mother, cried for all the lost little children. I don't know what she had been thinking, letting me see and understand what those headstones were. Maybe she'd been so surprised by her discovery that she hadn't thought to protect me from the idea that children, children just like me, might die. The thought had stayed with me, terrifying me in the night.

"Come over here, son."

"I don't want to," I said.

"Did your mother tell you about the little girl she thought she saw out here?"

I shook my head. She hadn't. If she'd ever seen a girl, she hadn't mentioned it to me. I could tell he didn't believe me.

"Your mother is . . . not . . . well," he said. There were these long pauses in his sentences, as if he were searching for words, a way to say something without actually saying it. Like: *Your mom's a nutcase, kid. She's a crazy woman who saw people out in the woods. Don't be like her.* He drew in another deep breath, bowed his chin toward his chest.

"She hasn't been well for . . . a while. I wish I'd . . . understood that better, acted to help her more quickly—

helped her at all. I wasn't there for her when she needed me—in the way she needed."

Kneeling there, he rested his hands on the gravestone, looked as though he might pull it from the earth.

"Her thoughts, her ideas about certain things—they aren't reliable."

I had no idea what he was talking about.

"When she lost those babies, one after the other—it undid her a little." He wasn't talking to me. He was talking to himself, to the woods, to anyone who would listen. "She was sick with grief. I think her mind started playing tricks on her."

"But then she had Ella," I offered. The words died between us, though.

"It wasn't . . . enough," he said. "To fix what was broken. I should have seen it. Maybe I didn't want to see it."

I stood there watching, seeing him as I hadn't ever seen him before. He was a stranger.

"I'm trying to tell you that there's no one out here. There's no little girl. Look."

I moved in closer to him and followed the beam of his flashlight. The stone was worn down, the letters and numbers barely visible. I leaned in close and read what I saw there.

CHAPTER TWELVE

Fatboy is headed home from Molly's place. It's late but he takes the subway from her Brooklyn Heights brownstone.

He descends the gray, filthy stairway past graffiti-covered walls and onto the platform. Here the lights flicker, and water drips from unseen leaky pipes. He watches a rat skitter across the tracks as he sinks onto a bench to wait for the train. He dozes in his seat, and in his dreams, wraiths move through the shadows on the tracks.

Fatboy's New York City is different from the real, pretti-fied, gentrified, heavily policed, cleaned-up millennial New York City. Fatboy's New York City is a towering, twisted dystopia of deserted streets and abandoned buildings, blinking streetlights, and crumbling concrete walls. The shadows are thick with bad characters, and the sky is persistent gunmetal. The images are gray scale, with flashes of bright color—neon signs, and flame-red fire hydrants, the copper wire of Priss's hair, the hot pink of her high-heeled shoes.

Suddenly he is startled awake to find himself surrounded by a gang of thugs. They loom tall, with gold teeth and blank eyes. Fatboy snaps to, and looks at the men around him. He is not afraid yet.

"I don't have much," he says. Just another mugging in the city. He empties one pocket, pulling out two wrinkled twenties, bright green and yellow. They lie on his outstretched palm. "Forty bucks and a dime bag."

In his other palm, he holds out a small bag of weed. One of the men uses a black-gloved hand to knock it all to the concrete platform.

"Hey," says Fatboy. He rises to standing, his face flushing fuchsia with anger. "What the fuck?"

Once upon a time, Priss would show up and start kicking ass. But not tonight. Fatboy has told his avenger, his protector, that he doesn't need her anymore. Part of him believes that she'll come anyway. But the platform is empty except for his assailants. Fatboy is on his own. *I can do this,* he tells himself. *I can take these guys.*

When they move in on him, though, he doesn't stand a chance. He puts up a fight—feels a momentary rush of power and confidence. He gets a few blows in. But ultimately he takes a beating, blows turning his face purple and red. The thugs fold in on him, their wide backs filling the panel until Fatboy disappears into the blackness.

When Fatboy comes around, he's lying on the subway tracks—the bright white moon of a headlight blazing in the tunnel ahead of him. He tries to pull himself up, but he's hurt bad. As he struggles, a lightning bolt of pain rockets down his back into his leg. He looks down and discovers that his leg is twisted in an ugly, unnatural way—a hideous blue-and-red zigzag against the silver of the tracks. He lets out a desperate cry of pain and fear, but the station is deserted and the train is coming on fast.

He's sweating, weeping now, thinking about Molly and all the things he's not going to be able to do with her now—their wedding, their honeymoon, the family they both wanted to start right away. He calls her name, a wail of despair.

The world around him is shaking, roaring with the approach of the train. He can't hear anything else. A rat he saw earlier skitters over his leg. He manages to roll over, starts clawing his way off the tracks. The horn on the approaching train begins to blare in panic. The conductor sees him, but she can't stop the train. Fatboy knows that. It's over. He's going to die here *tonight. He's about to close his eyes and accept his fate. But then, she's there. Priss, standing in the shadows.*

"Don't just lie there, you pussy."

She grabs him hard and starts to pull. He screams in pain. But then he digs deep, pushes himself. And they roll to the side, just as the train rushes past, never stopping or slowing.

They lie together, panting.

"Priss," he says. "Thank you."

She strokes his head and then wraps her arms around him. "You still need me. You know that, don't you?"

At my drafting table, I stared at the page in front of me, reading what I'd put down. It wasn't at all what I had intended to write. The words floated in front of me, swimming before my tired eyes.

I had wanted a scene where Fatboy proved to himself that he could survive the bad, cold world without Priss. More than that, I wanted something to happen that proved to him that the world itself wasn't as big and scary as he imagined it to be. Instead, I wound up with another event that spiraled out of his control, where Priss had to step in to save the day.

I bit back the rise of frustration and anger, a desire to tear the pages from my notebook and fling them into the trash. I felt like a child, being forced to do something I didn't want to do. Why had I not written what I sat down to write? After all, was I not the boss here? Were these not my hands, my words, my images? Who was calling the shots in my subconscious—me or Priss?

I turned the page in the notebook, determined to write another version of the scene, but draft after draft, when it came time for Fatboy to fight and win, it didn't happen. I simply was unable to put the words down, couldn't see the pictures in my mind. The late night turned into the wee hours, turned into dawn. Finally, spent and exhausted, I abandoned the drafts—the pages, the sketches lying flat and accusatory on the table. The truth was, I didn't see Fatboy as the master of his circumstances. What did that say about me?

CHAPTER THIRTEEN

Megan didn't like the loft. She wanted us to get our own place, something that we bought and decorated together. Binky and Julia wanted to help, which made me a little uncomfortable. They were *so* tied into Megan and what was going on with her. Was that normal? I didn't know. I'd never had a normal family.

Initially, I'd agreed to moving. But the morning after my stunning narrative failures, I found myself floating the suggestion that I keep the Tribeca place as my studio. This idea was *not* met with a warm reception.

"Keep it?" she asked with a tilt of her head. She had a forkful of egg headed toward her mouth and it paused midair. The apartment was washed with light, the *Times* spread out around us—her with the Arts and Leisure section, me scanning the Week in Review. Patsy Cline was singing "Crazy" from one of Megan's playlists streaming to my Bluetooth speaker. She'd arrived earlier and made breakfast for us.

Wedding plans were in full swing. It had just been a little over a week since I proposed and already we had a date (six months away), a plan to do it on the beach at Binky and Julia's, a caterer, and a growing guest list. Did these things always go so fast? I thought people were generally engaged for a year or more. I mean, not that I was getting cold feet or anything.

"So I can work," I said. The words felt bumpy in my

mouth, as though I knew they shouldn't be uttered but swallowed. "Fewer distractions."

She looked around the loft, as if considering it.

"The rent on this place is six thousand a month. Can we handle that in addition to a mortgage?"

I shrugged. "I don't know."

In case you think I was being a typical guy, looking to keep some vestige of my male freedom, was having a fantasy of someplace to party with the boys or bring home the occasional fan girl, that wasn't it. The loft had actually meant something significant to me when I first moved in. It was the symbol of my success, a big "fuck you" to the Mikey Beeches of the world—all the people who had taunted me, bullied me, accused me, and judged me. I had overcome obstacles, worked hard, and made my life what I wanted it to be. I had reasons, real reasons, to make a mess out of my life, but I hadn't. I used my art, my talent, to lift myself up out of the mire of my childhood. I was proud of that.

Few graphic novelists reach the level of financial success I had achieved at a young age. Most people spend years drawing, writing, flogging their work at comic book conventions across the country, sending their work to agents and publishers, never breaking into the big leagues. I went to work for Marvel out of school, thanks to the help of one of my professors who got my foot in a door that would never have opened for me otherwise. I was talented, sure. But there are lots of talented people who never get a break like I got.

I spent a few years as a colorist working on the art team for the comic *X-Factor*, gaining tons of experience, learning all about the industry, meeting deadlines, working with a team. And in my off-hours I wrote *Fatboy and Priss*.

I'd only been out of school for a couple of years when

I sold *Fatboy and Priss* to Blue Galaxy, the small publisher that turned my comic into a huge success. It had started small but grew steadily into a cult phenomenon. My first apartment in New York was a five-story walk-up studio on Avenue C. I had a bed, a drafting table, and a chair, one frying pan, one plate, one set of silverware. A year ago I'd moved into a $6,000-a-month loft in Tribeca, New York City's hippest, most expensive neighborhood. The place was a part of the new and improved me, the slim and successful me. I didn't want to give it up. I took a chance and told Megan all of this, most of which she already knew.

"You're not giving anything up," she said. "You're *growing* up. We're getting married, starting a new chapter in both of our lives, right? I don't think we can do it in your *bachelor pad*."

She leaned on the words, heavy with irony and disdain. I didn't love her tone. Why did women always have to act like that? As if men were these stupid, selfish, clueless children who needed to be corralled and controlled or else toddle into the street?

"Is this open for discussion?" I asked.

She got that tightness to her mouth that by now I knew meant she was upset.

"Of course," she said. But her tone said: *No, you man-baby, this is not open for discussion.*

"Great," I said. "We don't need to decide today."

More silence. She finally got those eggs into her mouth, then took a bite of toast, a swallow of coffee. She was staring out the window, the paper in front of her forgotten.

"What about the place in The Hollows?" she said. "Couldn't you use that as your writer's retreat? I mean, surely you'd have fewer *distractions* there than here."

Wait for it. She took another sip of coffee. Then, "If that's *really* why you want to keep it."

Now it was my turn to be quiet. I had just told her why I wanted to keep the apartment. Why didn't she believe that? There were already little problems—maybe every couple has them even from the very beginning. Little things that might just go away, or might be tiny fissures that will split wide open when pressure is applied. She had never met Priss, and I had told Megan that Priss was gone from my life for good. But we both knew that this wasn't quite true. It bothered her, she'd told me, that she felt like I didn't *want* them to meet. We didn't talk about it much, but the issue was there.

Plus, I was still doing some recreational drug use—pills, weed, too much drinking for Megan's taste. She'd asked me to cut back, and I had, some. But not enough. It had come up a couple times, kind of lightly. *Do I smell weed?* Or, *Are your eyes glassy?* The truth was, I didn't want to be completely sober. Weed took the edge off some of the anxiety issues I suffered. And pills like Adderall and Ritalin kept me focused and productive. I could get them online; they weren't exactly illegal. I wasn't drinking to the point of blacking out anymore, so that was something, wasn't it? Sober, I was anxious and unfocused. Better living through chemistry, right?

And now we were talking about The Hollows house. I thought I'd made my feelings on the subject pretty clear. But Megan wasn't getting it. Looking at her, I could feel the pull of that place. It wanted me to come back, and it was using Megan to lure me.

"What is that supposed to mean?" I asked.

My tone was harsher than I had intended. It bounced back at me way too nasty, too angry. I saw her eyes grow wide with surprise, then fill with tears.

"Nothing," she said. She drew in a sharp breath and looked away. Wow, did I ever feel like shit. I had never made Megan cry before, not from being a jerk.

"I'm sorry," I said. I moved around the table to her and knelt by her side. "I'm sorry."

"Maybe this is going too fast," she said. She wiped her eyes on the sleeve of her shirt. "Maybe you're not ready. It's okay if you're not."

"I *am*," I said. "I'm *so* ready. I love you."

"Okay," she said, nodding, still not looking at me.

I leaned in to kiss her, and she kissed me back. I was expecting a chaste make-up kiss, but was surprised by its heat and hunger. It was an invitation. I stood and pulled her to her feet and she wrapped her arms around my neck. Oh, she was sweet and warm and my body came alive with wanting her. Her fingers laced themselves through my hair. I pulled off her top and gazed at the long willow of her torso, the perfect white swell of her breasts, the pink roses of her nipples. I lifted her and she wrapped her legs around me. She was a perfect flower of a woman, dewy and blush.

In the bedroom, I lay beside her and held her as close to me as our bodies would allow. I buried myself in her. I pressed my face into the hollow between her neck and her shoulder. She moaned low and breathy for me, pulled me in deeper and deeper. Her hands on my back, her breath in my ear, the caress of her leg on mine—I was lost in her, the peaceful deep of her goodness, her warmth. Why couldn't we just stay there like that? Why did the ugly world always have to be waiting just outside the door?

As we lay quiet afterward, I heard Priss's voice. *She played you, Fatboy. She pulled it all out—tears and sex.*

No, that's not Megan.

That's all women. They all bring out the big guns to get what they want. And why not? It works. You're putty in her hands.

You don't know her.

• • •

Later that afternoon, Megan left to go to work. And as soon as I was sure she wasn't coming back to the loft for whatever she might have left behind, I popped an Adderall. Then I looked up a number I'd been meaning to call for a while: No Paine Construction.

My dad's old partner got right on the line.

"Ian!" he boomed. "Good to hear from you, kid." Then, softer, "How's your mom?"

"She's holding her own, Mr. Craine."

"Hey, kid, for the millionth time, call me Jack," he said. "How's the funny business?"

"Pretty good," I said. He made me smile. He found it amusing that I wrote "comic books" for a living. And it *was* a pretty silly way to get by, if you thought about it.

"I keep looking for your comics in the paper," he said.

"Someday maybe," I said, just to be friendly. Most people did not get what I did. They didn't understand writers or artists and they definitely didn't understand graphic novelists. But that was okay.

"So, Jack," I said. "I think I want to tear down the old house."

"Oh, yeah?"

"I'm getting married in a couple of months—"

"Whoa! You're kidding. Man, does that make me feel old or what? Congratulations, Ian. Your mom must be happy."

I actually hadn't even told my mom. That was another thing Megan was kind of miffed about. I literally didn't have one person I wanted to invite to our wedding. Not one. Colleagues, acquaintances, childhood friends? No. My mom would never come; she couldn't handle the trip, the event. She wasn't well enough.

"She is," I said. "She's really happy."

"So the new missus has ideas for The Hollows property, huh?"

"Exactly," I said.

"I got an architect on staff now, you know. We can set up an appointment, help you with the plans for the new place."

"Definitely," I said, trying to sound enthused. "But in the meantime, can we just schedule the demolition?"

"Sure," he said. I heard him tapping on a keyboard. "We're a bit swamped but I have a gap in a couple of weeks. It shouldn't take more than two or three days to do the job. What about the stuff inside?"

"Junk it."

A pause. "The furniture, the appliances?"

"Just junk it all or sell it, whatever it is you guys do with it."

"You sure? There's nothing you want from there."

"Nope," I said. "Everything of any importance was cleaned out long ago."

Photos, beloved childhood books, legal documents, my old sketches, a couple of paintings my mom did, some of her old clips, her diplomas, baby keepsakes—my old blanket, Ella's. It filled exactly three boxes and they sat in the guest room closet here in the loft.

I heard him tapping. "All right, kiddo, you're in the schedule."

"Great, Jack," I said. "That's great."

"Hey, Ian," he said. "What about the other place?"

"Oh, yeah." Priss's house.

"Want me to rip up that old foundation? We didn't do it right the first time, and it's a bit of a hazard. No charge."

I felt the bite of fear, a lash of something like shame. Maybe I was going too far. What happened when The Hollows was calling you back and you gave it the big middle finger? Then I caught myself. That was crazy thinking.

Megan said it herself: *You give that place too much power.*
The same was true for Priss. Maybe Fatboy couldn't get
his shit together. But I, Ian Paine, *was* the master of my
own universe. Neither The Hollows, nor Priss—nor even
Megan—was going to tell me what to do.

"Yeah," I said. "That would be great."

More tapping.

"It'll feel good, I think," said Jack finally. He was
always such a nice guy; my dad really liked and respected
him. "Raze the past, start a new life. You deserve it."

"Thanks," I said. "That's the plan."

"It's a nice piece of land. We'll build you something
beautiful when you're ready, for you and your new family."

That was never going to happen. I would scorch the
earth before I would ever move "my new family" out to
that hell mouth.

"I'm looking forward to the day," I said, just to be so-
ciable. "I really am."

I ended the call feeling weak, even shaking a little,
with relief. I lifted a recent sketch of Priss and Fatboy.
She was pulling him off the train tracks. *That* was Fatboy,
not me. I didn't need Priss to live my life.

See. She didn't get what she wanted, I said in my head.
Didn't she?

But even under the relief, the bravado of my thoughts,
wasn't there a dark river of dread? Didn't part of me know
that I had stepped over some cosmic line?

Anyway, that's when bad things started happening.

CHAPTER FOURTEEN

After I had scheduled the demolition on the house, and the initial superstitious dread subsided, I rode a giddy sense of freedom. I was shedding all the negativity in my life—Priss, The Hollows, even the series, which had, as Zack had intuited, come to its natural end. The house was going to be leveled, and with it any chance that Megan could convince me to go back there. I hadn't seen Priss at all; she was obviously respecting my wishes. And I was tearing up the place where I'd first met her, so even my memories wouldn't have a home there anymore. I felt good—liberated and strong.

Meanwhile, I buckled down and started working like a machine, taking Adderall in order to work sixteen-hour days on the last *Fatboy and Priss*. I had one bottle left, a little orange vial of blue pills—just enough for a month. I was taking it only in order to meet the deadline, I told myself. I felt guilty because of the promises I'd made to Meg. But I swore to myself that when I was done with this book, I was done with the pills.

I'd stopped smoking weed during the workweek, and whenever Megan was around. *It makes you gross and lazy*, she told me. And I knew she was right. I was just a lump on weed, voraciously hungry and zoned out. I'd also promised to give up anything harder perma-nently. Moderate drinking was still okay, though. (God knows Binky and Julia tossed back two martinis a night, and Megan had never met a glass of Cabernet that she didn't like.)

I wanted to give up all the drugs. I would have done anything for Megan, anything to be the man she wanted me to be. But, *honestly*, I didn't have the mental juice to do what I needed to do without help. I tried not to worry that I had permanently fried my brain with everything I'd taken over the years—weed, blow, X, mushrooms, mescaline, ruffies. They—the ubiquitous "they," with all their threats and warnings—say the kind of drugs I was taking can permanently alter the chemicals in your brain. I told myself I'd deal with my various addictions and all the problems associated with such after the wedding, after the book was turned in and accepted, and after Megan and I were married and lying on a beach in Hawaii. Then I'd do some self-examination, walk into my new marriage working to be a better man.

But right now there was work to be done and very little time to do it. Adderall made me a superachiever: focused, tireless, fearlessly creative. And I needed that. I was struggling with the narrative, wrestling with Priss and what needed to ultimately happen in the book. It was like she was fighting me, clinging to her own existence.

One night around three a.m. I crashed hard. I must have fallen asleep at my computer, just spent. Graphic novels are often a team effort. There might be a creator, and a writer to begin with. Then there's a penciler, who does the initial sketching for the book, the inker, and finally the colorist. I do it all for *Fatboy and Priss*. The writing, the art. I am the creator, the artist, *and* the writer.

It's a paper-and-pencil proposition. I write out the story longhand in a notebook—totally old school—creating a loose outline of how I want things to go. But I never know exactly how things are going to end. Then I start penciling the panels, very vague sketches of how the story is going to evolve in pictures.

Once that's in place (with some ambiguity toward the end) I start inking. After that, I scan the inked pages into my computer. And working in Adobe Photoshop, I do the coloring, shading, all the fine-tuning of the images, as well as the lettering.

I have always preferred to work alone. But it's a hard and lonely effort at the best of times. And this book was practically a Sisyphean effort, every page and panel a slog. I am sure that a shrink would have had a field day with why I was having trouble separating Fatboy and Priss, leading them to a final conflict in which Fatboy might free himself. But I wasn't thinking about any of that. I couldn't; I was just trying to get the words down, the images on the page.

And I must have hit the wall that night. The drugs wore off, and there wasn't enough caffeine in the world to keep me up. My abused body and mind took the rest they needed—without my consent.

When I came to, Priss's face was staring at me from the screen. She looked angry. And the sun was glaring in my windows. My face was wet, as it was lying in a pool of my own drool. I jumped up.

"Oh, crap," I said, reaching for my iPhone.

The screen was a virtual catalog of my fuckups. It was one thirty in the afternoon. I had slept nearly ten hours—missing the Big Meeting at Blue Galaxy with my editor, the marketing and sales department, and the company president, who had all gathered to talk about the exciting finale of *Fatboy and Priss*. I'd shown the outline to Zack and they were all jazzed. There was a voice mail, a couple of texts from my editor:

Hey, buddy, we're all waiting.

Hey, Ian, hope everything is okay. Joe has another meeting; he can't wait much longer.

Okay, I guess maybe we'll need to reschedule. Hope everything is okay. I told everyone you had the flu. It was kind of hard to put this together; you know how schedules are these days.

But worse even than that—and that was pretty bad— I'd missed my appointment with Megan and the wedding planner.

From Megan:

Hey, where are you?

Megan got really pissed when I was late—and I was late a lot. She said it showed a lack of respect for others. *It's like saying that your time is more important than everyone else's.* Plus, I had already stood her up once that week, missing dinner because I lost track of time. She'd waited at DBGB on the Bowery for forty minutes. She knew I was working, so she showed up at the loft with carryout. She was cool about it but I could tell she wasn't too happy.

You're fifteen minutes late. I'm starting without you. Which means you'll have to accept my decisions about some of this stuff.

P.S.—I didn't really care about the *wedding* per se. I cared about marrying Meg—but as for food and cake and flowers and music and all of that, I was happy with whatever made her happy.

Next text: *Wow. You're really not coming, are you? Did you turn your phone off?*

She attached a picture of some kind of flower. Calla lilies? Isn't that what they used at funerals?

Then there was a picture of a three-tiered cake— decorated with roses.

Then: *My mom is here and this is embarrassing. Why do I think you're passed out on your desk?*

Final text: *Seriously, Ian????*

"Ah, fuck!" I yelled at no one and nothing. I stared at the offending phone. "Why didn't I hear you?"

The weird thing was that my phone had been right next to my head. No one's ever that sound asleep, right? I tapped my way to the settings screen. The ringer *had* been turned off—but not completely. Someone had set the phone to block calls from Megan and my editor only. Had it been me? Would I have done that? No. Why would I? If there were two people in the world I wanted to talk to, it was Megan and Zack. But if I hadn't done it, then who?

In my hand, the phone started ringing. The caller was blocked, and I couldn't bring myself to answer. A kind of panicked paralysis had set in. A few minutes later—as I *still* sat in a stunned, angry stupor, trying to figure out how to lie my way out of this mess—the apartment phone started ringing, a number very few people had. I moved over to the kitchen, where the phone hung on the wall. The caller ID read: SHADY KNOLL PSYCHIATRIC HOSPITAL. I answered even though I didn't want to.

"Mr. Paine?"

I felt like the room was spinning suddenly. My race to get to the phone, the drugs mucking with my system, fear—who knows why. But I felt horrible, and had to lean against the wall for support.

"Yes."

"This is Dr. Jameson from Shady Knoll." I'd met him before. He was an annoyingly nice, attractive man who seemed to be making quite a bit of money off the mentally ill.

"What's wrong?" I said. The words sounded thick and slow even to my own ears.

"I am afraid we have a problem," he said. He had a soft, pleasant voice. "Your mother is missing."

It took a few seconds for the words to make sense to me.

"I don't understand," I said. "How?"

"Your mother has some freedoms here at the hospital, as you know. She's allowed to take the bus into town, etc. But she didn't come back last night for dinner. We've been looking for her since last evening around six thirty, along with the local police. But we have not located her."

"Why am I just hearing about this now?"

"We tried to call last night," he said. "Several times. Did you not get our messages?"

I looked at the phone in my hand, tapped to recent calls. Three messages from Shady Knoll. No idea why I didn't hear those calls either.

"Mr. Paine," he said. "Do you have any idea where she might have gone?"

"No," I said. "I don't know. But I'm coming up."

I am an asshole; I can admit that. I used the situation with my mother to get me out of the deep shit I was in with both my publisher and my fiancée. Within twenty minutes, I was in the Scout heading toward the FDR. I called Zack first, because he was going to be easier to deal with.

"Hey, Zack, I'm so sorry, man. My mother, you know she's mentally ill? She has been missing since last night. I'm so sorry; I just got slammed with this."

He was all "Oh my God" and "Is there anything I can do?" So that was easy.

Megan on the other hand was *not* easy, not buying it, and didn't understand at all.

"Why didn't you call and tell me?" she said. I could hear her mother in the background, the sound of traffic. She was breathy, as if she was walking. "I'm going to be your *wife*. This is not something you have to handle on your own. You get that, right?"

"I'm sorry."

She let go of a little sniffle. The whole wedding thing really made girls crazy; she was much more emotional than usual. There was an unfamiliar edginess to her.

"Where are you?" she said finally.

"Out looking for her." A lie. But a white lie, right? I *was* on my way up to The Hollows to look for my mom. I could still hear Megan breathing at the other end of the line, rhythmic with her walking. She didn't believe me. Or she wasn't sure if she should.

"I'm sorry," I said. "I'm sorry I let you down today. And that I didn't call sooner to share this with you. It's just that it's embarrassing. I don't want this to be a part of your life."

That part was not a lie. It *was* embarrassing that all I had to bring into Megan's life was pain and trouble.

"Do you need me to come up?" There was an eager note to her voice. "I could take the train."

I could tell that she *wanted* to come, that she truly wanted to help me shoulder this. I don't know if I've ever felt that from anyone before, not since my dad died. I was my mother's caretaker. And Priss was always running her own agenda, using whatever was going on with me as an excuse to act out. But Megan selflessly wanted to help. Why couldn't I let her?

"No," I said. It's so mean not to allow someone who loves you to take care of you. "Not yet. I'll call you if I need you to come."

"Okay, Ian," she said.

I felt like crap as the city whipped past and the East River snaked gray and cold beside me. I could have easily admitted my lie, pulled off the highway, picked her up, and taken her with me. By the time we got to The

Hollows, she would have forgiven me. But the truth was that I didn't want to.

"I'll call you later," I said. "I love you."

And I hung up before she could answer me. I know. I know. I was a horrible person and I was going to be a terrible husband. And I think it was just starting to dawn on both of us at about the same time. Just know this. I really did love Megan, with all my heart. But that doesn't count for much, does it?

When I arrived, I could tell that my mother had been at the house. The front door stood ajar. There was a glass on the counter, half filled with water. In my room, I could see that someone had been lying on the bed. There was a slim indentation on the spread; the pillow had been hugged. I had come straight to the house, sort of unthinking. I couldn't imagine anyplace else she might go. I hadn't told her about my plans to tear it down. But maybe she knew, somehow. She was tuned in like that. Or maybe she had just overheard it somewhere. People gossip in The Hollows, for lack of anything better to do. And everyone knows everyone.

I walked through the kitchen, and headed out the back door, which also stood open. It was a gorgeous day—the sun warm on my skin, the air dry with a light breeze. I was counting the seconds until this place was an empty lot.

The Whispers called me into the woods—their energy was teasing, a little angry. And then I was walking, quickly moving through the trees. I hadn't been there in years but I knew the way, knew where I was headed. I walked and the birds sang. I moved past the old house that wasn't there. I tried not to look at it, didn't want to see what was there or wasn't there. Pretty soon a bulldozer would come and tear out whatever was left.

I walked the rest of the way to the small graveyard. I had read that The Hollows Historical Society had plans to restore the site, rebuilding the church and fixing up the graves, but it hadn't happened yet. And there was some really dull-looking spray-painted graffiti—GONZO WAS HERE and AMY AND LAURA BFFS—marring the stone walls since I'd last visited.

My mother sat on the ground, linking flowers together, singing to herself.

> *Little flowers in the garden*
> *Yellow, orange, violet, blue*
> *Little angels in the garden*
> *Do you know how I love you?*
>
> *Little flowers in the garden*
> *Growing tall toward skies of blue*
> *Little flowers in the garden*
> *Oh, your mama so loves you.*

She turned as I approached, and smiled. I felt like I was nine again, before Ella, before my mother went away and didn't come back.

"Mom," I asked her. "What are you doing here?"

Her smile faded as I drew near to her. She had aged so badly, looked ten years older than she was. She was frail and gray, her face marred by deep lines. Her eyes were dark hollows of fatigue and sorrow.

"You called me, Ian," she said. "You told me to meet you here."

I felt a catch of fear in my throat, a notch that I tried to swallow but that stayed lodged where it was. It was tricky, because my mother was crazy and I had been messing with my own brain chemistry. Had she imagined the call? Or had I, in some drug-addled state, indeed rung her and asked her to meet me? Or had it been someone else, someone fucking with us?

"Didn't you?" she asked. She looked so sad suddenly. "I've been waiting for you. Do you remember how much fun we used to have out here?"

It had never been fun. This place was a *graveyard*. It was sad and creepy and always had been. But I always loved being with her. There were few people as unfailingly kind, as unconditionally loving as my mother was before she became ill. I missed that woman, even now.

"I remember," I said.

I sat beside her and saw what she was doing. She was weaving wildflowers together and then hanging them on the graves of children who had died long before she herself was ever born. Pastel links—blue, violet, rose, tangerine, buttercup—were draped carefully on gray stone.

It had been Priss. She'd set my phone to block those calls. She'd lured my mother out here, thereby luring me back home. She was the agent for this place, always playing tricks, keeping tabs. And here I was, back in The Hollows Wood—the Black Forest, as the locals call it.

"Who was she?" I asked out loud even though I didn't mean to.

My mother tilted her head and regarded me quizzically, then she hung her flower chain on the grave of Priscilla Miller. It was the grave my father had shown me that day long ago. It was the reason he didn't think Priss was real. He thought I'd come out here with my mother and seen her name, used it unconsciously to create an imaginary friend. Or at least that's what I imagined he thought. After he'd pulled back the weeds and showed me the gravestone, we'd returned home in silence.

"Don't you know?" she asked.

"No. I really don't."

She stood and dusted herself off. There was pollen in her hair and on the sleeves of her T-shirt, a bright yellow dusting.

"Do you know what's odd?" she said. "The reason I can't come back here or anywhere?"

"What's that?"

"I can still hear her crying," she said. "I'll never stop hearing her."

For a moment I thought she was talking about Priss. But she was talking about Ella.

"I know, Mom," I said. "I'm so sorry."

"No," she said, looking at me with a concerned frown. She put her hand to her heart. "*I'm* sorry. So deeply, forever, impossibly sorry."

"I know."

I rose to take her into my arms, and in my embrace she felt like bones in a leather sack. If I squeezed hard I could crush her. She was so weak from years of medication and inactivity. She was rotting inside her own body, though she had only turned fifty-five last year. She was punishing herself; she'd never lived another second after Ella died. Maybe she didn't have a right to—plenty of people would say that she didn't. But depression or postpartum psychosis or any kind of mental illness is a rabbit hole. It's a whole other world down there. The decisions you make in that place don't hold up in the real world. No one understands that.

"Come on," I said. "Let's get you back. Everyone's worried."

"Who's worried?"

"The staff," I said. "They don't know where you've gone."

She pulled away from me and looked up into my eyes.

"Why did you call me? Why did you want me to come back here?"

I didn't know whether I should tell her that I hadn't called her. I didn't want to frighten her but I didn't want to lie either. When Priss was up to her tricks, people started getting hurt. I was angry, but I was afraid, too. How furious she must be to start playing these games, hitting me where it hurt the most. What would she do next?

"You didn't call me, did you?" she said.

I shook my head, and some battle played out on her face—embarrassment, confusion, sadness. She put her hands on top of her head and rubbed. It was something she did when she was distressed or feeling confused, a self-comforting gesture. I touched her arm; if I had wanted to, I could completely encircle it with my fingers.

"Someone called you," I said. "Just not me."

She looked at me, relieved. "It sounded like you," she said. "A mother knows her son's voice."

"Let me take you back," I said. "I'll tell you all about it on the way."

"Can we stay a little while?" she asked. "It's such a beautiful day."

And so we sat among the graves, with the birds and the butterflies. And I tried not to think about Priss and what she had done. But I was starting to get a sense of what her wrath might look like when it was directed at me. She had a special gift for finding your tender places and making them ache.

As I was leaving the hospital, after getting my mother settled, I saw Megan sitting in the passenger seat of the Scout. I'd left the door unlocked. The beautiful, warm day had finished cold, and she was shivering. I turned on the ignition without a word and cranked up the heat. I was happier to see her than I'd have imagined. A kind of relief washed over me in Megan's presence—she smoothed out the jagged places inside of me.

She moved over close and I took her in an awkward embrace, hitting the horn and startling us both. She pulled away, pushed her dark, thick hair behind her ears. She looked tired and sad and I knew it was because of me.

"You found your mom," she said. "Is she all right?"

"She's okay," I said. "Someone called her and told her to meet me at the house. So she went there and waited."

She gave me a frown and a little tilt of her head. "Who would do that?"

I found I couldn't look at her.

"Priss?" she said.

"I don't know," I said. I let out a sigh of fatigue and frustration I'd been holding in. "Maybe."

"Why?" she asked.

I was looking out into the night. The parking lot was nearly empty, and the trees were bending in a wind that had kicked up. For a second I thought I saw someone standing by the trees that edged the lot. But the moon passed behind the clouds and darkness settled into the shadows.

"She's angry," I said. "Angry that I'm getting married, that I'm in love—that I don't want her in my life anymore."

Priss was angry that I was trying to tear down the house, to move on from this place once and for all. But I didn't tell Megan that. She'd have been angry, too. Another decision I'd made without her.

I felt Megan's eyes on me, and I turned to face her. She wore a worried, uncertain expression. I spilled my guts about everything else. I told her that I'd been taking Adderall in order to finish my book and how I'd passed out last night, woke up to find I'd missed my meeting, and my appointment with her. I apologized for lying, for not bringing her up here with me, for taking drugs when I'd promised I wouldn't. I told her about my falling sales, and the end of *Fatboy and Priss*, about the trouble I was having with the project.

She didn't interrupt me, not once, just let me pour it all out. When I was done, she waited. She had her hands folded in her lap, her eyes on her knees.

"So that's it, right?" I said. "You're done with me."

If she were my friend, and not the girl of my dreams, I'd tell her: *Run. Get away from this guy. The drug problem, the crazy ex-girlfriend, the psychotic mother, the unstable psyche of an artist-slash-writer? None of it makes him husband material. You throw in with this guy, and he's going to ruin your life.*

She pushed out a little laugh then held up her ring and looked at it. If I was honest, I was disappointed that she hadn't wanted the big one. This one seemed too small to adequately express my love for her. Add vain and shallow to my list of bad personality traits.

"Do you want me to be done with you?" she asked.

The moon moved from behind the clouds, casting the night in silver blue. Now there was definitely someone standing there on the edge of the lot. Or was there? My head was swimming, with stress, fatigue, and a pill hangover. How much abuse can your body take? I was well on my way to finding out.

"No," I said. I took her hands. "*No*, I don't want you to be done with me. I love you—like I've never loved anyone. I'm my best self with you; I really am."

Did it sound hollow? Or was I just a hollow person, with little access to any true or deep feelings?

"Then let me be here for you and your mom," Megan said. "Let me help you. We have to be partners in this life;

we have to hold each other up and lean on each other. Otherwise, it won't work, you know?"

I could tell that she was thinking about Binky and Julia, about how special, how strong and real, their relationship was. Sure, they bickered and argued. But they had something; anyone could see it. They were solid, the foundation of Meg's life. She wanted that with me. Could I give it to her?

"I know that," I said.

I didn't know, though. My parents loved each other, and my father stood by my mother when others wouldn't have. Even when she shut us out, he took care of her. Still, I'd never had a good model, really. I wasn't even sure what a normal, healthy relationship looked like. Meg was young, younger than me, but she'd had other relationships, good ones. She knew what people were supposed to do for each other.

"I need to tell you . . ." she said. "I've had a couple of bouts with clinical depression."

This came as a bit of a surprise. I had seen the darkness moving within her in fleeting moments, a specter of sadness. But mainly she was a bright light, leading the way for anyone who needed it. I tried to imagine this practical, positive-energy girl in the throes of depression. I couldn't. "Really?"

"Yeah, once in high school," she said. She rubbed at her forehead, then wrapped her arms around her middle. "And again toward the end of my senior year in college."

"What brought it on?"

She shifted in her seat, glanced out the window. I followed her eyes. Did she see someone out there, too?

"Oh, I don't know. I guess I felt a lot of pressure. I told you about my brother."

I'd learned the last time we discussed it how her brother, Josh, walked out onto the beach, just a toddler, unseen by Binky and Julia. He'd walked into the Atlantic and apparently drowned. His body washed up a few miles down the shore. *They got over it, in some ways. But they never did, really. I think you can see it in my mom especially. There's this sad place inside her and she can fall into it if she's not careful.*

"I just felt all this pressure to be perfect, to never hurt my parents, never give them anything else to be sad about," she said now.

"I get it," I said. "I'm sorry."

I knew all about that, about holding yourself responsible for things that had nothing to do with you. It was a terrible burden, especially for a kid.

"I'm just saying," she said. "I know that place, how dark it is, how all the colors drain from the world. How there are dark thoughts, really dark, that make perfect sense when you're there but nowhere else. Like, once you've passed out of it, you can't believe you were ever in that place, thinking those horrible things."

I wasn't sure if she was talking about me or my mother, or both of us. But it was a relief to hear the words from her, that she wasn't perfect, that she understood the darkness in me.

"I'm sorry you had to go through that," I said. But she waved her hand. She was not one of those people who asked "why me?" when a bad thing happened. She was more a "why *not* me?" kind of person.

"A lot of people battle depression," she said. "And they get help and it's okay. Both times I talked to someone, got the right meds. I worked through it, you know? I owned it and took responsibility for it. And I moved on."

She moved to put her hands on my face. "When you're stressed and things are really hard, I want to be there for you. That's what people who love each other do."

"Okay," I said. I put my hands on hers and bowed my

head in gratitude. I didn't deserve her and I knew that. But I was keeping her just the same.

"Let's start by getting you some help for the drugs."

"Yeah," I said. Some of the tension in my body released. "Okay."

I swung the car around the lot and passed the place where I thought I had seen someone standing. There was nothing but a stump of a tree that looked as if it had been hit by lightning. My eyes were playing tricks on me.

We barely spoke on the long drive home, each of us lost in thought. I looked over at her, and took her hand. She let me, but she didn't look at me and smile, as usual. She kept her eyes focused outside, on the passing night landscape.

Then things started getting worse.

CHAPTER FIFTEEN

Megan was coming home from an extra-long day with Toby. She was tired as she walked up Broadway to the subway, not in the greatest mood. She'd had a hard night with me the night before, hadn't gotten much sleep after we returned to the loft from The Hollows. I'd convinced her that I'd turn my attention to my problems once the book was done. But it wasn't sitting easy with her. She was worried that I was putting off dealing with my issues, and that there would always be a reason I couldn't pay attention to them.

She had a lot on her mind—my stuff, the wedding, an agent she'd queried had asked to see her novel, and Toby had been acting up all day. He hadn't had school, was coming down with something, and was just intractable and cranky from the minute his mom left for work. He never napped, so Megan didn't have time to work on the pages she wanted to send to the agent. She was remembering how her mother wanted her to focus on her writing and give up her job, but she didn't want to do that. She was anxious and frustrated.

Plus, she'd just had the weirdest feeling. A kind of nervous, unsettled vibe, she told me.

All day, I was jumping at shadows. I felt like someone was watching me.

But she was inside her head, not really paying attention to the world around her like she should have been.

She had her earphones in, too, listening to Indian flute music and trying to get Zen amid the chaos of the city and her life.

The platform was crowded, and the train was delayed. She waited the better part of half an hour, getting ever more tired and impatient, like all the rest of the commuters after a long day. She got too close to the edge of the platform, leaning over to see if the train was coming. That's when she felt it, a nudge, a little push, someone's body pressed against hers. She pushed back; she was a New Yorker after all. She knew how to claim her space in a crush.

"Hey," she said. But when she turned around, she couldn't tell who had been nudging her.

More people streamed down the stairs. And still the train didn't come. The platform was growing louder, hotter, and people were agitated. There was a kind of throb, a tension that was building. And she felt so exhausted, so annoyed. She closed her eyes and thought of the beach house, imagining her parents cooking dinner, a fire going, the surf crashing outside. It was her happy place, her secret garden. She'd told me that early on. The city stressed her out, as much as she loved it—or the idea of it. At heart, she was a beach girl, quiet on the inside, enjoying quiet without. Sometimes Manhattan felt like an assault on her senses; she shut herself down, went elsewhere when it got to be too much.

One train raced by the station, packed with passengers, but didn't stop. There was a collective groan. She could see the platform across the tracks on the downtown side, and it was equally crowded. Her jacket felt heavy, too hot; she was sweating. She was considering going back up top, just hopping in a cab. But she'd already paid for the ride. Megan was frugal. *Every penny counts*, Binky was famous for saying. She waited.

She sidled close to the edge again, leaned over just a little. She saw the white of the approaching headlights. And that's when it happened. A body pressed against her. She pushed back but it didn't give this time. In fact, whoever it was kept pressing in.

"Hey," she said for the second time.

But it seemed like the crush of the crowd on the platform kept moving forward. On the track in between the two platforms an express train raced past and the station filled with its roar. For whatever reason, the conductor blared his horn. Megan tried to turn around, but then she felt the force of one hard push.

It was too powerful, too heavy a shove, and she lost her footing. And suddenly, unbelievably, she was losing her balance. Then she was tilting, falling over the edge—the weight of her bag sealing the deal. She landed hard on the wood and metal below, the gravel crunching beneath her. She knocked her head, but she didn't feel the impact. She was only distantly aware of a siren of pain, the thrum of fear.

All she could take in was the approach of the train, the screaming all around her from both sides of the platform. And then she was washed over with a kind of peaceful paralysis. *This is it. I don't get married. I don't get my book published. I don't have a baby. I don't get to say good-bye to my parents, to Ian.*

And she was okay with it, in that moment. She got it. None of us are promised anything. She remembered something her mom told her when she was a child: *You get what you get and you don't get upset.* This all happened in a flash of seconds.

But New York is a city of heroes. And two young men, a stockbroker and a bodybuilder who didn't know each other, jumped onto the tracks at the same time. They were able to lift her past the third rail to get her to the space between the local and express tracks in the fewer than thirty seconds they had to do it. The train roared past them, a killing metal wave of light and sound. The stockbroker started to cry, Megan told me. And she comforted him, thanking him and the other man for saving her life.

By the time the police and paramedics arrived, the crowds had cleared the platform.

"Did you see who pushed you?" the cop asked. She remembered that the cop was baby-faced, looked too young to be wearing a uniform. The gun at his waist was shiny and new.

"No," she said. "I never saw anyone." Neither had the other men.

"We'll get the CCTV video," said a detective. She was a young woman, wearing jeans and a Rangers jersey, her hair done in a spiky blond crew cut. "It'll take a couple of days."

That night at my apartment, after Julia and Binky had left, Megan was in good spirits. Giddy, actually, talking a mile a minute. She had skirted death and had moved from frightened and shaky to angry, then on to manic. I assumed there would be another dip in her mood, probably nightmares. She had a minor concussion and a black eye. But she was otherwise unscathed.

I was a wreck, wanting nothing more than to get drunk or high to take the edge off my fear and anger. Who had pushed her? If it hadn't been for those two guys—whom I was filled with gratitude toward and an irrational jealousy of—she'd have died. Lights out, just gone, her body mangled on a subway track. Who would do that to a girl like Megan, someone who'd never hurt anyone?

Binky had been to Katz's and picked up Meg's favorite

matzo-ball soup. And she was slurping it happily on the couch. She'd gone quiet.

"God," she said after a big bite of matzo ball. "It's *so* good."

"Megan," I said. I sat next to her, put my finger gingerly to the swollen black puff under her eye. There were so many colors—violet, pink, plum, a kind of green. "You're sure you didn't see who pushed you? Try to think of who was standing around you."

If she'd seen Priss, she'd have recognized her from the books, the drawings all over my place. Priss couldn't hide herself. She was too beautiful; all the flowers turned toward her when she walked into a room, attracted by her light and heat.

"I wasn't paying attention," she said. I noticed that her hands were shaking. "It could have been anyone."

"When are they going to have the CCTV footage?"

She put the soup down on the coffee table and looked at me. "I don't know."

I kept thinking of the panels I'd drawn of Fatboy falling onto the tracks. The single white light in the black tunnel, the thugs above him, the flash of their gold teeth, the expression of fear and pain on his face. It was too similar. What did it mean? Had Priss come into the apartment and seen the sketches? Was she trying to send me a message? Or was this just some kind of bizarre coincidence?

I walked over to my drawing table, which stood in the far corner of the loft, and brought the pages over. She flipped through them, and I heard her gasp.

"The tunnel, the headlight," she said. She went paler than she had been. "It was just like that."

She put the pictures aside and dropped her head into her hands. I sat beside her, wrapped my arms around her. She still smelled like the emergency room, antiseptic and strange.

"When did you draw these?" she asked finally. She moved away from me, pushed herself into the corner of the couch.

"A couple of days ago," I said. I picked them up and started looking at them. "Maybe a week."

She said something, but I didn't hear it. I was immediately lost in the drawings, thinking about the lines and the colors and how they didn't look quite right. The white wanted to be bluer. The tunnel needed a shadow outline of the oncoming train. Fatboy had to look more horrified. He was about to die in the most hideous possible way. In the sketch, he just looked merely scared, not mortally afraid. There should be more of a blankness, that slack expression of pure terror.

"Ian!" she said. I snapped back in.

"I'm sorry," I said.

"*What* are you trying to tell me?" she asked.

"I don't know," I said.

She wore an expression I hadn't seen before but would see many times again—dismay meets disappointment, concern meets anger. "You're scaring me."

I started seeing a psychiatrist after Jones Cooper's visit. They didn't have enough evidence to charge me with the Beech fire. Really, they didn't have *any* evidence. But everyone in town believed it was me.

The good news was that Mikey Beech and all the other bullies were giving me a wide berth. There was a nervous chatter in the hallway when I passed now, long, anxious looks. No one stood near me in the locker room, where I still had to change and sit on the bleachers even though I'd been excused from gym class until further notice, on order of my new shrink. (Because that's what I needed, to get *less* exercise, to be *more* of an outcast.) And no one sat at my table during lunch, where I unapologetically gorged myself on cafeteria food—pizza, hot dogs, hoagies, fish sticks, what have you. I didn't have a single friend.

My dad wasn't exactly the forward-thinking type. So I'm surprised that he took the step of seeking psychiatric help for me. Looking back, I realize that he was afraid; he'd failed to see the signs of trouble with my mother—or ignored them, more like. And it had cost him everything—his daughter, his wife, much of his business. I guess he'd learned his lesson.

There was a family and adolescent psychologist in town, but she was Detective Cooper's wife. So I wound up seeing a child psychiatrist at a place called Fieldcrest, a school for crazy kids that offered some outpatient services.

It was another thing that would seal my fate in The Hollows. Once this news got out, I became a complete pariah. In The Hollows, once you *were* something—the popular girl, the burnout, the football hero, the crazy kid—you were never anything else. The Hollows liked to put you in a box and keep you there forever—like in a coffin.

So once a week I got to sit in this plush office with Dr. Crown. He was an older man with a ring of hair around his shiny pate and a pair of round wire spectacles. Every week he wore a different colorful tie with some kind of cartoon character on it. I guess he was trying to be relatable, and it *is* the detail that I remember the most vividly about him. In a landscape of brown, beige, black, and maroon—in his office, his outfits, and his coloring—there was always the shocking color of his tie. Electric blue with the Tasmanian Devil, bright orange with that weird Bugs Bunny monster, red with Mickey and Minnie and tiny hearts all over. (Cool side note: The shrink in my comic has ties like that—art imitates life and all. It was really hard to come up with a new one for every time he appeared; I was running out of cartoon characters. Last time out, I'd resorted to SpongeBob.)

We started off talking about Ella's death, my mother's institutionalization, the bullying I was enduring at school. Dr. Crown was a careful, engaged listener. But I knew what we were really there to talk about: my imaginary friend Priss. Because nobody believed that she was real—not my grandmother, not my father, not the good doctor.

"When did you first meet her?"

"After Ella was born."

"And how were you feeling at the time?"

"I don't know," I said. "Fine."

I didn't want to tell him how angry and jealous I'd been then, how forgotten I felt. It didn't seem right. I'd have done anything to have my mother and sister back. I was deeply regretful for hating Ella; I missed her so much—her fuzzy head, her powdery smell.

He looked at me over his glasses and waited.

"Ella cried all the time." I examined the pile on the carpet, the water stain on the ceiling. "My mom was always with her."

"It's normal to be jealous and angry about a new sibling. You don't need to be ashamed of that, if that's how you felt."

More silence. It expanded and swallowed me. I wanted to go home.

"Is that how you felt, Ian?"

"I guess," I said. "A little."

"So at a time when you were feeling angry, jealous, maybe a little lonely, you met Priss out in the woods behind your house. Will you tell me about that?"

I told him about the day we met, how we played out in the woods. Then I recounted the night that Ella died, and how Priss saved me.

"She's real," I told him. "She is."

He gave me a kind, small smile, a slight nod of his head. "I believe that she's real to you."

"No," I said. I felt something go hard and mean inside me. "Not just to me, you asshole. To *anyone*. She's a real person."

The doctor pulled himself up from his relaxed posture, took off his glasses, and leaned forward just a little.

"Let's be mindful about how we speak to each other in here, Ian. This should be a safe place, a respectful place for both of us."

I'm not sure I remember quite what happened next. I just remember a rush of rage so intense that it turned the world red. My father came through the door, and then there were hands on me.

I remember the look on Dr. Crown's face. He wasn't surprised by my rage or the intensity of it. He wore a calm, impassive expression as he helped my father subdue me. He had seen it when I walked through the door, that raging angry beast that lived inside me. He spoke in soothing tones about taking deep breaths and coming back to the moment, and slowly I returned to myself, exhausted and weak. My father laid me down on a couch, where I began to sob.

She's real, I just kept saying over and over. *She's real.*

CHAPTER SIXTEEN

On the day of Fatboy and Molly's wedding, the sky is a heavy gunmetal gray, with a dark looming shelf of clouds moving slowly over the ocean. They are getting married at her father's country club on a bluff overlooking the sea.

Rows of white chairs set against the green lawn, an altar of lilies and roses, doves in a basket waiting for their release, the stately white country-club building surrounding the space like a pair of comforting arms. And that sky, that dark, dark sky threatening rain.

The guests arrive, crisp suits and floral dresses, high heels and gleaming leather loafers. They are the beautiful ones—the wealthy, the intellectual elite, the manicured, the coiffed. They are Molly's people.

Fatboy stands alone in the dressing room where he has donned his tux. He is red-faced and sweating, tugging at the hard collar, messing with the tie that's not quite right. He has invited no one. There is no "friends and family of the groom" side. All of these people are here for Molly. Fatboy had asked his mother if she would come, but she was too afraid. Of course, he didn't invite Priss. His father, his grandmother, and sister are all dead. He has never had a real friend. He has been alone until Molly. Now you have us, his mother-in-law-to-be said. But he saw worry as much as kindness in her eyes. Fatboy thinks she must be wondering: What does Molly see in him?

The guests filter onto the lawn, and Molly's father comes to walk with Fatboy down to his place at the altar. Her father *will give Molly away, and then, in a break with tradition, he'll stand up as the best man. There really is no one else, and her dad is too kind to let Fatboy stand alone. There is the usual speech about how Fatboy needs to take care of his daughter, and you're a part of the family now, son, and you can count on us. The sky starts rumbling and the guests stare nervously at the clouds above. Attendants run out with umbrellas just in case.*

When Fatboy sees her, Molly coming down the aisle, all his fear and nervousness falls away. She is an angel and he loves her. And when he looks at her, he can see that she loves him, too. For some reason he thinks of his baby sister, and something his mother said a lifetime ago. If you're good to her, she'll adore you forever. *He's going to do that. He is going to be the man that Molly deserves. He is going to take care of her and love her forever.*

She reaches him and the pastor begins to speak. They take their vows. And then the heavens open and it starts to pour, a big bolt of lightning slices the sky. The guests flee, but Fatboy and Molly stay put. Attendants rush to cover them with umbrellas, and they finish reciting their vows, and exchange rings alone in the rain with just the pastor and Molly's parents braving the weather.

They are all laughing and giddy as they start moving toward shelter. Molly is holding up her dress, keeping it off the ground and staying close to the ushers holding their umbrellas. She doesn't see right away the shadowy figure walking up the aisle toward them.

Then she does. "Who's that?" Molly asks.

Fatboy's heart starts to pound as the figure draws closer.

"I think there's been some mistake," the shadow says. "I didn't get my invitation."

Fatboy stares at her. She is nearly translucent in the next skein of lightning that opens the sky. The crack of thunder is deafening.

"Well," she says. *"Aren't you going to introduce me to your wife?"*

Priss.

Outside, a storm had been unleashed and rain was battering the windows.

"Life is not a comic book, Ian." Megan held the pages in her hand. She looked at them with disdain and then lifted them at me as if proving a point.

I know, I thought. But I wish life *were* a comic. Then I could draw the world and write the ending I want for us.

But I just stayed silent, because that's not what she wanted to hear. She wanted to hear that I was grounded in the real world, solid and able like Binky. Never fall in love with a girl who has a great father. You'll never measure up, and you'll kill yourself trying. Not that I was exactly trying. I'm just saying.

"You don't write something on the page and then it happens," she said. "It's a coincidence. A weird one, okay? But a coincidence."

"Unless . . ."

Her mouth dropped open a little as she put the papers down. I could see her hands shaking, and she was so pale she was almost gray. She should have been resting.

She lifted her palms. "Unless *what*?"

"Unless she was here and saw those sketches. Maybe it gave her ideas."

Megan lowered herself back onto the couch. The rain was really coming down now, big silver tears streaking the windows, which were glowing orange and yellow, picking up the light from passing cars and the streetlamps.

"Is that the kind of person we're talking about?"

"She's never hurt anyone I care about before," I said. I was really thinking aloud—which, guys, you should *not* do when arguing with your distraught fiancée. Think before you speak. "But then again, I've never had a real relationship before."

Megan had, of course. She'd had two significant men in her life: Her high school sweetheart, whom she was with through her sophomore year in college. They both went to the Country Day School in Riverdale, and then on to Columbia.

Then there was the guy she met at Columbia, whom she'd dated until about a year before we met. He was a medical student. Both of her exes were smart and handsome, breakups amicable enough, and each of them remained her friend. And either of them would have taken her back in a heartbeat; that was clear. I'd met them both on separate occasions, and each looked at me as if I had stolen his ice cream cone.

You're not the kind of guy I thought she'd end up with, Biff had said. Okay, his name wasn't really Biff. It was Kirk. Kirk Pasich. But it *could* have been Biff—beefy, preppy, well coiffed, charming. I felt like the Hulk beside him, and not in a good way—in an angry, clumsy, awkward way. I was aware of my tats, and my wild black hair, and the fact that I hadn't taken a shower, and couldn't remember the last time I'd shaved.

Oh, yeah? What kind of guy did you expect her to end up with?

Uh, me, Kirk said, and he gave me a kind of sad, self-deprecating smile that I couldn't get motivated to knock off his face. I felt bad for him, actually. I hoped to never be in the past tense of Megan's love life. What a desolate place that must be.

I patted him on the shoulder. "Sorry, dude," I said.

He shook my hand, offered a sheepish grin.

That was the kind of people Megan knew. Nice people, good people. She collected them and they stayed in her life forever. Because she was kind and sweet, funny and expansive, generous and thoughtful. All the things I wasn't. Is that what they mean when they say someone completes you? But what about the other person? What does she get?

"You think she'd—*hurt* me?" Megan said now.

"I really don't know," I answered.

The truth was, I never knew what Priss was going to do, not even on the page. She defied me even as I tried to write Fatboy's happy ending. She wasn't going to let him go, not without a fight. She wasn't supposed to show up at the wedding; she just did. I was wrestling with her in ink and in life, and losing on both planes of my existence. I didn't feel good about myself.

I could tell that Megan didn't feel good about me either. She was probably thinking about Kirk—how clean, how strong, how upright he was. How she'd never been in a mess like this with a man like him. She'd wrapped herself up in the blanket and curled into a little ball, leaned against the couch arm. The thunder rumbled and the lights dimmed a moment, then came back up. Then she dug into her pocket and handed me a card.

"You need to call the police and tell them about this woman," she said.

Her voice had grown stern, her eyes dark. There was that expression again. I stared at the shape of her face. How could I put that on paper—what lines, what shadows, what colors?

"If you really think she's a suspect, then you need to tell them who she is, where she lives, where she works, and where they can find her. You know—all the things you won't tell *me* about her."

I held the card in my hand, nodding, staring at it.

"Ian?"

"Okay," I said. I sounded young, defensive—a kid agreeing to do something he didn't want to do.

"If it's her, then your *friend* pushed me onto a subway track." Her voice had gone shrill, gone up an octave. "I seriously nearly died the most terrifying, ugliest possible death. Are you *getting* that?"

"Of course I get that." I tried to sound soothing, but I think it just came off as patronizing.

"Then why aren't you *angrier*?" Her voice grew softer, her eyes filled.

"I *am*."

But I was really more frightened, and I think she could see that. There was a flash of disappointment in her eyes. It cut me. No woman wants to know that you're afraid. She doesn't want to hear that you're scared and not sure you can control the situation, and a little bit of a coward. When she's frightened, she needs you to be the hero, the man with the gun. I wasn't that; I never had been. I didn't know if I could protect her, or even myself, from Priss.

I was just standing there shrugging with my hands out—not the posture of a superhero.

"What do you want me to do, Meg?" It even sounded a little whiny.

She got up then, tossed the blanket to the floor, and made for her things. She pulled on her shoes.

"Where are you going?" I asked, moving after her.

"Home," she said. "I want to go home."

"Uptown?" I said, blocking her passage. "I'll take you. I'm staying with you. You have a concussion. Be mad at me, okay. But I'm staying with you."

Her face softened, more of the old Megan, the real one, the one I met in the park. Was she changing? Was I changing her? Can you do that? Can you change a person for the worse—bring out things that weren't there before you entered her life? Or were they already there, dormant, just waiting for you to let them free?

"No," she said. She rubbed her eyes. "Home to Long Island. I can't work tomorrow anyway; I already called and told them I can't watch Toby this week."

It was best if she just stayed and got some rest. I tried to reason with her, but she just kept moving around, gathering up her stuff—her iPhone, her scarf and hat.

"Your parents just left, they won't be back there yet," I said finally.

"Well, I'm not staying here," she said, looking around the loft. "If she has access to this place then I'm not safe here."

It was pouring outside; it was Friday night. It was going to take us forever to get to her parents' place.

"Okay," I said. "I'll drive you."

I picked up her bag and walked with her to the door. She looked back at the loft.

"I hate this place," she said, quietly. "It's so cold."

I felt an irrational lash of anger, and was surprised to realize I was clenching my teeth as I locked the door behind me.

CHAPTER SEVENTEEN

I discovered comic books in a supermarket. My mom used to let me sit by the spinning rack, looking, and flipping through the pages while she did the shopping. I remember the first one I picked up, how it flapped in my hand, fell open to pages rich with color and the most amazing images.

Initially, I just stared at the pictures, mesmerized by the beauty of the women, the power of the men, the fantasy of the universe they occupied. *Batman, Superman, The Avengers,* the *X-Men, Daredevil*—how much better it was than anything I had ever seen in the gray, dull life of my suburban upbringing. School, the supermarket, our isolated house, the thick woods, the squeaky swing set in my backyard. Nothing real ever compared to what I saw in those magazines. If I'm honest, it never has.

My mom was happy to buy me whatever comics I wanted. At fifty cents or a dollar, they kept me busy for hours. First looking at pictures, then realizing there was a story, then trying to draw what I saw on the pages. I'd always had a gift and a love for art, so it was natural for me to try to re-create what I was seeing. This was before Ella was born, so I was young—maybe seven or eight. Even then, I wanted to climb inside those books and disappear. I wanted to get bitten by a spider, or fall into a vat of toxic waste and emerge a superhero with powers beyond my imagining.

"The kid lives in a fantasy world," my father would complain, looking at the stacks of comics. But I could see that light in his eyes, too. Every boy wants to be a superhero. "Hey, let me see that *Batman.*"

Eventually, I found a place in town, Second Hand Knowledge, a used-book store tucked inside a shabby strip mall off the main drag. It was a windowless box of a shop with moldy carpet and a water-stained ceiling. There were shelves and shelves of used books with bent-out spines and coffee-cup-stained covers, dog-eared pages— mystery, romance, science fiction, old classics. There was a man behind the counter, his red ashtray always overflowing with butts, his teeth and fingers stained yellow. He knew everything there was to know about comics.

There was a back room, well lit and clean, where he kept the comics—bagged and boarded, in pristine condition. I kept my comics mint for him, because unlike old paperback novels, I knew he wouldn't take the comics unless I'd treated them with respect. I'd bring in the ones I could let go of and trade them for the ones I wanted. Everyone knew the shop owner as Old Brian—though he wasn't that old, maybe in his forties when I first knew him. He lived over the store, and never left the strip mall . . . he ate at the pizza place, got his groceries at the 7-Eleven. He *seemed* old, though, walked slowly with a limp, was stooped over, head gone prematurely bald.

I should have seen him as a cautionary tale, someone so lost in a world of make-believe that he'd forgotten to live his life, that he'd grown old while he was still young. That for all he knew about comics—the larger-than-life characters, the big, purple stories, the dystopian cities, the mythical universes—there wasn't anything else in his life.

But I thought he was the coolest guy alive—because he was the first person other than my family to treat me with any real kindness and respect. He was my first friend.

He answered all my questions, taught me everything he knew. He never teased me or told me I was an idiot. And later, when I was older, even after I became Fatboy and the school freak, he gave me my first job. He called me "comics manager" and paid me $6.50 an hour.

That store, those books, my art—they saved me. More maybe even than Priss. Because it was while facing the sketch pad, with a pen in my hand, that I have always had the most power. There, I know who I am. I know what to do. I can use lines and color to create and understand the world. I can disappear inside those pages, and emerge a superhero like Clark Kent entering the telephone booth and coming out Superman. I went in as one thing, came out as another.

I guess I was about twelve when Brian gave me the job. I remember that my dad had to take me to the court-house to get my working papers, which I thought was the greatest thing in the world. He gave me permission to hop another bus after school that took me to town rather than out to my house. And the school bus would let me off by the pizzeria. I'd stop and eat, and then go to work.

Old Brian showed me how to board and bag the first editions on the first day.

"Comics are an important American art form," he told me. "And they deserve to be treated with care and respect."

He had a stack of boards and a pile of cellophane bags. He took one in each hand.

"First, you put the board in the bag," he said. He demonstrated, slowly slipping the gray cardboard into the shimmering sleeve. I tried not to notice that his finger-tips were yellow from cigarette smoke. "Then you put the comic on top of the board. Like so."

He was really into it, reverently slipping *Batman: Haunted Knight* into the plastic.

"Then you peel back the strip and seal the bag."

He handed it to me, and nodded to the shelf where it belonged. I placed it there.

"Good," he said with an approving nod. "Now remember: never, ever use tape when you're boarding and bagging. That adhesive can damage your comic."

"Okay," I said.

"Let me watch you do one."

I took a board and a bag, and put them together exactly as he'd shown me. Then I slipped a copy of *X-Men: Dark Phoenix Saga* from the stack he had told me was especially valuable.

"You have good taste, Ian," said Brian. He leaned a slender arm against the shelf. "She's one of my all-time favorites."

"Mine, too," I said. I stared at the cover for a second—her wild red curls, impossibly lush body, maniac grin. Jean Grey was a woman pushed to the brink and beyond. I slid it gently inside and handed it to Brian. I knew he'd keep that one behind the counter. I thought about that issue sometimes; it was worth about six thousand dollars the last time I looked for it.

"Good," he said again, and gave me a pat on the shoulder. "You get it. Go to town."

I was in heaven, sitting there on a little rolling stool, putting the comics in their protective sleeves, watching them glitter and shine, arranging them carefully on the shelves. I don't know how much time passed, but eventually I heard someone push through the curtain. I turned to see a slim old woman in a gray wool coat move into the room—not your usual comic book customer. Probably buying for a son or a grandson, I thought. She walked around the room, looking at the books, then she ran a hand through her short gray hair and issued a sigh.

"Can I help you, ma'am?" I asked the way Old Brian

had taught me. *Be open, be helpful and friendly, no matter what.*

I stood up to face her. She looked vaguely familiar but I couldn't place her. It was like that in The Hollows. There were no strangers.

Her eyes were dark and glittering. She was small, smaller than I was, but she seemed stronger, more powerful somehow. There was something about her gaze that made me want to avert my eyes, and I dropped them to my shoes. It wasn't that she was unkind or intimidating. It just felt like she saw me in a way that people usually didn't. She looked right past my acne, my overweight slouchy self, and into the heart of me. What she saw there, I didn't know. *I* didn't even know what was under there.

"I don't know too much about comics," she said. "Do you?"

"Yeah," I said. "I know a little bit. I'm learning."

I knew a lot but I didn't want to brag.

"So, if I were going to buy my first comic, what would you recommend? Pick one for me."

I walked over to the shelf by the door, grabbed a copy of *Watchmen*, and handed the heavy book to her. "It's a classic," I told her. "Everything that's great about the form."

She held it in her hand, looked at me, and smiled. "Thank you, young man."

"You're welcome." My first sale! I was stupidly proud of myself.

I thought she would turn and walk away but she didn't, she kept looking at me.

"Can I get something else for you?"

"I think we have someone in common," she said. "You're Ian, right?"

"Yeah," I said.

"Do you know a girl named Priss?"

The name sounded strange on the air. I just stared at her—someone else who knew Priss. She was the first adult I had encountered who had actually seen her.

"She's my friend," I said. "Do you know her?"

She gave a crooked little nod. "I do know her. How is she?"

I shrugged. I wasn't sure how to answer. She was just Priss—wild, unpredictable, loyal, lonely. But I didn't have the words for all that, so I said nothing. The woman seemed about to say more when a couple of kids walked into the room laughing in big guffaws. Two boys, geeks like me—one bespectacled, skeleton thin, the other round and sloppy with a ripped, stained red sweatshirt and greasy hair. They fanned out and started looking at the shelves.

When I looked back at the woman, she was moving through the curtain. I couldn't follow. It was Brian's number one rule: don't leave kids alone in the comic book room. I helped the big one find a *Spider-Man* he was looking for, and the other was just along for the ride, gazing longingly at the shiny covers. I felt bad for him; I knew what it was like to want something and not be able to afford it.

By the time I followed them up to the register, the old woman was gone.

"That woman . . ." I said to Brian after the boys had left.

"*Watchmen*," he said. Brian could only identify people by the books they bought. "She left this for you. You know her?"

I shook my head as he handed me a folded white piece of paper.

Call me if you want to talk about Priss, she had written in a thin, scrawling hand beside her name and a phone number. It was a name I recognized, but couldn't place. *And be careful.*

"She was a little creepy, huh?" said Brian. He wore a frown of concern. "You okay?"

"Yeah," I said. I stuffed the paper in my pants pocket. "It's cool."

I remember being almost giddy with relief, even though the encounter *had* been unnerving. Someone else had seen Priss. This woman, whoever she was, knew her. It wasn't that I had doubted that she was a real person. I wasn't crazy like my mother. I knew the real world from delusions. She had a scent, a touch, a shadow—a physical presence in the world. Now I could prove to my dad that Priss was not a figment of my imagination. She was real, and not just to me. That's all I could think about; the warning scratched on the paper registered not at all.

Julia and Binky did, in fact, beat us back to the Hamptons. Megan had sent them a text message from the road to tell them we were on our way. She'd done quite a bit of texting—more typing than I was used to seeing her doing. And her phone was binging every few minutes. What was she telling them? Our ride out was awkward and silent. We barely exchanged a word. She was already unstrapping her seat belt as we pulled into the driveway, and was out the door the second after I'd stopped the car. She slammed it hard behind her.

Julia was waiting for us, and seemed to pick up on all our negative energy the moment we walked through the door. She shot me a strange look and ushered Megan upstairs, leaving Binky and me in the foyer staring after them.

They liked having her home; I could tell. She was still their little girl in a lot of ways. Too many ways, I was starting to think. But maybe that was Priss's voice in my head. Maybe it was normal to go home to your parents when things got rough—if you had parents to go home to. Maybe I was jealous. I'd been on my own, emotionally speaking, since my mother went away; it hadn't always been easy. Megan lived like someone who had a safety net beneath her. I never felt like that; I was always looking down at hard concrete and broken glass.

"Drink?" said Binky.

"Please," I said.

I followed him to the bar, where he poured me two fingers of scotch into a crystal lowball. Then we made our way out to the deck. It was cool, the air full of salt and sand, but the rain falling on Manhattan was not falling on Long Island. The surf crashed loud and fast against the shore.

"I like you, Ian," said Binky. He said it easily, offered a warm touch to my arm. "And that's not always an easy thing for a father to say to the man who's marrying his daughter. As a dad, you don't want to give that little girl away. You can't understand that now, but you will when you have one of your own. I hope you do; I hope you have a bunch. We just have our Megan."

He took a swig of his drink and I knew I wasn't supposed to talk yet. It was one of those talks, one where you were required to shut the fuck up and listen.

"We lost a child," he said. "Did Megan tell you?"

"She did tell me," I said. "I'm sorry."

He took another deep swallow of his drink and kept his eyes on the yawning black distance in front of us. "That pain, that grief, that guilt . . . it takes you apart and puts you back together again. You're not the same person afterward. You go on for your other child."

Why was he telling me this? Was this going to be some speech about how I needed to protect his daughter? Had Megan told them about my mother? I'd never asked. I didn't keep it a secret, or ask her to. But it wasn't something people went around shouting from the rooftops. It was too horrible even to be sensational gossip. *My mother killed my sister and would have killed me if I hadn't had a disobedient streak. And she's been in a mental hospital ever since.*

Binky moved over to one of the Adirondack chairs and sat down, the ice clinking in his glass. I sat beside him.

"Even though Meg doesn't remember the incident or her brother, I think she has had it the worst. Time heals us, even if you don't think it will. Julia and I, impossible as it seemed in the moment, moved on without him. We had to. But Meg, I think, was defined by our grief. In a way, she was formed in it. She has always been such a good girl, so careful with herself, so well behaved and conscientious. I always wondered if she was taking such care for us, you know? To spare us more pain."

I thought about what Megan had said about her bouts with depression, the pressure she felt to be perfect.

"She's told you about her depressions?" Binky asked, as if reading my mind.

I said that she had, and he nodded slowly.

"Right," he said. He drained the glass and put it down on the arm of the chair. I did the same. He wouldn't drink more; I knew that. But I wanted another. Left to my own devices, I'd probably have had three.

"But how much time do you really spend talking about *Megan*?"

There was an edge to his voice that put me on the defensive. "What do you mean?"

"I mean it seems to me like an awful lot of time is spent on you. Your dark history, your mentally ill mother, your problems with work, your recreational drug use. Megan is a caretaker. It's in her nature to comfort and fix. That unfortunately, unwittingly, is how we raised her. But in a marriage, you're supposed to take care of *each other*."

I saw a form way down the beach, just a thin line moving in our direction.

"I know," I said. "I do take care of her. I will."

"What about this woman?" asked Binky. "This friend of yours."

I felt an embarrassed flush heat my face. God, did she tell them *everything*? There was something childish about that, I thought.

"It's a problem," I said. I leaned forward in my seat, suddenly feeling uncomfortable. "I'm taking care of it."

"See that you do," said Binky. "I don't want to be the asshole father-in-law who doesn't think anyone is good enough for my daughter. And I like you, Ian."

The fact that he had to say it a second time was making me doubt his sincerity. He went on.

"I think at your *core* you're a good guy. But I'm starting to get concerned for my daughter. I'm wondering if you guys are ready for marriage, if you know what it means."

There was a lash of fear, followed by anger. The form was drawing closer, getting bigger. It wasn't much of a night for a walk on the beach; the surf was angry and the wind wild.

"Megan seems to think this woman has something to do with what happened tonight," he said. "Is that true?"

"I don't know," I said. How could he know that? Did she text him from the car?

"She says you haven't called the police," he said.

I hadn't called the police. I couldn't. I told him so.

"I don't understand," he said.

"They won't believe me."

He was staring at me hard now; I could feel his eyes boring into the side of my face. I was getting that cornered animal feeling I sometimes got. I was hot, even though the air was cold. I kept my eyes on that person walking up the beach; I stood to get a better look. The shape was familiar to me. The most familiar shape in the world. *Oh God, how did she find us here?*

"Why won't they believe you, son?" Binky said. His voice had the gentle, level tone that people take when they think there might be something wrong with you. "Make me understand that."

I couldn't answer him, just kept my eyes on Priss as she drew closer.

"Ian," said Binky. His voice was stern, fatherly. I heard him rise from his seat, but all I could see was Priss. "I need you to tell me why you think no one will believe you."

I started moving toward the staircase. I had to get to her before she got to this place. If she came here, if these two worlds collided, I couldn't bear it. Everything here at Binky and Julia's was clean and good and right. It was safe. It was wholesome. I wouldn't let her defile that. Before I could get to the stairs, I felt Binky's hand on my arm.

I turned to face him and found that red veil of rage coming down over my eyes. I don't want to tell you what happened next.

CHAPTER EIGHTEEN

Even though I'd basically attacked Dr. Crown, he still wanted to see me. So, once a week, my dad and I made the trek out to his office after school. I endured these visits, mainly because I knew we'd stop at Burger King on the way home.

"How are you doing, Ian?"

That's how Dr. Crown began every session, looking at me with what I'm sure he thought was a warm smile. To me, it seemed condescending to the point of goading. I think he was a nice man, probably good at his job. I hated him.

"Fine," I said. (In case you're wondering if this and the phrase "I don't know" were the most oft uttered words of my boyhood, they were.)

"Anything going on at school that we need to discuss?"

"No."

"Have you had any feelings you couldn't control?"

"No."

There were two big topics of conversation, things we worked on. One was my rage problem; I apparently had one. The other was Priss; no one believed she existed. They thought I was making her up, my imaginary friend and scapegoat for the Beech fire. Of course, no one had ever come out and said that precisely. There was zero physical evidence connecting me to the fire, which was why the investigation had been dropped.

They were trying to lead me to my own conclusions about Priss, using pointed questions such as: Why is it that Priss doesn't go to school? How come she won't show you where she lives? What's her last name? How is it that she's out in the woods at all hours of the day and night? Is she an orphan? Does she have a family? Where are they?

I had answers for all their questions, at first. Priss was homeschooled; her mother used to be a teacher. She wasn't allowed to have friends because her mother didn't let her bring people home. Her mother worked at a hospital now, so she was gone a lot and Priss came and went as she chose. Priss never knew her father. Her last name . . . well, Priss said it was a secret.

These were the answers Priss had given me. Do they seem specious? Does it seem like her story had a lot of holes? Whatever. I knew she was real. No one was going to convince me otherwise. Especially now that I knew someone else had seen her.

I had given up on trying to convince my dad and Dr. Crown, and "admitted" that Priss wasn't real, just a friend I'd made up in my terrible loneliness. I had apologized for worrying everyone. No, I didn't play with her anymore. It was silly, childish. I'd moved on. It was just easier that way.

But in reality I was spending more time with Priss than ever. I was sneaking out into the woods while my father was working or sleeping. And she was always there, waiting for me, ready to play or just lie among the graves and watch the clouds or stars. She was all I had, the only one in the world, other than my mother, who didn't think I was a freak, a liar, and an arsonist.

Then there was the rage thing, which was a little confusing. Apparently, when I got really angry, I kind of lost it. There was the incident at school where I had threatened to burn Mikey's house down, according to witnesses. I had vehemently denied this, but so many people had seen it, that even I started to wonder. Then there was the attack on Dr. Crown. He said that a kind of blank look came over my face before it set into a mask of fury. I lunged at him, called him a cocksucker and a string of other unpleasant names, closed my hands around his throat. My father apparently stepped in, subdued and held me until I calmed down. After which point I wept, went briefly catatonic, then fell asleep.

The weird thing was that I had only the fuzziest recall of this, so vague and odd that it was less real to me than a dream. It seemed like a lie, except that I could tell by the fear on my father's face that he was telling the truth. There was always a part of me that didn't believe I had this capacity for blind rage. There was always a part of me that thought maybe all these people were making it up, trying to fuck with me in some vast conspiracy that spanned years, and different schools, different cities, people who were strangers to one another. But that was probably not realistic.

"How have things been for you at school socially?" asked Dr. Crown.

"Socially?"

"Tell me about your friends, your interests," said Dr. Crown. "How's art club?"

Art club: middle school's only haven for freaks, an oasis in a sea of misery. There at the long, wooden, paint-splattered tables, beneath the colorful mobiles that hung from the ceiling and the artwork of ages papering the walls, Miss Rose at her easel with the overhead fluorescents off, the music playing from a squat pink boom box by the open window—there I was at peace, at one with myself and the pencil in my hand.

"You're very gifted, Ian." That's what Miss Rose had said to me early on, and I carried the sound of her voice with me, remembered her words when I was feeling like a loser. "You'll have a career in the arts if you want one."

I had art class every Tuesday and Thursday, and art club every Wednesday and Friday after school. So almost every day I could disappear into that room. On Friday afternoons Miss Rose let me stay after the late bus and wait for my father to come get me after he got off work.

"It's good," I replied to Dr. Crown.

"You're very talented," he said. He reached over to his desk and picked up two pieces of paper, large, heavy stock like the paper I favored for my sketches.

"Where did you get those?" I said, recognizing them immediately.

"Your father visited with your art teacher on parents' night. She showed him some of your work. Didn't he tell you?"

"No," I said. I leaned forward and stretched out my hand. His eyes lingered on the drawings for a moment, and then he handed them to me.

"Who is that?" he asked, pointing to the one on the top.

"No one," I said. I stared at her; I didn't have her yet— the color of her hair, the line of her jaw, that particular light in her eyes. None of it was perfect. I was years from getting her just right. If I'd had a pencil in my hand at that moment, I'd have started erasing, redrawing.

"Is that Priss?" he asked.

"Priss isn't real," I said.

He gave me a quick nod. "But is that how you imagine her?"

"I don't know."

"The girl in that picture. Well, she's not really a girl. She's a woman, a very sensuous, well-developed young woman."

I felt my throat tighten, heard a kind of roar in my

ears. I cleared my throat, tried to calm myself the way Dr. Crown taught me to—with my breath, with my thoughts. *Everything is okay. I can let the anger wash through me, acknowledge and release it.*

"Have I upset you?" he asked. "I'm sorry. Perhaps your father should have asked you before he showed these to me. I thought he had."

He did seem sorry, and looked concerned with a wrinkle in his brow as he leaned forward in his chair. But I was shaking, my breathing growing ragged. Why had Miss Rose given these to my father? Why had my father given them to the doctor? I felt deeply betrayed, ashamed. *Everything is okay. I can let the anger wash through me, acknowledge and release it.*

"You always describe her as a young girl, about your age," the doctor went on. "Waiflike and pale. But this woman is powerful, sexual."

I kept staring at her. The eyes were almost right— amused, knowing, and something else. Something dark. I felt some of my anger start to die down, looking at her.

"Sexual fantasy is normal at your age, Ian." How old was I then? Twelve going on thirteen?

"It's not like that," I said. The blinds in his office were dusty; the couch beneath me was hard and uncomfortable.

"I used to read comics when I was your age," he said. "I had the world's biggest crush on Barbara Gordon. You know, Batgirl."

It was the right tactic. I suddenly saw him as something other than a distant authority figure, someone who was trying to get into my head to tell everyone how fucked up I was.

"Really?"

"Really." He nodded. "She was hot."

We both started to laugh a little, and I felt my anger dissipate—at least toward him.

"She reminds me a little of Dark Phoenix," said the doctor, nodding at the sketch. "She has that edge to her. Rage."

I hadn't seen it until he mentioned it. But he was right. Dark Phoenix was one of my early favorites, so certainly she was a strong inspiration. But Priss was her own thing.

"Not that I think it's derivative," he said quickly. "I mean, your drawing is totally original. I can just see how you might have been influenced."

I felt myself opening up to him as I talked about how I'd found another world within the pages of those comic books. It was a place where the battle of good versus evil was easy to understand. Where the good guys were heroes—bold, brave, and powerful—who never failed to vanquish the bad.

"The real world is never so simple," said the doctor. "I understand. In your life, the ultimate symbol of good, of nurturing and love, did something unspeakable. It must be comforting to dwell in a world where things are easier to understand."

"She didn't mean it. It wasn't her," I said. There was that familiar rush of defensive anger. "She's sick."

"That's true," he said with a careful nod. "Your mother was suffering from postpartum psychosis. She is mentally ill. But the impact of her actions has been life rupturing for you. And it's okay to experience the full range of emotions associated with that—even rage. If we can deal with your feelings head-on now, they won't consume you. You won't seek other ways to comfort yourself, to blow off steam."

I nodded, even though I didn't understand what he meant. I was already living in a fantasy world, eating myself into oblivion. It wouldn't be a long time before I started experimenting with drugs. He was a good doctor, who offered solid advice, but I was too far gone. And frankly it was just easier to *eat* my feelings than to deal with them.

I don't remember the end of that session. I do recall getting the feeling that the doctor thought he'd made some kind of breakthrough with me. Maybe he believed that there was some connection in my mind between my mother and Priss. There was only one problem with his theory. Priss wasn't a larger-than-life comic book character. Priss was real.

The next week, there was a fire at my school. It happened over a weekend, late at night. So no one was hurt. Only one room suffered damage. The art room.

I ran across the beach with Binky calling after me from the porch. But by the time I reached the place where I had seen her standing, she was gone. I was sweating and winded, bent over with a terrible stitch in my side.

"Priss!" I yelled into the black night. The surf carried my voice away, drowning it in that eternal roar. "Priss! Stay away from them!"

But no one was there. I sank to my knees and the wet sand soaked through my jeans immediately; the surf lapped in and washed over my calves and shoes. The salt water was frigid, slicingly cold, and my legs went numb. The big beach houses stood back behind the tall sea grass, their windows glowing orange. I don't know how long I stayed there, kneeling and staring into the black, calling after a woman who obviously wasn't there. Finally, Megan came out after me.

"What's wrong with you?" she said. She had her arms wrapped around herself, kept her distance. The bruises on her face looked like shadows.

"I thought I saw someone," I said.

She glanced around us at the vast dark beach, making a point of gazing up and down. "There's no one here."

She was right. There was no one and nothing as far as the eye could see.

"Did you hit my father?" she asked. Her voice broke a little. "He wants to call the *police*."

"No," I said. Hit Binky? Had I hit him? "Of course not. I would *never* hurt you or your family."

She moved in closer. She still loved me then, still wanted to pretend none of this was happening. Or that it was something that *had* happened, and that would be over and forgotten, something that we would wonder about when we were old, watching our grandchildren play on this very beach, looking back at that very same house. She reached down for me and pulled me to my feet. I moved to her, grabbed her, and held her against me. She felt so good, so soft and warm.

"Ian," she whispered.

"I love you," I said into her hair. Lately, the words just sounded desperate, like I was trying to convince her, to convince myself. She sighed deep and long, pressed into me, and held on.

"I love them—Binky and Julia. You—all of you—are everything I could have hoped for."

She was shaking her head as she pulled back from me, big blue tears pooling in her eyes and then rolling down her dewy pink skin. The wind was tossing her hair. She shouldn't have been out there. She should have been resting. Binky was right; I wasn't taking care of her as I should be.

"My dad said you were staring at something on the beach. Something that he didn't see. You stood suddenly and started to run. He tried to stop you and you turned to swing at him. He dodged it mostly, but you clipped him on the jaw."

"No," I said.

"There's a bruise," she said. "He's got ice on it."

"I couldn't have," I said.

"He said that you didn't even look like yourself." She was shivering, pulling her sweater tight around her.

"Megan," I said. But then I didn't know what to say.

"You better tell me everything," she said. "You better tell me right now."

"Not here," I said.

I looked up and down the beach. If Priss had been there, she was gone. Unless she was hiding in the tall grass like the tiger she was, watching us.

Megan looked back at the house; I could see Binky on the porch. She started moving toward him.

"I'll meet you at the Scout," she said. "I don't think my parents want to see you again tonight."

I watched her walk away, and I wished so hard that I could undo everything bad that had happened over the last few days—hell, over my whole life.

I sat in the Scout and waited nearly an hour. Megan finally came out. Julia and Binky stood in the doorway, but they didn't try to stop her. Maybe they already had, and she'd prevailed. She'd obviously convinced Binky not to call the police. I didn't remember hitting him, but the knuckles on my right hand were swollen and red, aching.

Megan, pale and shaky, climbed into the vehicle. She ran a hand through her hair and fastened her seat belt.

"Is he okay?" I asked. I hated that I'd hurt him. How could we go on from there? How could he forgive me? It didn't seem like something you laugh about later: *Hey, son, remember that time you clocked me in the jaw. You know, the night your ex pushed Megan onto the subway tracks?*

It was slipping away from me, this new life I'd created. Just the way Priss wanted it to. She liked me best when I was lonely and high, an outcast who didn't belong anywhere. She didn't want me loved and happy, building a life that didn't include her.

Megan didn't answer me, just put her head in her hands.

"I'm sorry," I said. "I'm so sorry."

I started to drive and we wound up at this old diner off the highway where we'd been before. Megan ordered pancakes with bacon and scrambled eggs; she always ate like a truck driver when she was stressed. I ordered black coffee and wished I had a joint, something to take the edge off. But there was no escaping this. I had to tell her everything now, or lose her. I might lose her anyway. If she was smart she'd go running. And if I loved her, really loved her, I'd let her go.

CHAPTER NINETEEN

Detective Jones Cooper came to our house the day after the art room fire. It was Sunday morning, and I was playing video games. My dad was reading the paper. We were both feeling down because we'd been to see my mother the day before and it hadn't gone well. It seemed like she was never going to be able to come home.

"I want to die, Nick," she said. "Why didn't they let me die?"

"We have a son," he whispered to her. I was sitting right there, playing my Game Boy. Maybe they thought I couldn't hear them; maybe they were just too far gone in their own unhappiness to care. "He needs you. *I* need you."

"I don't even exist," she said. "I'm a ghost."

"Don't say that," my father said. "Please."

My father and I went out to dinner that night, him staring at his food, me shoveling it in, not talking. We hadn't really talked since the blowout we'd had after my last visit with Dr. Crown. And I hadn't been back to art class. Miss Rose showed my father my work, then he and Dr. Crown had used it against me to get inside my head. I hated them all. The only person I was still talking to was my grandmother, and she was around less and less. Who could blame her?

When the knock came at the front door, something inside me went cold. I got up and left the room, went upstairs, and closed my door. My father had bought me an artist's draft table for Christmas. And that's where I spent my time when I wasn't plastered to the television. I stood at my window and saw a squad car, as well as Cooper's maroon SUV. My stomach bottomed out. What had she done now?

I heard the door open and close downstairs. And then there was silence, a stretching silence that went on too long. Finally, I crept from my room and stood on the landing, listening.

"This is the second incident of arson in The Hollows in under a year," I heard Cooper say. "Both of which followed an altercation with your son. Ian is going to need to come in for questioning."

"This is ridiculous," my father said. "You *know* us."

"I'm sorry, man," said Cooper. "This isn't personal."

They let me ride in my father's car, though I would have preferred the squad car. I'd never been in one, and I was childish enough to think it would have been cool. The gravity of the situation hadn't dawned on me. And to be honest, a kind of apathy had settled. Too much stress, unhappiness, loneliness. I was shutting down in significant ways.

It must have showed, because Cooper was different with me during this second questioning. He was more distant, treating me less like a troubled kid needing his help and more like an adult suspected of a serious crime. The gloves were off. He walked me through the station and led me to an interrogation room, a gray room without windows. We sat with a narrow metal table between us. My father stood in the corner.

"What did you and Miss Rose argue about?" Cooper asked.

There had been an argument; I remembered that much. I remembered that I wanted to confront her. Dr.

Crown said that I had a right to talk about my feelings, that I didn't have to keep them buried down deep. *Because feelings don't stay down. Unexpressed anger and sorrow have a way of finding unhealthy releases if suppressed.*

"She showed my drawings to my father."

"And you didn't want her to do that?" He raised his eyebrows, as if musing, trying to understand.

"No."

"Why not?"

"My drawings are private." I could feel the anger start to come alive. There was a tightness in my throat, a little race in my pulse.

"But it was parents' night. Your dad came to see your work, right?"

"She didn't ask me if she could display them for parents' night. I would have said no, if she'd asked."

He nodded, rubbed the crown of his head. He settled back into his chair.

"I can see why that would upset you. I think I would be angry, too. You argued about it?"

I shrugged. The truth was, I didn't exactly remember what happened. I went to art class, same as always. When I saw her, I felt the rise of anger, the sting of betrayal.

"Ian," she'd said. She'd worn that warm smile. Her raven curls were pulled back; her dark eyes always looked like she was just about to cry from happiness. "Your father was so impressed with your work."

"She described you as 'enraged,'" the detective said now.

"No," I said. "I don't know."

"The other students say you were yelling. You called her a bitch, told her you hated her." He looked down at his notes. "You screamed, 'How could you show him? I trusted you.' Sounds like you were pretty mad."

I could feel my father looking at me. If he'd been smart, he'd have told me to keep my mouth shut, wait for the lawyer. But he wasn't smart, not about things like that. People like my father always think that you tell the truth and everything works out fine. In fact, the opposite is often true.

"I don't remember saying that," I said.

Jones Cooper looked at me hard, a deep frown creasing his forehead. "So you don't remember your argument with Mikey Beech. You don't remember your argument with Miss Rose. But these things happened. A lot of people were there to bear witness—each time."

I listened to the buzz of the fluorescent lights, my father clearing his throat, the *tap-tap-tap* of my own foot. There was no noise outside the room.

"Are there any other blank spots in your memory, Ian? Say, for example, last night. Or on the night of the Beech fire."

"No," I said. "I didn't do that. I didn't set any fires. Okay, I get angry sometimes. I guess I say things I don't mean. But I wouldn't do anything like that."

"You know what, son?" Jones Cooper didn't take his eyes off me. They were dark, unyielding—black holes that sucked in everything. "I don't believe you."

I tried to stare back at him, but I couldn't hold that gaze.

"Honestly?" he said. "I think you're a stone-cold liar."

"That's enough, Cooper," my father said. I could hear a note of impotent anger in his voice. "Ian, not another word until the lawyer comes."

"That's fine," said Detective Cooper. "You're gonna need one."

He left the room. And my father and I dwelled in an expanding silence.

"What's wrong with you?" my father asked.

"Nothing," I said. I turned to look at him. He was standing away from me, looking pale. "It was her, Dad.

It was Priss. She did it. She likes fire; she likes to watch things burn."

His mouth dropped open, but he didn't say anything. The look on his face—I'd never seen it before. It was unreadable. But it filled me with dread.

"I met someone," I told him. "An old woman who says she knows Priss."

My father shook his head, looked confused. "Who?"

Before leaving the house for the police station, I'd grabbed the piece of paper from the drawer by my bed. I'd had a feeling I was going to need it, that today was going to be the day that I had to prove that Priss was real. I handed him the note, told him quickly how the old woman had come to see me at the shop, what she'd said.

I expected him to react with relief, to jump into action. But that's not what he did.

"Oh, good Christ." He rubbed his face vigorously. When he looked at me again he seemed so angry, so hopeless. He took a quick step toward me and I flinched, thinking that he was going to hit me. But he did something that hurt even worse; he started to cry.

"Ian," said Megan. She looked distressed, taking in all the details of my long, sad story, my strange history with Priss. "Are you telling me that Priss isn't real?"

The diner was empty except for an old waitress behind the counter and a cook visible in the kitchen. A pie case turned by the cash register and emitted an unpleasant whirring noise. Heavy in the air was the smell of grease and burned coffee. Megan had cleaned her plate, but her coffee sat untouched. It had gone cold.

"No," I said. "She's real. I've just never been able to *prove* that she was real."

She leaned back from me, looking down at her hands.

"You know that doesn't make any sense, right? You know it sounds totally crazy."

I didn't say anything. I had the sense that the waitress was eavesdropping, but when I turned to give her a withering look she wasn't even there.

"Yeah," I said. "I know."

"Why do you think she's real?" Megan asked. I loved this about her, her willingness to roll up her sleeves and get to the bottom of things. Unlike me, she didn't judge; she examined, explored. "In spite of all evidence to the contrary, why do you think she's real, Ian?"

"Because my mother has seen her," I said.

The words hung in the air. Yes, my mother—the baby killer, the mental patient who has been hospitalized on and off for twenty years—has seen Priss. I went on. "And I don't control her, you know? I mean, she's *outside* of me. She does things I don't want her to do. I'm—afraid of her."

Megan still hadn't said anything. I could see her working through what I'd told her, turning the information over.

"And this other person who knows her?" said Megan. "Eloise Montgomery? Why didn't she help you? Why couldn't she prove to your father and to the police that Priss was real?"

How to put it? "She was *unreliable* in some ways," I said. "Not everyone thought she was *all there*."

Megan frowned, and I could see she was about to probe for clarification. But I reached for her hands and squeezed them tight. That heart-shaped diamond glittered like all the hope I held inside. It was small but pure, flawless. She had been right to choose it; it was so much nicer than the one I had chosen. I had selected a ring for flash, for what it told the world about me; she'd chosen one for beauty, for simplicity.

"I'm not crazy," I said.

Her eyes filled, and she turned her hands to clasp mine.

"I know you're not," she said. "I believe you."

My breath caught in my throat. "Thank you," I said. "Thank you."

"So, how do you reach Priss?" she asked. "When you want to get in touch with her, do you call her? Do you go see her? Does she have a job?"

"I call her," I said. "Or I go see her. She has a place on the Lower East Side, a total dump walk-up on Rivington Street."

I didn't want to tell her that Priss was a squatter. She moved from place to place, staying with the same ragtag group of friends in various abandoned places throughout the five boroughs. It was becoming a harder and harder existence, as even the worst neighborhoods were gentrifying. She'd never worked, as far as I knew. She'd inherited money when her mother died. There was a house in The Hollows, supposedly; she went there sometimes. I didn't want to tell Megan any of this because it sounded like a lie. Priss's answers to questions about her life always sounded like lies to me, and double that when I repeated them to someone else. But I had learned not to push Priss, not to question her. She didn't like it.

"So call her," said Megan. "Ask her to meet us somewhere."

"Why?" I said. "What does that accomplish?"

"We can tell her to leave us alone, or we're going to inform the police that we suspect her of being the one who pushed me onto the subway tracks."

It was a practical solution, offered by a very smart, but totally naive and pampered young woman, one who believed that everyone around her was as upright and honest as she was. She thought that she could reason with someone like Priss. I tried to imagine how Priss would react to a confrontation like that. It wouldn't be pretty. I felt myself cringing.

"That might not be the right way to go," I said. I was getting a big headache; it was a slicing pain between my eyes.

"You have to stand up to her, Ian," said Megan. She lowered her voice to a fierce whisper. "You're afraid of her and she knows it. She's terrorizing you. She's terrorizing me. I mean, she's homicidal—she may have tried to *kill* me. What will she do next?"

Megan was right. Priss had gone too far.

"Okay," I said. Lamely. Weakly. Unconvincingly. (Pick an adverb, as long as it means I sounded like a loser.)

It was a bad idea, but I wanted to appease Megan. If I refused to call Priss, how did that look? I took the phone from my pocket and called up her contact info, and I pressed the field to make the call. Her picture, from the cover of the most recent edition of *Fatboy and Priss*, filled the screen.

"Put it on speaker," Megan said. Her eyes fell on the image of Priss and stayed there. There was something in her expression that I hadn't seen before and couldn't name. I pressed the speaker button. The waitress, now pretending to read a paperback, was definitely listening.

The generic greeting was broadcast into the diner, a mechanized voice droning: *"You have reached 212-555-8128. Please leave a message."*

"Priss," I said. "We have to get together and talk, okay? Why don't we meet at the Shake Shack around one today? Let me know."

I ended the call and looked at Megan, who gave a solemn nod. She looked so tired, and I felt like a monster for putting her through all of this after everything else she'd been through tonight. She needed rest, not drama.

The first light of dawn was a thin glow on the horizon

as we got back into the Scout. I brought her back to her parents' place.

"I'm going to get some sleep here," she said. "I'll meet you at your place at twelve thirty and we can go over together."

"I want to apologize to your dad," I said.

"Later, okay?" she said. "It'll be all right."

She didn't look very confident, and I couldn't blame her. I reached for her. Instead of an embrace she gave me a light kiss on the cheek, pushing me back gently with her palms. It wasn't that she was cold, but she had the aura of self-protection. I think she wasn't sure if she could trust me. Maybe she was afraid.

"I love you, Ian," she said. She sounded as desperate as I was. I wondered if maybe what we had wasn't real enough, strong enough to endure this much stress, this early. We hadn't even laid the foundation for our life together and already the ground was shaking. She shut the door and walked away quickly before I could answer her. I left her driveway, feeling a deep hollow of loneliness open wide inside me.

Zack was an early riser. It wasn't even seven when I saw his cell-phone number on my caller ID. I'd scanned my early pages yesterday and sent them to him, to make up for the missed meeting. He must have read them fast. I was still in the Scout, stuck in traffic getting back into the city, snaking up the LIE.

"This is great, Ian," Zack gushed. "I've been up all night reading, looking at the art. I just had to call, even though I didn't think I'd get you. I know you're not an early bird, exactly." He laughed manically; too much coffee too early for too-young Zack. He was like a puppy on speed.

I could see him leaning over his desk, pressing the phone to his ear.

"I mean it's perfect. The three of them on the bluff, Molly in white, Priss coming out of the storm. The art is amazing! Your best yet! And the story! I mean, I'm on the edge of my fucking seat. How close are you to being done? I'm not even asking as your editor, but as your fan. I *need* to know what's going to happen."

"I don't know," I said. "Not long. I'm working on it, night and day."

"Okay," he said. "No pressure. Take your time. You can't rush this stuff, I know that."

"Yeah," I said.

"Hey," he said. "Give me a call if you need to talk or work anything through, okay?"

He really wanted that, wanted to be the guy I called to hammer out plot points. And don't get me wrong; I appreciated his eagerness. But I worked alone; I couldn't do it any other way. Fatboy, Molly, and Priss were standing on that bluff, with the storm raging around them. I had no idea what was going to happen next. I wouldn't know until it happened. But how was I going to get back to that place, when my real world was shaking apart? What I needed was some more Adderall.

"Okay," I said. "I'll do that."

When I got back to the city, I parked in the lot about a block from my building and walked home. But when I put the key in the lock of the downstairs door, it didn't fit. This happened from time to time: someone lost their door key; the locks had to be changed. I buzzed the super's apartment, once, twice, three times. No answer. Shit.

I sat on the stoop of my building and waited. Finally

one of my neighbors, a svelte yoga mom whose Lululemon garb, blond highlights, and gel manicure just screamed my-husband-is-a-hedge-fund-manager-and-I-gave-up-my-middling-career-in-PR-because-I-want-to-be-there-for-my-kids-you-know, reluctantly let me in.

"I live on three," I said when we passed into the lobby together. She never once spoke to me, simply hadn't pushed the street door closed behind her. She didn't look at me when we got on the elevator, or when I got off. She just tapped on her BlackBerry, not even lifting her eyes. I didn't even exist in her universe; if I'd been a cockroach, she'd have at least moved away from me or glanced at me in disgust.

"Thanks for letting me in."

The elevator door closed and I was alone on my floor. I saw a bright orange piece of paper tacked to my apartment door. A flyer for a rave, a take-out menu, a gym discount ad? No. Eviction notice. I stood there staring, not comprehending.

"What the fuck?" I said aloud to no one.

I ripped the notice off and held it in my hand. It *did* look official, with a number to call. The marshal would arrive on Friday, it said, to personally remove me from the premises, etc., etc. But there was *no* way. My rent was transferred automatically every month from my checking account. Even if there'd been some screw-up, the management company would have just called. I'd been living in the apartment for more than a year and had never even once been late with my rent. There must have been some mistake. Still, I was shaking.

My apartment key still worked, so I let myself in and called the management company, but only got voice mail. I heard a rushing in my ears so loud that it drowned out all other sound. I went straight to my laptop to check my checking account.

The Internet access was slow and I waited. Outside, the city was coming to life, horns honking, sirens in the distance, cars thumping over the metal manhole cover in the street. Through the window across the street, I saw a girl making herself a cup of coffee. Life was moving forward, normal and easy. Meanwhile, I felt like the ground beneath my feet was starting to shift, revealing itself as something unstable, not to be trusted.

When I finally logged in, I just sat and stared. The checking account was a grid of red—negative funds, a list of checks and ATM withdrawals that had come in and been covered by overdraft protection, converted to a credit balance that had exceeded my limit. My balance was negative. It wasn't possible.

When was the last time I'd checked my accounts? Hadn't I just received a hefty royalty payment from my publisher like a month ago? There had been an e-mail from my agent saying that they'd sent me a wire transfer. Hadn't there?

Then the phone was ringing and I saw that it was the management company. I picked up right away.

"Hello?"

"Mr. Paine?" The voice of a young woman, tentative and soft-spoken. I felt some measure of relief—here was a nice person, a competent person, someone who would take care of this mess. "This is Natalie from building management. I'm returning your call."

"I came home to find an eviction notice on my door," I said. "There must be a mistake. Can you help me?"

She cleared her throat. "There's no mistake, Mr. Paine. We've been over this a number of times."

"Excuse me?"

A crackling silence on the line.

"You and I have been over this several times, sir. I told you during our last conversation that you had ten days to pay the three months' rent due, plus the rent for the upcoming month, or we would have to proceed with eviction."

"Uh . . ." I said stupidly.

"We have been more than generous. You have been a good tenant and we understand that with your book contract getting canceled you got behind. But unfortunately, this is a business, Mr. Paine, and we have no choice at this point but to ask you to move out of our apartment."

Our apartment? There were words I wanted to say, but they were all jammed up in my throat.

"Now," she said with a note of apology, "I'm going to end this conversation, Mr. Paine, before you see fit to level any more verbal abuse at me."

"Verbal abuse?" I said. "Do I know you? Have we spoken before?"

She emitted a little laugh. "Are you for real?"

"I'm sorry," I said. Man, that headache that had started in the diner now felt like it was splitting my skull in two. I put my head down on my desk. "I don't know what you're talking about."

I heard her blow out a breath. "You should get some help, Mr. Paine. A lawyer, a doctor, whatever."

Then she hung up the phone. The whole room was spinning as I tried to make sense of the conversation I'd just had. My rent was three months past due? I'd had a previous conversation with Natalie in which I'd verbally abused her? Had she said my book contract was *canceled*? All the money was gone from my checking and savings accounts. I was being evicted from my apartment.

The roar that had been building inside my head was deafening, expanding. I tried to control my breathing the way Dr. Crown had showed me so many years ago. But the room around me was disappearing into a familiar red fog. A crescendo of light and sound built on itself until the world was only that.

The lawyer my father hired showed up shortly after I'd confessed to him about Priss. This guy had his work cut out for him. The police were already at my house. By the time they were done searching, they'd found paint thinner in my backpack as well as a cigarette lighter in my coat. It wasn't much as far as evidence went. But combined with witnesses claiming they'd seen me raging at Miss Rose, all the suspicion surrounding the Beech fire, my family history, and my ever-more-repulsive appearance . . . let's say things didn't look good for me.

The lawyer, a wiry, balding man with a beaklike nose and a collection of ill-fitting suits, suggested a plea: vandalism and reckless endangerment.

"If you plead to this, we're looking at a couple of months of community service, group therapy for anger management," he said. His voice was nasally, and as high-pitched as a woman's.

He was looking at my father, talking more to him. As a minor, I didn't get much of a say in what was happening to me. Still, I understood that they were trying to get me to admit to something I hadn't done.

"But I didn't *do* it," I said.

The lawyer looked down at his file, which he'd retrieved from an impossibly thick leather satchel stuffed with other manila files just like mine. All those people in trouble, relying on this uninspiring man to save them.

"No one believes that, kid," he said. "The evidence and police opinion are against you. Sometimes you just have to take what you can get. And this is what I can get for you. Otherwise, we go to trial and you take your chances. I doubt they'll charge you as an adult, if you're found guilty. But you could wind up going to juvenile detention. That's not going to be good for you."

"No," my father said. He'd raised his voice and both the lawyer and I jumped. He pushed a thick finger hard on the table. "No, Ian. You plea, that's it."

There was a yawning hole of desperation opening inside of me as I looked back and forth between the two men.

"Do you believe me, Dad?"

He looked at me with an expression that someone else might have read as stone-faced, but the corner of his mouth twitched a little and his eyes were moist. In an uncommon gesture of tenderness, he put his hand on mine.

"I believe that *you* believe she did it," he said.

"This girl," said the lawyer. "She doesn't exist. There's no record of her living or going to school here in this town. No one has *ever* seen her."

"I—" I started. But he held up a hand.

"Don't start with the whole Eloise Montgomery thing," said the lawyer. "That woman is not a reliable witness. And invoking her name is not necessarily going to work in your favor."

I didn't understand why no one was willing to discuss Eloise Montgomery, why my father had taken the note she'd given me, shoved it in his pocket and never returned it. She was an adult, wasn't she? Didn't that alone make her more reliable than I was? Why wouldn't someone at least question her?

"We don't have a homeless population in The Hollows," the lawyer went on. "There's no one squatting on the property behind your house."

"But—"

My father silenced me with a hand on my shoulder.

"So continuing to insist that this girl started these fires makes you seem like a liar. The court doctor does not consider you delusional. You are not schizophrenic. You know right from wrong, real from fantasy. If you're doing this because you think it's going to help you, you're wrong. The best thing you can do for yourself is to own up, pay the price, and try to make good from here on out."

"People know you've had a rough time of it, Ian," my father said. "That's why they are offering you this plea. No one thinks you're a bad kid. Just angry and sad—a little messed up."

A shroud of despair wrapped around me that day; I felt myself shut down. I let it cloak me in darkness, and I disappeared inside it for a good long while. I was powerless in my life, as all kids are. But my life wasn't like the lives of other kids—it was a train wreck. I couldn't help Ella, or my mother. Now I couldn't even help myself.

"Fine," I said. "Whatever."

And the plea was signed. I was sentenced to one hundred hours of community service—picking up garbage on the side of the highway (you can imagine what this did for my image) and six months in youth group therapy for anger management.

"Mikey Beech needed a lesson," Priss said. It was the night after my father and I signed that plea. My despair had turned to anger at Priss. I waited for my father to go to sleep and then I easily snuck out. I knew she'd been waiting for me out at the graveyard. "And Miss Rose betrayed you."

"You shouldn't have done those things," I told her. I was weak with Priss, watery and insubstantial. My anger was impotent in her presence, and it turned on me, became a heavy sadness, a crushing fatigue.

"Somebody has to stand up for you," she said.

She sat beside me and put her arms around me. And I sank into her, not as a friend, or even as a boy awakening to his desires, but as a child rests against his mother. I took her strength, let her bolster me, comfort me. "Nobody ever stood up for *me*," she said.

And I could hear a jagged edge of bitterness and anger in her voice.

"Do you know what they did to me?" she asked.

I looked over at the gravestone that tilted and glowed white in the moonlight: Priscilla Miller.

"No," I said. I didn't want to have this conversation with her. I didn't want to know who she was, what she was, or what they had done to her. But I asked anyway, because I knew she wanted me to. "What did they do?"

"What *they* do—the bullies, the betrayers, the ignorant. What do they do to things they don't understand and can't control?"

She looked like a little girl, but she was not a little girl. Not anymore. I guess I always knew that on some level, that she was not what she appeared to be.

"I don't know," I said.

Because I didn't know. I was just a boy and I didn't understand yet how ugly was the world, even though I'd experienced more than my fair share of horror and misery. I didn't know how utterly bankrupt, how unforgiving, how soul-crushingly indifferent people could be. Her embrace was cold, like holding the wind.

"They take a special thing and try to break it," she said.

Her voice had turned into a whisper and it mingled with the wind, and became one with the chorus of the trees, of the night. A million voices trying to tell me their sad stories, but there were too many. The Whispers. I couldn't tell one from the other.

"What did they do to you?" I asked.

I closed my eyes and leaned closer to her, but then I tumbled to the ground. And for a moment I thought that I was alone, the full moon hiding behind a thick blue cloud cover.

"Priss?"

Then she was over by the trees, her wild hair licking up in the wind like flames. I saw the fire all around her, a blue-orange blaze. She was an angel and a demon, beautiful and terrible. I moved to pull her to safety. But the heat drove me back, searing my skin, a wall of pain that kept me away. We locked eyes and I saw all her fathomless sorrow and rage. She lifted her arms up to the sky and started to scream, a shattering, primal wail of pain and terror. I felt it in my gut and in every nerve ending in my body. And her scream was living in me then, my wail joining hers.

CHAPTER TWENTY

I guess I don't have to tell you that Priss didn't make it to our little meeting at the Shake Shack. Megan and I waited for an hour, doing our time on the burger line, ordering, eating silently at one of the metal tables. We sucked on our shakes and didn't say a word, Megan's eyes scanning the perimeter of the park. She was waiting for a tall, buxom redhead to approach us. I was waiting, too. Priss wasn't one to answer when called. She had always come and gone from my life as she pleased.

Still, I looked for that flash of red, that slash of color in the gray and black and white of a cool early-spring day in New York City. The buds hadn't appeared on the trees yet; there was no bright green pushing up from the brown, no explosion of blossoms. I tried to imagine them, Megan and Priss, occupying the same space, exchanging words. I couldn't.

"This is where I first saw you," I said. I looked over at the park where the children were playing. I was hoping I could make Meg reminisce, see her smile. But she was pale, her mouth a sad little line. She had the purple shiners of fatigue under her eyes, in addition to those bruises. It was more than an hour past the time we'd asked Priss to meet us. The afternoon was growing ever grayer, the veil of afternoon falling—contrasting with the yellows of the taxicabs and their bright red tail-lights.

"It wasn't that long ago," she said.

"No," I answered. I took her blue-mittened hand. "But I can't remember my life before you."

It was the kind of corny thing that I said to make her blush. But she didn't even smile. She pulled her hand back.

"So, Ian, I've been thinking." Her soft, pretty face was set like stone.

I hadn't told her about the apartment, or my financial situation, or my disturbing conversation with Natalie from the management company. Because, frankly, it didn't look very good, did it? I was asking her to believe something that no one else had ever believed. And I sensed, particularly since Priss hadn't showed, that I was pushing Megan to the brink of her very understanding nature. Past the brink. How could I tell her that somehow I'd allowed my checking account to go into overdraft, hadn't paid my rent in months, and didn't even realize it? Does that sound right to you? Would you want to marry that guy? Meanwhile, all of my credit cards were near their limits. I had about two hundred dollars in cash in my wallet, and that was pretty much it.

Megan had wrapped herself up in her arms, a posture she'd retreated to every so often since last night.

"Maybe we need to take some time off," she said. Her tone was a closing door.

Believe it or not, I did *not* see that coming. All her talk about unconditional love and being there for each other no matter what? I bought all that. I thought she *meant* it. But adult love is not unconditional, is it? That's a myth, a fantasy they sell you. You have to earn that shit, work to keep it alive, feed it, nurture it. Otherwise, it shrinks and grows cold.

I had closed my eyes to take in all the implications of her words, and when I opened them, she was crying.

It wasn't just tears in her eyes. She sank her head into her hands and she was shaking, releasing these shuddering breaths. The two girls at the table next to us gave me a dirty look. Both of them, like: *What did you do to her, asshole?*

"Megan," I said. I leaned in toward her. "Don't do this, okay?"

"I told the police about her," Megan said. She seemed to steel herself by taking a deep breath. "Priscilla Miller, right?"

Had I told Megan her last name? I didn't remember.

"They want to talk to her," she said. "And they want to talk to you."

She slid a business card across the table. I'd lost the one she'd given me yesterday. She must have talked to them again. Detective Grady Crowe. Great, here we go again.

"I told them how she lives on the Lower East Side," she went on.

I stared at the card, then put it on the table.

"I told them about the other things you said she did, when you were younger."

"You did?"

She nodded. I could tell that she was unsure of her actions. She had that look that good people get when they've managed to stand up for themselves. She couldn't muster self-righteousness, but she had done what she'd thought was right—or what her parents had encouraged her to do. It felt bad to her, though, like tattling. I read all of this in the wiggle of her eyebrows, the flush on her white cheeks.

"They are going to have that security video today or tomorrow, Ian. So we'll know then if it was her or not."

I felt a little flutter of panic that I couldn't explain.

She was drawing away from me, pulling herself out of

intimate distance. She leaned away, cast her eyes down. A week ago she'd have been leaning close, some part of her—her hand, her foot—touching me. That was Meg; she was touchy, cuddly like that. Now she pulled herself to standing.

It was then that I noticed Binky sitting on the park bench over by the playground. He was wearing a thick parka and a wool hat, holding a newspaper. But he had his eye on us. When he saw me looking, he stood up and approached us. I stood as well.

"I'm sorry," I said when he reached us. He didn't have any visible marks on his face. I couldn't have hit him *that* hard. "I never meant to hurt you."

He lifted a hand.

"I know, son," he said. He gave me a kind, patient smile that reminded me irritatingly of Dr. Crown. "I know you're dealing with something. I don't pretend to understand what. But I hope you get your act together."

Before I could say anything, he told Megan that he was going to get the car. He'd meet her at the corner. And then he was gone into the crowd.

"You need to call that detective, okay?" she said. "Tell them what you told me."

"You don't believe me," I said. She'd believed me last night; I knew she had. It must have been Binky and Julia who made her doubt me.

She dug her hands deep into her pockets and shook her head. "I'm confused," she said. "I don't know what to believe."

"Meg," I said. "Please."

"Let's talk tomorrow," she said. "I just need to get some rest."

She held my eyes for a second and I could see her— the sweet, funny, quirky girl who loved me. I could still have her back. I just needed to straighten out the mess of my life, and get Priss to step off once and for all. Then it would be okay. Right?

"You need to make a choice here, Ian," she said. "It's me or her. You can't have us both."

She walked off then, and I didn't have the voice or the energy to call her back. I took the long walk back to my place, waited for someone to let me in, and then went up to my apartment. They hadn't evicted me yet, and I was still thinking I could talk my way out of whatever was happening to me.

But when I went back inside, the place had been trashed. The couch was turned over, the throw pillows shredded. My big-screen television lay facedown on the floor, the cable and Xbox cords ripped from the fittings. Dishes and glasses had been taken from their cabinets and smashed on the counter, the tile floor of the kitchen. My bed had been tossed; clothes from the drawers and my closet were hanging from lamps.

The only place that remained intact was the corner of the loft where I worked. My computer, the pages I had scanned in yesterday, all sat undisturbed where I had left them. My pens, paints, and pencils were all as orderly and organized as they always were.

I stood, looking at the mess of it all. Had she done it? Knowing I'd be waiting for her at the park, had she come in and done all this damage? Or in that blank space after I hung up the phone with Natalie, when the veil of red had come down, had *I* done this to my home? Was there a part of me that wanted to destroy everything good in my life? That's what Dr. Crown would say, no doubt.

He believed that Priss existed to express the apocalyptic rage I had inside me. I felt abandoned by my mother when she sank into postpartum depression after Ella was born. That's when Priss first showed up in the woods behind my house. And then, when my mother killed Ella and tried to kill me—the rage, the shame, the horror, the betrayal I felt was too much to bear. I couldn't direct those feelings toward my mother, whom I loved and missed desperately, so I created someone to express them for me at whoever the object of my rage happened to be. It all works, as far as theories go. It makes a kind of sense. There's just one problem with it: Priss is real. My rage is real, too, I guess. They are not mutually exclusive.

I didn't bother cleaning up. What was the point? I hadn't been able to reach Zack, which was a bit odd. I'd left a message; I wanted to hear his voice, wanted him to confirm that I still had a contract. Likewise, I couldn't reach my agent. Which was also odd.

So with my life in a shambles around me, I walked over to my drafting table, sat down, and disappeared into the only place where I'd ever truly been happy. Maybe, I thought, if I could tame her on the page, my life would get easier to handle.

"There's no mistake," Molly says to Priss. A mammoth streak of lightning splits the sky, casting them all in a yellow glow. "You weren't invited to our wedding because you're not welcome here."

The rain is coming down in sheets, the sky a thick gray black. Molly's parents are also there and they wear expressions of fear and surprise. They each have a hand on their daughter.

"Is that true?" Priss asks Fatboy. "Am I not welcome? Is there no place for me in your new life?"

"Tell her," Molly says. She is looking at Fatboy with an angry frown. "Tell her to go hurt someone else."

Fatboy opens his mouth, but a crash of thunder silences him. He never wanted them to meet, never wanted them to exist in the same frame in his life. He almost can't handle it. Molly's parents try to pull her away, but she won't go.

"*Tell her*," *says Molly.* "*It's time.*"

"*Why don't you let him speak for himself?*" *says Priss.*

And then they're screaming at each other, angry faces, red lips, flashing eyes. Priss's orange hair is wild. Molly's white gown blows around her like a mist. And then Priss reaches out to push Molly, and Molly, shocked, stumbles backward. Fatboy grabs for her, but Priss is already on her—and they are moving to the edge of the bluff. He wants to help Molly, but he's paralyzed, can't move his arms or legs, like in a dream where you're weak and powerless against an assailant.

"*Priss*," *he yells. But his voice is just a whisper in the storm. Molly's father reaches for Priss, but she strikes him back with a powerful blow to the jaw and he falls into Molly's mother. Priss is strong, so strong. She is all power, no reason, when rage takes over. No one can talk her down; no one can stop her.*

"*Let go of her*," *he yells again.*

"*Do something, you coward*," *yells Molly's mother.*

But they all three are weak, hanging back and afraid, as Molly and Priss fight like berserkers—punching and clawing at each other. Molly's dress is splattered with blood. Priss has a warrior's slash on her face where Molly has scratched her.

They move closer and closer to the edge as the storm rages. Finally, Fatboy starts to move toward them.

They are in silhouette now against the night sky, locked together in a violent struggle. Fatboy feels numb, disconnected from the scene. Molly is all that is right in his life—love, a future, a family, stability. Priss is all that is wrong—rage, addiction, angry sex, madness. The choice should be clear. But it's not. It's not at all. Darkness is a cocoon. It asks nothing of you but your complicity. A life lived in the light—a job, a wife, a home, a family—that requires your presence. It's work.

He feels like his feet are made of lead as he slogs toward them. In the dark, he can't tell who is who. Molly's dress is so wet and torn now, it clings to her body. The rain is battering him, soaking him. Then, he sees lightning strike the ground

between him and the bluff and soon after hears a giant det-
onation of thunder. The world seems to still in the silence. He
watches in horror as one of them—Priss or Molly—falls from
the bluff. His own wail of protest echoes through the night.

I fell asleep at the drafting table. And when I woke up
with a start, Priss was standing over me. I stared at her,
and then down at the sketches on the table in front of
me. Again, not what I wanted—not at all. It felt like a
dream—and that dream lay manifest on the page before
me. She was looking, too, issued a mocking little laugh.
She seemed pale and young, as she had on the day we first
met. She hadn't looked that way to me in years, like the
child she was.

She's not a child, Ian. Never let her convince you of that,
my crazy mother warned me.

Finally, she strode away, her pencil-thin heels clicking
on the hardwood.

"What happened to this place?" she asked. "What did
you do?"

"Me?" I asked her. "I didn't do anything. What did
you do?"

"You always try to blame me for the things that go
wrong in your life," she said. She moved a torn cushion
off to the side and then sank onto the couch. "When are
you going to grow up?"

I always thought of her as big, larger than life. In the
book, her breasts are enormous, her waist a sliver, fanning
out into broad hips and big, powerful legs. Her eyes are
almond-shaped, cat eyes. But in life, she's just a wisp of
a thing. Still there's a power that radiates from her flesh.
She's radioactive. The damage she does is silent, insidious. It wastes you from the inside out. She's sweet like
lead paint, tastes good on your tongue. But her poison

works its way into your blood, shuts you down from the inside out.

"You didn't do this?" I asked.

"Of course not," she said. She even had the nerve to look offended. "I've only ever loved you. I protect you."

"You hurt people."

She laughed at that. "Do I? Are you sure about that?"

She stood and slithered her way into my arms. And my arms, traitorous, wrapped around her. She pressed her body against me, and I felt myself grow hard. That aching desire for her burned a hole in my center. Her lips, hot and soft, were on my neck, and then her hands were unbuttoning my jeans. The warm press of her breasts, her cool hands on my flesh. Ah, God, I could never resist her.

A deep animal hunger took me over. I spun her around and took her from behind, bent over the ruined couch, pushing myself deep, deeper as she moaned and her breathing came sharp and ragged, desperate. She cried out, at first in pleasure, then the tenor changed—pain, anger. I held her down with my hands hard on her back, my hips pressed tight against her. I could feel her writhing to get away. But she couldn't. I was too powerful for her. And the knowledge of this made me drive myself deeper into her. She wasn't that strong after all.

"Ian," she said. Her voice was blistering with anger. "You *fucker*! Let. Me. *Up!*"

I came inside her, and let out a moan of pleasure I couldn't contain. It was a deep, guttural roar and I was a lion, king of the jungle. Then I moved away from her, pulled up my pants, which had fallen around my ankles. She hauled herself off the couch slowly as if in pain, put herself back together. And when she looked at me, she wore an expression of malicious glee.

"Happy now?" she said. "You can add rape to your list of crimes."

I was too breathless from my anger at her to react to her words. Then I was weak, too weak to stand. I sank to the couch. Rapist? Was I that? But it was just like her to goad me into doing something horrible, to distract me from the horrible things she did.

"Did you push Megan?" I asked.

"What do you think?"

She was shaking. It was slight, almost imperceptible, but I could see the quiver in her fingers.

"I want you to tell me," I said.

She moved into the kitchen, broken glass and ceramic crunching beneath her feet. She took a bottle of vodka from the fridge, a glass from the cabinet—the only one that hadn't been smashed, and poured herself a glass. She tossed it back and poured another.

"Like the Beech fire, and the art room blaze?" she said. "And all the rest of it?"

Yes, there was more. A lot more.

"All those things you blame on me," she continued.

"All those things you *did*."

"Let's just be clear. I never did anything you didn't want me to do. And you know it."

"Did you push Megan onto those tracks?" I asked again. For some reason, I desperately wanted her to say yes. And I wanted her to say no just as badly. Maybe this was all just a horrible accident, an ugly coincidence.

"Why would I do that?" she asked. "You love her. You told me that. She loves you. Why would I want to hurt her?"

"Because . . ." I said. I felt foolish saying it. "Because you're jealous. You don't want me to love anyone but you."

She let out a derisive chortle. "You think an awful lot of yourself, don't you, Fatboy?"

"Just answer the question."

But she didn't answer. She finished her drink and, with a little wobble in her gait, walked toward the door. I watched her move, wanting her to leave, wanting her to come back. Outside, it started to rain again and I found myself wondering about the book. Who had fallen off the cliff—Molly or Priss? Who was stronger? Who had a greater will to survive? Why didn't I, the author, know the answer?

Before she reached the door, the buzzer rang, announcing someone outside. I got up to answer. She looked at the video monitor and there was a man standing there, holding a shield up to the camera at the street door.

"Don't open it," she said. She tried to block my passage to the intercom. But I pushed her roughly aside. I had never been angrier with her, the love I had for her a distant echo.

"I have to," I said. "It's time."

She was here in my apartment. When the police came up, I was going to tell them everything. And she'd have to answer the questions herself for once. There was no other way out of the apartment except through that front door. No fire escape, no back exit. She was trapped now, she'd have to show herself to someone other than me.

I pressed the unlock button without asking who it was. Priss gave me a shrug and headed into the bedroom, where she slid the door closed. Did she think I was going to let her hide in there?

A few moments later, there was a hard knock on the door.

"Detective Grady Crowe, New York Police Department." It was the name on the business card Meg had handed me.

The man outside my door was thick through the middle, with a purposeful five o'clock shadow, and better dressed than one might expect from a detective.

"Ian Paine?" He held up a leather wallet holding a gold shield and an identification card. He wore a gold wedding band on his left hand. For some reason I found myself thinking that my father had never worn a wedding ring. *Jewelry is for fancy boys*, he'd say with a laugh. He didn't need a ring to show his commitment to my mother. He loved her, stood by her until the day he died.

"That's right." I had only opened the door a little, blocking it with my body.

"I'm here to talk about Megan's case," he said. He looked me up and down, tried to peer around me into the apartment. "Her subway assault."

"Yes," I said. "Of course."

"She said you might have some information involving a woman named Priscilla Miller. She suspects that Ms. Miller might be the assailant. Do you think that's true?"

"I honestly don't know."

He gave a quick nod.

"Can I come in? I have something you might be interested in seeing."

Truth was, I already had cold feet. I thought about refusing him entry. I had a right to do that. But how would it have looked. I let him inside, momentarily having forgotten that the place looked like downtown Beirut.

"Wow," he said, looking around. He had a big aura, took up a lot of space. I suddenly felt crowded. "Not much of a housekeeper, are you?"

"Someone trashed my place," I said. It sounded lame.

He raised an eyebrow at me. "When?"

"Just now. I was out with Megan, and when I came back this is how it looked."

He walked around, blew out a breath. "Hell hath no fury, right? This girl must be a piece of work."

Actually, it's *Heaven has no rage like love to hatred turned, nor hell a fury like a woman scorned* from *The Mourning Bride* by William Congreve. Most people think it's Shakespeare, but it's not. I thought about Priss listening at the door. Why didn't I walk over and slide it open to reveal her standing there? I can't answer that question.

I gave him a little laugh. "Yeah. She can be pretty psycho."

"What can you tell me about her?" he asked. He had this tone, it had an amiable, almost conspiratorial edge to it. Like a we-all-know-how-women-can-be kind of thing. But I'd spent enough time with the police to know all their little tricks.

"Because I honestly can't find anything about her," he continued. "She doesn't have a record at all. In The Hollows, New York—that's where you're from, right?" He made a show of checking his notebook. "There are no recent birth records or death records of anyone by that name, no record that anyone by that name ever got a Social Security card, went to school, got a driver's license."

I didn't say anything, just perched on a bar stool.

"But I put in a call to The Hollows PD. They connected me with a retired cop turned private detective, a man named Jones Cooper. He was very familiar with you, Mr. Paine. He gave me an earful."

"I bet," I said.

"He says that there's no Priscilla Miller. That she's your hallucination. That she's your imaginary friend."

"He does think that, yeah," I admitted. Now would be the perfect reveal. *He may think that,* I could have said. *But here she is.* I could have pulled her from her hiding spot in the bedroom. But something powerful inside kept me on my bar stool. I was bound and gagged by it, whatever it was.

"Hey," he said. He pointed to the shelves of books in the hallway. One level was devoted to my book—all the U.S. editions, plus the foreign editions, multiple copies. It looked pretty impressive, all of them lined up. I was proud of it. "I am a big fan, by the way. I've been reading *Fatboy and Priss* as long as you've been writing. I am a comic book junkie, have been all my life."

"Thanks," I said. "Thanks a lot."

"In the books," he said. He was on a roll. "And I know it's just fiction, okay? But Priss is, like, Fatboy's superhero, right? I mean, she does all the things that Fatboy wants to do but can't do, won't do, for himself. He's meek and gentle, prone to depression, medicating with food, drugs. But Priss is not afraid of anyone or anything. It's like she's his anger, you know? His rage."

"That's true," I said. "But that doesn't make him complicit. We all can have dark impulses. Not acting on them is a virtue, not a weakness."

All I had to do was to tell him she was in the bedroom. Why didn't I do that? I don't know.

"Do you have dark impulses when it comes to your fiancée? I mean, marriage is a big step."

"What?" I said. He was good. "No. I love her. She's all I ever wanted."

He looked at me carefully, raised a dark eyebrow, and then offered a sympathetic nod. He walked around the apartment.

"You, on the other hand, have a record a mile long," he said. "Your juvenile record is sealed, but Detective Cooper filled me in on the whole arson thing. You got mad, set things on fire."

"No," I said. "Not me. Priss. My dad made me take

that plea. He was afraid. We'd lost my sister Ella to crib death, and my mother was in a mental hospital."

I thought I saw the door to my bedroom move, as though Priss was leaning against it listening.

"That's rough," he said. "A horrible thing for any kid to go through. It had to do some damage, right?"

He offered a concerned frown, then he gave his head a little tap with his finger.

"I had therapy." I still called Dr. Crown sometimes, just to talk when the memories came back, when the veil of depression threatened to fall, when anger got the better of me. But it had been a while. I'd been well—until Megan. Now I was really starting to think I might need to give Dr. Crown a call. Maybe I would, right after I got rid of this cop.

"Right," he said. "You've been good. It's been a while. There's a drunk and disorderly a couple of years ago, some fight you got into outside of a nightclub. You did a lot of screaming, had to be subdued. That was a misdemeanor, a ticket. Then, last year you punched some guy in the face, broke his nose. You pulled assault for that. But the judge gave you a fine, because the guy was an asshole. You have two moving violations—speeding. One parker, got your car towed. No fires in a while. You on meds?"

"No," I said. *Nothing legal, Officer.* "I grew up."

"Good," he said. "Good for you."

My patience for this guy's shtick was wearing thin. "You said you had something you wanted me to see," I said.

"I do."

He pulled a smartphone from his pocket, did some tapping, handed it to me. It was a video, a crowded subway platform. I knew immediately that it must be the CCTV footage from Meg's subway incident.

"Most people don't realize that there are cameras

everywhere these days," said the detective. "Especially in New York City. It's a veritable grid of electronic seeing eyes."

The movements of the people on the platform were choppy and unnatural-looking. And I stared transfixed, searching for Megan. I finally caught sight of her, the familiar shape of her head, the delicate lines of her profile. Her face was paper pale on the black-and-white feed. She had her headphones on, leaning against the metal beam. I watched as she walked toward the edge of the track, leaned over to look for the oncoming train. Then she moved back to her spot near the beam.

"You should be seeing it right about now," said the detective.

I stared at the screen, and suddenly I saw a hooded form moving through the crowd, pushing toward Megan. The sea of waiting commuters parted as the figure moved nearer to her. Megan was oblivious, staring off into space.

She did look tired, as she said she'd been, and a little down. I remember what Binky said: *It seems like you two spend a lot of time talking about you. But have you really been there for Megan?* I hadn't been.

"Do you see him?"

I noticed that the detective didn't say "her." But *was* it a man? I couldn't tell. The form was hooded, hunched over. Something about the fuzzy quality of the footage, the crowd . . . I just couldn't judge the size of the figure; it was a black blur.

"You said 'him,'" I said.

The detective gave me something that might have been a smile. "Keep watching."

I saw Priss then. Not on the platform but here in my apartment. Still I didn't say anything. She'd pushed the bedroom door open, and was standing in the shadows of the dark room. What was she doing? All the cop had to do was turn around and see her there. Then he'd see that she was real. But he'd also see that I was hanging out with the girl who was suspected of pushing Meg onto the subway tracks. I had stayed silent about her being here in the bedroom all this time. How would that look?

I put my eyes back to the screen and watched as the black form in the film moved closer. And then there was Megan once again. She pushed herself from the metal beam and walked over to the tracks, inching closer. *Stop*, I wanted to say to her. *Get away from the tracks.*

The hooded form picked up speed. It was big; I could see that now. Bigger and taller than a lot of people on the platform. And the shape of the head was unfamiliar. It wasn't Priss. It wasn't her. I felt a mingling of relief (she's not *that* bad!) and fear (then who is it?).

But Megan stepped back again. I felt the agitation that fills the air of a crowded subway platform when a train is running late during rush hour.

"Did you know that the incidence of stranger crime is an anomaly?" Crowe asked.

"I'd heard that."

"This dangerous *other* that we all fear? In actuality we have the most to fear from the people closest to us."

"Right," I said.

Priss had now stepped out of the room and was moving toward us, stealthy as a cat.

On-screen, Megan moved toward the edge of the platform again. And this time the form was on her. Two big hands reached out toward her back, the people around her oblivious, staring at the tiny screens in their hands or out into space. The shove was hard and definite, and she was just far enough over that she toppled, her bag swinging forward, the weight of it taking her down.

The crowd sprang to life then. Hands went to eyes

and mouths, some people stepped back, a couple of people immediately started dialing—presumably calling 911. Others stepped forward with cameras poised. Two men—from opposite ends of the platform—seemed to move in unison toward Megan, then jumped onto the tracks. They quickly moved her out of the way of the train. After it had passed, hands reached down to help and I watched as Megan was lifted up, then lay motionless on the platform while a woman knelt beside her, put her hand on Meg's head. The two men climbed up off the tracks.

I was transfixed, watching all of this, and I had lost sight of the black form. But then I saw it, moving toward the camera, head down. Just as it was about to move out of range, it looked up. The features were an ugly blur, the face of a demon—black holes for eyes and a gaping wound for a mouth.

"Recognize him?" asked Crowe. He wore an unpleasant smile.

"No," I said. I shook my head vigorously. "I don't understand. Is there something wrong with the camera? It looks like a ghoul."

There wasn't time to stop her. She held the hammer high above her head and brought it down hard. A hot, warm spray of blood sluiced across my face. Crowe stared at me wide-eyed, jaw slack for a moment, then fell in a heap to the ground. Priss stood looking down with an expression of mild concern.

"Priss," I said. I could barely breathe. *"What the fuck?"*

"They are going to lock you up like your mother," she said.

"What are you talking about?" The room was spinning. A wave of nausea hit me, and next I was puking into the sink.

"Just get out of here," she said. I heard the detective moan. "I'll handle this."

"No, Priss," I said. "Don't do this."

"Look," she said. She nodded toward the phone that was still in my hand. The frame had frozen. I stared as the features of the ghoul came into focus.

CHAPTER TWENTY-ONE

I left the building and ran and ran, through the city streets and the darkness and the filth of garbage bags and the crush of pedestrians. I ran until my chest felt like it was going to explode and my thighs were on fire, my calves cramping. I don't know how long I was out there, walking and walking. The time since I left Megan in the park seemed warped and blurry.

The sun was aglow on the horizon as I found myself in the first place I'd ever visited with Megan, on the bench beside the bronze *Alice in Wonderland* statue near Seventy-fourth in Central Park. The rain had stopped and the sun was coming up. I sat soaked and freezing and called Meg for the hundredth time with a phone that was miraculously still working. She finally picked up.

"Ian," she said. "*What* do you want?"

"I need to see you," I said. I was shivering.

"Did you talk to the police?" she asked.

"I did."

"You told them about Priss?"

Anything I said now was going to be a lie, so I just kept my mouth shut. My brain was in overdrive, trying to process everything that had just happened. I was having some kind of mental brownout.

"That's what I thought," she said when I didn't say anything.

"They know about her already," I said quickly. "You told them, and they're investigating."

I sensed that she was about to hang up. "I need to see you. Please, Meg. Please."

A pause, during which I could hear her breathing, feel her considering. "Where are you?"

"I'm at the *Alice in Wonderland* statue," I said, looking up at it. In the semidark, it seemed grim and menacing, not cheerful and fun as it had always seemed.

It was just a couple of blocks from her place.

"Give me a little while," she said. She had stopped loving me, I could tell. Now she was just dealing with me until she could figure out how to give that ring back. She would meet me now out of a sense of obligation, listen to me, and then tell me she needed time or space or whatever it was people say when they are trying to be nice about wanting you to go away for a longish time, if not forever.

I waited and waited, almost gave up. But she did finally come. Already, everything that had happened in my apartment was taking on a dreamlike patina. I was distancing myself from it. By the time she arrived, the sun was up and the nannies were strolling babies, and the commuters were hustling by looking harried and important with coffee in one hand, cell phone in the other. I felt almost normal. Whatever that means.

She showed up with lattes and sat beside me but not close. She handed me the drink and it tasted heavenly— milky and sweet. She looked delicious, too, and just out of reach. We were just two normal people sitting on a park bench, sharing a morning coffee.

"I almost didn't come," she said. Her eyes already looked better, not as black as before. More lavender and gold.

"I know," I said. "I'm glad you did."

She was wrapped up in a big sweater and red scarf. Her shoulders were tense, and she kept her hands cupped around her latte.

"Detective Crowe was supposed to call me when the video came in. But I haven't heard from him," she said.

"Look," I said. I tried to keep the desperation out of my voice. But I'm not sure that it worked. I leaned toward her but she didn't lean into me. In fact, she moved back a little.

"I was thinking that maybe you and I just need to get away. Let's go to the Caribbean or something. Just take a break from all of this, spend a week alone and reconnect. I love you. And we've let a lot of outside negativity bring us down."

She shook her head, moved farther away from me on the bench. "I don't know," she said. But her body language said: *No way, dude. You must have lost your mind.*

"I'm totally done with Priss," I said. "She's not going to bother us again."

"How can you know that?"

"I just need to clear my head," I said. "Get out of town for a while. We can leave today."

"We both have responsibilities, Ian," she said. Her tone was slow and measured. It was a voice I'd heard her use with Toby. I felt the first tickle of anger. Did she think I was a child? "I have a job and you have a deadline, right? There's an open investigation into my assault. I have a concussion; I don't even know if I can fly."

"Sometimes you just have to say 'fuck it,' you know?" I said. "We'll drive someplace if you're worried about the concussion. Vermont? Some B-and-B upstate?"

"You know," she said. She was holding on to that cup of coffee so tightly that I thought she was going to crush it. "I'm not the kind of person who says 'fuck it' to my responsibilities."

Was I really going to marry such a prude? I felt it start to boil in my center, the powerlessness, the desperation, the confusion. It was a dangerous cocktail, a bubbling brew.

"Well, okay," I said. I tried not to sound angry and peevish. But I did. She heard it and her face went hard. "But *I'm* going to get away. I need to. I can't handle all of this."

"All of what?" she said. Her voice had come up a couple of octaves. "*I'm* the one who got hurt."

I remembered that she didn't know about my eviction from the apartment, or about the detective, or about the surveillance video or about my bank accounts. And for some reason this just made me angrier. She didn't even *know* that my life was falling apart, when not long ago, it had been better than it had ever been. I had been sipping cognac by the fire with Binky while Julia and Megan prepared a wonderful meal for my birthday. From that to *this*. How was it possible?

"Come with me," I said. I tried to push the anger back. "Please."

"I'm sorry," she said. "I can't. And you shouldn't go either, not now."

She put the coffee down and pressed her arms tightly against her sides, seemed almost to double over in pain. When she looked at me again, I expected her to be crying. But she wasn't. She looked stronger than I'd seen her look over the last couple of days.

"I'm—" she started to say, and then stopped.

"What?" It was churning inside me.

"I don't want to tell you like this." She looked away again. I knew what she was going to say. *I'm calling off the wedding. I don't just need some time off. I never want to see you again.*

"Tell me." I was going to make her say the words.

"I'm pregnant," she said finally. "They told me at the hospital."

In an instant, all the colors around me seemed brighter; I drew in a sharp breath of surprise. It was the purest rush of joy I'd ever felt. All that anger just dissipated like a fog.

"That's . . . amazing," I said. I didn't have any words for the happiness I felt. It was a gift, wasn't it? Why did she look so sad? "It's awesome, Meg."

I reached for her, and she let me embrace her but she was stiff within my arms.

"It's not really a good time," she said. "For us. For me. I'm not ready. *We're* not ready."

Then she stood, and I did, too. I grabbed for her wrist, but she pulled her hand back from me. And for some reason that act of withdrawal enraged me all over again; the anger came rolling back through me in an ugly, unstoppable tsunami of emotion.

She was abandoning me, taking herself, her love, our child, all the good she brought into my life—taking it all away. And the veil came down once more. What did I say? What did I do?

All I know is that she was backing away from me then, her mouth an O of shock, her eyes wide with hurt and surprise. People around me stared with frowns of confusion and disapproval. Nannies grabbed children into their embraces and carried them off. Megan started to run. I don't think I went after her. I don't know.

Fatboy wakes to a bright light glaring down on him from above. It is harsh and blue; he has to shield his eyes. He tries to move his arms and he can't. There is a blinding pain in his head and a scream lodged in his throat. Who was it? Who fell over the bluff?

His eyes adjust to the light. He is lying in a hospital bed, his legs and arms bound. He can't move. The light streaming in from the barred window is bright and strange.

"Mr. Paine," says a voice, easy and measured. "Don't be alarmed. Everything is all right."

That seems pretty unlikely. Fatboy looks around the gray-and-white room, and as his eyes slowly adjust to the light, he sees a small balding man with glasses and a Technicolor tie sitting in a chair by the door.

"Dr. Black," Ian says. "What am I doing here?"

"What's the last thing you remember?"

It all comes back in a rush—the wedding, the storm, Priss, the fight on the bluff.

"Oh my God—Molly," says Fatboy. Panic is a living thing trapped in his chest. "Where is she? What's happened?"

"Tell me what you remember."

Fatboy tells him the events as they come back to him, foggy and disjointed. All the while the doctor is writing on a notepad in his lap.

"Who was it? Who fell?" Fatboy asks when he's done.

"No one fell," says the doctor. "Everything is all right."

"I saw someone fall."

"Do you know where you are, Ian?"

Fatboy did know where he was, the surroundings oddly familiar. But, at the same time, he didn't know. That feeling of panic . . . it started to grow.

"I need to get out of here," he says. "I need to find Molly."

"Maybe later," the doctor says easily. "Right now we have to worry about you feeling better."

Fatboy strains against his restraints, trying and failing to get up.

"Where am I? What am I doing here?"

"Ian," says the doctor, leaning in closer. "You're at the Shady Knoll Psychiatric Hospital. You've been here for the last five years."

Nooooooooooooooo.

• • •

No, no, no. That wasn't right. It was a total cop-out in fact. That all of it—Molly, their new life he was supposed to have, all his success, was just the fantasy of a madman, locked away inside a loony bin somewhere. Crazy. Just like his mother.

The sketches were raw, just charcoal pencil and some slashes of oil pastel color—scarlet and ultramarine, blue violet. But the images were terrible, grim and full of fear. It was just a way not to choose, to let Fatboy retreat to the safety of his own cowardice. If there was no Molly, no promise of a better life, then Fatboy would never have to decide whether or not to grow up. He would never have to own his life.

I never tore up sketches. Nothing ever went into the garbage. But I had to try again. I knew I had to do better.

Fatboy wakes in a panic to a bright light glaring down on him from above. It is harsh and blue; he has to shield his eyes. There is a blinding pain in his head, and it takes him a minute to remember where he is. The hospital. He raced there in the back of an ambulance with Molly, who had been pushed from the bluff by Priss. He had been dreaming about the doctor, about the psych ward. He is drenched in sweat.

Molly is broken, shattered, in a coma—and he has been beside her for two full days. He is slouched in a hard, gray chair. As he comes awake, the room resolves into focus. Molly, white and peaceful, lies on a hospital bed, casts on her arms and legs, a chaos of tubes and wires traveling from her arms, her nose, her mouth. Her prognosis is uncertain. The doctor has told him that the child she was carrying has been lost. He was so sorry. But Fatboy didn't even know she was pregnant. Had she even known? She must have. Why hadn't she told him?

He takes her hand. "I'm so sorry," he whispers. "This is all my fault. I should have protected you. I was too weak."

But her face is still, her fingers limp and lifeless. The only sound in the room is coming from the heart monitor and the machine that is breathing for her. He feels her slipping away. He lays his head on her bed and weeps. "Don't leave me, Molly. Please."

Molly's parents arrive in the doorway and Fatboy kisses Molly's hand and leaves the room. They hate him, blame him for what has happened to their daughter. And their faces are hard and cold—all dark lines and deep shadows of rage. He doesn't blame them, leaves them to have some peaceful time with their daughter. Her mother has brought flowers and her father holds a bear that Fatboy recognizes from Molly's room at home. Maybe it will help.

He leaves the hospital; it looms a great white monolith behind him. He walks out into the daylight, the sun high and orange. He gets into his truck and starts to drive. When he puts his hand on the wheel, he notices the gold band on his left hand. His wedding ring, the symbol of his commitment to Molly. He belongs to her, and she to him in a real and tangible way. He starts to drive. Whatever happens now, they are a family.

He has to think. He has to fix what he has allowed to be broken. Something Molly said to him suddenly gives him clarity. You have to choose. You can't have us both. That has been the problem all along, ever since he first knew Priss. He has always chosen her over everything else. He must sever whatever it is that connects them and he must do it once and for all. There is only one person who can help him. Eloise Montgomery, the psychic, the only one who really knows the truth about Priss.

The blue Scout heads north on the FDR, taking Fatboy back home to The Hollows.

When I came to myself, I was in the Scout, parked illegally on Lispenard Street. The sketch pad was balanced on my legs, leaning against the dash, my box of pencils open on the passenger seat beside me. How long had I been there? Why was I working in my car? It was dark again. I was disoriented and confused; was it a dream, that meeting with Megan? Had the detective really come to see me with that video?

No, none of it seemed real. I looked in the backseat. There was a duffel bag, the one I used for traveling, and it was stuffed. My folded drafting table and my large portfolio as well as my full art-supply box were packed and secured in the back of the Scout. What was that smell? Gasoline.

In the distance I heard the approach of sirens. And I looked through the windshield up to the windows of my apartment. I saw an orange glow within, a dancing, moving bloodred light. Oh God, I thought. Oh, no.

I put the key in the ignition and pulled slowly away from the curb. There was no panic now, no wondering where I was headed or what I was going to do. There was only one way to drive and one place to go. And I realized, finally, that I couldn't have gone anyplace else if I'd tried.

PART TWO

And When She Was Bad, She Was Awful

CHAPTER TWENTY-TWO

About a week after I'd started the community-service part of my sentence for the art room fire, Eloise Montgomery came to see me at Second Hand Knowledge again. I don't know why Old Brian hadn't fired me. I guess he figured misfits had to stick together. So, as usual, I was boarding and bagging some books in the back room when that small, spindly woman pushed her way through the curtain for the second time.

She looked me up and down with an assessing but not unkind gaze.

"Can I help you?" I asked. I had promised my father that I wouldn't talk to her again. Maybe she just wanted another comic book.

"Do you know who I am, Ian?"

According to my dad, everybody (except for me) knew who Eloise Montgomery was. She was a bigger freak show than even I had become. She was a psychic, someone who talked to the dead—among other things.

Once upon a time, she'd been a normal lady. But one day, she and her family got into a horrific car accident that killed one of her daughters and her husband, and left her in a coma. When she recovered, she found that she'd been gifted with visions of missing and murdered women and girls—of things that might happen, of things that had happened hundreds of years ago, of things that were happening right now.

Since then, working with a local detective, she had been responsible for solving hundreds of cold cases, the rescue of abducted women and girls, and the retrieval of bodies long lost. She'd been on *Oprah*.

I found I couldn't answer. I just stood and nodded my head.

"I think you have a problem," she said. She looked around at the comic books then back at me. "Do you?"

I shrugged. "I don't know. What do you mean?"

I had lots of problems. She needed to be more specific.

"Can you take a break?" she asked. "I'll buy you lunch."

I wasn't at all sure I wanted to have lunch with Eloise Montgomery. Especially since direction from my dad on this matter went something like: *Don't you ever go near that goddamn crazy woman.* But I found myself asking Old Brian if I could take my lunch break and following her to the pizza place a few doors down.

We sat toward the back but still managed to attract a few curious stares from customers. I can only imagine what they were thinking. And if my father found out that I was with her, he was going to kill me. *Aren't you in enough trouble? Don't people hate you enough without your associating with the town crackpot?* Some people thought Eloise was a hero, others thought she was a witch, still others like my dad thought she was just plain crazy. I didn't know what to think. But I was curious enough to sit across from her in the red vinyl booth and order two slices of pepperoni and a large Coke.

"I'm sorry about what happened to your family," she said.

I nodded, didn't say anything. I'd heard that a lot and I never knew how to respond. I found if I was quiet, people either went quiet as well or just walked away.

"I shouldn't be talking to you," she said. "But I tried to

talk to your father and he didn't want anything to do with me. He shut the door in my face."

She didn't look like a psychic. She looked more like a church lady, erect and stern-faced. Plainly dressed in a white button-down shirt and black pants, she wore no adornment at all—no makeup or jewelry, no nail polish on her short square nails. She was so thin that I could see the tendons on her arm dance beneath her skin when she moved her fingers. But I couldn't take my eyes off her. There was something magnetic about her, something fascinating.

"But I don't have much choice in these things," she went on.

Finally, curiosity got the better of me. "You talk to ghosts?"

She bowed her head, and when she looked up she wore something that might have been a smile.

"Not exactly."

I was disappointed. I took a bite of pizza, a swallow of soda. I remember thinking that nothing was ever as cool as you imagined it to be. Even sitting face-to-face with a real-life psychic . . . it was the same as being with any other adult. Boring.

"Are you familiar with the law of the conservation of energy?" she asked.

It was the first law of thermodynamics. And I was familiar with it because I was in an advanced-placement physics class. In spite of all my many problems, I was pretty smart. Except for PE—and who can believe you even got a grade for that?—I had straight As.

"Energy can be changed from one form or another, but it cannot be created or destroyed?"

Again the smile that wasn't quite a smile. "I'm impressed. Yes, that's right."

I shrugged. "So?"

"So this is what I believe. I believe that we are all energy fields, and that we are connected by an infinite cosmic net. Each of us, every living thing, every person, plant, and animal is a point of light upon this net. When our physical body dies, our energy remains in the web."

"Okay," I said.

"I'm like a receiver, just more tuned in than most others to these energies. I receive transmissions. They are not always clear or understandable, or even truthful. Sometimes I never know why I received them and can't do anything about them. Other times it's very clear what I have to do, who I have to warn, or call, or just go visit."

She had leaned into me, was speaking with a whispered intensity that reminded me of the way my mother talked to me in the psychiatric hospital. Maybe my father was right. Maybe Eloise Montgomery was crazy, too. There seemed to be a lot of that going around The Hollows.

"I have to get back to work." I suddenly felt uncomfortable, wanted badly to leave. I started sliding out of the booth.

She seemed to realize she was making me nervous, pulled back a bit. "Some spiritual energy is negative."

The pizzeria had emptied out and only the old man who owned the place remained. I watched as he used an enormous wooden spatula to slide a pizza in the blazing oven. When he opened the door, I saw and heard the flames inside and I thought of Priss being devoured before my eyes. I didn't say anything.

"Those negative energies are attracted to other negativity—like rage, despair, or grief. They can attach themselves to our own energy fields and intertwine."

I stared down at my empty plate and wished for another piece, but I was too polite, too embarrassed, to ask. If left to my own devices I would have eaten a whole pie. I already knew that I ate way more than others, and tried to keep my appetite in check when people were around.

"Do you understand?" she asked.

I didn't have the first idea what she was talking about.

"I should go," I said again. I made to get up, but she put a hand on my arm.

"Your friend," she said.

I slid back into the seat and leaned closer. "Priss?" I whispered. "She's real."

"Of course she is," she said. "She's real and she's dangerous."

With a twist of dread, I saw my father. Old Brian must have called him. He came marching past the big picture window of the pizza shop and banged through the door, causing the bell to ring loudly. He scanned the restaurant and then came toward us.

"My dad's here," I said.

She turned to look, then turned back at me. "You have to stop talking to her. Get away from her and stay away."

I shook my head. "I can't."

"Hey," said my dad. His voice filled the restaurant. "Eloise, get away from my kid."

"Don't get attached to her," she said. She was speaking quickly, fiercely. I leaned into her. "If you do, she'll intertwine herself with your life. You'll get to the point where you won't be able to tell the difference between her feelings and yours. She's not your friend, not really."

"What the hell are you doing?" My father's voice boomed, bouncing off the linoleum floors and the drywall. "I could have you *arrested* for talking to my son."

"Nick," she said when he came to stand beside our table. She closed her eyes as if to summon her patience. "Calm down."

"Don't poison his mind the way you poisoned hers." His face was red, and his hands were shaking. What did he mean? He reached down and pulled me roughly up from my seat.

"Dad . . ." I said.

"*Shut up*, Ian," he said. Then to Eloise: "Stay away from my family."

"Ian," said Eloise. "It's important that you don't give her too much power."

My dad raised a quaking finger at her. "*Don't* talk your craziness to him."

"Please . . ." started Eloise.

But my father was dragging me out of the shop. I tried to tell him what she'd said, ask him why he was so angry. But he didn't want to talk. In the car, my dad drove home, mouth in a tight line, hands gripping the wheel hard. He didn't say anything until we were in the driveway.

"That woman has been a scourge on this town," he said. He brought the car to a stop in front of the house. "Stay away from her. You hear? You have enough problems without that witch filling your mind with more garbage."

"Okay," I said.

It was too late anyway for any warnings from Eloise Montgomery. I was already deeply, painfully attached to Priss. The truth was, even then, I'd have been lost without her. She was my most helpless addiction. And I had no intention of staying away from her, even if I had understood what Eloise meant. She'd been talking to me as if I was an adult. But I was just a kid, lonely and sad. And Priss was all I had.

CHAPTER TWENTY-THREE

A dim gray light washed in around the window blinds. My head was heavy, filled with fog. I heard the words Eloise Montgomery had uttered more than a decade ago ringing in my ears. But I hadn't really heard them when she'd first uttered them. Like so many things I didn't want to deal with, I'd buried her advice and warnings deep. Anyway, I had just been a kid. What good advice was ever seized upon by an adolescent boy?

I lay still, listening to my childhood home, still in the clothes I'd been wearing yesterday. There was a large rust-colored water stain on the low ceiling. It looked like a mushroom cloud, burgeoning, spreading, a quiet, deadly mass. I was the last man in the postapocalyptic world of my life.

A leaden fatigue dragged at my limbs, and I felt as if I could lie there forever, never moving again. The thought of it was almost a comfort. I imagined myself slowly starving to death in my twin bed, my corpse rotting, becoming one with the cheap mattress. Who would miss me? Megan for a time, and my mother. Then I thought of Megan's news—a baby, our child. I pulled myself to standing and went downstairs, the wooden stairs creaking beneath my weight.

"Priss?"

I tried to flip on a light, but there was no electricity. Of course not. The bill had been automatically deducted from my account, which was, of course, overdrawn. I tried

not to think about it—any of it. I still hadn't heard back
from my agent or from Zack, in spite of leaving repeated
messages. What did it mean? My life, the one I'd had just
a few days ago, seemed so far away. I was in a capsule or-
biting the earth, no way to go home. I felt the childish
urge to weep and pressed it back, but just barely. I know.
What a pussy.

My phone sat silent on the countertop in the kitchen.
There were no messages, and its charge was running low.
I stared at it, willing it to ring. But no. No one was calling
because I didn't exist.

Beside my phone was an orange bottle of blue pills,
standing at attention like a little soldier. What was it?
Ritalin? Adderall? Ruffies? Where had it come from? I
didn't recognize it from my personal stash. Whatever it
was, I needed something. I couldn't just be me right now.
I took two—then popped another for good measure. You
might be wondering: What kind of fool takes unidentified
prescription pills? Answer: Someone who would rather be
anything but who he was.

I didn't know how long it would take the police to
find me up here in The Hollows, but my guess was that
it wouldn't be long. Assault on a police officer, arson—I
would get blamed for both of those things. There must be
a manhunt under way already. I probably had twenty-four
hours at the most. I didn't know if anyone had seen me
pull into town. But the odds were high that someone had
noticed. In The Hollows, someone was always watching,
seeing what you didn't want them to see. What would I do
when the police came? Turn myself in? Run? Suicide by
cop? Lots of options, all of them bad.

"Priss," I called again.

I remembered now walking right past her last night,
without even acknowledging her. I could hardly stand the
sight of her.

"Like this is my fault," she'd said as I moved my stuff in from the car. At first, I wasn't biting. I didn't have the energy for an argument. She sat on the couch, put her feet up, and crossed them at the ankles, making herself at home.

"It's not so bad here," she said. "Quiet."

"Don't get comfortable," I snapped. She had always known just how to push my buttons, to hook me right in. I had no choice but to engage with her. She put her hands behind her head, fanning out her arms like the wings of a cobra. "It's scheduled for demolition. I'm tearing this fucker down, leveling it."

Her smug smile had faltered a bit. It wasn't what she expected from me. It didn't take her long to recover.

"And *then* where will you go?" she'd asked. She looked at me with low lids, a nasty smile. "Back to the loft? Or were you planning on moving in with *Megan*? How *are* those wedding plans coming along?"

I wanted to leap on her, take her neck in my hands, and squeeze until her eyes grew red with blood and her body went limp in my grasp. Instead, I closed my eyes, drew in a deep, cleansing breath. *I can let the rage pass through me. I don't have to hold on to it, use it. I can release it.*

"What's wrong?" she said. She pulled her face into a little pout. "Trouble in paradise? Megan starting to get a clue as to what a hopeless screw-up you are?"

"Don't say her name."

"Meganmeganmeeeegggaaan."

I felt the clutch in my solar plexus, the clench of my fists.

"What did you do to that cop?" I asked. I barely had a voice; it sizzled in my throat.

She tilted her head to the side, twirled a strand of that fire hair.

"Nothing," she said. "Bought you some time."

"You burned down the apartment."

"*I* did?" she said. "That's funny. When are you going to grow up, Ian? When are you going to stop blaming everything on me?"

"*When you stop fucking up my life*," I said. But the words came out as a roar, angry—no, hysterical, impotent. The rage was building, a heat that was growing from my gut, rising up my throat like reflux. I couldn't control it. Who was I kidding? I'd never been able to control it.

She rose and the very earth seemed to rumble beneath us. She was the queen of rage. I was just her apprentice.

"*Did you think you could just be done with me?*"

Her voice was just a whisper, but it seemed to come from everywhere, from the walls and the ceiling, from the air. I felt the vibration of her anger in my nerve endings, an electric tingle. She flung out her arms. The whole house shook, photographs rattling on walls, cups chattering in cupboards, drywall shivering.

"Did you think you could just be done with this house, this land? We *belong* to this place, and it belongs to us. We don't get to go anyplace else, not forever. Our bones belong here."

"No," I said. I thought of the graves out back, the old house where I first saw her. "You, maybe. But not me."

The rumbling all around us grew louder, an oncoming freight train, a tornado, a hurricane.

"There is no *you and me*," she said. Still that horrible deafening whisper. "There is just *us*. We're one."

"No," I said again. I moved closer; I wasn't backing down. Not this time. "Megan is my *us*. She's pregnant, Priss. She's having our baby. Whatever our problems are right now, that will bind us."

She stared at me, and for a moment there was a flicker of something on her face, something so young, so afraid, so very sad. I realized I had always seen it in her, had always known on some level that she needed me as much as I needed her. A deep urge to comfort and protect her bubbled up through my rage like a cooling blue spring.

I took a breath and sank down onto the couch.

"Let me go, okay?" I said. "Please."

And then the storm was on us, the world shaking, shattering, the roar of it deafening. And Priss, screaming, burning. I ran from her, up the stairs, into my childhood room, and slammed the particleboard door while the house rattled and shook all around me and then went silent as a tomb.

When I went back downstairs, she was gone. How had she gotten there? Where did she go? You might be wondering about the logistics of Priss. The truth is this: I don't understand them myself.

She only has as much power as you give her, my mother had warned me once. That, too, was starting to make a kind of sense. All of this information I had in my head; it was floating around in there, amorphous, not taking shape, not always accessible. But as with any addiction, you have to hit rock bottom, lose everything to finally start paying attention to the advice people have been trying to give you. You can't hear it until you're ready to do something.

I'd say if there was a rock bottom, I was lying on it.

I'd all but lost Megan. I had been evicted from my apartment, was virtually penniless. I would certainly be accused of assaulting, possibly killing, a police officer. (Was he dead? Had she killed him? I had no idea.) I would definitely be accused of starting the fire I'd seen burning in my apartment. In a million years, no one would ever believe it wasn't me. Not even Megan. Especially not Megan. I just kept seeing the look on her face in the park, the surprise, the hurt. I was about as fucked as a person could be.

Still, because I was a screw-up of epic proportions, there was a kind of inertia. Might have something to do with the mystery pills. The world was a bit foggy, not quite solid. I sank again onto the couch and a cloud of dust erupted, causing me to cough and sneeze in loud, angry shouts.

Then there was silence again, the sound of my own congested breathing. What would I write for myself? Something had to happen. I had to take action. But I couldn't. In my real life, Priss was the instigator, the avenger, the doer. I was the angst, the do-nothing, the doormat, the impotent worrier. It was true in the book, too. It was why I couldn't write the ending I wanted for Fatboy. Because he couldn't make a move without Priss. He was just the puppet on the end of her strings. But not me. I am not Fatboy. I had to do something. How long did I sit there thinking that?

There was a light knock on the door then, and I stood frozen as if I'd just heard a sonic boom. The silence expanded and my heart was beating in my throat. Who was it? Megan? The police? After a moment, I moved carefully over to the window and saw a white Prius parked in the drive. Another knock.

"I know you're in there."

It was a woman's voice, soft but somehow strong. I flung the door open, thinking that it was Megan for some reason even though it didn't sound anything like her. Desperation plays tricks on your mind. But it was Eloise Montgomery, looking older and smaller—it had been over ten years since last I'd seen her and the decade had taken its toll. She looked even more tired than I was.

I took a step back from the doorway and watched as she moved slowly inside. I shut the door.

"You didn't listen to me," she said. It seemed like she was continuing the talk we'd had ten years ago, like somehow I'd summoned her to finish the conversation my dad hadn't allowed.

She clutched a cheap-looking pleather pocketbook to her side, her gaze demanding acknowledgment. I lifted my palms in a gesture of haplessness. She bored into me, seeing, assessing. I'm not sure what kind of judgment she made, but she finally let me go, her eyes scanning the room.

"I can't really blame you, I guess," she said. "You were just a kid. Your father's son. He never listened either."

I didn't know what to say to that, so I said nothing. She walked around a little, her bony fingers glancing on the edge of the couch, a picture frame, the mantel. Somehow her presence in the house made it look even more dumpy and worn down.

"But you're really in deep now."

She seated herself in the chair by the window, smoothed out her simple black skirt, and tugged at a threadbare blouse. The psychic business must not be as lucrative as I would have imagined.

"She's angry," said Eloise. "I can feel it everywhere."

I could have written that line. That's what the Eloise character would have said in my book. Of course, in my story, she's a fraud because everyone is always trying to rip Fatboy off. They are always trying to strip him of his meager accomplishments. And they usually succeed.

"I don't have any money," I said. "I'm seriously broke. So if this is the moment where you tell me you can 'clear' the house, or exorcise my demons, or show me how to walk into the light or whatever, you can just skip it."

Though indeed withering, her expression, I'm certain, didn't properly capture the depth of her disdain.

"You think I want your money?" she said. "That I'm a carny or a con?"

I couldn't take another woman being angry with me. Didn't it seem like they were always so mad about what you'd done or hadn't done? How is it that they are always right and you are always wrong? I bowed my head so I didn't have to look at her.

"I don't know what you want or what you are, Ms. Montgomery."

She stood and walked again around the living room, made a slow circle, and then came to a stop near the window. The room felt wobbly and warped. I wondered briefly what I had taken . . . those pills. Where had they even come from? I sat back down onto the couch. It was the only semicomfortable piece of furniture in the whole dump. I sank in, wishing it would swallow me. I read about that guy in Florida who was just lying in his bed one night when a sinkhole opened up. He fell into a fathomless cavern in the earth, never to be heard from again. I wished that would happen to me.

"Do you remember what I told you about energy?" she asked.

"Vaguely." I did remember, of course, had just spent some time reflecting on that long-ago conversation. I don't know why I just didn't tell her so. Maybe it was embarrassing that it was just now making sense to me.

"Negative energy doesn't just adhere to people. It adheres to places, too. People call it a haunting. I guess it's a haunting in a way, just not in the way of movies— no banging doors and demons pulling you out of bed. A haunting is personal, like a relationship."

"A bad relationship."

"Well, yes," she said. She blinked her eyes at me like a Vulcan, as if trying to process why I would waste energy stating the obvious. "Love lets go, Ian. Only fear holds on and drags you under."

"She's holding on to me?" I felt like an idiot having this conversation. She was a nut, wasn't she?

Eloise came to a stop before the mantel, picked up a photo of me, my father, and my mother. It was one of those department-store shots, Sears or something, in the cheapest possible frame. We all looked so stiff and unnatural. I remember that I got an ice cream after and how my mother was pleased. *I always wanted to do that*, she said. And suddenly this struck me as so goddamn sad. It was probably one of the best things she ever did. Man, did she ever fuck up her life and mine. Then there it was, that rumble of anger that follows sadness. But it was dull and distant—whatever I was on was keeping all my emotions behind glass.

"She's holding on to this place," Eloise said. "She has unfinished business here, or thinks she does. But *you're* holding on to her."

"I'm not holding on to her," I said. It sounded more like a bark, like the yip of a stupid little dog. I didn't like how defensive I felt, tried to soften my tone. "I'm *trying* to get away from her."

"You're trying to get rid of her like people try to kick a heroin habit. You want to give her up; she's killing you, destroying your life. But you're hooked on her. You want her, need her, feel lost without her. You're addicted to her."

I thought about Fatboy on the tracks with the train bearing down, Priss pulling him to safety. He wanted to give her up, but without her he was a victim, weak and powerless. I wanted to argue with Eloise, but I couldn't. She was right and I knew it.

She kept moving in the circle around the room; it was like she couldn't stop. A nervous energy kept her in motion. Maybe she was afraid, I thought. Now she was looking up at the ceiling.

"There's so much anger and fear here. Can't you feel it?"

I *could* feel it. It was like a noxious gas in the air, every breath I took in this house made me sicker.

I started talking then—I don't even know why. I just couldn't keep it all in anymore. I told this strange woman everything, even though I wasn't totally convinced of her sanity. Everything that had happened then, now, and how I had no place left to go and why. She listened carefully, never commenting or making affirming noises. When I was done, she stayed quiet.

"Who is she?" I asked. "What happened to her?"

Eloise Montgomery shook her head. "I don't know," she said. "I can only see so much, only what she wants me to see."

Okay, that sounded a little crazy. But I didn't have any choice but to stay with her. Even if I wasn't convinced of her sanity, I was less convinced of my own.

"What has she wanted you to see?"

"A long time ago, she showed me the night she died. She was just a child. Someone she loved, someone she trusted, did unspeakable things to her. She died in terrible pain and horror."

She paused here and closed her eyes as if out of respect, or as though she could feel the pain herself. "That suffering and fear has turned to rage. It lives here on this property, where she died, where her ashes are."

"Her ashes."

"There was a fire in the end."

Of course there was. Priss *was* fire, burning out of control.

"But *what* happened to her? You must know."

She pressed her lips into a line and looked out the window. In the harsh light that washed in, I saw how much her work cost her. She looked like a crone, ancient and desiccated. If she closed her eyes and lay down, she'd have looked like a corpse laid out. Maybe that was why she never stopped moving. Afraid someone would carry her off to the morgue.

"I don't know," she said. "I can just see her running, barefoot and cold, afraid."

Was she telling me everything? Why would she come here and keep things from me? But I could tell she wasn't going to say more. Maybe she couldn't. I didn't know what the rules were.

"How do I find out what happened?" I asked.

"The Hollows Historical Society has an old library—they have birth and death records, old newspapers. They have a cache of primary sources, too—letters, journals, some school files. There's a woman there, Joy Martin. She's a historian, an expert on The Hollows and some of the nearby towns. She might be able to help you."

She stood as if to leave, and I felt a kind of panic set in. She was the only person who had understood what I was dealing with. I really didn't want her to go. I moved after her.

"Why can't *you* help me?"

I put my hand on her arm. It was as spindly as a tree branch. She didn't pull away. She put her hand on mine, turned her storm-cloud-gray eyes up to me. It was the very gaze of compassion, caring but somehow distant. She would help me if she could, but she wouldn't let me pull her down into the quicksand.

"I *am* helping you," she said. She moved her hand from mine to place it gently on my cheek. "This is what I can do for you right now. If I can do more, I will."

She walked toward the door and pulled it open. Warm air and sunshine washed in, and she moved into it. I followed her onto the porch. I didn't want to beg, but I was about to.

"They don't let you go easy," she said. "You've wasted too much time, given her too much energy and power. She's strong. And she'll do what she must to keep you here with her. Forever."

"What does that mean?" I was as pleading and desperate as a whiny toddler.

"I'll tell Joy you'll be coming by. She'll help you. She's very knowledgeable about this town. More than most."

Then she walked down the drive toward her car. The sun moved behind clouds and I shivered in the chill that seemed to fall.

I looked after her. What had she just told me about Priss? She'd never said it outright, not really. We'd talked about negative energy. Did she just tell me that Priss was a *ghost*?

CHAPTER TWENTY-FOUR

I went to see my mother. It was pretty risky considering that the police were likely looking for me, but there were things we needed to discuss. Things I hadn't wanted to talk about until now, when addressing them was a five-alarm emergency. My mother knew about Priss; she'd told me as much. But I had filed away the information like one files away all the things crazy people say, in my mental trash bin. Now I found myself sifting through the things she'd told me about Priss. But my memories were foggy and disjointed.

The nurse at the front desk greeted me with a knowing smile even though I didn't quite recognize her. I found myself staring at her, the doughy quality of her skin, the hazel eyes, her thick lashes. There was something unsettling about her gaze.

"Ian," she said. "It's good to see you. Your mom will be so happy."

I had no idea what her name was, so I just smiled and said how nice it was to see her, then quickly moved on to the elevator bank and pressed the call button. The space was big and airy—flowers everywhere and soothing watercolors hanging on pale blue walls. With skylights letting in the sun and soft music playing, the place was trying to look like a cross between a hospital and a hotel lobby. It wasn't a bad place, all things considered. They'd taken good care of my mother. But I hated it.

I went to my mother's room and found it empty. Her space was plain, with just a narrow bed and a table by the window with two chairs. On her windowsill, she had a framed picture of Ella and me. In the photo, I was sitting in the rocker that still stood in my mother's bedroom and Ella was in my lap, wrapped in a pink blanket. Her blankie had these soft bunnies on it, and I had secretly wished it were mine even though I was too old to like bunnies. In the photo I looked down at her and she looked up at me, the two of us gazing with fascination at each other. I remember wondering that day how long she was going to stay.

On my mother's hospital bed, there was a blue-and-white crocheted blanket that she'd made herself. I knew there were a few cheap items of clothing hanging in the closet. It made me sad that she had so little. If I ever figured out what happened to my money I was going to buy her more things. Even though she needed nothing, wanted nothing, made me take back everything I bought her, I was going to get her some stuff. You know, the junk we all have—journals and iPads, jewelry, tchotchkes, books, magazines, hair accessories. All the little pieces of our personal mosaic—she needed some of those things. Didn't she?

The floor nurse told me to go up to the eighth floor, where I might find her. And I did. My mother was standing in the art room behind a canvas. There were two other patients as well: a bald and terribly thin older man, and a young girl with white-blond hair who looked pretty and sad and totally vacant as she stared at her blank canvas without even a brush in her hand.

My mother looked at me and smiled. She was wearing street clothes—a pair of jeans and a white button-down shirt. She looked almost normal. She'd put on some weight since I'd last seen her. She didn't seem as drugged out.

"Mom," I said, leaning in to kiss her. "I need to talk to you."

"Of course," she said.

It seemed as if she'd been waiting for me. Once she told me that she was always waiting for me, always expecting me to walk through the door. And that's how I always thought of her at Shady Knoll, patiently waiting for me even though I didn't come to see her often enough. Talk about guilt.

I followed her out to the library, which was empty of others and washed with sunlight. Spare metal shelves held a scant supply of worn and wrinkled books. We found two chairs near the window and sat. I leaned in close to her. Outside there was the sprawling green of the grounds, and tall oak trees standing sentry. It was a peaceful view, and there was something about it that calmed me.

"Mom," I said. I put my hand on her arm, drew her closer to me. "I need you to tell me what you know about Priss."

Her smile faded and a frown moved over her features like cloud cover. "Why? What's happened?"

"I just need to know who she is. When did you first see her? What did she tell you about herself?"

My mother shook her head. She was losing her hair, a side effect, her doctor told me, of the many years she'd been on medication. What remained was a brittle black-and-gray tangle. "It doesn't matter, Ian. No one ever believed me about her."

"I know," I said. "They don't believe me either. But she's real and I need to be free of her. I can't do that until I know who she is."

"I told you," she said. She grabbed my hands and pulled me in even closer. "You have to ignore her, don't give her your attention."

"But I didn't do that," I said. "I wish I had but I didn't take your advice."

It was too late for ignoring Priss. Maybe at first I could have just walked away from her and she would have attached herself to the next lonely and desperate person who crossed her path. But we were wrapped around each other, each of us giving and each of us taking something from the other in a psychic symbiosis. You can be addicted to all kinds of things.

My mother pulled her hands away and did that anxious rubbing of her crown. I imagined her rubbing away all her hair, it falling to the ground like leaves. Suddenly I felt bad for upsetting her. What was I doing here? This was a mistake; I should have gone to The Hollows Historical Society and not brought all this up to my mother.

"I'm sorry, Mom," I said. I stood and tried to gently pull her to rise with me. "Forget it. Let's go downstairs and get some lunch."

I wanted to be with her a little longer, even though I didn't have much time. If the shit hit the fan, I could be going to prison. I might never see my mother again. The thought was a stone I'd swallowed, sitting cold and heavy in my craw. She didn't get up; instead she pulled me back into my seat.

"I had three miscarriages after you," she said. "Did you know that?"

I sat back down beside her.

"Dad told me," I said. "I'm sorry."

"We wanted another child," she said. My mother had been pretty once, beautiful even. Not gorgeous. So few people are truly gorgeous in the real world. Flawless beauty exists only in movies and magazines, in the comics. The rest of us are the sum of our qualities and imperfections. But my mother once had laughing eyes and a wide mouth that always seemed upturned in a smile, as if she were in on some cosmic joke. She'd had wavy dark hair that framed a heart-shaped face. She'd been shapely, full-bodied. There was nothing of that woman in the anxious, washed-out person before me. "I loved you so much. I couldn't wait to make more babies."

She tried for a smile, but it was more sad than a smile had a right to be. It faded quickly and she looked out the window.

"But at times I have felt as if there's this terrible darkness in me. It's like a black hole, sucking in all the light, all the happiness."

She wrapped her arms around herself, reminding me of Meg. Meg had said something like that, too, when she told me of bouts of depression she'd suffered in high school and in college. *It's like all the color drains out of your world. There's nothing you want to see or do. I just wanted to sleep forever.*

"I wasn't always like that. It started after my first pregnancy. A few weeks after you were born, a kind of shroud fell over my life. It was gray and suffocating; I couldn't move. Your grandmother helped me then, too. But it passed quickly enough."

"Postpartum depression," I said.

"Of course, we know that now. Then, no one ever said anything like that. There was no diagnosis, no worry that it would come back. For me, it was like labor. Once it was done, I forgot how painful, how frightening it had been."

Another patient walked through the door with the shuffling walk of the overmedicated. My mother waited for her to move away, to take a seat on the other side of the room and open a magazine.

"I saw her after I lost my first baby."

"Priss? Where?"

"In the woods. I was out walking, close to the house because you were napping. I saw her, this pretty little thing, darting through the trees like a sprite. I called to her, but she ran away and I followed. The property is so isolated—so it was strange seeing a little girl there. I needed to get back to you, but I didn't want a little girl wandering around alone. It didn't seem safe."

I could see Priss running, teasing. I knew how irresistible it was to chase her.

"I finally caught up with her in the graveyard," my mother went on. "My first thought was that she must have been so cold. It was chilly and she just wore this little cotton slip of a dress."

"White, with yellow flowers," I said.

"Yes," she said. "That's right. She had an aura of sadness, of loneliness. And it reached out for me, connected to my own sadness and grief. She told me that she was sorry about my baby. And I asked her how she knew."

I waited for my mother to go on, but she seemed to drift away into her own thoughts. She looked smaller, more wasted than she had when I arrived. I put a hand on her shoulder.

"She said that so many little children had died there," Mom whispered. "And she showed me their graves."

She was trembling a little now. "I was so afraid suddenly. I saw what she was and I ran from her, back to you. I was afraid that she had lured me away from you and that when I got home, you would be gone. But you were still sleeping when I got back, safe and sound.

"And then I started to doubt what I had seen. I took the miscarriage hard, harder than everyone thought I should have at that early stage; was I losing my mind? I didn't dare tell your father. He was so worried about me already."

I imagined her running through the woods and bursting into the house, dashing up the stairs to find me safe in bed. I could see it all—my room as it was, with stars painted on the ceiling and a big stuffed bear on the chair in the corner, my mother pale with fear, leaning against the doorframe in relief.

"But the next day I saw her again," she said. "She was waiting on the edge of the woods. She wanted me to follow her. But I didn't, not that day."

"What did you mean that you knew what she was? What *is* she?"

"She's anger, Ian," my mother said. "She's misery. She's revenge. She's a deep, abysmal loneliness."

She was all those things; I knew that. But Priss was more. She was real, not just some bad energy trapped in the ether. She was a person, with needs and motivations. Eloise was right. She wanted something real that only I could give her.

My mother told me how with each miscarriage, she became more despondent. She started following Priss out to those graves every day as I napped. She wanted to comfort the children who lay there, comfort the souls of the children she hadn't been able to carry. This continued, on and off, for years. And then my father discovered what she'd been doing and made her promise to stop.

"He knew about her, even though he wouldn't admit it at first. He'd seen her, too."

I remembered how he'd said to me: *There is no little girl in those woods and there never has been.*

"But your father was too strong for her, too solid," she said. "He wasn't weak like me. He never let her lure him out to the woods. When she teased him, he ignored her. He finally told me as much. He said she'd been there forever."

But my father had never acknowledged seeing her, not to me. Wouldn't he have? I remembered him yelling at Eloise about not poisoning my mind as she had my mother's. I wondered how much of what my mother was saying was true, how much of it her delusions.

"So I started ignoring her, stopped following her when she came for me. And a few months later, I was pregnant with Ella. And I never saw her again, until the night Ella died."

She always referred to it as "the night Ella died." Never as "the night I killed Ella and would have killed you, too, if you hadn't run." But some words don't exactly roll off the tongue.

I could see her drifting away as she was prone to doing, getting deeper and deeper inside her own head and further from me.

"You saw her that night?" I said. "What did she want? What did she say?"

We had never talked about that night, what delusion, what madness had led her to do what she did. It made sense that Priss had something to do with it.

"Tell me what happened, Mom," I said.

My mom just shook her head, and her eyes grew wide and filled with tears. "She didn't say anything. It was the Whispers. They got so loud, a million voices all around me."

"What did they say?"

My mother's doctor walked in then. He was a slim and meticulously dressed man, with sharply pressed black pants and a royal-blue button-down. He did not look happy to see me. He told me once that my visits to my mother could be "destabilizing." I didn't know what that meant, and fuck him if he didn't think I was going to come and see my mother.

"Ian," he said. "It's good to see you."

His voice was cautious, suspicious as he stepped closer to us.

"Everything all right?" he asked. "Miriam? Everything okay?"

My mother wasn't looking too good. She was rocking

in her chair, staring at some point far off into the distance. She glanced over at the doctor but didn't answer.

"What have you been discussing?" he asked.

"That's really none of your business, is it, Doctor?" I said. I was surprised by the edge to my voice, and from the look on his face, I could see that he was, too. He plastered on a shrinky smile, but his eyes were twin laser beams of disapproval. I was sick of that look from people—from teachers and doctors and cops. I'd had a lifetime of it.

"Your mother's well-being is indeed my business, Ian. And she does *not* look well at all."

"Mom," I said gently. But she was gone, way gone.

"We've talked before about upsetting her, about showing up here unannounced."

Have we? If we had, I didn't remember it. But I stayed silent. I didn't want to seem crazy in this crazy place. What if they didn't let me leave? On the other hand, what a nice little escape it would be. Just say you're nuts and need to lie down for the foreseeable future. I could see the appeal of the situation my mother had chosen for herself. Nothing was required of her. She hadn't truly answered for anything. She'd killed my sister and destroyed my life. When it all became too much, the white coats came and took her off to rest for as long as she needed—like forever. Did that sound bitter? You know what? I *was* pretty bitter.

"How about we table whatever you're discussing until tomorrow or the next day?" he suggested when I didn't say anything.

"Mom?" I said. I couldn't leave without asking. "What does she want?"

The doctor moved over toward my mother and took her arm, gently eased her to standing. "I really must insist."

"Mom," I said. "Please."

She walked over to me and wrapped her arms around

me. I held on to her tight. In spite of it all, I loved her. You never love or need anyone in this life like you do your mother. And no one ever quite loves you the same way she does—even if she does go crazy and try to kill you.

She whispered fiercely in my ear: "Sweetheart, why don't you just ask her?"

CHAPTER TWENTY-FIVE

In my senior year of high school, I developed a serious, soul-destroying crush on my advanced-chemistry lab partner. Her name was Marley and she was the first person to be nice to me in a hundred years. Her family had just moved to The Hollows from South Carolina, and she was almost as much of an outsider as I was. Well, not quite.

I was a ghost at The Hollows High, moving through the hallways unseen, lurking silent in the back of classrooms, sitting alone at lunch eating enormous piles of food. No one came near me, but no one messed with me anymore either. It was understood that if you earned my wrath, bad things happened to you. So by senior year, there wasn't as much as a snide glance in my direction. Even the teachers were terribly careful with me.

And so I lumbered through my life. My only saving grace was my weekends and summers in the city. I was taking art classes at Parsons School of Design, where I hoped I would go to college. It was a massively expensive proposition. But my father never said a word about the cost. He knew I was an artist and he wanted me to pursue that dream. He knew it was the only healthy, productive thing I had in my life.

When I look at my old yearbooks now and I see a morbidly obese, acne-masked monster, I am surprised people didn't come after me with torches. Maybe in another era, they would have.

But, oddly, Marley didn't seem to view me that way. We were assigned to work together since I was the only one in chemistry class who didn't have a partner. Usually, the teacher, Mr. Gardener, worked with me. I expected Marley, pink-cheeked and petite, to register some revulsion, but instead she shook my hand and smiled, warm and sincere. She looked right past the external me and held my eyes.

"Nice to meet you, Ian," she said. There was the loveliest lilt to her voice. She moved a self-conscious hand to sweep a riot of black curls away from her eyes. "Thanks for being my partner. Chemistry is *not* my best subject."

"I'll help you," I said. My voice crackled as if from disuse.

"Oh, you're a doll," she said. She lowered her voice and whispered as if I were her intimate pal. "It's so *hard* to be new."

That day, she came and sat with me at lunch. "Do you mind?"

The Hollows was not a welcoming place. Provincial and backward, people didn't do well with outsiders. But Marley had looks and charm going for her. Eventually, I knew she'd find someone else to sit with. In the meantime, I enjoyed her company as she chattered endlessly about how much she missed her friends back home, and how mad she was at her father for moving the whole family for his job, and how happy she was to have me as a friend. I'm not sure I ever uttered a word.

Suddenly I was looking forward to school every day. And there was something about Marley, or maybe just my feelings for her, that made me look at myself differently. It was the crush, however ill-fated, that got me to start taking better care of myself. I stopped eating so much junk food when I got home from school. My grandmother didn't live with us anymore now that I was old enough to take care of myself. But she still did our grocery shopping. I asked her to get more healthy foods.

"Like what?" she asked, genuinely not sure what I meant.

"You know fruits, vegetables, granola. Maybe some fish and chicken that I can cook. I'm going to start cooking for my dad at night."

She shrugged. "Sure," she said. I started making her a list, and she bought the things I requested.

I went to the library and got a cookbook: *101 Healthy, Easy Meals*, and *Arnold's Bodybuilding for Men*. It's amazing how love can inspire us to change ourselves.

Of course, I never had a chance with Marley. I was simply the first person she met in a new school. I was easy, desperate, a sure thing in an unwelcoming place. And sure enough, she slowly developed other friendships.

She wasn't quite cheerleader or prom-queen material. But she was smart and pretty in a nonthreatening way. And soon she was sitting with the brains—the college-bound, student-government, debate-team crowd. Not the cool kids exactly, but the kids that the cool kids went to when they needed help with their homework or else get kicked off the squad, team, whatever. They held a place of not coolness exactly, but at least respect within The Hollows High hierarchy.

She must have heard everything about me from the other kids, but she never once stopped being kind to me, remained my chemistry partner, and still occasionally sat with me at lunch, just to be nice, I'm sure. She was like that, kind of a natural politician and networker.

Meanwhile I was dropping pounds pretty quickly. After dark fell, I had started running. I didn't want anyone to see me lumbering, red and sweaty, breathless and suffering, through the streets of The Hollows. So I waited until night, after dinner, to get out there. I started working out with the weights Old Brian kept in the storeroom of the bookshop. There was a bench and a rack of free weights that he'd bought, hoping to get in shape, and never touched. He said I could use them anytime. So I started coming an hour before my shift, working out and then showering in his apartment over the store.

Without all the junk food, my skin cleared up. There was, though, a lot of scarring and I wouldn't exactly say that I looked good. But I looked better. My mother was the first one to notice, since she didn't see me every day.

"I'm so proud of you," she said. "It's so hard to change yourself. Are you in love?"

By the time prom season rolled around, I'd dropped fifty pounds, had some decent muscle tone, and could actually look at my own face in the mirror without blurring out my vision. My dad never said a word about the change. But he started running with me at night. He just turned up in the driveway while I was stretching one evening, wearing his sneakers, an old pair of gym shorts I'd never seen, and a "No Paine Construction" T-shirt.

"Thanks for dinner," he said. "It's nice to have some home-cooked meals."

We'd had chicken and broccoli with rice. I wasn't a world-class chef, but at least it wasn't burgers and fries, or fried chicken, or pizza or subs or whatever my dad picked up on his way home from work. Even my dad was slimming down a bit.

I drove to Marley's house on a Saturday to ask her to go to the prom with me. I couldn't stand the idea of asking her at school and having her turn me down, or laugh at me or run screaming or any of the other myriad humiliations I had imagined. I figured the rejection would be better if it happened off campus; that way I could spend the weekend licking my wounds before donning the emotional armor I put on to survive school.

But I *was* liking my chances; she'd hugged me on Friday when I told her that I'd been accepted to Parsons School of Design for the fall. I could still feel her hands on me, as if she'd left warm little imprints on my broad back.

Her mother opened the door, and I could see immediately where Marley got her charm and good looks.

"Oh, Ian," she said, bright and enthusiastic. "Marlena has told me all about you. You were her first friend in The Hollows. Come in."

She welcomed me into her sunlit, flower-filled foyer and called for Marley, who bounded down the stairs.

I hadn't seen Priss in a while. I'd stopped going out into the woods to look for her, and she wasn't waiting outside my window at night. It was a bit of relief, even though I missed her. But at least I didn't have to lie to my father and Dr. Crown about her. I was starting to wonder if maybe they were right. Maybe she wasn't real after all. Maybe Eloise Montgomery was a fake or a nut job. I didn't dwell on this too much, because if Priss wasn't real, then I was as crazy as, maybe even crazier than, my mother.

Seeing Marley on the stairs, I felt like my throat and mouth were filled with cotton.

"Ian," she said. She gave me one of her signature quick little hugs. "What a surprise. Want a soda?"

I followed her to the kitchen, where she started to pour me a Pepsi. I lifted a hand.

"Just water, please," I croaked.

Arnold said absolutely no soda ever, it was poison for muscles. His bodybuilding book was like my new Bible. I was quoting it at home until my dad told me enough already. Then I saw him reading it one night after he thought I was asleep.

"So what's up, Ian?" she asked when we sat down at the kitchen table.

I cleared my throat and looked down at my hands. I felt myself redden and start to sweat a little, a real Prince Charming just sweeping the girls off their feet. I took a deep breath, the way Dr. Crown had taught me.

"I was wondering if you would like to go to the prom with me."

It came out in a tumble, an avalanche of words that crashed into nothing. Of all the reactions I imagined, surprised silence was actually the worst. It was a kind of purgatory, neither outsized nor cruel. Asking her to the prom was the last thing she expected of me; it hadn't even crossed her mind that I might have a crush on her. Her face—surprised, empathetic, sweetly embarrassed for me—was a real heartbreaker.

"Oh, Ian," she said. She put her hand on my hand. "That's so sweet. But I've already agreed to go with Mikey Beech."

I felt like God was laughing at me. He'd played some kind of cosmic joke. I didn't even know Marley *knew* Mikey Beech. But, of course, captain of the lacrosse team, homecoming king, school heartthrob—everyone knew him. He'd had a high-profile breakup earlier that year with a blond goddess named Juliet. He'd broken up with her for reasons no one could explain. Certainly, there was no one richer, more beautiful, more perfect and empty-headed than Juliet. And all the girls had been wondering who he'd set his sights on next—Jodi, Tami, Grace? Nope. Apparently, it was Marley.

"I'd have *loved* to go with you, though, Ian. Really," she said kindly, even though we both knew it was a bald-faced lie. "Thank you *so much* for asking."

Her cat rubbed against my leg.

"Aw, look," she said. "Spunky Doodle likes you."

I hated cats. I felt that ugly heat I knew too well. I imagined taking Spunky Doodle by the tail and twirling him over my head while Marley looked on in horror. I could see him, released from my grasp, sailing through the picture window that looked out onto a perfectly manicured lawn and pool deck. I could hear his terrified yowl, the shattering of glass, the sickening thud as he landed on the concrete. I pushed myself away from the table and stood. Spunky Doodle hissed and moved away, startled by my sudden movement.

"That's cool," I managed. Why hadn't she just hit me in the head with a sledgehammer? At least then I would have had the gift of unconsciousness.

"Ian," she said. She put a gentle hand on my arm. "I'm sorry."

She meant it; I could see that. She liked me, and maybe she was really my friend in some easy, superficial way. I couldn't wait to get out of there.

"Oh, yeah," I said. "No problem. I just thought since you were new, maybe you didn't have anyone to go with." Lame, I know. I felt suddenly like I was going to throw up. *Oh God, please don't let me.* "I guess I'll see you in chemistry."

I moved quickly down the hallway lined with smiling pictures of Marley, and pushed out through the heavy oak door. I don't remember what she said as I was leaving, just the sound of her voice—sweet, apologetic, soft—as I closed the door behind me.

I stumbled past the pink-and-white perennials and managed to get into my car before puking on the passenger-side floor. What a loser. Seriously.

I drove home and headed straight into the woods, where Priss was waiting by the hollowed-out oak tree. Interesting, isn't it, that she's always there when times are dark, when I'm at my loneliest, saddest, angriest, most despondent?

"You're kidding me right?" she said. "Prom? What

a crock. A rented tuxedo, sluts in cheap dresses thinking they're princesses for the night, only to get their cherry popped by some steroid-eating loser. Come on. You're better than those people."

She'd grown stunning—taller, fuller. Her body belonged to a woman even though she was only a teenager. I found myself mesmerized by her and the sound of the Whispers. It was a white noise all around me, hypnotic and strange.

She moved in close to me, and the next thing I knew I was in her arms. And then her mouth was on mine. My first kiss—and it was a fire starter. Then she breathed into my ear, soft but fierce, "I love you. I'll always love you."

She set me on fire inside.

"Stay with me, Ian," she said. I was trembling as she took my hand. "Don't leave me here alone."

I didn't know what she meant, wasn't even listening, so overwhelmed was I by her touch, by her heat. I followed her deeper into the woods, where she made me feel things I'd never felt before.

Marley wasn't in school on Monday. And by the end of the day, we all learned that she was missing. All eyes turned to me again. Something horrible happening after an altercation with Ian Paine.

Her mother claimed that our conversation had ended badly, with me storming angrily from the house. It hadn't been like that; I *knew* it hadn't. I'd been in therapy; I'd done my anger therapy homework. I was better. But by the end of the day, the police were at the school and I was being hauled in for questioning.

I remember feeling numb, disaffected, and I don't recall having any feelings of fear or worry for Marley. I was just stunned that something like this was happening again after I had worked so hard at keeping my head down, keeping away from people. So I think my affect was very flat the day they brought me in, and this came across as indifference. The interrogation, the desperation of the police and Marley's parents was grueling.

Tell us where she is, Ian. Is she still alive? Take us to her and things will go much easier for you.

After hours of this, the shell I was in cracked and fell to pieces. At one point, I put my head down on the table and started to cry. *I don't know where she is. Please. I don't know.*

My father got another lawyer. The police released me due to lack of evidence to charge, but then followed me everywhere, searching the woods behind my house. Flashlight beams danced like will-o'-the-wisps, and voices rang out through the night, urgent and loud. Dogs barked and bayed. I waited for Priss to come, but she didn't.

What have you done? What have you done now, Priss?

I saw my dreams of college and New York City slipping away. I remember what Priss had said. *Don't leave me here alone.* If she had done something horrible to Marley, I would be charged and convicted. Of that I had no doubt. Is that what she wanted?

They found Marley two days later. She'd been out in The Hollows Woods and had fallen down an abandoned mine shaft (something that happened quite a bit in The Hollows—usually to little kids ignoring warning signs). She'd broken her leg, but she was alive.

How did she wind up in the woods? She'd been driving out to see me. She felt so bad about turning me down for the prom that she wanted to apologize again. On her way, on the isolated rural road, she'd turned the blind corner and almost hit a little girl with bright red hair who'd been darting through the gloaming.

The little girl looked so lost and afraid in her cotton

shift that Marley pulled her car off the road and called out to her. When the girl didn't stop, Marley followed in her vehicle, pulling farther down the path off the main road. But the little girl disappeared into the woods. Finally, Marley followed, until she caught sight of the girl again. *I realized that it wasn't a little girl after all. That she was more my age, more like me. She was crying, though.*

Marley called out to her: *What's wrong? Can I help you?*

Because that's the kind of person Marley was. The girl stopped running, and Marley moved closer. Then she felt the ground break apart beneath her feet, almost rip like paper. And she fell down the shaft.

I could hear her laughing, Marley said. *I called for her, but she never came to help me.*

Eventually, the police had spotted Marley's abandoned car and that was how they found her. Obviously, I was cleared and the police surveillance rolled away without apology. Even though I had nothing to do with what happened to Marley, it was another nail in my social coffin.

When I went in to work the next day, Old Brian let me go.

"I'm sorry, kid," he said. "It's hard enough keeping this business afloat. People have stopped coming because you work here. I don't think this latest incident is going to improve matters, and I'm barely surviving as it is."

He gave me two weeks' severance, and I left his shop—not angry, just sad and lost. But I had already been accepted at Parsons and I knew my days in The Hollows were coming to a merciful end anyway. I wondered if I could take my GED and opt out of the rest of the year. New York City was a clean slate, a new life. I was eager to find my way there.

When I arrived back home after getting fired, Jones

Cooper was waiting for me in front of the house. My stomach bottomed out at the sight of him leaning on his maroon SUV, looking up at the trees.

As I climbed out of the Scout, I heard the Whispers. They chattered, nervous and grim, like voices at a funeral. Did he hear them? Did they speak to him, too? He seemed like the kind of person who might be able to hear them. I had come to understand that there had to be some kind of darkness in you—sadness or fear or anger. You had to believe that there was more to the world than just what you could feel and see and taste. You had to be the sort of person who thinks some places might have a soul, just as a body might.

"What now?" I asked him.

He told me what Marley had said about the girl in the woods. I felt something like relief. Someone reliable and solid had seen Priss. She *was* real.

It was cold, and spring was making no sign of itself. The trees were barren, and the sky was a charcoal lid above us.

"I don't know who she is," he said. "Or *what* she is. But I've lived in this town a long time. There are lots of things about it that I don't understand."

He had on a strange look, sad and faraway. Jones Cooper was revealing himself to be someone I wouldn't have thought him to be. I had thought of him as a hardcase; he was like my father, no give. I still hadn't said anything.

"I heard you got into some art school in the city," he said into the silence. He covered his mouth and gave a little cough. "Is that right?"

I shoved my hands in my pockets against the cold. I wanted to move past him and go inside. He was not my favorite person, and being around him made me uncomfortable.

"Yeah," I finally said.

"Do yourself a favor." He kicked at a stone with the toe of his shoe. "Go there and don't come back."

I found myself nodding. The Whispers had started and I turned to look back at the woods. There was a strange pitch to the chatter now, angry and fearful. Cooper's eyes followed mine, but if he heard what I heard he didn't show it.

"That's the plan," I said.

He looked at me a minute longer, with the searing, assessing gaze I had squirmed beneath too many times. He started moving back toward his vehicle.

"Good," he said. "Have a nice life."

That night I dreamed of Priss. She snuck into my room and climbed naked into my bed. The soft warmth of her enveloped me. She whispered: *I'm coming with you.*

CHAPTER TWENTY-SIX

A haunting is a personal thing, a relationship. That's what Eloise had said. And I was finally turning this idea over in my mind. There is give-and-take in this relationship; mistakes are made. It's liquid; it changes and evolves. In the movies, the whole haunting thing seems very black and white. The haunting ghost is always evil, the haunted one is a hapless victim. But in nature, nothing exists in a vacuum. There is a constant energy exchange between separate entities, a net that connects us all.

The Hollows Historical Society was housed in a red clapboard building off the main square, around the corner from a yoga studio and down the street from the Java Stop, the trendy coffee place. It has been there forever, but I don't recall ever paying any attention to it.

The Hollows has actually turned precious since I was a kid, morphing from a backward, semirural, ticky-tack dump, to a faux-hip, tony little burg. That's what had so charmed Megan. She didn't know it was just a thin façade over the true face of The Hollows.

But it had fooled plenty of people. The Manhattan rich had discovered The Hollows, bringing with them their appetites for fine things, and the cash to motivate others to provide those things. Real estate prices had skyrocketed since the eighties, and even during the downturn they didn't falter overmuch. Certain people always have money. And for whatever reason, some of those people had decided on The Hollows as a retreat from the city. It boded well for me. Once I had torn the house down, I was going to sell the land. Then I was going to use that money to buy myself a place in Manhattan—even if it was just a shoe box on the Lower East Side. And I was never going to leave my city again.

But thinking about it made me remember how all my bank accounts were empty, and how I hadn't heard back from my agent or my editor, how Natalie had said I told her that my book contract had been canceled, and how none of it made any sense at all. Oh, yeah, and how my apartment had been on fire last I saw it. And how I was probably going to prison for the rest of my life for murdering a cop. Did they have the death penalty in New York? I didn't even know.

I felt the dawning of a migraine, which I hadn't had in years. A kind of halo was appearing around my vision and I could feel a tingling in the crown of my head. If it hit, I'd be incapacitated until it passed. I'd have to lie in a darkened room until the mind-crushing pain and waves of nausea passed. And that could take a while. I pulled the Scout over to the side of the road and put it in park. The little red house looked dark; I wondered if anyone was inside.

As I was getting out of the car, the phone rang: Zack.

I know what you're thinking. I should have dumped the phone, not been making calls. If the police were looking for me, an iPhone is basically like a tracking device. I was a blip on a screen somewhere. But I didn't have much choice. Besides, the phone was about to die. Once it did, I had no electricity at my house to charge it, no car charger. I didn't even have a wall charger to steal electricity at the library or the coffee shop. When my phone went dead, it would stay dead until my life returned to normal.

"Hey, man," I said.

"Hey, Ian," he said. "Sorry for the delay in getting back to you. You know my wife's pregnant? We had kind of a false alarm, thought the baby was coming early. But we're all good now."

I felt a twinge of sadness thinking about Megan.

"Glad all is well," I said. What had he heard? What did he know? Was it all over the news about the cop, the fire? I tried to be cool.

"So how's the work coming along?" he asked. "I can't wait to read those pages."

"It's coming along," I said. I was just going to go with the flow. "I'm having some technical difficulties. So I decided to leave town for a couple of days to try to knock out the ending."

"Great idea," he said. He sounded weird, tense. But maybe it just had to do with his pregnant wife. "Where are you?"

I ignored his question.

"This might sound crazy, Zack. But just humor me, okay?"

"Sure."

He sounded suddenly excited, eager. He thought I was going to ask him about plot.

"Everything's okay, right? With my contract?"

There was a beat of silence.

"Yeah," he said. He sounded perplexed. "Of course. This is the last book in your contract, and we discussed moving on after it to something new. Right?"

A wave of relief crashed over me. Okay, okay. That was good. I wasn't *totally* losing my mind. I was just experiencing huge gaps in my memory of how I was behaving with other people. But my whole *life* wasn't a hallucination. That was something, right? I know: the bar was very, very low on what I considered good news.

"Yes," I said. "Right."

"Hey, Ian, you doing all right, buddy?"

"Why do you ask?"

Why do you ask, Zack? I missed the most important meeting of the year. I've been calling you obsessively for two days. For all I know it's all over the news that I'm a cop killer and an arsonist. What could be wrong?

"You just seem—tense."

"Well, you know . . . the wedding, the deadline. And . . ." Should I tell him? Why not? "Megan's pregnant."

"Wow," he said. He let out a long breath. "Congrats, man. That's great. I know how you feel, though. It's all really big stuff, right?"

"Yeah," I said. "It is." I basked in the normalcy of the conversation.

"So, where did you say you were?" I imagined him sitting in a room surrounded by police, all of them leaning in toward the phone. There would be a bright light shining off frame, the cops just shadows, and Zack would be looking nervous, maybe flushed and sweating. My comic book imagination.

"Just out of town," I said. "I needed to focus on Priss right now. On the ending, I mean."

"Okay," he said. He drew the word out, seemed to want to say more. "Just—stay in touch?"

"I'm going off the grid for a couple of days. I'll send the work when it's done. Thanks, Zack."

I heard his voice carrying over the air, but I ended the call. Then I called Megan. Of course she didn't answer. I left a rambling message about how much I loved her and how sorry I was and how I was trying to make everything better. I am sure I sounded crazy and that it didn't help my position any. But I had to keep trying.

"I am *going* to be a better man," I told her. "I'm facing the things that are working against me. I'm going to get help. Meg, I'm going to fight my way back to you and our baby. I swear to God."

Then I hung up, that halo burning blue white around my world. I moved from the car and headed up the path toward the little red clapboard house.

The door was open and I pushed inside with the ring of a little bell. I expected to see an old woman, hair in a bun, wire glasses, sitting at some old-timey desk. She would have all the answers to my questions, like some soothsaying crone. That's what it would have been in my comic; that was the kind of librarian I was going to give Fatboy.

Instead, there was a smartly dressed, fit woman, with a neat black bob—a youthful fifty-something, maybe. She was still seriously fuckable, if I had those kind of thoughts—which I didn't. Much. She sat behind a long, low-profile worktable, a silver laptop open in front of her. I couldn't help but notice her nails, square and candy red, like little lozenges.

"Can I help you?"

She didn't look up from her work, tapping furiously on her keyboard.

"Eloise Montgomery said you could help me."

I closed the door behind me and immediately was ensconced by the place—its aroma of roses, the floor-to-ceiling shelves of leather-bound books, the warm amber lighting. The swirling chaos of my world was firmly shut outside and something like relief washed over me.

"You must be Ian," she said without looking up.

"Right."

"I've done some preliminary research on the grave-yard behind your house, and on your property," she said.

She still hadn't looked at me. The noise of her keystrokes reached a crescendo and then abruptly stopped. She swiveled to me, gave me a quick glance, and reached for a tall pile of books and files on her desk. She rose, hefting the stack onto her hip.

"We have some study tables in the back of the library," she said. She moved toward an archway to her right. "Follow me."

I moved behind her past rows of vintage photographs—The Hollows' first school, first church, first iron mine. There was a group of miners with dirty faces holding various tools of the trade, smiling uncertainly for the camera. There was a group of men who I recognized from my school days as the town's founders. Stiff, angry-looking, and big-jawed, they were the kind of hard men who settled towns and blazed trails, blew holes in the earth to take from it what they wanted. The opposite of the kind of man I was. I couldn't even take care of myself, of the few people who relied on me. Again, I was blasted with thoughts of Megan and our baby, buffeted by waves of sadness, shame, and fear. What was going to happen to me, to them?

"I have here the sales history of your property, the church records of the graveyard behind your house. There are some news articles I thought you might find helpful, some books. There are also some journals that might be of particular interest to you," she said.

She put it all down in front of me with a thud. I looked at it, enervated. It made me want to put my head down and go to sleep. What can I say? I am a child of the search-engine generation. I want to type my questions into a box on a screen and have the answer magically appear before me. I didn't necessarily want to work for it.

She seemed to sense my despair, took pity on me.

"There was only one person born in The Hollows in

the last hundred years with the name Priscilla Miller. She had a short and unhappy life. It's all in here."

"Where do I start?" I asked her.

She laid her hands on the pile, peered at me over the frames of her reading glasses. "Start at the top."

I did.

CHAPTER TWENTY-SEVEN

Fatboy returns to The Hollows. It is a gray and miserable place, with a run-down town center and a ramshackle church. The recession has hit the area hard—homes are in foreclosure and clearly abandoned with dark windows and overgrown yards. "Out of Business" signs hang in the windows of the bookstore, the ice creamery, the antiques shop. The other shops on the square—the diner, the hardware shop, the grocery—are empty.

The Hollows only had one industry, the iron mines. And those mines ceased to yield decades earlier. Now there is just a network of abandoned and dangerous tunnels beneath the streets and homes, deep into The Hollows Wood, up into the foothills of the mountains.

It is a place of charcoal grays and dirty whites and dusty blacks. Even the sun is a misty ball of light. Only the moon has a slightly blue tinge. The sky always portends rain; the wind is always gusting. There is nothing cheerful, or sunny, or green about Fatboy's hometown. It is left fallow, abandoned by anyone who had anyplace better to go.

Fatboy arrives at The Hollows Historical Society building. It is housed in the old church and maintained by a bespectacled old gargoyle of a woman named Misery. Maybe she has another name, but no one knows it. That's what she has always been to the residents of The Hollows. She knows Fatboy and he knows her, even though he's sure they never met. But that's the way of The Hollows, everyone knows everyone.

"Well," she says as he walks through the door. "It's about time. What have you been waiting for? An invitation?"

There is a towering stack of materials on her desk. She nods toward a long wooden table, indicating that he is to sit, and he does. She brings the reading materials over to him, and he starts to read, sifting through piles of news articles and journals, books, and city records. Who is she? What does she want? Slowly, this girl, this woman, this mystery, starts to take shape. He always thought that Priss was the person he knew best. He suddenly realizes that he doesn't know her at all.

First he finds her birth record, a tattered piece of parchment, faded with time.

Priscilla Miller was born on March 4, 1910, the six-pound daughter of Martha and Thomas. She entered the world at 3:33 a.m., born at home, which was the norm, attended by a midwife nun. The details are scrawled in black ink, a thin hand lettering that seems hurried somehow, dashed off. The document doesn't look quite real; it's flimsy and insubstantial.

Her family lived a hardscrabble life in a one-room cabin deep in The Hollows Wood. They were what the townfolk referred to as Hill People—isolated, uneducated, and strange. The Hill People were said to be the descendants of escaped slaves and criminals. They were shunned and hated, and so they kept to themselves, moving farther and farther back into the foothills of the mountains. All these details are noted in the midwife's journal. Mention is also made of the child's "unsettling" red hair as "very nearly a deformity."

The librarian has compiled other records. Priscilla had siblings, an older brother, Caleb, and a sister, Clara.

She went to lessons in the old schoolhouse in town, a long walk from her home. Fatboy sees her name in the register and wonders if she walked all that way every day. Obviously not in winter, when the big snows came. Wasn't it an oddity for a girl from the hills to go to school? Her brother went there, too, until he was old enough to work in the mines at the age of eight.

An old newspaper article reports on the collapse of a mine shaft, and the librarian has highlighted two names on the list of the dead: her brother, Caleb Miller, twelve, and her father, Thomas Miller, thirty-five. Fatboy had heard about this mining accident, learned about it in his middle school history class. Several hundred men were killed, devastating the town, and leaving widows with children they suddenly had no way to support. The church was overwhelmed with need and the town banded together, the wealthy donating money and offering jobs, families taking in other families.

The event was always hailed as a symbol of everything that was right with small-town life. There was a saying in The Hollows: There's a net here that can only be seen when tears are shed. But Fatboy knows that's not true for everyone. For someone like Martha Miller, Priss's mother, a woman living on the fringe of society, maybe too proud or too timid to ask for help, there was no net, not really. Maybe at first, but as days turned to weeks and months, the helping hands would have slowly disappeared.

He could see them huddled in the cabin, Priscilla, her mother, and infant sister, Clara. Possibly they lived on stores for a while; maybe they had a garden and a smokehouse. But how long could they have survived?

Another article told of how some women in the hills had fallen into prostitution after the mining disaster. Some pages from the nun's journal, which had been earmarked with the librarian's yellow sticky notes, detailed the young novices' trips into the hills. They brought food and supplies. They brought offers of work for laundresses and seamstresses. Some of the younger women, those without children, returned with the nuns to town to work and live at the convent. But most did not.

They greet us with such blankness and distrust, barely able to utter their thanks. What will become of them when winter falls?

There is mention of Martha Miller and her two daughters. The librarian has highlighted a copy of the journal page. She is a known prostitute now, taking men into her home while her daughters sleep. She greets the nuns with open hostility, refuses their charity, asks where God was when the mine collapsed, taking her husband and son. I see the light of madness in her. She is sick with grief.

Fatboy stays hunched over the stack of papers, sifting, reading. All the pieces of the puzzle of Priss are laid out before him on the wood table, the lamp burning above him. But they are not coming together to form a clear picture.

What do you want, Priss?

Then the marriage certificate: Martha Miller to Nicholas Paine.

Nicholas Paine, born 1890, died 1950. Fatboy's great-grandfather, legendary for his cruelty and temper. He was a builder, like his son and grandson after him. The original company was called Paine and Son. Later, No Paine Construction.

There are no more records of Priscilla and Clara. No school records, no marriage or death certificates. The Hill People buried their own dead back then—some still did.

What happened, Priss? What did they do to you?

Then Fatboy hears his mother's voice: Why don't you just ask her?

"How's it going?"

I leaped up as if I'd been Tasered. Joy Martin issued an apologetic chuckle.

"Didn't mean to scare you."

I turned to look at her. "Did you compile all of this?" I asked.

"I did," she said. She pointed to the nameplate on her desk with one of those bright red nails. "That's my job, research librarian."

She looked somehow out of place among the old books and papers. She was all sleek and modern, all straight lines among the fuzzy vagaries of historical records.

"I gather the data. It doesn't tell the whole story, but it's a start. If you're lucky, there is enough information to start to form a picture of what might have happened."

I had to wonder, how much of what we believe about the past is actually true? In the retelling, so much is added and taken away, so much is just doing what I was doing, connecting the dots between separate events to weave a story. How much of it is extrapolation, or just plain fiction?

"What did Eloise Montgomery tell you?" I asked.

"That you have company on your property and you need to deal with it."

We might have been talking about a rodent problem, as if all I needed to do was rid myself of moles or raccoons.

"What else do you know about her?"

"Priscilla Miller?" She took off her glasses and rubbed at her eyes. She looked even younger without them. "What you see there, and some rumors, plus some stories that have traveled through the generations. Folklore."

"How reliable is that?"

"Sometimes it's more reliable than the data you see in front of you. More accurate," she said, and then paused, looking for the right words. "Energetically speaking."

"Sometimes the data doesn't tell the whole story."

"No," she said. "As a writer, you would understand that."

She took a seat. The light washed in bright through a big multipaned window. And I was reminded that it was a warm, sunny day. This was not Fatboy's hometown. It was a real place, and outside, people were living their lives. It was only my life that was on hold.

"So what's the story?" I asked.

"It's not pretty."

I lifted my eyebrows at her. "Nothing about life is pretty at the moment."

"Women didn't have a lot of options in those days, especially not around here. After her husband died, you probably read, Martha turned to prostitution. Then a few years later she married Nicholas Paine."

"My great-grandfather?"

She gave me a nod of assent.

"He was a very wealthy man, at one point he owned over a thousand acres of land. The acreage on which your house is built is the last of it. With his ready supply of lumber and his skills as a carpenter, he became a successful builder. He is credited with building over half the structures in the older parts of The Hollows."

I knew that, of course. My father bragged about it endlessly. *Our family built this town*, he used to say. That's why they could never leave. My mother wanted to go, but he couldn't. Her dreams lay fallow while he kept building and building—homes and restaurants, offices and shops, making The Hollows bigger and better. And yet my parents stayed in the same house, on the same property. *This is my home.* And he meant it in a way that people don't mean it anymore. He meant that he'd come from this place, and he was of it, and he would never leave. And he didn't. After he died, I scattered his ashes in the woods, just as he'd asked me to.

"Some people say it was love, that Martha was the only woman Nicholas Paine had ever loved," said Joy. "He lifted her and her girls out of poverty, bought the land on which her house sat. Then he built her another house, big and modern—running water, indoor toilets, heat and electricity."

I thought of Priss's house, that little shack that wasn't there. That must have been where Martha lived with her girls.

"My house is the one Nicholas Paine built?"

She nodded. "He built it on that site, yes. But the original house that Nicholas Paine built burned to the ground. Another was erected in its place, the place where your grandfather, a son by a later marriage, grew up. Then, decades later, your father gutted, remodeled, and expanded the structure again."

Burned to the ground. I remembered that night in the woods, watching Priss being engulfed by flames, her cries carrying out over the night.

Joy went on. "But other people say it wasn't *her* he loved at all. Not Martha."

I knew what she was implying. Priss was so beautiful, even as a child, impish and luminous like a fairy. I knew how consuming it was to desire her.

"There was speculation that he married Martha so that he could have Priscilla," Joy said. "After all, by the time he married Martha, she was used up. By all accounts she was nearly mad—addled by grief and loss, fallen, doubtless abused by the men who paid her for pleasure. He was a wealthy man, never married, who could have had anyone. Why would he choose some hill woman, a prostitute no less?"

The data is just the penciling of the truth, the sketch of what might be there when you start to fill in the colors. I was starting to see them all. And Joy was right: it wasn't pretty.

"You said the house burned to the ground?" I said.

"That's right."

"She died there that night. Priscilla and her sister, Clara?"

I thought of the graves, the old dilapidated church. She seemed to read my mind.

"She's still there," said Joy. "Buried in that little grave-yard just on the other side of your property line. Have you seen her grave?"

"I have," I said. "But there was no record of her death? No investigation into what caused the fire."

"I did not find a death record. They had a home funeral and buried the girls themselves, which was not at all uncommon then, and still happens today in some parts. The fire was investigated and was deemed to have been caused by bad wiring."

"That's what the records say."

Out on the street, I heard a car door slam, some voices. But the sounds seemed distant, as far away as everything else in the world. Joy sat with her hands folded, looking down, as if praying.

"The story is that Martha killed them," she said. I could see that Joy cared about the story she told. It wasn't just an impersonal history to her. "That she discovered Nicholas with Priss and blamed the girl."

"She killed both children?"

She raised her eyebrows and gave me a sad smile.

"Clara was, by all accounts, as beautiful as her sister. It was only a matter of time."

"What happened to Martha?"

I thought of my own mother, her crimes against my sister, against me. That dark place she said existed within her. Was it there before my father brought her to live on that land? Or was it living in that place? Was it like a poison in the water? Did we drink it in? Had it informed the events and choices of our life?

"After that, Martha went completely mad. Paine intended to institutionalize her, but she managed to get hold of his straight razor about a month after the fire and slit her wrists in the bathtub."

I tried to imagine the misery and pain, all that energy— fear, shame, dark depression sinking into the earth. I *could* imagine it; I could *feel* it in me.

"As for the whole truth of it, what exactly happened

the night of the fire, I don't think anyone knows that. It's buried on that land."

She was wrong. Someone did know what happened. And she wanted to tell me. Oddly, I started to think about something Binky had said when we'd been talking about my relationship to Megan. He'd asked how much time we really spent talking about Megan. Hadn't it always been about me and my problems? He wanted to know.

In that moment, I started to feel something for Priss that I had never experienced before: compassion. She'd suffered for longer than anyone deserved to suffer. I still didn't know what she wanted or if I could give it to her. But thanks to my mother, at least now I knew what I had to do.

CHAPTER TWENTY-EIGHT

As I left Joy and started down the long hallway back toward the door, my phone rang. I saw Megan's name on the screen, and I was shot through with happiness and hope. I answered right away. I had to tell her all of this.

"Meg?" I answered. "Megan, I have so much to tell you."

There was a pause and a kind of sigh. Then, "No."

Then silence, a kind of choking sound on the line. My heart did an ugly little dance.

"Meg?" I said.

I'd stopped in front of those old photographs. Why do they always look so creepy? A hundred years from now, will my photographs look strange and stilted, even haunted, to my grandchildren? "What's wrong?"

"Ian, it's Julia."

Julia, Megan's mom. All my happiness dissipated, replaced with a big dump of fear in my belly. Why would she be calling me unless something was really, deeply amiss?

"What's wrong?" I said again.

"Where is she, Ian?" Her voice was a hiss, just south of hysterical. "You tell me *right now* what you've done to her."

"What?" I said. "Nothing. Julia, what are you talking about?"

"She's *gone*," Julia said. But it was more like a moan, the last word pulling like taffy. She took a deep, shuddering breath. "You were the last one with her. People saw you screaming at her in the park."

Her voice had a wobbly pitch of terror and rage. It wasn't a scream or a sob, but it was somehow both—a mother out of control of her child's well-being. Her energy crackled over the line. I found myself suddenly trembling, adrenaline pumping—flight or fight.

"Ian," she said. "You tell me where my baby is or so help me God . . ."

"I swear, I don't know what you're talking about. What's happened? Please. Why do you have her phone?"

She started to wail then, and I heard other voices talking over her screaming. *She's missing, she's gone. My baby.* Then Binky was on the line.

"Ian," he said. He sounded calm, soothing, but I could feel his fear, too. "I implore you. Just tell us where she is."

"I don't know," I said lamely. "Please, just tell me what's happened."

My head was a siren of pain, and the world was spinning all around me. I was moving toward the front door, still clutching the phone even though the line was suddenly silent.

"Binky!" I yelled, stopping in my tracks.

I pulled the phone away from my ear and looked at the slim black device clutched in my hand. It was dead. My phone was completely out of power.

"No, no!" I shook it stupidly, issuing a string of expletives.

Then I started moving again. My mind was a dervish, planning, scheming. I'd get in the Scout and go to their house. They could see me, do what they wanted to me, but they'd know that I hadn't, would *never*, hurt their daughter. We'd find her together.

She was just hiding out, taking some time to think. Didn't she say she did that sometimes? Wouldn't anyone who'd been through what I'd put her through want to get away? And when we found her, all would be forgiven. We'd help Priss together. The house would be demolished and we'd never go back to The Hollows again. It was all going to be okay. Right? Right?

But at the door, I saw that I had company. The police had surrounded the Scout. There were three squad cars, maybe ten cops in crisp blue uniforms. They all looked suitably grim and important.

"Oh, shit," I said.

I turned to see Joy behind me. I expected her to go screaming out into the street. Instead, she looked me up and down again. Then, "There's another way out."

I didn't know why she was helping me but I followed her through the building, into a small kitchen, then through a door. We walked down a rickety set of wooden steps into the basement. We wove our way through shelves and shelves of books and records, cardboard boxes, old computers. The mold and dust stung the inside of my nose, clung to the back of my throat. Finally, she hefted open a thick metal door. It led into pitch black. A tunnel. She looked inside, and then back to me.

"Just keep walking until you can't walk any more, then reach up and unlatch the door," she said. She might have been giving me directions to the A&P, she was so unflappable and cool. "Though you might consider waiting until dark before you exit."

I didn't have that kind of time. "Where does it let out?"

"About a mile from here, near the railroad tracks."

"Thank you," I said.

She didn't answer, just closed the door with a heavy clang and locked it behind me. I didn't have time to be scared or hesitant, or even clumsy. I only had Meg on my mind as I ran through the pitch darkness, keeping my hands on the wall. I was deaf and blind like a mole, moving through the earth, only touch to guide me. How would I draw it? I thought. Just panel after panel after panel of black.

CHAPTER TWENTY-NINE

After hurrying awhile in the dark, I slowed my pace. I had a stitch in my side, and my lungs ached with the effort of running. I must have gone a mile or more. What was this place? A remnant of the Underground Railroad, an old mine tunnel? Maybe Joy was locking me in here, and the police would approach from either or both directions. Why had she helped me? Maybe she saw something in me—my innocence, my desperation.

But for the moment, there was silence, not even the sound of dripping water or the scurrying of rats. Just hard concrete beneath my feet and a great yawn of nothingness.

I tried to get my head together. Whatever I had taken earlier in the day was wearing off. In addition to my headache, I was starting to feel shaky and nauseated. I kept moving; I had to get out of here, get to Megan, wherever she'd gone.

"Priss," I screamed into the darkness. "What have you done with her?"

I thought she'd emerge from the darkness, laughing. But she didn't. I was totally alone. I picked up my pace. And just when I thought I would stay there forever, trapped, alone with my own panic and insanity, I came to the end of the tunnel, running hard into a wall. I reached up and found the latch, just as Joy promised.

I have never been so glad for the daylight. I took big gulping breaths as if emerging from deep water. I climbed up and lay on the ground, looking up at the tops of trees and bright sunlight, high cirrus clouds. It took me a minute to notice the idling white Prius. Eloise.

I pulled myself to my feet and raced to the vehicle, crashed into it. I didn't even ask Eloise how she knew where I was, figuring Joy had told her. She started driving without a word.

"Stay down," she said.

"I need to get back to the city," I told her. I tried to sink down low, but my big body and her small car were not working well together. I pulled myself into an awkward crouch.

"Your business is here," she said.

"My fiancée," I said. "She's missing. She's pregnant."

She glanced at me with something like pity on her face, but she kept driving. I slumped against the seat, trying to piece it all together, trying to understand.

"Is it revenge that she wants?" I asked. "I am the descendant of Nicholas Paine and she wants me to suffer as she has? She wants to destroy everything I love?"

Eloise gave me a look she seemed to have mastered, the teacher summoning patience for her terribly slow student.

"That's not a motive," she said. She had her hands at ten and two, her eyes on the road. She drove exactly the speed limit. I had no idea where she was going. "Revenge is not a motivator."

"You must be joking," I said. "It's a motivator as old as time."

"No, the desire for revenge is a secondary impulse," she said. She was driving faster now, keeping to the back roads. She knew this place as well as I did. Like me, she was of The Hollows. We were both trapped here, I thought. Why didn't she seem to mind?

"People act out of love or they act out of fear," she said. "Those are the only two primary motivators."

I could tell she wasn't someone worth arguing with; you couldn't change her any more than you'd change the flow of a river or the phases of the moon.

"Where are we going?" I asked. "I need to find Megan."

I was aware of a sound, distant but persistent in the air all around us. *Thwack-thwack-thwack*. Slowly, it started to dawn on me that it was the blades of a helicopter. Then I saw up ahead that a roadblock had been established. A line of twenty cars were stopped, waiting, as the police checked inside each vehicle.

"This is bad," she said. She pulled off onto a side street, moving slowly. Did anyone see? Surely that was something they looked for, people turning from the line, heading in another direction. She drove a short way, around a bend, out of sight of the other vehicles. She pulled along the edge of The Hollows Wood. I calculated that we were about five hard miles through the woods from my house—not that I could go there. Where *could* I go? Nowhere, that's where. One thing was for sure: I couldn't get myself arrested. I had to find Meg.

"I'm getting out," I said.

Her eyes darted back the way we'd come and then to me. Something in her gaze acknowledged that yes, that's precisely what I should do.

"Where are you going?"

"I don't know."

I wondered if she had some idea where I should go. She hadn't been that much help, really. Maybe she'd come through now with some great piece of advice.

"How about your place?" I suggested when she didn't say anything. I was only half kidding.

She shook her head. "You can only hide so long," she said. "It's not going to help you to hole up."

"I know," I said. I couldn't keep the exasperation out of my voice. "I have to find her and give her what she wants, right? Except I don't find her; she finds me. And she takes what she wants."

Eloise looked back again toward where we'd come. I followed her eyes, expecting to see the police pulling up. But no.

"Ian," she said. "You have it, too."

"What?"

"It's not the same as what I have," she said. "But you have some measure of my ability. Otherwise this wouldn't be happening to you. You're tapped in, you're picking up frequencies. Maybe just her frequency, but you're connected."

"Not by blood," I said.

"No," she said. "That's the least thing that connects us."

I felt so lost, so utterly inept. The hero always knows exactly what he's supposed to do. And he does it. He fights those inner battles of fear and self-doubt, and then he goes on to take on the big, external demons. He fights and wins. I was not that man. Eloise must have seen it then. She closed her eyes and shook her head, put a strong hand on my arm.

"Find her," she said. "End this. Or she'll crush you. She's so close to taking everything—your fiancée, your baby, your life. This might be your last chance."

These words were not inspiring. I fell from, more than exited, her car. Before she could issue any more soul-crushing warnings, I entered the woods and started to run. Once again, I didn't even know where I was going.

Fatboy is running through the woods, the tall black trees towering above him, branches whipping at his face, leaving angry gashes. The woods seem to fold and tip into him, tripping him, making him stumble. The Whispers around him are low but ubiquitous. Welcome home, asshole.

"Priss," he yells. His voice echoes and bounces, coming back at him in the Whispers—taunting, mocking. "What do you want?"

The woods turn around him, like a fun-house maze. He's not sure where he is, or even how to get out of the woods. Finally, his running slows. He can't run anymore. He starts walking, the sky growing dark. Even though he hadn't been heading there, he comes to a clearing, and through the trees, he sees the back of his childhood home. That's the trick of The Hollows. It always gets what it wants.

I stood in the clearing, looking at my house. I was drenched with sweat. I hadn't wanted to come here, and yet I had. It was deserted, and so quiet. No police. Was it possible that they hadn't linked me to this place yet?

No. Megan would have told Binky and Julia about it. It's the first place the police would have come. If I had done something with Megan—if I had harmed her, abducted her—surely I would have brought her here. Yes, of course. If I had killed her, I'd have brought her body back to this place. I'd have put her in the back of the Scout and carried her body out to the graveyard. Wouldn't I?

I could envision it, very clearly. I could think of how I'd draw it. I saw myself hefting her from the trunk. Bodies were heavy. Even Megan, who was a small woman, short and small-boned, would weigh more than one expected. So it would be a physical struggle.

She'd be wrapped in that Moroccan rug she'd had in her living room, the one Binky and Julia brought back from a recent trip they'd reluctantly made without her. I'd have been weeping, sick with grief and regret as I trudged through the woods. *I'msorryI'msorryMegI'msososorry.*

The trees would have bent in to watch, and the Whispers would be deafening, like the wind in a storm. I could envision it, panel by panel.

Maybe those were strange thoughts to be having, but I lost myself to them for a while—feeling the sickness of misery and dread I would surely feel if I had done something horrible to Meg.

I lingered under the tree cover, watching. Maybe the police had come and gone. Or they'd come here first and found the house empty. Or maybe they were hiding, taking up a space among the many shadows, hoping I'd turn up. When I stepped into the clearing the shadows would take their human form, as uniformed police, and they would descend upon me. Maybe they were watching me right now.

If I could just find my charger, hide for a while somewhere while my phone juiced back up, I could call Binky. And then what? Make him understand that I would never hurt his daughter.

Then, suddenly, I remembered the video. The video that had sent me running from the apartment. I had managed to press it away, deep down inside me. Now I saw it playing out now before my eyes.

I collapsed against the tree, and let myself sink to the ground. I saw the hooded figure cutting through the crowd toward Megan, her standing, oblivious to the approach of danger, listening to her music. I saw the hulking monster on the platform, the one who pushed her, and then smiled for the camera. It was not some nameless maniac assailant. It was not even Priss.

It had been me. I had pushed her onto the tracks, and hadn't even stayed to watch her die. I saw my own face in the video, wearing a horrible expression of malicious glee.

But I had no memory of this event. None. I couldn't even put myself there, despite what the detective had shown me. The detective knew when he came to my apartment that it was me. Why hadn't he arrested me on the spot? Why hadn't he called and warned Megan?

I got to my feet then, stumbled through the woods toward the graveyard. I was weeping. I mean, really sobbing like a woman. Who was I? What had I done? What was I capable of doing?

The little church rose up ahead of me, and when I reached it, I let myself fall among the graves. Priscilla, Clara, Martha. Fallen, broken, abused by circumstance and design.

"I'm sorry," I said to Priss, who wasn't there, to Megan, to our unborn child, to my sister, to my lost mother. "I'm so sorry."

And then she was there, as she always was when things were at their worst. I could see her standing behind the church—a child, a fairy, the most delicate wood sprite. We locked eyes and everything around me, all the thoughts in my head, disappeared as I was pulled into her deep blue, drowning like Ella.

"Priss, what have I done?"

And then I was with her, in another time, another world. I saw her, just a little girl, running through the night, thin white legs pumping, her face a mask of tears and terror. Her breath was ragged in my ears, her panicked heartbeat one with mine.

All the Whispers were saying the same thing over and over: *"Mommymommydon'tmommyplease."*

She ran until she fell, twisting her ankle with an ugly snap. She lay a second, then pulled herself up and started limping. But the sound of footfalls, her name being yelled into the night—they were right behind her. I felt it all in my own bones and blood—her terror and confusion. But there was nothing I could do for her. I was inside her. I was dreaming her. Her pain and fear were mine. I couldn't help her any more than she could help herself.

When I came back to myself, I was lying on the ground, doubled over. I lay there writhing from what I'd seen and felt. I thought of Eloise and what she'd said about me—that I could see things like she did. If I couldn't, this wouldn't be happening to me. There wouldn't have been this wide doorway inside me where Priss could walk through.

And that's how the police found me, weeping on the ground like a child. I never even heard the helicopter that had been tracking me through the woods with its heat-seeking technology or the police as they moved through the trees. They cuffed me and took me in. I heard the Whispers as the police car carried me off. They were laughing, of course.

CHAPTER THIRTY

Déjà vu. I am here again, surrounded by grim and accusing faces. I have been here many times—after the fires, and Marley's disappearance, after rages in bars which led to brawls, for allegedly pushing someone into traffic, after miscellaneous drunk and disorderly episodes—throwing a chair through a window at an East Village restaurant, crashing some glasses off a bar, tipping over a table.

But I haven't stood only before cops and judges. Once I was called before the disciplinary committee at Parsons for trashing the office of a teacher who'd given me a poor grade. Another time my pill dealer showed up with some muscle, claiming that I'd come to his place and robbed his stash. He was a skinny kid with spiky hair and thick black-framed glasses, not intimidating in the least. But his enforcers looked like escaped convicts on steroids, damaged, angry, high on pills. The thugs pushed their way into my East Village walk-up, roughed me up a little, then stood over me with the same face: accusatory, unyielding. Why was I always in the wrong? They didn't want the pills back; they just wanted the money. I paid them, even though I'd have sworn on my mother's life that I hadn't taken his pills. I was a pussy like that, and they were bigger and meaner. (Later that day, in the treasure box, I found a huge baggie stuffed with a rainbow, every possible color of brain-altering chemical candy. How had it gotten there?)

Every time, in the face of every accusation, I whole-heartedly pled my innocence. I wasn't lying. I *believed*. I had no memory of most of the incidents; others were fuzzy and indistinct. All of them involved Priss in some way, her whispering in my ear, or telling me what I should do, or that she'd handled it, or what that asshole on the other end of the bar had said to her.

When are you going to stop blaming me for your problems, Ian?

"Are you high, Mr. Paine?" asked the squat, dark detective who sat across from me now. "What are you on?"

I thought of the bottle of blue pills. I had no idea what they were or where they'd even come from. I couldn't have answered him if I'd wanted to.

Anyway, the problem at the moment wasn't that I was high. The problem was that I was *sober* and growing more so by the minute. My head was pounding, that migraine still looming like a storm on the horizon. I was shaking, nauseated. Had I been on something, I'd have been in much better shape.

I was starting to think that pills were my big issue. The pot, the booze—those were predictable. Weed was great—it made me happy and lazy. Booze gave me confidence, connected me to the extrovert within. But pills were cutting these jagged little holes in the fabric of my life—they altered me. I was someone different depending on every color—spaced out on red, hyper but focused on blue, blank on black, inexhaustible on purple. Dr. Crown had prescribed a mild antidepressant for me years ago. And ever since then, I'd been on something or other— Ambien to sleep, Ativan for anxiety. Not to mention the recreational drug use, the stuff I got from dealers. You really weren't supposed to mix either. And I did. All the time.

"I want a lawyer," I said.

He leveled a reptilian stare at me, cool and menacing.

"Where is she?" he asked. He kept his voice low. "Is she alive?"

The question jarred me, brought reality crashing back into focus. Megan was *missing*. It wasn't a dream or something I'd drawn; the woman I loved had fallen down Priss's rabbit hole.

Panic pulsed through me, and my belly went to acid. What did Priss want? Did she want me? Did she want Megan? Did she want our child? Did she just want to destroy my life, what was left of my sanity? And why? For vengeance?

It didn't seem like that could be right. Eloise had said that revenge wasn't a primary motivator. And as I thought about it, it *did* seem watery and insubstantial as far as a motive. Because there is no revenge, not really. I knew this because of my mother. You might seek punishment for someone who wronged you, and you might even find it. But nothing fixes the wrong thing, nothing makes it better, or hurt less. Not even hurting the person who hurt you. That just makes you feel worse. The only one you can really punish is yourself.

People act out of love or they act out of fear. It had sounded overly simplistic to me at first. But I was starting to believe that Eloise was right. Because fear and love have a million different shades and textures, present themselves in all sorts of complicated hues and colors.

No, Priss didn't want revenge. Our relationship was so much more complicated than that; we had been together for a long time. We were completely entwined in so many sick and unhealthy ways that I didn't even know where I ended and she began. I had to get out of this police station to find her. But my hand was cuffed to a metal bar on the table.

"Mr. Paine? Are you with me?"

The detective had been talking, and I'd heard his voice. But I'd been listening to my own manic thoughts; he was no competition.

"Yes," I said.

"You had an altercation with your fiancée in Central Park. What were you fighting about?"

I closed my eyes and tried to remember exactly what had happened. What had I said to Megan that caused her to look at me with such pain on her face? But there was a white noise blocking out my memory of the encounter.

I wanted to say: *I asked her to run away with me and she wouldn't. I wanted to take her somewhere far from Priss and all her little games. But she wouldn't go.* I could hardly say that, could I? It didn't sound good at all. It sounded downright crazy, actually. So I didn't say anything.

"Tell me about the fire in your apartment," he said. He'd obviously decided to change tack.

"What fire?"

"There was a small fire," he said. "The super put it out fairly quickly. Looks like something was left on the range top. Papers. What were you burning?"

A small fire? The super had put it out? In my memory, I saw the flames licking at my windows. Okay, I hadn't burned the building down. That was good.

"Nothing," I said. "I didn't start that fire."

"Witnesses saw you leaving with a bunch of your belongings shortly before the fire alarms started going off."

I remember sitting in the parked Scout, watching the orange glow. But the time between meeting Megan in the park and that moment was gone. Whatever small measure of relief I'd felt just now disappeared with the bubble of dread that was swelling in my stomach.

"No," I said.

"Any idea who started it, then?"

I shrugged. What a punk I must seem like to him. Did he see my fear? My confusion? Or did he just see a criminal, an arsonist and possibly a killer, sitting before him? But his wide face was blank, his demeanor rock solid. Jones Cooper had shown temper, emotion. He was mad at me for being a screw-up, for lying. This guy—Ferrigno, he'd said his name was—gave nothing.

"Who else has access to your apartment, then?" he asked.

Another question I couldn't answer.

"Look," I said. "I need to get out of here." And this elicited a patient smile from the detective.

"We have a lot to talk about," he said. "Whatever other commitments or plans you happen to have are going on hold until we find your fiancée, okay? Her parents are here, you know."

The thought of facing Binky and Julia made me physically ill. I could only imagine their terror. And of all the accusing faces I'd met in my life, theirs would be the worst.

"I don't know where she is," I said. "I wish I did."

I heard how it sounded, hollow and disaffected. But I couldn't be further from that. I was jittery with my need to get out of there and find Meg.

They probably had enough to hold me for a while as a person of interest, even if they couldn't charge me with anything yet. On television, they have to let you go for this reason or that reason. But in real life, they have all sorts of little tricks for keeping you. I thought the next question would be about Detective Crowe, but it wasn't. I certainly had no intention of bringing this up.

The detective got up and started pacing. "Can you run down the day for me? Give me a time line?"

Uh, no, not really.

I grasped at it. With effort, I pieced it back together.

I came back from Long Island, found out that I was being evicted from my apartment, that my money was gone, went with Meg to meet Priss, who never showed, came back to find my place trashed. Priss was there when I got back. Detective Crowe came to see me. I saw a video of myself pushing Megan onto the subway tracks. Priss knocked him out; I ran like the coward I am. Feeling the boom about to be lowered, I went to get Megan. I remembered her in the park, looking at me with that shocked expression of pain. Then I was in the Scout, the back of it packed with essential belongings.

I didn't tell him any of that, but I felt irrationally proud that I had at least some grasp on what had recently transpired in my life.

Instead I said, "I need a lawyer."

He came back to the table, took a seat.

"We're running out of time here, Ian." He was going for gentle, earnest.

"I want a lawyer."

From a small table by the door, he retrieved an iPad. He brought it over and pushed it toward me. I could see from the frozen frame that he was about to show me the surveillance video from the tracks.

"I'm serious," I said, as if I needed to make that clear. "I need to talk to a lawyer. Right now."

He pressed the triangle on the screen and it played. I wanted to look away, but I couldn't. I was transfixed by that hooded figure moving through the crowd. I watched poor Megan get pushed again, saved again. I watched the train enter the station, Meg lying on the platform, a crowd forming around her. I watched the figure walk toward the camera.

"Stop it," I said, moving to grab the tablet. "I've seen it."

But he moved it out of my reach, held it up so I could see. But when the hooded figure turned his face up to the screen, Ferrigno pressed the pause button. Then I just stared at it, leaned in close, and took it from him. It wasn't me on the screen. It was Fatboy.

CHAPTER THIRTY-ONE

Or rather someone wearing a Fatboy mask, part of that merchandising initiative my publisher had launched late last year—the rubber mask with obese jowls and an angry red-and-white field of acne, empty holes for eyes. He wore a crazed, toothy smile in that mask; I don't know why. In the books, Fatboy almost never smiles. There had been Priss masks, too, and long red wigs. But those didn't do as well—maybe because the rest of Priss was so hard to imitate. Her huge bust and impossibly small waist, those meaty but shapely thighs, that heart-shaped ass—she was a male fantasy. No woman alive ever looked like a comic book girl.

I sat staring, transfixed. The figure looked smaller than it had the first time I'd seen it. But the black hood, the black T-shirt . . . both were innocuous. There were no other clues as to who it might be behind the mask.

"Who is that?" he asked. He nodded toward the frozen frame.

"I don't know." My brain hurt; I was having that mental brownout again, the internal lights flickering. I was dull and heavy, more like myself than I liked to feel. I'd have given anything to pop something, anything, in my mouth, to feel that wash of something other than my own addled thoughts.

"Was there someone else in your apartment when Detective Grady Crowe came to talk to you?"

I didn't have an answer. I had wondered when this subject was going to come up.

"He said you kept looking behind him. Then, when you saw that video, you ran. He gave chase but you took the stairs and he said you were in pretty good shape, and him not so much. By the time he got to the street, you were gone. He couldn't get back into the apartment."

So, she didn't hit him? He wasn't dead or hurt? Oh man, I didn't need a lawyer, I needed a doctor. I needed a room next to my mom at the crazy house. I pressed my head into my free hand.

"Work with me," Ferrigno said. He kept his voice soft and low. It was almost soothing. "What's happening? Where is Megan?"

I couldn't talk to this guy. I couldn't tell him any of this. Surely, they'd lock me away and I'd never find my way back to Megan. I needed help and I could only think of one person who could help me, improbable as my choice was.

"I want to talk to Jones Cooper," I said, after long seconds passed by.

Detective Ferrigno stood and walked over toward the door. I thought he was going to leave but he leaned against the wall. He had a gray, unhealthy look to him, a big paunch, dark rings under his eyes. He was a guy who wasn't taking good care of himself, and it was starting to take a toll.

"Jones Cooper isn't a cop anymore," said the detective. "He's retired, a couple of years now. I'm afraid you'll have to talk to me."

I knew Cooper was still in town, that he was working as a private investigator. I'd read about it in *The Hollows Gazette* during a visit a couple of years back. He'd saved some girl from drowning. When I'd been younger, he'd rescued a boy from a mine. He was that kind of guy, the everyday hero type, the guy you called when there was trouble.

"I'll talk to him and no one else." I was in no position to be making demands. But I figured that they were pretty motivated to find Megan.

"You have to talk to me," Ferrigno said again. He moved back across the room and leaned forward on the table between us. "Let me help you."

I moved in closer to him.

"If you don't let me talk to him, we'll never find her." My voice had come out in a kind of weird, crackling whisper.

A frown creased his brow, and he leaned back.

I saw that look, that confused, skeptical look I knew so well. It was the look people gave you when they thought you were nuts. Some kind of battle played out on his face as he assessed the situation, calculated his options. I held the detective's gaze until he got up and left the room.

Jones Cooper arrived within an hour of my request, looking fit and fresh-faced. Retirement agreed with him. And it was a relief to see him, someone familiar, someone honest. When he sat across the table, a dam burst inside me. I told him everything, really laid it all bare, the total truth about everything, then and now. He took it all in with a series of nods and affirming noises; a camera mounted at the far end of the room winked at me with a red eye. They were recording it all, I knew. And that was fine. I had nothing to lose at this point. All I cared about was Megan.

"So," he said when I was done. "You're saying that Priss has something to do with this. You think she's done something with Megan."

He didn't believe me; I could see that.

"I don't understand how it works," I said. I sounded like a desperate, crazy liar. "But I know that she manipulates things. Like luring Marley into the woods, or my mother back to our house, in turn causing me to follow."

"Okay," he said. "I get it."

"Eloise Montgomery told me that I need to figure out what she wants."

I knew he and Eloise knew each other. I'd read about that in the paper, too.

"Did she?" he asked. He cleared his throat, got a little frown. He didn't like her, or he distrusted her—or something. Maybe she just made him uncomfortable, as she did me. "When did she tell you that?"

"Years ago," I answered. "And just recently."

He gave me a careful nod, seemed about to say something but then changed his mind.

"I have to go there to see her, back to the graveyard," I said. "I think that's what she wants."

He stood. "Okay," he said. "Let me see what I can do."

He paused at the door, again seemed about to say something. Then he turned the knob to exit.

"Do you believe me?" I said.

It was a childish question and one I'd asked many times of many people. I'd never yet gotten the answer I wanted.

"I believe that you believe it, son."

"You said that you did," I said. "All those years ago, you told me that you believed me, finally, about her. You told me to leave The Hollows and not come back."

"I wish you'd taken that advice."

"How could I?" I said. "This place. It calls you back. It doesn't like it when you try to leave forever. I think you know that."

He pursed his lips and gave a slight shake of his head—pretending that he didn't know what I was talking about.

"You said you believed me back then."

Cooper rubbed his jaw. "I told you that I know enough about this place to understand that there are things beyond my explaining. And that's why I'm here."

It was all I was going to get from him.

"Okay."

What had I expected from a man like him, so grounded, so locked into the real world? I envied him his solid footing, while I was sinking deeper into the quicksand.

He left the room then. When he came back a few minutes later, he unlocked the cuff that held me to the table. I rose, rubbing my wrist, which had a big, angry red mark on it, and followed him out the door.

Everyone in the station watched me go—including Binky and Julia. The two of them stood in an office, behind a big glass window, Detective Ferrigno beside them. Julia looked as if she'd aged twenty years; I wanted to comfort her, assure her that I'd never hurt Megan, but I kept seeing that Fatboy mask, that look on Meg's face. Shame has always been a wall between me and other people, keeping me separate, alone. Julia laid a hand on the glass. She was crying. Her eyes said: *Please, bring my baby home.* I made her a silent promise. *I am going to do that. I will give my life to do that.*

I suppose they let me go only because they figured I would lead them to Megan. I knew no one believed me, not even Cooper. No one was trying to help me; no one cared if Priss was real or not, or what she wanted. Finding

Meg was their only agenda, as it should have been. I didn't expect anyone to believe that it was *my* only agenda, too.

Outside, I climbed into Cooper's big maroon SUV. On his visor was a photograph of a pretty middle-aged woman and a young man who was a slimmer, cooler (tats, earring, punky hair) version of Cooper. The car was meticulously clean, dash shining, not a piece of lint on the carpet.

In my books, the detective is a bad man, someone corrupt and sadistic. He's quasi-obsessed with Fatboy, thinks he's the liar, the criminal who has escaped the detective's grasp. The detective is one of the book's villains. But Cooper was not a villain. He was a good man, the kind of man I wanted to be if I ever grew up. Why was it so hard to be that kind of man?

We drove through the gloaming and the world was pink and gold. The Hollows was a pretty place when it wanted to be, drawing you in, enticing you to stay awhile. It was lovely and welcoming, until you wanted to leave.

We pulled up to my house, and it was still and dark. I got out of the car and so did Cooper. The sun had nearly set, but there was still light glowing in the western part of the sky. Cooper moved around to my side of the car. I could see that he was armed, the leather of his shoulder holster visible through his open jacket.

"I have to go in alone," I said.

He nodded, shoved his hands in his pockets. "I figured as much."

I started to walk toward the woods.

"You know it's over, right?" he said. I turned to face him. He went on. "I mean, if you're trying to pull a fast one. There's no other way out of these woods. You're physically surrounded. There's the chopper, the state police, and all of their surveillance equipment. You're not just going to walk into those woods and disappear."

"No," I said.

He was right. But there was a lot more, too much, that he could never understand. I walked into the trees. The Whispers had gone silent.

CHAPTER THIRTY-TWO

Fatboy approaches the graveyard. The moon is a giant red ball, hanging low in the sky, and the night sky is starless pitch. The whole graveyard is washed in a shimmering orange, the light from the moon. An owl watches, eyes glowing gold. The Native Americans believed that the owl was a symbol of wisdom and strength, the great hunter. But other cultures saw it as the symbol of death and illness, the destroyer that sweeps in soundlessly to carry off your young. Its eyes follow Fatboy as he moves among the graves—Martha, Clara, Priscilla. And the tiny graves of the other children—who were they? How did they die? Miscarriage, illness, accident, murder. Death claims us all, even the most innocent among us.

He is still and watching as she emerges from the trees. Not the woman he knows, but the girl she has always been, will always be. Fatboy sits on a tree stump and the trees sway and whisper all around him. He understands now. All this time he has been coming into the woods, Priss has been comforting him, championing him, defending him. She does for him what she couldn't have done for herself.

He holds out his arms to her and she walks to him, seats herself on his lap, and lays her head upon his shoulder. He enfolds her, holds her as he would his own child, the one growing inside Molly.

"Tell me what they did to you, Priss."

She lifts her head and whispers in his ear.

He sees her. She's just a little girl alone in the night,

frightened in her bed. He watches as the door drifts open and a large, dark form snakes in with the light.

Oh, you're beautiful, so beautiful.

The little girl still remembers her father and how good he was. How he made her toys and carried her on his shoulders, and how she knew that nothing bad could ever happen when he was home. He had been strong, not like her mother, who was weak and frightened—shattered by the loss of her first husband and only son. Her mother was a delicate person, uniquely fit for caring for children and making a home but for little else.

"He'll take care of us," *her mother said of Mr. Paine. And after the long nights of listening to her mother lie with a parade of strange men—some of them polite, some of them angry, all of them dirty and ugly to the core, Priss hoped that her mother was right. Because someone needed to take care of them—even Priss could see that. She no longer went to school; she alone now cared for Clara because her mother was too tired, too lost to be of any good to them.*

"Don't judge me," *her mother begged.* "A woman only has one source of power."

Was that true? Priss didn't know.

Didn't her mother know what was happening to Priss? That the man who was supposed to act as her new father was putting his hands on her, using her body, making her dirty and sick inside. She didn't dare tell. He said she'd better not say a word, or he'd kill her—and there was Clara still, who was just as lovely, maybe even lovelier.

Then her mother found them. Him, that nasty old man, in her daughter's bed. And all she did was turn around and walk away, leaving them to it. Priss died inside that night. And her mother did, too. Priss could see her sinking deeper and deeper into that black place she went to. She stopped looking at Priss, stopped touching her. Even before they'd lost Daddy and her brother, her mother had sometimes gone so dark, a ghost moving through the house, not talking, not washing.

"It's just the melancholy," her father would say. "It will pass."

And it always had before. But not this time. She sank deeper, further. She wasn't coming back.

And then Priss was walking up a darkened hallway toward the new indoor bathroom. She pushed open the door, and saw her mother leaning over the tub. Mama was singing the song she always sang when she gave Clara a bath:

> Little flowers in the garden
> Yellow, orange, violet, blue
> Little angels in the garden
> Do you know how I love you?

"Mama?" she ventured. But her mother didn't turn around. There was something so strange about her voice.

> Little flowers in the garden
> Growing tall toward skies of blue
> Little flowers in the garden
> Oh, your mama so loves you.

Priss walked slowly, the wood cold beneath her feet. When she drew near to her mother's narrow, bent back, she saw Clara, lying gray and still beneath the water's surface, her eyes open, mouth open. Priss saw the fear, the confusion on her sister's life-less face. She drew in a sharp breath, everything in her running cold with fear, and started moving backward. But her mother turned and saw her.

"Time for your bath, Priscilla."

She was dull and blank, not her mother at all, but a ghoul. In her eyes, there was a sucking, nightmarish emptiness. A hole without a bottom, swallowing the light. Priscilla turned and ran, with her mother shrieking after her. She stumbled down the stairs and out the front door, into the woods. She heard her *mother thundering after her, screaming her name into the night.*

Pleasemamapleasedon'tpleasedon't.

The words came out in the stream of her breath. She might have gotten away, found a place to hide, even made it to town. But she stepped on a stone and turned her ankle hard, falling to the ground. She got up and limped, but her mother was behind her.

She laid herself down finally, so tired and hurt. Her mother came to stand over her.

Pleasemamapleasemamadon'tpleasedon't.

All she remembers is her mother leaning down and picking her up, carrying her home while she wept. There was no fight left in her. Maybe, just maybe, it was all a dream.

The next thing she was aware of was the burning in her throat and lungs, and the leaden fatigue that numbed her mind and made her limbs feel like lead. And even though she saw the flames creeping toward their beds, there was nothing in her that could lift her from the bed. They were all gone—her father, her brother, Clara. Even the mother she knew had been inhabited by something dark, not of this world. Her real mama never would have hurt them so. And so when the flames came, she almost welcomed them, even though the final things she heard were the sounds of her own keening.

Fatboy sees the flames licking through the trees and Priss isn't on his lap anymore. He runs, runs toward the burning house where he'd first seen her standing in the doorway. He can hear her screaming inside, and he bursts through the door—for the first time in his life not thinking about himself.

But he is late, far too late. He sees Priss and Clara in their beds, both of them still and lifeless as the flames engulf them, the wall of heat driving him back outside, where Martha slumps against a tree, staring into the flames.

"You killed them," he screams into the night. "You killed them both."

But she is a million miles and a hundred years away. She doesn't hear him.

I sat outside the house that wasn't there and watched the flames lick the night. I found a spot beside a tree and sat. There was no heat, no smell. It was just a picture in a book. The image of Priss lying in her bed, letting the flames swallow her, stayed seared into my mind's eye like the red impression left after staring at the sun.

And then I was aware of Priss standing beside me. Not the woman I knew, but the girl I first met when I was only a boy myself.

"I'm sorry," I said. "I'm sorry for everything that happened to you."

I meant it. There was a deep sorrow within me, a well of compassion I never knew existed. She was silent, watching the flames until they disappeared and everything around us turned to quiet night.

I could sense that we were not alone. I knew that the woods were surrounded, as Cooper had promised they would be. I thought I could hear the distant sound of chopper blades. They were looking for Megan, and so was I. I couldn't let Priss make me forget why I was here.

That's what she wanted, wasn't it? For me to abandon the present, to live with her in the memories of her ugly past—and mine. Isn't it easier to wallow in anger and misery over the wrongs that have been done to you than to let go, to forgive, and move forward? What is it about unhappiness that is so comfortable, so familiar? Priss and I had kept each other locked in place—my rage and addictions keeping me in her thrall, her righteous anger feeding mine. We'd both been victims. But we weren't victims anymore; we'd become perpetrators.

"You didn't deserve it," I said. "I wish I had been there to protect you. I would have."

She moved over and sat on my lap, and I took her into my arms. She was real, flesh and bone, but so cold, so brittle.

"But you're here now," she whispered. "And you'll never leave me, will you?"

I felt the tickle of fear. Eloise had told me to find out what Priss wanted and give it to her. Did she mean that I had to give myself over, if that's what Priss wanted? I couldn't do that anymore. Could I?

"Where's Megan?" I said.

She pushed herself roughly away from me. When I looked at her again, she was the woman I knew. I bit back that familiar twist of fear and desire. *You're trying to give her up like people try to give up heroin.* I still wanted her, even though she was destroying my life. I could feel her pull.

"She came looking for you," she said. She folded her arms. "She thinks she loves you."

It was the thought of Megan that made me strong. I stood and faced Priss, prepared to stand up to her once and for all. Megan told me that it was time to choose. In my heart, I had already chosen. I just needed to say the words. If only I wasn't so tired.

"We've been together for a long time," I said.

"Forever," she said.

"But it's time for me to let you go," I said. I moved in closer. "I need you to find peace. You can't go on like this. Raging through the millennia. Aren't you tired, Priss? Don't you want to rest?"

She bowed her head but didn't answer. She just took my hand and led me back toward the graveyard. I didn't want to follow her, but I did. All around us I could hear the Whispers, soothing now like a lullaby.

Little flowers in the garden.

"What do you want?" I asked. I wasn't just asking Priss. I was asking the Whispers, too. "What do you want from me?"

"Aren't you tired, Ian?" Her question was an echo of mine. Coming back at me, it was almost hypnotic. "Aren't you tired of fighting everyone and everything? Neither one of us ever really belonged anywhere except with each other."

She was right. Everything else had always been a struggle—other people, school, work, the day-to-day of life, even Megan. All of it required that I hold big parts of myself inside. But out here with Priss, it had always been so easy. I never had to hide anything from her. She accepted all of me, even my worst, ugliest self. For better or for worse, she was my soul mate.

We had met, like any two souls meet. We had wrapped around each other and never parted. Eloise was wrong. Our relationship wasn't a haunting. It was a love story.

Yellow, orange, violet, blue.

The dilapidated church was a hulking shadow. And the graves had all but disappeared in the wild grass. It was untended and forgotten, which was a shame. The souls there deserved remembrance. I sank down to the ground, fatigue tugging at my limbs. I allowed myself to lean against the thick trunk of an oak. The reasons I'd come here—to claim myself, to find Megan—seemed distant and dreamlike. In my pocket, I discovered a bottle of pills that I knew hadn't been there. I took them out and held them in my hand. How I wanted to swallow them. All of them. Let them take me wherever they wanted.

Little angels in the garden.

"Before your mother came, I was forgotten," she said.

"There was no one who knew my name. She was the first person to see me in ages. No one else had ever wanted to play—not even your father."

I felt a cold trickle, a sudden dawning. *She's not your friend*, Eloise had said. *Not really.*

"She used to come out here when you were sleeping," Priss said. I could see my mother walking through the woods, remembered what she'd said about following a little girl through the trees. "She was so sad. And there's so much sadness here. It finds the empty places and hooks through, pulls tight, like vines on a trellis. I thought she'd stay with me."

She knelt down, then straddled my legs and moved her fingers through my hair.

"But she had you," she whispered. "And then Ella. She wouldn't stay with me. There was too much calling her away."

The sound of Ella's name on her tongue brought me out of the stupor into which I'd been slipping. I was suddenly awake and alive, listening. "Miriam had such a deep, dark place in her, just like my mother. It opened up and swallowed her."

Do you know how I love you?

"She went away," said Priss. "But then you came. And from that first day I knew you'd stay with me."

She pressed her lips to mine, and I drank in all that warmth. But then I pulled myself back.

Little flowers in the garden.

"I can't stay here," I said. I put a hand on her white, white face. This was as tender as we'd ever been with each other. "You have to let me go. I don't belong here."

"You do," she said. "*We* do."

And she was a little girl again, sitting on my lap, desperate and sad. I could see what she wanted suddenly, what she had needed all those years ago. What she had needed when she'd been alive. I ran my hand down the back of her hair. It was brittle, strands coming away in my hand, little slivers of copper wire.

"But it wasn't me that you wanted, was it?" I said. "It was my mother."

Whatever it was about this strange, haunted place, whatever lived here, it had taken her mother. And she had wanted mine.

"I loved her," she said. "She saw me and she would have taken care of me. But she left and you stayed. *You* wanted to be with me."

"Because I had nothing else," I said. A flicker of anger came alive within me. "Because this place took everything bright and good in my life."

That was the vacancy that Priss had occupied. If my mother had been whole and well, if my sister had lived—I wouldn't have been vulnerable to Priss and the energies that had us both trapped here. There would have been no room for her. But isn't that true of all addictions? It's just a way to fill the dark places some of us have inside. The hole in me was the size and shape of my mother. Priss expanded to fill it, became that and so much more.

"You love me," she said. She said it simply, without her usual flair for drama. "You always have."

Of course, it was true. I had always loved her. But it was a love that grew from loss and sorrow. I'm not sure if that made it any less real. Maybe it was even more powerful because of that—it clung, held on, fought for its own survival.

My love for Megan was something different. It was tame and healthy—not wild and thrashing, not desperate and smothering. It was grounded and right, a foundation on which we might build a real life. But I could see I wouldn't be able to make Priss understand that. She was a child's spirit. She wanted to be loved. She wanted to be cared for in the way that every child deserves. She raged when she didn't get her way. And her rage was a feral, dangerous thing.

"I do," I said. "I do love you."

She wrapped her arms around my neck, sank into me, sweet and soft. And I knew that I could stay here with her. A part of me even wanted to. Except that now there was something calling me away as well.

That's when I smelled smoke. I spun in the direction of my childhood home. The area where it stood glowed a harsh white beneath the tree line. Then, far in the distance, the thin music of approaching sirens. My heart clutched, and the real world came crashing back.

"What did you do?" I asked her.

She pulled herself away and moved into the trees with a smile.

"What I've *always* done," she said. "Exactly what you wanted me to do, whether you'll admit it or not."

And then she was gone.

CHAPTER THIRTY-THREE

With everything I had in me, I ran. The ground was soft beneath my feet and the woods seemed to slow my sprint toward the house. I tripped twice, but finally stumbled into the clearing. Where was Cooper? Where were the cops? I thought they'd all be there, waiting. But no, it was just me and the burning house.

The flames were eating through the roof, great orange, red, white, blue fingers clawing at the starless sky. The heat and the roar of the fire were living things, wild beasts growling, warning me to come no closer. But, for once, I overcame my inherent cowardice and ran toward the house and up the porch steps. As I burst through the door, the blistering air and heavy, choking fumes knocked me back. But I pushed my way in, immediately starting to cough.

"Megan," I screamed. But my voice was already lost to the fire, my throat crackling with it.

Distantly, I heard a rhythmic banging. I pulled the collar of my shirt up around my nose and pushed my way toward the back of the house, where the sound seemed to originate.

The whole structure was creaking and groaning, and the sound of the flames was the sound of the Whispers, chattering with malicious glee. Curtains were curling, linoleum tiles cracking; the couch was on fire. And the heat was a presence, settling on my skin, snaking up my nose and down my throat.

Priss was right, I realized suddenly. I *loved* watching this ugly, sad little place burn. It was so much better than having it demolished while I sat in New York City, far from the action.

I watched my childhood and all its shitty, mean memories be consumed. The smoke was insidious, a drug, the ultimate quaalude. I felt myself grow wobbly and weak, taken over by the poison in the air. I could have easily laid myself down among the flames and let them take me. I would have died like Priss died nearly a hundred years ago. Physically able to save myself, but so wrecked inside that I just let the flames have my body. There was a kind of poetry in that. It was an apt ending to a sad, sad story.

But it was the banging that brought me back to myself. Slow and rhythmic, right beneath me. I pulled myself back from the quicksand of my self-destructive thoughts—just barely.

I tried to scream for Megan again, but I couldn't get enough air in my lungs. This was how it happened, I realized. It wasn't the flames but the smoke—just like they always said. Priss just let it take her, because she was a little girl who had lost everything, because she didn't have any fight left in her. But I wasn't Priss. I had a lot to live for, and I was going to fight for once. For once I was going to act like a man.

In the kitchen, I stopped and listened past the raging noise of the fire. The banging had stopped. I called Megan's name again, or tried to. It came out as a strangled cough. I made it up the staircase and moved from room to room—my parents', mine, Ella's old nursery. I pushed my way through thick smoke, then went back downstairs.

Back in the kitchen, I heard the banging again, this time faint and weak. That's when I remembered the door to the basement. I rested my hands upon the surface; it was cool to the touch. I threw it open to see a yawning darkness and climbed down the steps. It was another world down there, free from flames and heat. It was as quiet as a tomb. I could breathe, the air blessedly clear. Upstairs, I heard something heavy fall and the very foundation of the house creaked and shuddered.

My father had refinished a room down there, the guest room for a family that never had any guests. I remembered that it had a twin bed and a high small window. Sometimes in the summer, he slept down there.

I saw his workbench and tools off to the right. He used to bring things back here from building sites and fix them—or he'd build cabinets for some of the jobs. He'd make the occasional table or rocking chair. He was good at it; he liked fixing broken things. Giving something that didn't work a second life. I was one of those people he always complained about. *People just throw things away nowadays. They just replace, never repair.* I couldn't wait to get rid of the old things.

It was so quiet. "Megan," I said. "Are you down here?"

Megan? Are you down here? I hated it when Priss mocked my voice. It really made me angry.

"Where is she?"

Where is she?

She moved out of the darkness. But she wasn't the little girl or the woman I knew. She was an old woman, bent over and gray. She wore that same cotton shift, but her limbs were as spindly and thin as knotted old wood, and her hair was straw. She was as ancient as the trees and mountains, as the hills around The Hollows. Those eyes, though, those blue, blue eyes, were as bright and hypnotic as ever.

I was not afraid of her; I never had been. What I *have* feared is my life without her, whatever she is. Without her, I would just be myself in this cold and wicked world.

And I have always been so desperately afraid that I could never be enough.

"What do you want, Priscilla? If you let them go, I'll give it to you."

If you let them go, I'll give it to you.

She moved in close to me, and I let her. She smelled of centuries—mold and dust and decay. There was something oddly comforting about the scent. It was familiar like the smell of wet ground, or rain, or fallen leaves in a pile on the lawn. I put my hands on her dry and withered shoulders, and she whispered in my ear. But, of course, I already knew the answer, had known it all along.

"Yes," I said.

She drew back from me, and smiled. Then she laid herself down on the ground by the stairs and I watched as she became the woman I have desired and loved. Then she was the little girl who saved me one desperate night in the woods. And finally she turned to a pile of ash on the floor at my feet. I knelt beside her and wept for her. Boys do cry. We cry all the time.

I lifted my head and called for Megan. And my voice sounded like the wail of an animal.

"Where is she, Priss? What have you done to her?"

When I looked back, I saw that in her place before me lay Megan. She was ghostly pale and frighteningly still, with one leg terribly bent, a pool of blood beneath her head.

I burst into action, stumbled and nearly fell over myself trying to get to her. I knelt beside her and whispered her name. Her eyes fluttered, and she looked at me.

"I saw her," she whispered. "I did."

"You saw Priss?"

"I saw her," she said. "You were right. She's real."

"I have to get us out of here," I told her. I had no idea if I could. Above us I could hear a riot of sound, crashing and the roar of flames. I lifted her, and she cried out in pain.

"No, Ian," she said. There was panic and pain in her voice. "You can't."

But there was no choice. Carry her out and possibly hurt her worse than she was already hurt or allow both of us to die in the basement of my childhood home. There was no way I was going to die here, or let Megan and our child die here.

I lifted her as carefully as I could. She lost consciousness again as I carried her up the stairs. The smoke was moving toward us like a noxious beast. I was weak, and I started to feel overcome again as soon as I made it up the stairs.

But still I moved, one foot in front of the other as the flames raged and the house groaned around me. A beam from the ceiling fell in front of me, blocking my way to the back door. It wanted us to stay, to die here with Priss. But I turned and headed into the flames that seemed to block our way to the front. If we died here, it wouldn't be because I had given up.

Then I saw her everywhere, all around me in the flames, her shape, the color of her hair. Wherever I saw her, that was where I headed. And so, following the shade of Priss, I managed to move us through the fire. Finally, I stumbled out the front door and onto the porch. I turned back and watched the flames become a wall and heard the roof collapse. I turned with Megan still in my arms and ran. A crowd of policemen with guns drawn surrounded me.

Put the girl down, and put your hands in the air.

The firefighters raced past me, and I heard a woman screaming. Julia. Someone took Megan from my arms. And I fell to my knees, put my hands on my head. But the world around me was just a field of stars. I turned back to the burning house and looked for Priss, but she wasn't there.

CHAPTER THIRTY-FOUR

Weeping, Fatboy stumbles through the night and finds his way to the garage of his childhood home. Just as he remembers, there is a can of gasoline that the maintenance guy uses to fill the lawn mower. He picks it up and carries it inside.

In the drawer next to the stove there is the box of matches. It has always been there, to light the old oven. He takes it out and stuffs it in the pocket of his baggy jeans. Then he starts to walk around the house, leaving a careful trail of gas from the kitchen to the small living room, up the small stairway into the three bedrooms, then back down again.

He starts with the curtains in the front of the house and lights them on fire, watching as the flame starts out as a tiny lick of light and quickly grows. The flames twist and turn like dancers. He is transfixed by their heat and light. Then he walks, scattering lit matches along the trail of gasoline. The flames travel quickly.

He knows what to do. He has done it before. He has set fire to a bully's house, to the classroom of a teacher who betrayed him. He is the fire starter, not Priss, though he has always had her whispering in his ear, telling him what to do. He knows that now. All the memories, the blank spaces, are frighteningly clear. Since he found her in the woods so long ago, they have always been together. They have twisted around each other, a helix of anger and fear, creating nothing but damage.

He wished, always wished, that he was a better person, but he wasn't. Every bad thing for which he blamed her, he has done himself. He pushed his partner in front of that car. There was a rage inside him, a beast that made Priss look like a kitten. It was the rage that was his enemy, his addiction.

Fatboy watches his house burn to the ground. He sits against the tall oak on the other side of the driveway and takes in the show. He is happy to watch the place burn, glad that his past is about to be turned into a pile of ash. His future is suddenly clear.

He cannot go back to Molly. He knows that. He never deserved that kind of life—a happy, normal life with a wife and child. He could not leave The Hollows, or Priss. They are all one entity, indivisible from each other. He understands what she wants, what she needs. She needs him. He needs her. She needs him to stay here with her forever.

Priss walks out from the trees and he rises to greet her. She moves into him and wraps her arms around him. He puts his mouth to hers, and she tastes and feels like fire. She is all heat, fuel for the rage that burns inside him. They were made for each other, many lifetimes ago, and so they will remain.

She moves away and leads him by the hand. He follows without a fight as they both walk into the fire and are consumed.

Zack was a guy who liked a happy ending. But, you know, things didn't always work out that way. And it *was* a happy ending of sorts. Fatboy and Priss did belong together. He could never live without her, not after he'd faced his own guilt. In a way, it was like the ultimate love story. They couldn't survive without each other and they wouldn't have to. Didn't we all want a love that lasted into eternity?

"That depends on how you look at it," I said. "Did Fatboy die?"

"He walked into a burning house and never came out," said Zack. "There aren't too many ways to interpret that."

"Are you familiar with the first law of the conservation of energy?"

"Uh, no, I guess not."

"Energy cannot be created or destroyed. It can only change form."

A baffled silence. "Okay."

"It's the right ending, Zack. Trust me."

"I mean, don't get me wrong. It's a *great* ending—exciting, explosive. But *emotionally*, I think your readers are going to want more than this."

He seemed really young to me suddenly. And I felt old and battle-worn, trying to explain the world I knew to a child. *We don't always get a happy ending, son*, I wanted to say. Life is about compromise. Sometimes you get good enough.

"What do you think they want?" I asked. "The readers, I mean."

"I think they want to see Fatboy break free from Priss. They want him to do penance for his sins. But ultimately, I think they want him to end up happy with Molly. Free."

"And what about Priss? What happens to her? Seems like she's always getting the fuzzy end of the lollipop, doesn't it?"

"No," he said. "They let each other go. She gets peace, release. She moves on to whatever is next."

It made me think of something Eloise had said: *Love lets go.*

But does it? Does it let go? I'm not sure it does.

I looked at the sketch pad on my desk. There were the preliminary panels for my next book. I was eager to start a new chapter.

"Isn't that what *you* want for him?" he asked. He was so earnest and imploring, I thought about giving in. I really loved Zack. He was the only person who was into my story world as much as I was. They say every writer has one reader, the one they write for again and again. I guess Zack was as close to being that reader as anyone.

"Just think about it, okay? We have a little time."

"He's happy, Zack. You get that, right? It's what he always wanted."

I could hear him tapping his pen on his desk, considering.

"I guess I'll think about it, too," he said.

I ended the conversation with a promise to check in later, and turned toward the window, where a bright light washed in from the noonday sun. Outside, the crisp autumn day was gold and orange, still clinging to green. The sky was a cloudless cerulean blue. I wasn't rewriting the end of the book. It was precisely as it needed to be. I could feel that; I had a feeling Zack was going to come around to seeing this, too.

Fatboy and I had parted company. After I wrote him walking into the fire, I felt him leave me for good. I released that part of myself that was afraid and filled with rage. I let him burn.

I was alone in the art room, as I often was. It wasn't exactly an artsy crowd, though there were a few people who seemed to take comfort in painting. Occasionally, I shared the space with a haunted-looking woman in her forties trying to kick an Adderall addiction. She had an affinity for a Georgia O'Keeffe–style of flowers in bright oils. There was an eighteen-year-old meth head who painted the same stand of black, dead trees over and over. But neither of them had been around for a while.

I sketched for a bit, mostly Megan as she looked the last time I'd seen her, flushed and pretty, her belly round and smooth, breasts swelling against the pink of her dress. She *was* fecundity, beauty, expectancy. I was trying to get that, that blush of hormones and health. Like so many beautiful, natural things, it defied capture. Made things—cityscapes, machines, weapons—all of that was easy. Negative emotions—

anger, hatred, rage, jealousy—were all hard lines and dark shadows. Light, wellness, happiness, the natural world—all of that was harder. So much of it was not about what the eye saw, but about what it couldn't see.

I had phone and e-mail privileges now, which I hadn't for a while. For a long time I couldn't have cared less. I couldn't think of anything but my own ruin. And then there was the sickness, the writhing agony of drugs leaving my system. It's a river of pain—mental, physical, and emotional. Unless there's something waiting for you on the other side, I'm not sure there's any way to cross it alive. There wouldn't have been for me, I know that. The only thing I ever wanted more than to get high was to build a life with Megan and our child. And that's the only thing that got me sober.

I had been clean for sixteen weeks. And let me tell you frankly: sobriety sucks. I don't know how people do it. There you are in the world, just yourself, with nothing to take the edge off all your fear and pain and self-loathing. There's nothing to bury your demons, no way to cast off your inhibitions and let loose. All the things that bother you, hurt you—you have to face them, talk about them with your therapist. You have to deal with your life. Why would anyone want that?

But people did want that. And people wanted that for me. Mainly, Megan.

Have you considered that we might build a life where you wouldn't have so much to bury? That if you deal with the things that are causing you such devastating psychic pain, you might not need to "take the edge off."

At sixteen weeks sober, living at a rehab facility, working, communicating somewhat with the outside world, I was a long way from that place. But I was on the far shore; I'd made it through the mire. Now I just had to get to my feet.

Hi, my name is Ian Paine. And I'm an addict. I have been

*addicted to many things . . . booze, pot, pills, my own desire
to self-destruct. But I have been sober for sixteen weeks—and
counting. One day at a time and all that.*

My phone dinged in my pocket. There was an e-mail
from my dad's old partner.

Hey, bud, he wrote. *Thought you'd like to know that the
main house, and the other structure on the property, came down
completely today. The fire did most of the hard work. We dug up
the foundations and filled in the holes. It's a fresh start for you
and your family. Consider the demo my wedding gift.*

I looked at the clock on the wall and realized I was
running late for my session. I packed up my stuff—my
sketches, my pencils, the new blank pad—and headed to
therapy.

My therapist—well, there's no other way to put this. She
was hot. She beamed a lush-lipped, white-toothed smile
at me as I entered her office and took a seat.

"Ian," she said. "How are you today?"

She stood and shook my hand, gestured to the couch,
and then sat in an oversized leather chair across from
it. I settled in. My hours with her were long and painful, my only comfort was her long, shapely legs, her silky
blue-black hair. She tried to hide it, her hotness, in loose
dresses and big, dark-framed glasses. But it was like trying
to hide the blaze of a klieg light.

"Getting there," I said.

"Getting where?" she asked, never one to let a col-
loquialism slide. She was not a native speaker. She was
Brazilian, her accent thick and sweet like cocoa.

"You know," I said. "There. To the place where I want
to be. Sobriety. Normalcy. Megan and our baby."

"You must be proud of the progress you've made so
far," she said.

No, I wasn't proud of my progress. That was one of the more annoying things about this place. Everyone was so self-congratulatory. Every tiny victory was met with thunderous applause. But people were here only because they'd fucked up their lives and probably the lives of everyone else they knew. We were clawing our way back to a starting point, seeking forgiveness, atoning for our many sins, paying for crimes we'd committed. Was I supposed to be *proud* that I was *somewhat* less of a fuckup than I'd been four months ago?

"I am," I said, with my imitation of a confident nod. "Thanks to you and all the people here."

"We just hold the door open," she said. "You have to choose to walk inside and do all the hard work when you get here."

I gave her a modest but acknowledging nod. I knew it was what she wanted from me. One had to take responsibility for one's own sobriety. Because in the end, you're the only one who can keep you that way. To give away your power to others is the first step back to your addiction—whatever it is.

She had my file on her desk. I knew they were getting ready to kick me out of this place. I had completed the program. It was time for me to reenter the real world, which was weirdly scary and a big relief.

"Ian," she said. "As you know, you have completed the program here at New Reflections. This will be your final week with us."

"Okay," I said. "That's great."

"How do you feel about that? Would you like to discuss it?"

I rubbed at my shoulder, which had been hurting. That was another thing about being sober. I was tuned in to my body in a whole new way. And I didn't really like it.

I had all kinds of aches and pains. I used to just pop a pill for whatever ailed me. Those days were gone.

"I am eager to start my life again," I said. "Our baby is due in three months, and we have plans to build a new house. So there's a lot to look forward to."

She nodded, waiting. As usual, I tried to figure out what she wanted me to say.

"But I suppose I'm a little nervous," I went on. "This is such a safe environment, so predictable."

"We are always here for you," she said. "And you'll continue as an outpatient for another six months or as long as you wish."

I would not be returning to the candy store that was Manhattan—that island of temptation and debauchery. Meg's apartment was on the market, and she was renting a place for us off the precious little main square in town. Yes, Megan and I were moving to The Hollows. We would use the money from the sale to build Meg's dream house, the place where we would raise our family. With a little help from Binky and Julia, who, though not pleased with anything that was currently happening, were predictably supportive.

What could they do? Meg had chosen to stay with me, against all advice and good sense. She loved me; I was the father of her child. But there were conditions: one was that I stay sober and the second was that we not return to Manhattan. It was such a perfect trap that The Hollows had laid for me that I almost had to laugh. Almost.

Does this seem like an odd choice? That I would return to The Hollows after all my passionate declarations to the contrary. Sometimes the choices we make are not choices at all, but concessions to forces beyond our control.

"And, as you say, you have a lot of reasons to be well," said the doctor.

Megan saw Manhattan as a threat to my sobriety. It was the place where my various addictions had unlimited supply. I had a million opportunities to do the wrong thing. And it was widely agreed in the sobriety community that one should not return to the old hood if it could be helped. New self, new start, new place—you got it— new reflections. Even if, for me, the new place was the old place.

From beneath the file, the doctor pulled out a newspaper—*The Hollows Gazette*.

"I was interested to read about the restoration project you're planning," she said.

She handed me the paper, and I looked at the article of interest.

"Oh," I said. "Yes."

With the help of Eloise Montgomery, who had been to visit me several times once visitors were allowed, I have arranged for the old church and graveyard on the land that edges my property to be restored. Joy Martin, of The Hollows Historical Society, agreed to work with the same architect who was building my house, to save what could be saved of the old structure and rebuild the rest. The gravestones would be restored and reerected, the grounds cleaned and relandscaped. And I agreed to maintain the property.

A recent royalty payment, which included my cut of the sales of that Fatboy mask, had left me flush again. There was money, and with the new contract I was about to sign, in addition to the movie rights to the series that just sold to a major studio, there would be money for the foreseeable future. I would use that money to rebuild my life, yes, but also to right some wrongs—and not just my wrongs. Because in The Hollows it was not enough to atone for your own sins. The land demanded more.

The church would serve as a memorial to all the men who died in mining accidents in The Hollows. There would be a plaque that recounted the history of the in-dustry and what it has meant to our region—for better and for worse. There would be photographs on the walls, as well as a book containing the names of the dead.

"I think it's very healing," the therapist said. "To honor Priss in this way."

"She deserves it," I said.

Dr. Sanchez is the only therapist I have ever had who did not demand that I denounce Priss, pretend that she was some figment of my imagination, that she never existed. Don't get me wrong. Dr. Sanchez didn't believe that Priss was a real entity, a haunting, a ghost that almost destroyed me—she thinks Priss was a product of my pill-addled psyche, an archetype for my rage, a symbol of all my repressed anger toward my murderous mother. In other words, she believed that Priss was real to me—and that I had to deal with her as I would deal with any other person in my life. Part of recovering from addiction is to make amends to those you have wronged, and to for-give those who have wronged you. There can be no more holding on to the past. Love lets go.

I finished my session and went back to my room, where I took a shower and put on a pair of jeans, a blue-and-white-checked shirt that Megan had bought me. I was meeting her in the cafeteria for lunch. She'd had her doctor's appointment today, and I was looking forward to going with her to the next one. So far, she'd had to go to her checkups alone—which I hated. But I had a lifetime to make amends, and I planned to do so.

Don't let her turn you into one of those millennium nerds, Ian. One of those neutered, so sensitive, stay-at-home-dad types. Her voice was still with me, sarcastic, knowing. But I was going to let Megan turn me into whatever she wanted me to be. At least I wouldn't be an addict and an ass-hole.

• • •

Megan was waiting for me when I arrived in the cafeteria, smiling brightly. I kissed her, sat down next to her.

"How'd it go?"

She kept on smiling, slid a piece of paper over to me. I flipped it over and saw a grainy sonogram image. A little peanut, floating in space. I stared at the perfect profile—round cheeks and upturned nose. The little hands were clasped together.

"The sonogram was today?" I said.

I felt surprisingly sad, left out. It was something I'd fantasized about, that moment when, through one of the miracles of modern medicine, I could see our baby on a screen. I should have been there to hold Meg's hand, to wipe away her joyful tears. Megan's smile faded a little as she realized what I was thinking.

"Oh," she said. She put her hands on top of mine. "I'm sorry. I should have waited. You're right."

"No," I said. "No. It's okay. I'm happy."

"The face," I said. I held up the sonogram image again, looked at it closely. "I can see you."

"I thought so, too! I wouldn't let them tell me if it was a boy or a girl," she said. Her excitement, her joy, was contagious. Whatever sadness I'd felt, faded. It was okay. It was just one moment; I'd be there for all the others. Lucky for me.

I don't know who pushed Megan onto the tracks that night, but it wasn't me. It couldn't have been me. That Fatboy mask; there are tens of thousands of them floating around New York. And a certain element has taken to using them in the commission of crimes. This fact has saved me. The police have not charged me. Megan will not believe that it was me. But Binky and Julia . . . they despise and fear me. They are not sure who or what I am, what I am capable of doing. They only know I have their daughter in my clutches, and so they keep me close. You should see the way Julia looks at me when she thinks I'm not watching.

I know you, Megan said. *I look into your face and I see pain, yes. But I only see goodness beneath that. You are not Fatboy. You are Ian, my baby's father.*

Thank God for her, really. I would not, could not survive this without her. It was Megan who forced me to face down my haunting demons. It was my love for her that forced me to swim the river. What would have become of me on the other side? I shudder to think.

Sitting now in the sunny cafeteria, she chatted happily about the house. The plans were done. The baby was healthy in spite of the two bad falls Megan took. She'd been worried about that, she admitted now. But it was okay. Of course it was. And she'd been to see Joy Martin, who showed her some preliminary plans for the restored church and graveyard. She'd visited my mother, brought her some new clothes, as I'd requested.

"You know," she said. She took a sip of soup. "I know you never thought you'd be back in The Hollows. But I love it. It's so strange, but it feels like home to me."

I tried to ignore that tickle of fear that traveled down my gullet to my belly. Megan had picked up a big piece of chocolate pie from the case, and I took it from her tray and shoveled it into my mouth. I ate half of it in two bites. I had put on weight in here, nearly ten pounds. You had to have *something*, didn't you?

"I guess it *is* home," I said.

There must have been an unintended dark note in my tone, because I felt her go quiet in that way she has. I kept eating.

"Are you going to be okay here?" she asked when the pie was gone.

"Of course," I said. I wiped the cream and chocolate from my mouth. "It's what you want. It's what you both want."

She nodded, but she didn't look as happy as she had when she arrived.

"Yes," she said. "It is."

What did she want? Eloise had asked on her first visit to New Reflections. And I told her because there was no one else to tell. A mild look of surprise softened her features, then disappeared into its usual gentle neutrality.

And you're going to give that to her?

What choice do I have? I had asked. She didn't have an answer, and she knew it.

You said that we were all connected, I went on. *That we are all points of light on an infinite web.*

Yes.

Well, some of us are more connected than others.

More silence from Eloise.

Me and Priss. We can't be apart; it won't work.

CHAPTER THIRTY-FIVE

By the time I was released from rehab a week later, No Paine Construction had already cleared the new home site and had started laying in the foundation. Megan had brought me pictures. The new house was set back from the land where the old one had been. And a circular driveway would be laid where my childhood home had been. I was trying to see it all as a fresh start, one in which I'd torn down the past and started anew. I was surprised by the speed of the builders, but I guess I shouldn't have been.

When things are right, they're right, Megan said. And she sounded so sure of herself that I had no choice but to believe her.

I was jittery and nervous as I packed my things. I didn't have much, which gave me some clarity about my mother's situation. In a place like this, you need next to nothing. I wasn't as happy as I had imagined I'd be, graduating rehab. I was starting to understand why my mother had chosen her institutional existence. It was easy, once you got the hang of it; you made no decisions—not even about what to eat or when. I wished I was more excited to be going home. Of course, the place we were renting off the square wasn't really home.

"Don't be concerned if you're not giddy with relief," Dr. Sanchez had warned me earlier that day. "There's a long road ahead of you, and you're smart enough to know that. Just keep your life small right now. Focus on Megan and the baby, your work. Stay home, cook. Do things you haven't done before."

"Right," I said. "That's exactly my plan."

There had been a small party that morning with my various counselors and some other patients, who looked at me with expressions ranging from envy to terror. Lots of awkward hugs and averted eyes. Everyone was on their own trip there; some of us would make it and some wouldn't. I wasn't totally sure in which group I would fall.

And then that was it. I walked out the front door.

Megan picked me up in the Scout. I could tell that she was nervous, she was chattering away. After we'd driven a mile or so, I put my hand on her arm.

"It's okay," I said. "It's going to be okay."

She pulled the car over to the side of the road and started to cry, just these big, body-racking sobs. I held her, buried my face in her hair.

We'd never talked about the night of the fire. We'd talked about everything else, our relationship, what she wanted, what I wanted. We'd talked about the baby, about parenthood and everything we dreamed of and feared about it. But those last few days before I wound up in rehab, and everyone wanted to blame everything that happened on my addictions—we'd never talked about that. It kind of felt like talking about someone who wasn't here anymore, the Ian who was addicted to pills and hallucinating big chunks of his life.

We just sat there like that, on the side of the road. The trees were gold, orange, and brown, falling leaves dancing across the road.

"That day in the park?" she said finally. She wiped her eyes.

"Yeah." I'd always been afraid to ask her about it, what I'd said to her that made her look so shocked and afraid. I honestly didn't know.

"It wasn't you."

"No," I said. "I was totally screwed up, taking a bunch of different pills. I was someone else altogether."

In rehab, we learned about separating the real person from the drugs, how when you're dealing with an addict, it's really the substance that's doing the talking. It's like a possession—the booze or the drugs or whatever has snaked its way in and taken hold of the addict, is holding him in its grasp. Or a haunting. Always felt like a bit of a cop-out to me. But what did I know?

She shook her head. That pink diamond glittered on her hand, catching the sun. I noticed, for the first time during her pregnancy, dark circles under her eyes.

"That's not what I mean."

She ran a hand through her hair. I wondered, not for the first time, why she would stay with me, why she loved me. I thought about what Binky said, how they'd unwittingly raised her to be a fixer and a caretaker. Was that why she stayed? Because I fulfilled some deep need within her that she didn't even know she had?

"I mean, it didn't even *look* like you. Your voice. It was *different*."

I reached for her hands and held them, but I didn't know what to say. I had made a promise to myself to always treat her tenderly, to always take care of her. I was going to do that, whatever the reason she'd chosen to stay with me. I was going to be a better man. I kept saying this over and over to myself, like a prayer.

"You said, 'You belong to us now. Try to leave me and I'll kill you both.'"

I blew out a breath, as if I'd been punched in the gut. "I'm sorry. I'd never hurt you. You know that."

"I do know that," she said. "It wasn't you. But it wasn't the pills either."

She'd figured it out. I could see that look on her

face—the trepidation and doubt when you've discovered that the answer to a question doesn't make sense in the real world.

"When you called me later, it *was* you. I heard your real voice and I could feel how frightened and alone you were. I didn't understand what was happening to you, but I came to get you. I took the train to The Hollows and a cab from the station. But when I got to the house, you weren't there. So I went inside to wait."

She took a breath here, seemed to think about how to go on. I imagined her walking into the cold, dark house, calling my name.

"I walked around the house, saw all your stuff. Finally, I was so tired that I just lay down on your bed. I hadn't slept. I hadn't spoken to my parents since you saw my dad in Madison Square Park."

She wore a deep frown. "I was mad at them. I know they were just scared, but they were bullying me, trying to get me to come back out to Long Island, and I just needed to think. So I hadn't talked to them. They'd been calling. I didn't imagine that they'd be worried enough to call the police."

Poor Binky and Julia, such good parents and such good people. Some folks just don't know when to stop parenting, though.

"So I guess I just drifted off. But when I woke up there was a little girl standing in the doorway."

She sounded incredulous, and I imagined Priss standing there with that look on her face, that innocence, that sweetness.

"She was so pretty, and small, and she looked so afraid," Meg said. "I thought I was dreaming. 'Who are you?' I asked. She said, 'I'm Priss.' But, of course, I already knew that. I recognized her from your books and all the old sketches you showed me from when you were younger. I wasn't afraid. I should have been, but I wasn't. 'What do you want?' I asked her."

She stopped and sought out my eyes. "Does this sound crazy? Am I crazy?"

"No," I said. "I know how it is with her."

"She came nearer to me, and somehow she showed me things. I saw you—a younger you—setting fires, playing with her in the woods, making love to her. She was always different—first a child, then a teenager, then a woman. She grew with you. Then I saw you in the subway station. Except somehow it wasn't you; it was her."

She had a dreamy, faraway look as she spoke. I could see it all playing out before my eyes.

"She left the room, and I followed. Down the stairs, through the house, and into the kitchen."

Megan went on.

"'He belongs to me and to this place,' she said. 'He can't leave. And neither can you.'

"But she was crying; she was so sad and so lonely, and I could feel that loneliness inside me. It was a million years old. And I realized then what she wanted. She just didn't want to be alone anymore.

"'It's okay,' I told her. 'We'll stay.'"

When I didn't say anything, Meg kept going.

"She smiled at me and I moved toward her. I wanted to comfort her, to hold on to her. Somehow I was thinking about you, and my poor brother, and your sister, and our baby. There was something wide open in me, willing to take her in. She was just another lost thing.

"But I didn't understand that she wasn't really, physically there. And in that weird dream state, I didn't see the cellar stairs behind her. And then I was falling and falling. And I don't remember anything after that until you came to get me."

The wind was picking up outside and a car sped past

us, startling us both. Megan seemed to come back to herself, and then she started driving again. I knew where we were headed before she turned onto the back road, and then onto the long narrow path that led to the house.

As we pulled up the drive I saw that the house was gone. And farther along I saw the construction site, a bustle of activity, trucks parked and men wearing hard hats and carrying tools and two-by-fours. The foreman, a muscular young guy, gave Megan a wave and she waved back. He looked tan and healthy, smiled a little too broadly at my pretty wife. I shot a quick glance at myself in the sideview. I was pasty- and fatigued-looking. Maybe I could start working out again—sooner rather than later.

"I thought you would want to see it," she said.

We both climbed out of the car, and I walked around to lean on the hood of the Scout. King of all I surveyed.

They'd cleared away some of the trees to set the house back farther on the property. I could see that they had filled in the old foundation and etched out the shape of the circular drive, scattered some grass seed.

"I didn't want to talk about it while you were still in there," she said. "I didn't want to undermine what they were trying to do for you."

I looked into those deep, dark eyes. She had it, too, whatever I had that left me open to Priss. Some darkness, or some deep intuition—whatever it was, there was a doorway in both of us. I didn't think it could be closed.

"I know you have a drug problem, a bad one," she said. "But I also know it was something more. I saw her. I felt her."

What a relief it was to be known, to be understood, to be forgiven—to no longer be alone in this place. That, more than love, is what we all want, I think. That, I knew, was what Priss wanted.

"You made her a promise," I said. "So did I."

I heard the Whispers then, and I saw Megan's gaze dart toward the trees. She turned back to me.

"Want to take a walk?" I asked.

"Maybe you should go alone," she said.

The house that wasn't there *really* wasn't there now. The old foundation had been cleared and the ground filled in with fresh black dirt. It looked like a grave, and I barely paused there on my way to the little church. *Stay away from the places and people that got you into trouble before.* I remembered that first night so long ago very clearly. I was sad and alone, angry at my mother for loving Ella so much that I felt left out. That's what left me vulnerable to Priss. Just like my mother, whose grief opened the door for her.

Negative energy adheres to other negative energy. That's what Eloise had said. My anger only grew and grew, turning to an ugly, violent rage. I was fuel for Priss's fire, and she was fuel for mine. I kept waiting for her to drop into step beside me, but she didn't.

I came to the church finally and saw that a great deal had been accomplished already. The grounds had been cleared of all the weeds and brush and overgrowth. The tilting, rusted-out old fence had been torn away. The gravestones had been straightened and stood in neat little rows. Leaves had fallen from the trees all around, forming a damp, golden blanket that glinted in the high afternoon sun. The church had been cordoned off with yellow tape tied between posts. A sign read STRUCTURE UNSOUND. STAY AWAY.

The tape flapped in the breeze, making a tapping sound that mingled with the Whispers and the calling of the birds high in the trees.

When Priss had leaned into me that last night, she didn't tell me what she wanted. She didn't utter the words.

She inhabited me, as she'd done many times before. And I knew.

I was the first person to ever ask her what she wanted. Priscilla Miller the girl was powerless, a child who fell victim to circumstance. She was utterly helpless, like all children. The worst possible things that could happen to a child happened to her. They destroyed her. And her rage and sadness adhered her to this place, which had an energy of its own. It was buried here in fertile ground and it grew like a planted seed, though her memory was badly neglected.

She wanted me to tell her story, and I did that in the final installment of *Fatboy and Priss*. The world, or my small part of it, will know Priscilla Miller and how she was wronged.

She wanted me to see her and know her, and acknowledge her. But she also wanted me to forgive her. It was me who did many (but not all) of those awful things—who started fires, and raged, and got into bar fights, and stole pills from my dealer. And yet, it wasn't. My relationship to Priss is something that I cannot explain. We have held each other in comfort, and we have held each other back. Like any haunting, like any addiction, it is a relationship, deep and complicated, and so personal.

I walked over to her grave and let my fingers touch the cool stone.

Love lets go. That's what Eloise had said. But it wasn't true—not for Priss and me. She didn't want me to let go, and I did not want to. I wanted to be free from rage and sorrow and addiction. And so did she. But she did not want to be alone, here in this place. And I wouldn't leave her. We will stay.

That afternoon, I repeated the promises that I made to her in the burning house. I wanted her to know that I would stay. And even though I didn't see her, I knew she heard me. I know because the Whispers went quiet with a soft sigh. Everybody got what they wanted. Then I went back to my wife and my child.

Maybe you think I'm crazy, that my brain was addled by addiction, that poor Megan was just a pathetic enabler, fostering my delusions. And maybe you're right. It's certainly easier to think so.

But there is one thing I know for sure. And nothing— not therapy, not sobriety, not sanity—can convince me otherwise. Whoever she was, whatever she was, Priss was real.

When I saw her after that day—once the house was built and the church restoration had been completed— she was just a trick of light through the trees. She was a fairy, a wood sprite, bound to this place for reasons she couldn't understand but didn't mind anymore. Just like me.

ACKNOWLEDGMENTS

Everything begins and ends with my husband, Jeffrey, and our daughter, Ocean Rae. They are the foundation of my life. And nothing gets written without their love and support. I am blessed to have so much love in my life. Not to mention cuteness. They are both *very* cute. Jeff also cooks. Ocean *occasionally* cleans her room. We also have a cute Labradoodle named Jak Jak. He is somewhat less helpful.

My editor, Sally Kim, brought her usual brand of wisdom, curiosity, and insight to the editing of this novel. She never fails to add something invaluable in the gentlest possible way. I wish I had a nickel for every time she said, "I wonder if . . ." Actually, I probably do.

When my beloved longtime agent and forever friend Elaine Markson retired last year, Amy Berkower of Writers House stepped in, bringing with her many years of experience, but also great warmth, wisdom, and tremendous passion. She made what was a heartbreaking and difficult transition much less so. Thanks, Amy, for stepping in and stepping up. I can't tell you how much it has meant to me.

My special thanks to Jud Meyers from Blastoff Comics in North Hollywood, CA. There's nothing I admire so much in a person as the union of passion and expertise. Jud opened the door into his world for me and my experience was far richer than if I had ventured there myself. He sent me a stack of comics and graphic novels that I *devoured*, and then had to keep away from Ocean. Let's just say much of it was not appropriate for an eight-year-old—even though they were very shiny and colorful. (Ocean: That is SO not fair!) And thanks to pal and *New York Times* bestselling author Gregg Hurwitz for connecting us.

James E. Adams, MD, board-certified psychiatrist, spent his precious time on the phone with me talking about everything from childhood trauma to addiction. His insights and knowledge deepened my understanding of my characters—many of which could definitely use a talk or two with Dr. Adams.

The folks at Touchstone/Simon & Schuster and Pocket are an absolutely stellar group. Each and every person brings their own special gifts and talents to the table. My heartfelt thanks to: Carolyn Reidy, Susan Moldow, Michael Selleck, Liz Perl, Louise Burke, David Falk, Brian Belfiglio, Sophie Vershbow, Cherlynne Li, Wendy Sheanin, Paula Amendolara, Teresa Brumm, Colin Shields, Chrissy Festa, Charlotte Gill, Gary Urda, Gregory Hruska, Michelle Fadlalla, Bryony Weiss, Meredith Vilarello, Paul O'Halloran, Elisabeth Watson, and Melissa Vipperman-Cohen. And I can never heap enough praise on the top-notch sales team, out there on the front lines in this super-competitive business, getting books in every format into as many hands as possible. It's everything; thank you.

Last but not least, I have an amazing network of family and friends who cheer me through the good days and carry me through the challenging ones. I am so grateful for my parents, Joseph and Virginia Miscione, who have supported me in every way possible all my life, and are unstoppable as Team PA. To my brother Joe Miscione and his wife, Tara, for everything they do, including but not limited to facing out books on the shelves, inviting me to speak at Tara's book club, and general book flogging. Thanks to Heather Mikesell for being one of my first and most important readers. She also takes pictures of people she sees reading my books—which is always a boost! Thanks to Tara Popick and Marion Chartoff for their unfailing friendship. They've been with me every step of the way.

CRAZY
LOVE YOU

LISA
UNGER

This reading group guide for Crazy Love You *includes an introduction, discussion questions, ideas for enhancing your book club, and a Q&A with author Lisa Unger. The suggested questions are intended to help your reading group find new and interesting angles and topics for your discussion. We hope that these ideas will enrich your conversation and increase your enjoyment of the book.*

Darkness has a way of creeping up when Ian is with Priss. Even when they were kids, playing in the old woods of their small town, he could feel it. Still, Priss was his best friend, his only friend. Ian's time with Priss was his salvation from the bullies who called him "loser" and "fatboy" . . . and from his family's deadly secrets. Now Ian has escaped his home, his family, and the tortured shell of his childhood. A talented and successful graphic novelist living in the most expensive neighborhood of Manhattan, Ian has put his past behind him . . . except for Priss. Priss is still trouble. The booze, the drugs, the sex—Ian is growing tired of late nights together trying to keep the past at bay. Especially now that he's met sweet, beautiful Megan, whose love makes him want to change for the better. But Priss doesn't like change. Change makes her angry. And when Priss is angry, terrible things begin to happen. . . .

1. On page 4 of *Crazy Love You*, Ian says, "When the darkness calls, it's a siren song." This idea, the allure of the darker side of life, is one of the major themes of the novel. How does Ian's perspective on this idea change throughout his life and throughout the course of the book? Is it an idea you can sympathize with? How?

2. Ian is a classic unreliable narrator. How does his unreliability influence the development of the plot in *Crazy Love You*? At what point did you realize Ian might not always be telling the whole truth?

3. The comics that Ian writes—*Fatboy and Priss*—form a substantial part of the plot of *Crazy Love You*. How does the author use Ian's work as a tool to illustrate or hint at themes and plot points throughout the novel?

4. On page 10, Ian says of Priss, "The more I had of her in ink, the less I wanted or needed her in life." How does this reflect Ian's attitude toward life in general? Does the world of comics help Ian deal with real life? Or does it make it more difficult?

5. Why are comic books so appealing to Ian as a child, and why do you think he didn't grow out of them, as

so many kids do? Discuss your own relationship with comics (or lack thereof).

6. Priss has multiple incarnations as a character throughout the story. What are the boundaries between the different versions of her? Which is the "real" Priss? Is there one?

7. Throughout the story, the Whispers that Ian hears are an enormous influence on his life. What do you think the Whispers are? What do they symbolize in The Hollows? Have you ever experienced anything like the Whispers?

8. What was it in his life that made Ian so susceptible to Priss's manipulation? Why did Priss, in turn, have such a great need for Ian? What are the things in our own lives that make us vulnerable to things that harm us?

9. Ian's relationship with Megan and her family hinges on his difficulty with accepting the stability and normalcy of their life compared with his own. Do you share his doubts and misgivings about the closeness of Megan's family, or do you think he's just insecure? Why?

10. One of the most important themes of *Crazy Love You* revolves around fate. Is it possible to change our circumstances, or are we bound to our fate? Can the people in our lives be changed for better or for worse? How does Ian's judgment of this question evolve throughout the novel?

11. A prominent theme in *Crazy Love You* is the power and influence of addiction. How is Ian both a typical

and atypical addict? Does Ian's relationship with Priss constitute an addiction? Why or why not? Do you think we can ever really be *addicted* to another human being?

12. The difference between fiction and reality emerges as a major theme in *Crazy Love You*. The more we learn about Ian's life, the more the line between his art and his actual life starts to blur. What do you think of Ian's negotiation between his own life and his art? Do you think all fiction has some reality in it?

13. In Eloise Montgomery's words from page 292, the only two "primary motivators" are love and fear—everything else is merely secondary. Do you agree with her analysis in the context of Ian's story? Why or why not?

14. The reader's perspective on Ian and Priss's relationship evolves dramatically over the course of *Crazy Love You*. Do you agree with the peace that Ian arrives at in regards to Priss, or do you think he's delusional? Do you think Ian made the right choices at the end? Or is he still in Priss's thrall?

ENHANCE YOUR BOOK CLUB

1. In more ways than one, Priss plays the role of Ian's muse. From the muses of classical Greek myth, to the real-life muses of the Romantic poets, there are muses of some kind or another scattered across history: Research the history of muses in literature, and pick either a fictional or real muse to present to your group. How does Priss fit the role of a muse and how does she differ?

2. The world of comics is one that Ian holds close to his heart, and in modern culture he is not alone. Team up with one or more of your group members to make a comic of your own design—a superhero comic or something more personal. Your comic can be funny, serious, action-packed, or meditative—whatever strikes your fancy. Draw an entire book, or simply one detailed panel. Share your work with your group.

3. The history of The Hollows plays a crucial role in *Crazy Love You*. Although your town may not have as haunting a history as Ian's, you probably have a historical society or museum in your local area. Plan a visit, do some research about your town's past, and present your findings to your group.

4. Join the conversation! www.LisaUnger.com and www .facebook.com/authorlisaunger are great resources

for more information on Lisa Unger's novels and a way to meet other fans of *Crazy Love You*. Check out the videos on LisaUnger.com with your group and share your favorite parts of *Crazy Love You* with Lisa on Facebook.

A CONVERSATION WITH LISA UNGER

Ian is such a compelling and convincing narrative voice. How did you develop his character? Does he bear a resemblance to anyone in your own life?

Usually I can pinpoint an exact moment when I started hearing a character's voice. There's generally a germ or a seed that gives me a little buzz of excitement and leads me to do some research. And then I start hearing a voice, or seeing a scene over and over. That's when I sit down to start writing.

But I don't know why I started hearing Ian. He was just in my head one day. I knew that he was a graphic novelist and that he had some major problems that he was keeping at bay with his various addictions—pills, work, weed. He was in a dark spiral and in a toxic relationship that was enabling his various issues. But that was all I knew. When I first started hearing him, he had an apocalyptic hangover. So that's where we started our journey together, on the cold floor of his bathroom.

Comic books and comic book culture are an obviously important thread in *Crazy Love You*. Is it a world you were already familiar with before starting the novel? How did you do your research, if not?

I was not familiar with this world—at all. In fact, I had to call my author friend Gregg Hurwitz (who writes comics as well as stellar thrillers) and say: "You know, my new character is a graphic novelist and I don't know anything about this. Can you help me?"

He put me in touch with Jud Meyer from Blastoff Comics in North Hollywood. And Jud opened the door to this world for me. He shared his own experiences, sent me piles of books, and answered all my questions. I just dove into this very colorful and amazingly creative universe and loved every minute. Jud was a the perfect guide, as well as the sweetest, kindest person in the world. He was the best source a writer could have.

Ian as a kid finds incredible solace in comic books, so much so that he dedicates his life to that world. When did you discover mysteries? When did you realize that you wanted to write your own?

I think most creative people find a home in their art before they find one in the real world. Books were certainly my first love, and the darker, the more thrilling, the more complex, the better. So I was young (inappropriately so) when I started reading mysteries, thriller and horror novels.

My family moved around a lot, so even when I was the outsider at a new school or a new neighborhood, I was at home with books. Pretty early I had that moment when I went from being a reader to being a writer, from being someone who disappeared into other people's stories to one who wanted to create her own. Once I discovered that I could do that, I never stopped. I really relate to that part of Ian who prefers a fictional world to the often cruel and unforgiving real one.

Like many of your other books, *Crazy Love You* takes place, at least partially, in the town of The Hollows, which has almost become a character in its own right. What are the unique challenges and satisfactions of developing a setting over the course of several books? Is there a real place that you feel is closest to The Hollows?

When I first visited The Hollows, I didn't think very much of it. It seemed like it could just be Anytown, USA. I didn't really know where it was, somewhere in the tristate area. I had this vision of a place that was part rural, part a kind of village, with a hint of dark energy. Subconsciously, I think the town of Sleepy Hollow was a bit of an inspiration. I like the name and the history, its connection to a literary ghost story. But I didn't consciously think of any of that when I was writing. It was just a place with a strange name.

But once I visited The Hollows, I just kept going back there. And each time I went, The Hollows evolved, and I got to know it better. I learned something new about it every time, and yet kept revisiting the same spots. I started to see it as a place with a personality and an agenda. The Hollows wants something, and I'm not totally sure what it is.

The challenges of writing about a fictional place are the same as what's satisfying about it. It's totally my vision—streets, restaurants, homes, people, the woods, the river, the abandoned mine tunnels. There was nothing there until I put it there—which is both challenging and extremely cool. Making sure everything gels from book to book can be a little harrowing.

My brother swears that The Hollows is based on

the town where we grew up, called Long Valley, New Jersey. But, of course, it isn't that, though I can see why he thinks so. And maybe there are some similarities. But it's like all fictional places (and people). It is an amalgamation of my experiences and imaginings, part real but mostly real only in my fictional universe.

The history of The Hollows is an important facet of the novel. Is small-town history something you're particularly interested in? Are you familiar with the history of the place you live now?

I am interested in history, certainly. But mainly I am interested in personal history, the stories we tell ourselves about our past and how it affects our actions in the present. Most people aren't living in the present; our memories of the past impact our perceptions of the present, and our hopes for the future. And that is true of places, too. History is just a story that we tell ourselves. Some of it is true. Some of it so influenced by the teller that it is a biased version of the truth, and so not true at all.

A town has a collective history that shapes its identity, as well as the identities of the people who live there. What does it mean to be a New Yorker, a Parisian, a Floridian (in my case), or a resident of The Hollows? We come to identify with our location, and nowhere is that more true than a small town, especially when you've lived there all your life. Your identity becomes indivisible from that place. That's really what fascinates me about the The Hollows, its living history and how it impacts the people who live there.

One of the most fun aspects of *Crazy Love You* is the unreliability of Ian's narration. As an author, what

is particularly intriguing about an unreliable narrator? Is it more or less difficult than a traditional narrator?

All narrators are unreliable to some extent. In fact, anyone telling you a story is unreliable. They can only tell events through the filter of their perception, which might be very different from another person's perception. Of course, Ian is slightly more unreliable than most considering that he's pill-addled, mentally unstable, and far prefers to live within the pages of his graphic novel than in the real world. But I follow character voice. And I was willing to go with Ian wherever he wanted to take me. And that's true of even my more traditional narrators. They tell the story. I follow. So it wasn't significantly different from other journeys, just a little crazier.

The supernatural elements in *Crazy Love You* are part of what makes it unique and more complex or ambiguous than your more traditional horror fare. Have you always been interested in ghosts, psychics, and the like? What was it like to write in that mode? What is your own relationship with the supernatural?

I have a dark and curious imagination, so the supernatural has been a big source of fascination for me—not just spirits and ghosts, but psychic phenomena, fortune-tellers, tarot cards, anything that flirts with the other side. I have met people who were clearly gifted. And I've had some unexplainable experiences—enough so that I'm open to the possibilities. Since my fictional worlds are pretty dark, it didn't seem like such a big leap to follow Ian down the rabbit hole, especially since it took me a long time to figure out what was really happening to him. I *had* to follow him, just to figure out if he was crazy, addicted, or really experiencing something—beyond. The natural and supernatural exist side by side, a very thin veil between them. *Crazy Love You* is not the first time I've pushed the veil back, but I did go deeper than I have before.

One of the most compelling parts about Ian's character is his dedication to his work. What are the similarities (if any) between Ian's perspective on his work and your own? What was it like to write from the perspective of someone so wrapped up in his own art, so different from your own?

I actually don't think his art is very different from my own. He's a storyteller, just like me. There's a visual component to his art, but my fascination with my subjects is no less total. The major difference between Ian and me is that I am grounded in the real world in a way that he is not—and frankly doesn't want to be. I have a family and a home and responsibilities that keep from disappearing completely onto the page. When the book begins, he doesn't have any of that. He is young and single, wild, partying, troubled by a traumatic past. He is using drugs and his work to keep his demons at bay. He doesn't have anything in the real world to keep him rooted until he meets Megan. And, of course, that's when all the trouble begins—when he has to choose.

As a young and unhappy kid, Ian disappeared into the world of comic books—a brightly colored, exciting, easy-to-understand world where things were just *better*. I think that a lot of creative people find a home in their art at a very young age. It was definitely true for me. First I disappeared into books, then into my own writing. The world doesn't always embrace the sensitive and more creative among us, but the page is wide open, waiting for us to fill it with our art—whether that's poetry, or fiction, or paints and pastels. I don't think there's an artist alive who doesn't disappear into the world he creates and who often prefers it to the real one. I relate to him more than I don't.

Fate, or the perception of it, plays a big role in the lives of the characters in *Crazy Love You*. Ian in particular meditates frequently on the inevitable aspects of his life and wonders if it's truly possible for people to change. Do you believe in fate? Do you think that people ever really change, or that it's possible to change someone else?

I do believe it's possible to change yourself and nearly impossible to change anyone else. Our lives are a complicated helix of fate and free will, nature and nurture, meaning that we don't choose our genetics, or the things that happen to us, but that sometimes we can find the strength to take the wheel of our lives and start to navigate the terrain before us. When we marshal our resources, we have more power than we think we do over our circumstances. All through *Crazy Love You* I was rooting for Ian, hoping that something would motivate him to pull out of his downward spiral. But I also knew that the choice was his and his alone. We can't save anyone from his own dark appetites and desires. The choice to change is a deeply personal one.

Can you give us any hints about what you're working on next? Are you planning more books that take place in The Hollows?

I never talk about my next project, because it drains all the energy. But I will say I'm not done with The Hollows. Or, rather, it's not done with me!

Keep reading for a sneak peek at
Lisa Unger's riveting thriller

THE NEW COUPLE IN 5B

OVERTURE

You. Standing on solid ground, reaching. Me. On the ledge, looking down. All around me, stars. Stars in the sky, the city spread around me like a field of glittering, distant celestial bodies. Each light a life. Each life a doorway, a possibility. That's the thing I've always loved about my work, the way I can disappear into someone else. I shed myself daily, slipping into other skins. Some of them more comfortable than my own.

"Don't," you say. "Don't do this. It doesn't have to be this way."

I hear all the notes of desperation and fear that sing discordant and wild, a cacophony in my own heart. And I think that maybe you're wrong. Maybe everything I am and everything I've done has led me here to this teetering edge. There was no other possible ending. No other way.

Sirens. As distant and faint as birdsong. It seems as if, in this city, they never stop wailing, someone always on their way to this emergency or that crisis. Rushing to help or stop or save. From the outside, it seems like chaos. But when you are inside, it's quiet, isn't it? Just another moment. Only this time the worst thing is about to happen, or might, or might not, to us. Every flicker of light, every passing second, just a shift of weight and another outcome becomes real.

"Please." Under the fear, the pleading of your tone,

I hear it—hope. You're still hopeful. Still holding on to those other possibilities.

But when I look at you now, I know—and you know it, too, don't you?—that I've made too many dark choices, that there is no outcome but this one. The one that sets us both free right here and right now.

Pounding. They're at the door.

You know what's funny? Even on that day we first met, I knew it would end like this. Not really. Not exactly this, not a premonition, or a vision of the future. But even in the light you shined on me, even as you made me be the person I always wanted to be, there was this dark entity hovering, a specter. The destroyer. You were always too good for me, and I knew I could never hold on to the things we would build together.

Sounds rise and converge—your voice, their pounding, that wailing, the endless honking and whir of movement from this place we have lived in and loved.

The weight of my body, I close my eyes for a moment and feel it. The beating of my heart, the rise and fall of my breath. I tilt and wobble on the edge, as you move closer, hands outstretched.

"We'll be okay," you whisper. At least I think that's what you say. I can hardly hear you over all the noise. Your eyes, like the city below me, a swirling galaxy of lights.

You're close now, hands still reaching.

Just one step forward or backward.

Which one?

Which one, my love?

Keep reading for a preview of
Lisa Unger's engrossing thriller

INK AND BONE

PROLOGUE

Daddy was on the phone, talking soft and low, dropping behind them on the path. Nothing new. He was *always* on the phone—or on the computer. Penny knew that her daddy loved her, but she also knew that he was almost never paying attention. He was "busy, sweetie," or "with a client," or "just a minute, honey, Daddy's talking to someone." He was a good storyteller, a bear-hugger, always opened his arms to her, lifted her high, or took her into his lap while he worked at his desk. Mommy couldn't lift her anymore, but Daddy still could. She loved the feel of him, the smell of him. He was never angry, always funny. But *sometimes* she had to say his name like *one hundred times* before he heard her, even when she was right next to him.

Dad. Dad? Daddy!

Honey, you don't have to yell.

How could you not hear someone who was right next to you?

If Mommy was out and Daddy was in charge, then she and her brother could: eat whatever they wanted (all you had to do was go into the kitchen and take it; he wouldn't even notice); play on the iPad *forever* (he would never suggest that they read a book or play a game together); ride their plasma cars up and down the long hallway from the foyer to the living room. And it was only when they got too loud that he might appear in the doorway to his office and say: "Hey, guys? Keep it down, okay?"

He wasn't even *supposed* to talk on his phone on the hike—which was his idea. As far as she was concerned, hikes were just walks that never seemed to end. A walk with nothing exciting—like ice cream or a movie—at the end of it. It was just so that they could "be in nature"—which was Daddy's favorite place to be. And Mom wasn't there, because it was their time to just "be with Dad."

"Don't tell Mom, okay?" he'd said, as he fished his phone out of his backpack.

She and her brother had exchanged a look. It made her uncomfortable when he asked her to keep things from her mom, because Mommy had made her promise never to keep secrets. She said: "Anyone who asks you to keep a secret from your mom—a teacher, a friend, a stranger, anyone—is not looking out for you. No good person would ever ask you to do that."

She knew that her mom was talking about stranger danger and how people weren't allowed to touch her body (ew!) or "push drugs" at her. Mommy hadn't said *anything* about Daddy. She very badly wanted to ask: "What if Daddy asks me to keep a secret?" But she had a feeling that wouldn't be a good idea.

So she and her brother walked ahead on the shady path, leaving Daddy trailing behind talking in a soft voice to someone. She couldn't hear him and didn't care anyway. When grown-ups talked to each other it was *so* boring. She didn't understand their words, their tones, why—out of nowhere—they got angry at each other, started yelling. Or worse, got suddenly really quiet, not talking at all. Talking to each other in fake voices, then changing back to normal voices for her and her brother. Weird.

"Look, *what* do you want me to do?" Daddy said, his voice suddenly growing louder.

When she looked back at him, he glanced up at her quickly, then down at the ground again.

"Come on," said her brother.

He took her by the hand, and they ran up the path. All around them the trees were thick and tall, the air clean and fresh. There were no horns and sirens, just the sweet songs of birds in the branches. The crunching dirt path beneath her sneakers felt so different than concrete. The ground was wobbly and soft; she had to watch her step. But the air filled her lungs. She imagined them inflating like balloons, lifting her up into the leaves.

Her friends—Sophia, Grace, Averi—they all hated their older brothers. Brothers who teased and made fun, who scared them and hit them when their parents weren't looking, played innocent when their sisters cried. But her brother wasn't like that. She loved her brother; he helped her build the Lego Hogwarts Castle she got for Christmas, let her sleep in his bed when she was scared during storms. When her mom wasn't around (which wasn't often), he was the next best thing. Always there. Always knew what to say, what to do. Not like Daddy, who she also loved. But Daddy didn't *know* all the important things—like how she didn't like jelly, only peanut butter, how you weren't supposed to turn the lights all the way off at bedtime, just down really low on the dimmer, or that she wanted water only from the refrigerator, not from the faucet in the bathroom.

"What are we doing?" she asked her brother. She'd wanted to stay back with Mommy, but Daddy wouldn't let her. *Come on, kiddo. It's our time to be together.*

"Hiking," her brother said.

"Hiking to *where*?" she said, leaning on the word.

"Nowhere," he said. "We're just walking."

"I'm tired," she said. And she *was* tired suddenly—she wasn't just saying it so that they could go back to Mom. "My tummy hurts."

She *did* say that sometimes, because that was an automatic "let's go home" for her mom. Her dad didn't pay attention; he knew she sometimes was faking because she was bored or uncomfortable. *Just hang in there a little, okay?* he'd say.

"We'll go back in a minute," her brother said now. "Look at this."

It was a log that had fallen and was laying beside the path. "Remember that book: *Bug Hotel*—or something?" he said.

Oh yeah, that book about how when a log falls down, insects move in and find a home and help the log to decompose. Cool.

Her brother peeled back a wet brown layer of bark to reveal a congregation of tiny black beetles; she leaned in close to watch them move and shimmer, burrow into these little holes they'd made. She wasn't a girly girl. She didn't shriek about bugs the way her friends did. She reached her finger down, and one of them crawled onto her hand.

"He likes me," she said.

She turned her hand and let the tiny bug scuttle up her wrist and onto the cuff of her long-sleeve tee-shirt. Her favorite shirt, with the owl on it. She wore it all the time even though a hole had worn under the arm and the hem was coming down in the back.

Her brother was inspecting the log. There was already a deep, long hollow, and her brother was crouched down peering inside. While he was looking inside, she heard the birdcall she'd been hearing, this kind of sweet song, with lots of notes. She'd never heard one like it. Birds usually just sounded like they were cheeping to her, especially in the city. But this bird was saying something, something important.

Once when she'd been walking past the Alice in Wonderland statue in Central Park, she saw a man nearby with a monocular pointed up at a tall apartment building.

"What's he looking at?" she asked her daddy. The man had a table set up with brochures and photographs for sale. Her mommy would have said *I don't know* and that would have been the end of it, because they would have been running to this thing or that thing and there wouldn't be time to stop. But Daddy didn't ever care as much about being on time, so they wandered over.

The man had white hair and a plaid cap and a very nice blue coat. He reminded her of her grandpa, how quiet and careful he was. He talked about the hawks and other wildlife that nested right in New York City.

"Natural beauty is everywhere," he said. "It finds a place for itself even right here. You just have to know where to look."

He let her daddy lift her up to the monocular, and the man adjusted the lens until it came into focus and she saw two fuzzy gray baby hawks in their nest, their beaks open, surrounding their mama, who was red with white feathers on her chest and who had alert, bright eyes. Penny watched, mesmerized, until her daddy said it was time to go. When she moved away from the monocular, she saw only the building again—except now with the small cluster of brown up high on a ledge. She never would have seen it. After that, she started noticing birds in the trees and always tried to listen to their songs. The squirrels that danced across branches in the park. A woodpecker one day. Her daddy even showed her an article about someone who'd woken up to find a wild turkey sitting on his balcony. What the old man with the monocular said, about knowing where to look, it stayed with her. He was right.

Before they'd left for the hike, Daddy had downloaded an app on his iPhone that would help them identify bird-calls. He also had the binoculars. She looked around at the leafy tops of the trees, shielding her eyes against the bright yellow light (was it *ever* this buttery yellow in the city?). She tried to catch a glimpse of the bird that was singing, but she couldn't. She glanced back down the path—she wanted to show her daddy the log, to use the binoculars. Where *was* he?

"Where's *Dad*?" she asked her brother, a little whiny.

A single echoing crack came in answer. Then a kind of cry, a fluttering of leaves. She turned to her brother, who she could tell had heard it, too, because he was looking down the path toward where they had left their dad. The light shined on his white blond hair and turned the lenses of his round glasses weirdly golden.

"What was that?" she asked. He shook his head to say he didn't know.

"Dad?" he called out. The birds had gone quiet. Louder: "*Dad?*"

When there was no answer, her brother said they should go back for him, so they did.

They walked back down the path, her brother taking the lead. She felt wobbly, a quiver in her stomach, tears threatening. She couldn't even say why she was scared. What had they heard after all? Maybe nothing. They turned the corner to see the path empty. The rocky dirt surface was edged by trees that sloped down toward the river valley. "It's not that steep," her father had said. "But you could still fall a good ways and hurt yourself. So be careful."

She was the first to hear the low moaning.

"Daddy!" she cried. "Daaaddd*dy*!"

"Kids!" His voice was low and far away. He said some-thing else, but she couldn't hear what. They moved toward the sound, her brother edging toward the side of the path, looking down.

"Stay back," her brother said. She pressed herself up against the trunk of a tree, feeling the rough bark through her shirt. Her father was still calling to them. It sounded like he was saying *Get out of here! Run!* But that couldn't be right.

"I see him," her brother said. "He must have fallen. Dad, what happened?"

Then another one of those strange echoing cracks. Her brother froze stiff, then grabbed his leg and started screaming, fell to the ground. It was a terrible sound, high-pitched and filled with fear. It connected to something deep and primal within her, and sheer terror rocketed through her, a lightning bolt. She heard herself shrieking, too, a sound that came from her and didn't.

A black flower of blood bloomed on her brother's thigh. He'd gone a frightening white, couldn't stop screaming. It was a siren, loud and long, deafening. She wanted to cover her ears, to tell him to stop. Her father was yelling down below. Her name. Her brother's name. Then a command as clear as day: Run!

She went to the edge of the path and saw her father lying among the trees, sloping downwards, arm looped around a slender birch trunk as if he was holding on, leg bent strangely. And then she saw the other man. Dressed in jeans and a flannel work shirt, heavy boots. He wore a baseball cap, the brim shadowing his face. In his arms he had a gun, long and black.

She froze, watching him. Her brother's screaming had quieted; he was now whimpering behind her. Her father was yelling still. But she couldn't move; she was so afraid, so confused, that her body just couldn't move.

She heard something, a chiming. A little tinkle of bells. The phone. Her father's phone was ringing. She turned and saw it down the path, screen bright, vibrating on the dirt path. It broke the spell, and she ran for it. She was fast. She was the fastest girl in her third-grade class, always pulling effortlessly ahead of everyone else on the soccer field at relay races in PE. Coach said she was a rocket. But she wasn't fast enough today.

Another man, whom she hadn't seen, was coming up the path from the opposite direction. He got there first, crushing the phone beneath his hard black boot as she dove for it, skinning her knees, the dirt kicking up so that she could taste it in her mouth.

He looked down at her, his expression unreadable.

"Don't bother running," he said. He sounded almost sad for her. "He's got you now."

But she did run. Her daddy had always told her if a stranger tried to take her that she was supposed to run and scream at the top of her lungs and fight with everything she had. *Don't ever let them take you,* he warned. *No matter what.*

Why? she used to ask. The conversation frightened and excited her, like a scary movie. *What happens if they take me?*

Nothing good, said her father grimly. And the way he said it meant that the conversation was over.

She used to lie in bed at night sometimes, thinking of how she would get away from a bad guy that tried to take her away from her family. In those imaginings, she was always strong and brave, fiercely fighting and punching like the kids in *Antboy* and *Kick-Ass* (which she was way too young to watch but did with her brother on those nights when Mommy was working and Daddy was in charge).

It was nothing like this. She couldn't *breathe*; fear was a black hole sucking every part of her into its vortex. Her brother was now yelling, too, telling her to run. And she did. She got up from the ground and she ran past the strange-looking man, leaving her brother and her father behind. She was going for help. She had to be fast, faster than she'd ever been. Not just for herself, but for her daddy and her brother.

How far did she get? Not far when a great weight landed on her from behind, bringing her hard to the ground, knocking all the wind out of her. There was a foul smell and hot air in her ear.

"You come like a nice little girl, and I won't kill your father and your brother. I won't go back and kill your mother, too."

She couldn't even answer as the man yanked her to her feet and started dragging her back up the hill—past her brother who lay quietly crying on the ground.

"Let her go," her brother said faintly. "Please let her go."

They locked eyes; she'd never seen anyone look so afraid. It made her insides clench. She couldn't help it; she started to shriek and scream, pull back against the man. But he was impossibly strong; she was a rag doll, no muscle or bone. Her movements were as ineffective as the flap of butterfly wings.

When she looked back, she couldn't even see her daddy. And after a while, walking and walking with the man holding on to her arm, pulling her so roughly, talking so mean, it started to get dark. She had never been so far away from where she was supposed to be. Maybe it was a dream.

It couldn't be happening, could it? Could it?